Cloaks of Silver

The future has arrived.

It is what Alexa spent her childhood years desperately trying to reach, and now she has everything she ever truly desired. Her sister. A home. A secure life.

And, yet, something is missing.

Perhaps with every new need fulfilled, Alexa is becoming less grateful for what she has. Maybe what she gained is not really what she needs. Or possibly, she was wrong about her life, and she will never be capable of living successfully.

But where Alexa is failing, she is determined others will succeed. Everything she has will be devoted to her family and giving Bethany the future she deserved. If only life would play along. Because for them to truly embrace their futures, they will need to once and for all escape the clutches of their past.

Naomi Metzl was born in Sydney in 1981. Cloaks of Silver is the fourth and final book in the Marble Road series, following Alexa Samson as she builds her life and identity away from the horrors of her childhood.

Also available in this series

Cloaks of Silver

Naomi Metzl

Published by Midnight Sunrise Publishing

Printed by CreateSpace

ISBN 978 0 9924 3037 5

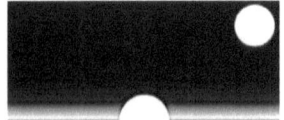

Midnight Sunrise Publishing

For my sisters,
Larissa and Tamara.
From fights to fun, joy to despair,
You have always been there for me.
As my protectors and bullies, my friends and foes.
Everything sisters should be.

And wilt thou leave me thus,
That hath loved thee so long
In wealth and woe among?
And is thy heart so strong
As for to leave me thus?
Say nay, say nay!

An Appeal
Sir Thomas Wyatt

Chapter One

ALEXA MEANDERED SLOWLY up the street, letting her hand trail along the high fences. It did not matter how many times she walked this path, she could not help but gaze wondrously at the huge houses, trying to come to terms with the fact that she actually owned one of these suburban mansions. It was the life she had always dreamed of, but history made it impossible to believe it was real. Or that it could last.

It was difficult to fathom that it had been less than two years since she finished school and escaped the nightmare that had been Redgrove College. That place – that world – felt like another lifetime ago, something only vaguely connected to the person she was now. Yet in too many ways, Alexa still felt like that girl; at the mercy of the world, just waiting for it to use her and toss her aside.

Closing her eyes, Alexa tried once more to convince herself her life had changed. That was behind her. She now had everything she ever wished for. There was not a single aspect of her life Alexa could legitimately complain about, and yet she was not happy. She was stuck in a strange emotional limbo she did not know how to explain or escape.

Everyone noticed Alexa's discontented state. When she looked to the recent alterations in her life to explain her mood, her theories were dismissed as nonsense, leaving her constantly searching for something else as the true source of her melancholy.

When Alexa mapped things out rationally, it painted a very pretty picture. Bethany was flourishing in her new life. They were finally living together in their own place, had their own lives and were free from the terrors of their past. They had some of the most amazing people supporting them. Yet, still, something was missing.

The move into the suburbs had been much harder than Alexa expected. She missed her beachside apartment; the taste of salt in the air and the distant whisper of the waves. The peacefulness of the coast was soothing in a way the broad, tree-lined streets never could be, and despite living in her new home for almost two months, Alexa struggled to love it. Its distance from the beach and longer commute to university were both legitimate grievances, but Alexa felt weak letting such small things impact her. After all she had gone through, such petty problems should be barely an inconvenience.

And while university was now an hour away, rather than an easy stroll, Alexa had no complaints about her academic endeavours. She had settled into nice friendships with Jessica and Jake from her course, along with Jake's girlfriend Amy, and beyond them was a wider group of acquaintances Alexa enjoyed keeping company with. It was social without being threatening and it made uni fun. However, university had never been a social undertaking. Alexa was determined to do well this semester to make up for the disappointment of the previous one – and distance herself from the mistakes she had made.

That tumultuous time still swirled within Alexa. Even now, months later, she felt the occasional stirring of a craving creeping through her veins. She refused to acknowledge, let alone indulge, them. She would not be an addict. Whatever happened in the future, Alexa was determined drugs would never form part of her solution. If she ever needed a way to deaden her pain so badly her hand reached for drugs, she would organise a permanent solution to her situation.

It concerned Alexa just how tempting suicide could still be; those feelings keeping her from believing this life was truly her own. Most of her peers at university came from relatively affluent families, and through her course Alexa had gained a greater appreciation of how heavily the odds were stacked against the poorer sections of society. It made Alexa determined to focus her career on helping those whose life resembled what hers once had.

Thinking about the kind of life she and Bethany could have been living made Alexa feel even guiltier for believing she had problems. There was no justification for her miserable outlook; although there was one person not at a loss to explain her current frame of mind. Bethany was convinced it was Marcus's absence that had Alexa so low, but Alexa found that answer as annoying as it was simplistic. While Alexa did miss Marcus, it was infuriating that anyone would believe her life revolved solely around a guy. Given the large house they now inhabited, Marcus's absence possibly added to Alexa's feeling of loneliness, but she would not accept it as the cause of the all-consuming sadness that seemed to have been woven into her soul.

Stopping by a high fence overgrown by greenery, Alexa stared at the house that was almost hidden by the shrubbery. The large three-storey mansion sat back from the street. A semi-circular drive wrapped around a forgotten fish pond and large front garden. Pushing open the heavy gate, Alexa strolled down the gravel drive wondering if the reason she found it so hard to love this house was because she found it impossible to believe it was hers.

The house had really been Bethany's choice. Alexa's bond to it was primarily through the happiness it brought Bethany. Rarely a day went by without Bethany professing her joy – enthusiastically, wondrously or even tentatively – that this was her home. That gave Alexa a sense of contentment in the purchase and since moving in she had done a lot to transform that into something that could be mistaken for enthusiasm. The very first thing Alexa had done on settlement was put in a pool. It did not quite compare to the rush of the waves, but she was learning to truly enjoy to soft flow of water over her body as she stroked up and down.

Not even bothering to go upstairs to her room, Alexa put on the swimmers she hid in the downstairs bathroom. She walked out into the backyard and, without hesitation, slipped straight into the pool. Hopefully, Bethany would not be home early. Her bedroom was on the ground floor, and with it she had claimed the only bathroom on that floor as her own. It left Bethany less than impressed when Alexa used it. Alexa had plans to build Bethany an ensuite; it would be the only path to household harmony.

As the number of laps increased, Alexa's anxiety eased. She never measured her swims, by laps or time, just stroked steadily, allowing her mind to wander. It was usually the pressure of some duty that pulled her from the water. Occasionally it was her tired body, but Alexa hated giving into that and often pushed through for just a little longer, as if to prove a point to herself, but whether she swam for five minutes or an hour, Alexa always swam. Multiple times a day. Morning, night. Light, dark. Rain or shine. Hot or cold. The pool was her sanctuary from the life she was still not sure she knew how to live.

Sitting on the edge of the pool, Alexa swung her legs through the water, enjoying the warmth of the drenching sun. The backyard was much smaller than when they had moved in, yet remained bigger than any suburban yard Alexa had ever seen. In tandem with building the pool, Alexa had built Bethany a workshop. The physical workspace had been constructed quickly and with relatively little expense. It was the fitting out that had caused issues. Alexa had to admit her shock at the cost was not all Bethany's fault, although Bethany rarely erred on the side of economy. When Sam and Ben supported Bethany's purchases, arguing quality tools had the advantage of longevity, Alexa was left with little input beyond paying the bills. All the minor irritations that accompanied those moments were made worthwhile by the pleasure Bethany found in her workshop and the gratefulness she expressed, but they did leave those would-be wonderful moments tainted with negative emotions.

Having wasted enough time wallowing, Alexa collected her clothes from Bethany's bathroom and traipsed upstairs for a quick shower before moving back down to her study. It was funny, she could swim for an hour without feeling tired, yet the prospect of going back up to her room to grab a book she had left on her bed was exhausting. Their home was truly that vast.

The ground floor housed the main living spaces, with the staircase separating the living areas from several rooms on the right. To the left was a large lounge room, which ran back towards a smaller dining room and very generously appointed kitchen. On the right was a large and bright room, which was Alexa's study, while the equally large back room was Bethany's bedroom.

The second floor was as vast as the ground floor and virtually unused. Bethany had designated it their guest floor, determined there would be room for anyone to stay whenever they needed. So far they had only furnished two of the rooms; a guest bedroom, primarily used by Charlotte, and the largest room became their second lounge room. Alexa occasionally read in there to ease her guilt over its disuse.

The third floor belonged exclusively to Alexa. It was smaller than the other floors, sitting over the front half of the house. The front left room was the master bedroom with French-doors that opened to the balcony that ran along the length of the front. A large ensuite and walk-in wardrobe completed the room. Alexa had fallen in love with it the second she had seen it, but presumed Bethany would also want it, so never expressed her desire for it. When Bethany chose the bedroom at the rear of the ground floor, Alexa had not been able to hide her delight. Bethany had immediately confessed her fears that Alexa would want her room. It turned out their criteria for selecting their rooms had been very similar. Just with opposite reasoning.

Alexa loved how self-contained her room was. In conjunction with the rest of the third floor, it felt like her own apartment. Bethany loved that her room was in close proximity to the living areas, making her feel like she had possession over more space than just her room. It was conversations like that which made Alexa realise how differently their fears and desires manifested themselves. Alexa wanted to keep her existence as small as possible, hoping it would keep her safe from passing dangers. Bethany wanted to stake as big a claim on the world as possible, in the hope that when, bit by bit, it was stripped away, she would be left with something.

Trudging back up to her bedroom to collect her book, Alexa looked longingly into the room next door. She had wanted to make it her study, but Bethany complained they would rarely see her if she did. It seemed ridiculous to use far-flung rooms across the house just for the sake of it, but, as usual, Bethany had her way. As soon as her workshop was ready, Bethany built Alexa a desk, constructing it in the front room in such a manner that it was practically impossible to move it to another room. Alexa did not complain. It was the most amazing desk she had ever seen. The only thing she changed was its position in the room. Bethany had set it up in the corner facing out the large front window, but Alexa could not sit comfortably with her back to the door. Once she moved the desk to the opposite corner, so it made a little corner office, she was content. When Bethany made a matching bookshelf, the room was all but complete.

Then Bethany complained Alexa was always at her desk. Even on a Friday night, it was where Alexa spent her time. Her previous ritual with Charlotte had fallen by the wayside with the distance between them. Alexa would not have let that stop the tradition, but things were going so well between Charlotte and her family. Alexa just wished she knew if things were as good as Charlotte claimed. It was why she had wanted Marcus to keep living in their beachside apartment.

Holding her head in her hands, Alexa tried to decipher how she felt about Marcus's absence. She missed him, but could not mourn his absence. That last fight over Lucy's missing wallet still stung badly enough that she could not wish him back in her life without hesitation. But it would be nice to have their friendship back. It was ridiculous to desire anything more. She had walked away from the first chance, and they had both stubbornly refused to take the second. Alexa sometimes wondered if they had done the right thing by always choosing to do the right thing. She had never stopped to seriously consider whether they should damn everything for their love, though she also knew her nature would never let her. Bethany would always have the greatest hold on her heart, and pride would prevent anything else.

Packing Marcus's possessions into boxes had been one of the hardest things Alexa had ever done. She had started the minute he drove off after choosing Lucy over her – choosing to believe Lucy's lie over her truth. To this day, even without evidence, Alexa knew Lucy lied when she accused Bethany and Charlotte of stealing her wallet. Alexa's anguish over that had not allowed her to change her mind about throwing Marcus out. Bethany and Charlotte tried to convince her to be there when Marcus came to pick up his belongings, but she refused. Seeing him again would have only risked her finding some way to excuse Lucy's behaviour, just so she could have him around again. It did not matter in the end. Marcus never came back. His best mate Brandon turned up instead and Marcus was never heard from again.

Alexa liked to believe she and Marcus would meet, perhaps after several years apart, when one or both of them were married. She only hoped Marcus never married Lucy. He deserved better than that. Or perhaps Alexa just wanted him with someone who knew nothing of their history. It was nice to imagine they would one day be allowed a friendship without condemnation, but she doubted it.

Sam and Ben often voiced their surprise that Alexa was still single, as though the only reason she had not dated before was Marcus. They refused to believe Alexa was not waiting for Marcus, but for someone as good as him, so every week, without fail, someone would ask her if she had met anyone nice recently.

The most annoying part of that question was that the answer was often yes, but to say that would lead to questions that could never be satisfactorily answered. Alexa met lots of nice guys. She had even met one who made her stomach squiggle in anxious anticipation every time she thought she would see him. When she eventually gathered the courage to speak to him, she quickly discovered he was in a relationship, but the real deciding factor was that he never looked twice at her.

When Alexa ventured to discuss that episode with her university friends, nearly all the single girls had similar experiences. It was just not that easy to find a boyfriend, and Alexa felt like they had much more going for them in the dating stakes than she did. It was strange for Alexa to feel pathetically normal. The only difference was, unlike some of the girls, she was not worried about being single. It was everyone else who had issues with her relationship status.

Jessica always laughed when they spoke about it, convinced Alexa was overstating the pressures she was under to find a boyfriend. After all, Amy's mother had been making ticking noises since her sixteenth birthday, while simultaneously banning her from dating. However, it only took one night out with Sam for Jessica to realise the unique circumstances Alexa was in.

"Man, I want to hang out with your family more often. Sam's a crack up," laughed Jessica. It was not the term Alexa would have used, but knew Sam had her best interests at heart. It just felt like he did not know her any more. "They realise finding a boyfriend's not the same as catalogue shopping, right?"

"I can't be sure about that," smiled Alexa. On occasion, she had been told to just pick a guy; there were plenty around. "They're just really fixated on Marcus and think if I date another guy he'll stop being a problem, but I did that with Damien. I'm not going through that crap again."

"If he's the kind of guy you pick off the shelf, we're definitely not letting you date that way," said Jake. "We'll browse for you."

Jessica, Jake and Amy enjoyed pointing out potential boyfriends, gauging Alexa's response to get a feel for her type. Alexa did not mind because all they wanted was for her to be open to possibilities and agreed with her only provisos – that she was attracted to the guy and felt safe. Jessica was sure such criteria could be easily met, but it was never that simple for Alexa. Physical attraction was not something she was very good at any more. Even with the guy at university, her imaginings had never included being intimate. Fear was something Alexa had a much closer relationship with and it was very good at keeping her attraction at bay. Jessica found that strange, but Alexa had not been able to disclose her history with men beyond Damien. Those stories were not suitable for a university discussion, but Alexa was heartened that the main reason she did not want to have that talk was not because she was scared of Jessica and Amy's reactions. Jessica and Amy were the closest female peers Alexa had ever had, and she felt as though they were more likely to help her through any of the troubles she faced better than a boyfriend.

"Lex. Lex, wake up."

Alexa jumped at the touch of her arm, her chair scuttling into the other side the desk with a painful thump. Looking up, Alexa was glad it was just Bethany. She had been having a nightmare. It was yet another thing they had fought about over the previous few months. There were still few nights where Alexa was not transported back to her five-year-old body and forced to flee with three-year-old Bethany from the menacing shadowy man. Every time, they wound up in a field of pipes. Every time, Ben found them and comforted them. And, every time, Ben ended up dead, as the shadowy man reached out for one of them.

"What's the point of me making you a daybed when you insist on falling asleep at your desk?" asked Bethany in a frustrated tone.

"What's the time?" asked Alexa groggily. With her thoughts swirling so much, it had not been a productive night.

"Almost one," answered Bethany.

"So you had a good night then," smiled Alexa.

"Yeah, I bumped into Sam and we hung out for a bit," smiled Bethany, her cheeks glowing. Alexa found it sweet Bethany was still so chuffed by Sam's friendship. "He just dropped me off."

"He didn't want to come in?"

"No, he has to work tomorrow and wanted to get home. He's coming over tomorrow night, remember. We're going to the movies. You're supposed come with us – get out of the house – have a life."

"I don't know, maybe. If I get everything done. I haven't cleaned the house for ages and there's heaps of washing."

"Lex, three days isn't ages," sighed Bethany. Alexa just shrugged. "You going to bed?"

"No, I'm awake now. I'll move to the daybed, don't worry."

Bethany must have been tired, because she just shrugged unhappily and went to bed.

Alexa woke much later than she intended. The cloudy sky kept the room darker than usual, but she felt better for the sleep in. Looking around the room as she stretched awake, she could not help but smile. Bethany had done an amazing job furnishing the study, but it had not been without its complications – like everything lately. After Bethany made the desk and bookcase, Alexa had spent so much time studying there that she kept falling asleep at her desk. So Bethany built her a bed. The speed with which Bethany could make and assemble furniture staggered Alexa, and she was sure all the money Bethany received from the interest payments went to buying materials. The resulting bed was beautiful, but Alexa hated it. There was just no way of telling Bethany; the cause being a source of deep, unspoken division between them. Every day Alexa's fear grew, to the point where she stopped going into the room. If not for Charlotte, Alexa would never have stepped foot in her study again.

The very first time Charlotte saw the bed, she recognised the problem. It was in those moments Alexa felt as though Charlotte was another piece of herself and wondered if it was Charlotte's absence she was struggling so desperately with. Without Alexa saying anything, Charlotte immediately set to resolve the situation. She begged Bethany to move the bed to her room. Bethany's reaction was scathing. Alexa had never seen Bethany be so rude to Charlotte. Bethany's sudden and dramatic reversal in attitude led Alexa to believe Charlotte explained the situation, but Bethany never said anything. With no fuss, she dismantled the bed and moved it to Charlotte's room. Once the move was made, Bethany asked Alexa what kind of bed she wanted. Alexa did not need a replacement bed, but Bethany was insistent. Their compromise was the daybed. It was perfect and Alexa loved it, but Bethany still had her way. Two weeks later, she made another bed – one Alexa did not fear.

Since then, Bethany had made it her mission to fill the entire house with her own furniture. Her bedroom was a beautiful shrine to her handiwork. If it was not constantly hidden under a mass of clothes, it would have been the best room in the house. However, the other rooms were catching up. So far Bethany had refurnished much of the dining room and added to or replaced individual items in other rooms. Alexa resisted every attempt to throw out the old furniture. She had spent good money purchasing it barely a year ago and could not so readily part from it. The compromise was its relegation to the second floor, which now felt like a shrine to Alexa's beachside apartment.

"Hal-ooh?" called a distant voice.

Alexa shook her head, looking up from her book as she sat on the lounge. Bethany had pestered her about living in her study as soon as she had sat down, so she moved to the lounge room to appease her.

"Sorry, Sam. What?" replied Alexa.

"I said, 'we're going to the movies. Do you want to come?'" asked Sam again.

Even though Sam was a frequent visitor now they lived so much closer, he and Alexa had not spent much time together. He mostly hung out with Bethany, and Alexa was grateful. Without Charlotte around, it took much more time to keep their large house running. Alexa's morning has been spent cleaning, washing and preparing food. People expected to be fed even when she could not be bothered cooking, so she found it easier to have stocks of refrigerated and frozen meals.

"What you seeing?" replied Alexa, looking up from her textbook. If she sounded interested, perhaps they would believe she was making an effort.

"I don't know. Decide when we get there. Maybe that trashy sci-fi flick," said Sam with a hint of excitement.

"I'll pass," smiled Alexa, holding up her book. "But thanks and, Sam, thanks for hanging out with Bethy."

"You always say that as if I'm doing it out of some strange sense of duty. Beth's great. Why can't I just like hanging with her?" asked Sam, sitting on the lounge with Alexa.

"You can and you should," said Alexa firmly, as she highlighted a sentence in her textbook. "I mean she has to be great, right? She's my sister and you love me, so by default you have to love her."

"Something like that," smiled Sam, leaning forward and tucking Alexa's hair behind her ear. "You're amazing, you know that?"

"Yeah," laughed Alexa. "I tell myself every day."

Alexa noticed Sam grimace at her comment.

"Ready?" asked Bethany, bouncing into the lounge room. Sam nodded and rose to leave. "You're not coming?"

"Gotta study," replied Alexa simply.

"Either you need to learn to study better or that's a terrible excuse," smiled Bethany. "It's Saturday night, you're allowed time away from your books."

"Not if I want to actually do well, get a good job and not just squander all our money."

Bethany rolled her eyes. This was not the first time they had had this argument. They viewed their financial windfall very differently, and Alexa was glad she controlled its distribution and expenditure. It was not as though she believed Bethany would necessarily waste their money, but Bethany was not a planner and rarely considered making provisions for the future. It was easy to understand. They now had a thousand times more than they had ever had before, and Bethany's life had taught her to live for the moment. Alexa's life had always focused on making sure Bethany could do just that.

Watching Sam take Bethany's hand, leading her to the door, made Alexa envious of the seemingly carefree way they were able to face the world. Worrying about every possible permutation that could transform their lives engrossed much of Alexa's time. Everyone except Charlotte thought she was being silly, viewing the world through an unreasonably negative lens, but Alexa did not think it irresponsible to be prepared. Yet beyond the ever-looming threat of Bethany returning to drugs, Alexa was not sure what else she feared actually happening. Sometimes it just felt as though disaster was ready to strike – brewing somewhere in the periphery. She could feel it, but not see it.

Giving up on study, Alexa headed out for her afternoon swim. The lengthening days meant she no longer swam in the dark at the end of the day, though the sun was low in the sky by the time she slid out of the pool and under a hot shower.

Looking around her mostly vacant floor, Alexa could not help but wonder who would eventually fill these rooms. The house was big enough that she and Bethany could live together forever with ever-expanding families, although the numerous niggling arguments of the previous few months made Alexa wonder how they would have survived living together had they not been forced apart – and how long they could survive living together now. They often needed every inch of space in the house to maintain harmony. Still, Alexa like to think that there would one day be children to fill the empty rooms.

In her future, Marcus and Charlotte were always there. Marcus held her children tenderly, as if they were his own. There was never another father around and Alexa wondered if she believed Marcus would one day father her children or if men never stuck to be a father to their own children. Occasionally, the Whites pushed their way into her visions, but Alexa never let herself indulge in those dreams. The Whites could never be a part of her life. They were far too precious to ever risk being involved with her again.

"Anyone home?" called a voice from downstairs.

"Ben?" replied Alexa, moving away from doorway of the would-be nursery and walking downstairs.

Ben was standing awkwardly at the bottom of the stairs. Alexa wondered if her face showed how uneasy she felt being alone with him. He had moved soon after them so that he was only a ten-minute walk away, but relations had never improved beyond the point of civility. Alexa wanted more, but did not know how to make it happen. Things seemed so easy for Bethany. She was constantly over at Ben's place and they regularly did things together. Bethany always invited Alexa along, but what Alexa wanted was for Ben to invite her into his life; make the same effort with her as he did with Bethany. Bethany argued that he did, but while all his invitations came through her, Alexa could never be convinced that Ben wanted her around as much as everyone insisted he did.

Further straining relations was Ben joining Sam in continuously questioning Alexa's life choices. When she was home, he thought she was studying too much. When she was out, he claimed she was not socialising the right way. It never seemed to matter what she was doing, he and Sam were second-guessing her. Bethany might pester her about things, but always in the context of unconditional support. Any support Ben gave was in the context of broad disapproval. It made their rare times alone together quite strained.

"I thought you and Beth might want some company," said Ben.

"Bethy's at the movies with Sam," said Alexa, continuing down the stairs. "I wouldn't mind the company though." Alexa could only imagine how happy Bethany would be when she came home to see them together. However, Ben's disappointed reaction did not inspire confidence. "You don't have to stay if you don't want to. Bethy'll be home tomorrow."

"It's not that. It's just – I – I was at the pub," Ben said grimly.

"Oh. Do you want me to call Bethy?" asked Alexa, unconsciously taking a step back. Even though did not look intoxicated, she did not want to take the risk. When it came to giving up drinking, Ben had found it harder than he imagined, giving him newfound respect for Bethany's struggles against her heroin addiction.

"No, no. I was kind of hoping to catch you, actually," said Ben, even though it looked the last thing in the world he wanted.

"You hungry?" asked Alexa.

When Ben nodded, she led the way into the kitchen. Ben paced behind her as she cooked. Alexa could not remember ever seeing him so agitated. It made her anxious. When she ventured to ask why he had been at the pub, he only stammered incoherently, ruffling his hair as he paced with greater vigour.

Ben had not drunk or smoked a single cigarette for many months. It had done him good. He had more energy and, he professed, more money. He took up running and squash with Bethany – another world they inhabited together away from Alexa – and had lost almost ten kilograms. With the extra money, he splurged on gifts for them. Alexa thought the value of the gifts exceeded any amount he could have possibly saved, but Ben would not let her refuse them. Bethany had never tried to.

"So what sent you in search of a drink?" asked Alexa after dinner, trying once more to discover the source of Ben's distress. "You've had plenty of tough days before and said you never felt tempted."

"This was different," sighed Ben, with a tinge of anger in his voice that scared Alexa. "This – this – it was Penny. We've still got mutual friends and one of them had a dinner party tonight. I was looking forward to going. I hadn't seen many of them for months."

"So? What happened?" asked Alexa, feeling guilty. She hated knowing it was her presence in Ben's life that led to his divorce.

"Penny was there," sighed Ben again, running his hands over his face. "I thought I'd be fine. It's been a year." Ben heaved heavily, as though he was containing a sob. "She's getting married. Two days after the court date for our divorce to be finalised! They were all talking about the wedding and she was so insensitive. I couldn't believe it. She's not the woman I married. She was angry and spiteful."

"What about?" asked Alexa, with a sense of doom.

"Me. The divorce. My apparent neglect of her. Years and years of bitterness. All the times I thought we were happiest, she was angriest."

"But you heard all that during the split. What was different this time? What made you want to drink?" asked Alexa forcefully. Ben's eyes flicked up, then quickly away. "She said something about us, didn't she?" Alexa continued. Ben nodded. "What?"

"When Penny found out that I'd moved," said Ben tentatively. "It came out that I'd moved to stay closer to you two."

"She blames me and Bethy for your divorce, doesn't she?"

"Not exactly," replied Ben, cringing with every word.

"Just me, then," snapped Alexa.

Ben nodded and Alexa turned away. She knew there was only one reason Penny would believe such a thing.

"Alexa —"

"What did she say?" asked Alexa angrily.

Ben moved to placate her, but she could only repeat her question in more demanding tones until Ben finally answered. "She ... she tried to make out that the relationship I have with you isn't one resembling that of a father and daughter," stammered Ben.

"She thinks I fucked you, doesn't she?"

Chapter Two

"ALEXA, PLEASE, DON'T say it like that," said Ben, moving towards her, but Alexa could not be near him. She stalked into the lounge room, pacing the same way he had earlier that night.

Ben tentatively shadowed her, clearly unsure how to approach her, but that only angered Alexa more. If it had been Bethany, he would never have been so hesitant.

"Is that what she thinks? Does Penny think I fucked you?" asked Alexa angrily. Ben did not reply. "Is that what she said!"

"Yes," he finally confessed.

"When'd she think it happened? When I came back from overseas? Before? While I was in your house?"

"The whole time," answered Ben immediately, as though now believing it was better to answer her questions.

Alexa felt betrayed. She wanted to scream. When Ben placed a placating hand on her shoulder, she threw it off. "This is your fault, Ben," she snapped, pointing angrily at him. "What did you tell her about me? How could you let her believe that? And why the hell did you insist on me staying with you when she thought that about me?"

"That's not fair," replied Ben, his voice a mixture of defiance and apology.

"And it's fair people think I broke up your marriage?" Alexa cried, horrified by Ben's response. "That they think we've been sleeping together?"

"No, of course not."

Alexa and Ben stood facing each other. Alexa's chest ached as her determination to be something better than what the world thought of her faded by the second. "Ah, hell, why don't you just take it?"

"Alexa —"

"Take it!" she cried, stepping in closer to Ben. "I bet it's been a while. Why not take what everyone thinks you've already had. Come on, name your price. I'll even give you a discount for being so good to Bethy."

Alexa pushed her body hard against Ben's, running her hands up his chest.

"Alexa, stop it," cried Ben, shoving her away from him.

Alexa stumbled backwards. She was about to trip over the coffee table when Ben suddenly grabbed her. He pulled her into his chest and held her tight, squeezing hurtful tears out of her eyes. With a deep breath, Alexa held her tears at bay and pushed out of Ben's arms. She did not want him touching her.

"I'm sorry," said Ben softly. "I didn't want to tell you, but thought if you ever happened to hear – I never wanted you to believe what she said was true."

"Believe it was true? What the hell does that mean?" gasped Alexa, backing further away. "Why would I ever believe it was true? I know what I've done. I know I've never slept with you, Ben."

Ben did not answer. Alexa could not understand what he could have possibly meant, and did not want to stay to find out. Storming straight past him, she dashed to her room and curled up on her bed, tears streaming down her cheeks.

Alexa tried to recall every interaction she had ever had with Ben as she interpreted the meaning of his last statement. There was only one reason for her to believe what Penny had said, and that was if Ben wanted them to be true. Ben's anger over Marcus's presence in her life suddenly took on a whole new meaning, and she hoped to hell she had not been encouraging him.

Worried that Ben was still in the house, Alexa locked the door and even moved her armchair against it. She curled back up on her bed, but sleep did not come. Her mind swirled so violently she thought she would be sick, and only in the early hours of the morning did exhaustion finally take over and grant her a couple of hours of fitful sleep.

It was still early when Alexa woke. The house was quiet, but she decided not to check whether Ben was in the spare room. Hopefully he would know to stay away, but she was in the kitchen less than two minutes when he walked in.

"I'm fine," Alexa said in a tight voice, hoping to get rid of him. "You don't have to stick around to check on me."

"Actually, Beth mentioned your Sunday breakfast was worth experiencing."

Alexa shrugged and began cooking, ignoring Ben's presence. He eventually took the hint and left. This was so far from what she had planned for Bethany to walk in on last night it was not even funny.

"Beth's right," smiled Ben, smelling the air as he walked back into the kitchen. "Where is she?"

"Still asleep probably. She might like the breakfast, but she won't get up early for it," replied Alexa flatly.

Ben nodded as he stood awkwardly on the other side of the room. Realising he would not leave, Alexa knew she had no choice but to confront him. "You know I've never tried to come on to you, right?" she said, holding Ben's gaze to make sure he knew she was serious. "I don't want anything like that with you – no matter what I said last night."

"Oh, hell, Alexa, I know that!" cried Ben, rushing to pull her into a tight embrace, but Alexa pushed immediately out of it.

"What – what about you? Is that how you see me? You think something might happen between us one day?"

"Alexa!" cried Ben, grabbing Alexa's shoulders and fixing her gaze. "I've never looked at you that way. I've known you since you were five. I wanted to adopt you not molest you. I swear, never."

"What are we swearing never to do?" asked Bethany, strolling into the kitchen.

"Ben had a weak moment last night. He was just promising it wouldn't happen again," answered Alexa immediately.

"Weakness isn't a good thing at Sunday breakfast, either," smiled Bethany, grabbing plates and serving herself up a big breakfast. "See, told you it was worth it, Da– didn't I?"

"I have to swim," said Alexa, feeling strangely uncomfortable.

"Then why'd you start cooking?" asked Bethany, holding Alexa's plate out with a perplexed look.

"Ben was hungry," answered Alexa as she scurried out the door, leaving Bethany looking worryingly at Ben.

Swimming back and forth, Alexa tried to clear her head. Up and down, over and over, she pushed further and harder, desperate to avoid focusing on the terrible thoughts swirling in her mind. It was impossible, and in the end her exhausted body betrayed her, forcing her from the water.

"It's not his fault what Penny says and thinks, you know."

Alexa pushed past Bethany and stomped towards the house.

"Ignoring me isn't going to make it go away," cried Bethany. "He didn't do anything wrong."

"Really? You don't think he has some responsibility to ensure his wife doesn't think I'm the reason he divorced her?" snapped Alexa, striding inside.

"She divorced him!" called Bethany, still trailing after Alexa.

"Because she thought I was fucking him!"

"But you weren't and he doesn't think of you like that."

"Everyone thinks of me like that!" cried Alexa, spinning back on Bethany at her bedroom door. "No matter what I do, everyone thinks of me that way. I'm the whore who worked as a prostitute, seduced her teacher and worked off your drug debt by sleeping with a paedophile!"

"We don't … I don't think … Lex, don't say those things."

"Bethy, what's the point in denying the truth? What's the point in trying to be something I'm not? Just leave it."

"You blame me, don't you?" asked Bethany tentatively. "That's why you don't want to talk about it."

"Why would I blame you? How could any of this be your fault?"

"My drug debt. My paedophile boyfriend. I'm the reason you worked in that brothel. I'm the reason Clinton found you there. All my fault."

"I didn't mean it like that," sighed Alexa.

"Then how did you mean it?"

"When people look at me, those things are all they see and I'm always to blame. When people meet you, they love you. They look past all the things you've done."

"Then you do blame me?"

"No, Bethy, I don't. I blame me," snapped Alexa.

"And Ben?"

"Yes, and Ben. I blame Ben."

Bethany tried to reason with Alexa until their circular argument frustrated them to the point of outright anger, and Alexa slammed the door in Bethany's face. Storming straight to her shower, Alexa turned the hot water on full. The searing water burned through her skin. When it became unbearable, she let the cold water run over her until she was shivering. The physical insult helped calm Alexa enough to clear her mind.

Returning to the kitchen, Alexa was almost thankful for the mess that had been left, though scoffed at everyone complaining about how much housework she did. Not content with just tidying up, Alexa cleaned the room thoroughly, pulling everything out of the cupboards, and rearranging the contents as she put it all back. It was strangely rewarding, and kept her mind occupied. Bethany came in a couple of times, before finally pulling Alexa out of the kitchen and into her arms. Alexa could not resist the embrace, hugging Bethany back just as fiercely. They did not talk, just sat on the lounge in each other's arms. It was why Alexa could never stay mad at Bethany.

"Sam's coming over soon," said Bethany softly, squeezing Alexa tighter. "We're going to hang for a bit then go out for dinner. Want to come?"

"No, I haven't studied all day," replied Alexa, shaking her head absently. "I might have another swim then get stuck into it."

"Lex, if you spend any more time in the water you're going to turn into a fish."

"Mermaid," muttered Alexa. Bethany giggled softly, before sighing heavily. "If I'm going to spend thousands of dollars on a pool, I'm not going to let it go unused, am I?"

"It's hardly unused. You swam this morning. Don't your uni friends have social lives? Don't you want a life outside this house?"

"You know I go out," snapped Alexa, pushing away from Bethany. "I know you know, because I get hassled every time I don't come home married to the perfect guy. So what's this really about?"

"It's about you moving on with your life, not hiding from it."

"Sounds like the same crap I copped before Damien and I still remember how that one ended," muttered Alexa.

"That was never me and I'd never have to say this if you'd just face up to things."

"Face up to what exactly? What facts am I hiding so desperately from?" cried Alexa.

"That your life sucks without Marcus," said Bethany seriously. Alexa could have smiled at Bethany's preposterously romantic views. "That you want to throw me an eighteenth birthday party, and I want you to as long as you invite him," added Bethany, trying to keep a straight face.

"And I've told you Marcus is gone," sighed Alexa. "If he wanted to be a part of our life, he would've contacted us by now."

"Perhaps he hasn't contacted you because you kicked him out and refused to see him so he sent someone else to get his stuff."

"He refused to take my word over Lucy's," replied Alexa simply. "I gave him a choice and he made it. He didn't pick me. We need to accept that. Besides, I deleted his number from my phone."

"I didn't," smiled Bethany gleefully, bouncing on the spot. "I have his number right here."

She was not lying, pulling a piece of paper from her pocket. Alexa recognised the number immediately.

"Angel, why?" While Alexa would have been happy to see Marcus again, she was no more interested in being pushed into a relationship with him than any other guy.

"Because I wouldn't be here if it wasn't for him. He saved your life – many times – thus saving mine – many times. If he hadn't stopped you jumping in front of that train, or revived you after Clinton hurt you, or all the great stuff he did, you would've died and so would I."

"So this is all about you? Nothing to do with me? Not some sort of misguided match-making scheme?" asked Alexa sceptically.

"Promise," smiled Bethany. "One hundred percent purely selfish motives. Don't care about you at all."

"Fine, I'll think about it," smiled Alexa.

"Don't chuck that out," warned Bethany, pointing at the piece of paper as she danced out of the room.

Alexa looked back down at Marcus's number, but the sight of it made her jittery, so she shoved it in her pocket. When Bethany and Sam left for dinner, Alexa pulled it out and examined at it. It would have been so easy. She imagined what Marcus would say, believing he would be happy to hear from her and tell her Lucy was gone. Then her better senses kicked in. Marcus chose to leave. Chose not to call. She knew why, but that did not make the rejection easier.

"Called him yet?" asked Bethany as soon as she came home.

"What exactly am I supposed to say?" asked Alexa, avoiding the real question.

"That he's invited to a party," smiled Bethany, always ready with an answer. "Call him."

"Tomorrow, Angel. It's late." It was true, but it was an excuse.

Alexa created a stack of them, using one every time Bethany asked the inevitable question. Even if Alexa could overcome her own reasons for not calling Marcus, it still seemed stupid to drag him back into their lives. Every time she had, his world had fallen apart.

"Fine, I won't have a birthday party then," said Bethany the following Friday afternoon.

Bethany had Alexa's attention this time. "You have to celebrate.

You're going to be eighteen."

"You don't let me celebrate your birthday," replied Bethany, her lips twitching, as though she might win two arguments in one go.

"Fine, no birthday then," shrugged Alexa, looking back down at her books. "It was going to be a hassle anyway."

The smug confidence slid from Bethany's face. Alexa started smiling until she saw Bethany lunge at her. Pushing away from her desk, Alexa realised too late that she was not Bethany's target and was not able to retrieve her phone from Bethany's hands before she danced away. "What's his number?" Bethany asked, smiling tauntingly.

"Don't know. Lost it," lied Alexa. She had thrown the number out two days ago, but it did not matter. It was burned into her brain.

Bethany sighed heavily, turning her body side-on to Alexa. "You forced me into this," she said harshly, handing Alexa a ringing phone. Marcus's name was flashing across the screen, causing Alexa's heart to beat harder with every impending ring. In a panic, Alexa hung up. "I'll keep going," warned Bethany, grabbing for the phone, but just as her hand touched it, it began to ring. Alexa's heart skipped a beat. Marcus was returning her call.

"Answer it!" urged Bethany.

Alexa was paralysed. Bethany fumbled with the phone as she tried to answer it. As soon as she had, she handed it to Alexa.

"Hi, Marcus. Sorry, I … it's —"

"Hello? Alexa, is that you?" asked a woman's voice.

Alexa's heart sank. "Lucy, hi. I just wanted to talk to Marcus for a second," she murmured, waiting for the inevitable tirade.

"I'm not Lucy. I'm Rhianna, Marcus's sister."

"Oh, Rhianna, hi," Alexa said hesitantly, unsure what else to say. She had no idea what Marcus's family knew about her. "I just wanted to talk to Marcus for a bit if that's okay."

"He can't really come to the phone right now," replied Rhianna in a tone that made Alexa suspect she meant something more.

"Right, well can you give him a message for me?" Alexa asked, trying to remember what Peter had been teaching her about phone etiquette. Bethany rolled her eyes as she lounged on the daybed, watching Alexa's uncomfortable exchange.

"A message? Seriously?" asked Rhianna harshly, making Alexa realise Marcus's family knew all about her. She was about to hang up when Rhianna continued in a critical tone. "Didn't you hear about the accident?"

Alexa was sure her heart stopped for a second, before thudding back into an erratic rhythm. "What accident?" she choked. Bethany sat bolt upright at those words, but did not move off the daybed.

"After all he told me about you I assumed you'd be here. You were supposed to be his best friend," continued Rhianna, obviously not comprehending Alexa's mangled words.

"What accident?" asked Alexa again, this time trying hard to speak clearly, even as her heart pounded in her throat.

"Lucy never called you? She told me she told all his friends."

"What happened?" cried Alexa.

"His car – the car he was in – got wrapped around a telegraph pole. He was lucky to survive."

"Is he okay?" Alexa gasped. All this time she had not called, angry that he had not taken her side in an argument, hurt that he had not called.

"He'll survive, but he's pretty banged up. They're not completely sure there'll be no permanent damage."

"Where is he?"

Alexa hung up as soon as Rhianna told her which hospital Marcus was in. Bethany peppered her with questions as she dashed upstairs to change before rushing out of the house.

"Want me to come with you?" called Bethany.

"No, I think I should face this mistake on my own."

Alexa drove quickly, checking her speed when it became excessive. The hospital corridors were busy, but Alexa paid them no attention. Reaching the door to Marcus's room, she was thankful to find him alone. His eyes were closed, but he did not look at ease. Both of his legs were in casts and slightly elevated. His left arm was in a similar state. There was a semi-healed gash on the left side of his forehead, but otherwise he looked somewhat less battered than she had imagined. Closing the door behind her, Alexa sat next to Marcus's bed, but did not know what to do. She had never imagined seeing him in such a broken state. Hesitantly, Alexa reached out and placed her hand over Marcus's uninjured right hand. In an instant, his hand grasped hers as his eyes snapped open.

"Alexa? Is it really you?" Marcus asked deliriously. Alexa nodded as his hand cupped her cheek with clumsy force. "I thought I'd never see you again."

"I'm sorry. I had no idea. You must think I'm a terrible person."

Marcus choked up a laugh, releasing her face to wipe away the tears that escaped his eyes. "Lucy said she called you and you told her you never wanted to see me again, but I learned not to trust much she says when it comes to you. She lied, you know. She never lost her wallet. She had it the whole time."

Alexa nodded. She wanted to know why Marcus had not called, but some things were better left unsaid.

"I wanted to call," he said, reading her mind. "I should've – just to say I was wrong – but I thought I was doing the right thing leaving you. I wanted you to get on with your life and I felt like I was holding you back."

"Lots of people thought that, but I just missed my friend."

"I missed you too."

"So what happened?" asked Alexa.

"Your birthday," answered Marcus. Alexa closed her eyes, hating that day even more. "All I could think about was you. I wanted to talk to you – see you – but couldn't. I kept thinking five years – five years til I could see you again. It felt like another lifetime. I just wanted it to pass. Brandon – my best mate – he didn't – I made up some story about having a bad day. We went out drinking. I was coming up with a new plan – something to pass the time. I don't know how much we drank or how the accident happened. I was so drunk I don't remember much except the pain of waking up here."

"What do you mean about five years? Why couldn't you see me for five years?" asked Alexa, feeling her heart swell.

"You're so young," said Marcus, stroking her cheek. "Just twenty."

"It's just a number," said Alexa in a soft whisper, trying not to be too mesmerised by his touch. "It's good to know I still drive you to drink," she added guilty.

"Don't even think about blaming yourself," said Marcus sternly. "I'm the idiot. I just remember this moment – don't know when – was sure I was going to die. All I could think about was how betrayed you looked that night, how I'd hurt you and that I'd never be able to say sorry."

Alexa saw tears building in Marcus's eyes and grabbed his hand, squeezing it firmly. "I could never hate you and you're not going to die," she said, forcing a smile on to her face, happy to see Marcus cough up one as well. "I just wish I'd been here earlier. I don't hate you. I won't ever hate you."

Marcus sighed heavily and squeezed her hand in return. "I get why you were always so desperate to get out of hospital. It's really quite depressing in here," said Marcus in a more composed voice.

"When are they releasing you?"

"I don't know. I've had all the surgery I need, but my legs have only just gone in the casts. With my arm in a cast for another month, I need full-time care. I've never been this useless."

"You're stuck here for another month?" cried Alexa.

"More, probably," smiled Marcus grimly. "Lucy had to move, with me not there to pay rent and bills. All my stuff's in storage. Don't have anywhere to go. My parents want me to live with them, but I'm not sure I could go back to my mother wiping my arse. Don't think I'll have a choice in the end."

"What happened to Brandon?" asked Alexa, though her mind was on other things.

"Few cuts and bruises and a large fine."

"That's it? For almost killing you."

"He was very contrite."

Alexa rolled her eyes. And Marcus thought she was forgiving. Marcus only smiled and stroked her face again. They did not talk much after that. Alexa found her mind busily planning, and it was easier to just enjoy the silence as Marcus stroked her hair. His eyes slid closed, opening every so often to smile at her, but she could see how tired her visit was making him. It just did not seem right to say goodbye yet. As Marcus's eyes opened again, they suddenly widened, his hand jerking away.

"Mum, Dad, what are you doing here?" asked Marcus in a jittery voice, as Alexa turned in panic.

"We thought we might visit our son, if that's okay. How are you feeling tonight?" asked his mother in a measured voice, eyeing Alexa suspiciously.

Alexa realised her identity was not a mystery and suspected her history was not either from the way his parents were looking at her, but for Marcus's sake she would not make a scene. "Hi, I'm Alexa. Marcus lived with me for a while," she said in a quiet voice.

"Yes, we know," replied Marcus's father curtly. "You were his student once too, I believe."

"Where's Rhianna?" asked Marcus, as Alexa gathered her things.

"She's outside on the phone."

"I should get going," said Alexa. "I'll come back and visit if you want," she dared to add. Marcus nodded timidly. "It was nice to meet you," Alexa muttered towards his parents, her eyes downcast as she rushed from the room.

Forcing herself not to run from the building, Alexa noticed a tall woman with spiky, light brown hair streaked with different colours walking towards her. The woman was smiling, but Alexa was unsure if she should acknowledge her. "Alexa?" asked the woman, stopping in front of her. Alexa nodded, shifting her position so that she had a clear path to the exit. "I'm Rhianna. It's nice to finally meet you."

"Really?" asked Alexa involuntarily, making Rhianna smile. It was the same smile as Marcus and made Alexa strangely predisposed to liking her, though she held out no hope of Rhianna returning the sentiment.

"How was he?" asked Rhianna.

"Better than expected after what you said," confessed Alexa.

"You didn't see him straight after. He was in a real bad way. Needed three lots of surgery just to save his life." Alexa could not respond. Rhianna sounded angry, as though she blamed her. "He's fine now," added Rhianna reassuringly.

"He wants to get out of here," replied Alexa automatically.

"Yeah, I know. I wish I could help, but I don't plan to stay here much longer. He's the only reason I've put up with Mum and Dad so long. I don't know how he's managed it."

"He doesn't want to go back there," said Alexa before she could stop herself.

"No, I don't blame him," smiled Rhianna slyly. "He's grown up these last few years. I'll give you credit for that." Alexa was sceptical. "You probably don't realise it, but Marc's talked to me a lot about you," said Rhianna, making Alexa's heart sink. "Brought us closer – something else I'll credit you for. He's a decent guy and did the right thing not getting involved with you before. He never wanted to be with you like that. Thing is, you're not his student any more. There's no reason you can't be together now, and you can't be worse for him than Lucy."

Alexa realised that she had a stupid grin on her face and quickly recomposed herself. She had never liked someone she had just met before as much as Rhianna. "I want to get Marc out of here," Alexa said, realising it was better to tell someone about her newly-formed plan. His family were not going to like her more if she kidnapped him. "You okay with that?"

"As long it doesn't involve sending him home or to Lucy."

Alexa smiled once more, but when Rhianna's mother stepped out looking for her, Alexa waved goodbye and dashed to the car. Her insides were quivering as she drove. She had never had so much to do and so quickly.

"What happened? Is he okay? Where is he?" asked Bethany as soon as Alexa got home. Alexa did not answer, barely able to comprehend the questions. All her focus was on the house and what needed to be done. "Lex? Are you listening to me?" asked Bethany, grabbing Alexa's shoulders and shaking her.

"How long would it take to make this place wheelchair-friendly?" asked Alexa.

"What?" asked Bethany. Alexa repeated her question in an agitated manner, waving her hand around the room as though that clarified the things. "For the basics, a couple of days max," replied Bethany. "Ground floor only, though. I can't build lifts."

"That's fine. When can you start?" asked Alexa quickly, thankful Bethany believed it possible.

"Is he coming home?"

"When can you start?" repeated Alexa in a frustrated tone.

"Now, Lex. I can start now."

Bethany pulled Alexa into a quick hug before rushing into the backyard. She spent all night in her workshop. Alexa could do little to assist, but tidied the downstairs rooms, removing all the excess furniture. It was a remarkably short time later that Bethany came in asking for help installing the ramps.

"Um, to do it quick, I have to make it a bit messy. Sorry," said Bethany apologetically. "I mean, it'll work and be stable. I just had to stick to really basic, so securing it – might need to patch it up later."

"Bethy," said Alexa, holding Bethany's face. "You have no idea how amazingly fantastic you are. This is incredible and I'd keep telling you how thankful I am if I wasn't so anxious to get it all done."

They slept briefly after the ramps were installed. Bethany was still a month off being able to sit for her provisional licence, so Alexa drove them to the hardware store. Bethany shopped and Alexa made no issue with the cost. As soon as they arrived home, Bethany started installing the handrails in the bathroom.

Alexa felt as though she was in some kind of trance. She wanted desperately to see Marcus, but did not want to go back with nothing to offer. Until she had a full-time carer, all the alterations to the house were simply decoration. Needing an immediate start and twenty-four hour care, Alexa had to offer a good wage, but figured it would only be for three months at the most. Marcus saved her life more than once; the least she could do was use some of her millions to give him the care he needed.

The idea of finding someone suitable in just a couple of days was daunting, but as soon as the resumes came in, Alexa started sorting. She received a surprisingly large number of applications and from people more qualified than she needed. However, it would not be qualifications alone that decided who got this job, which meant Alexa would have to personally interview the candidates. By Monday afternoon she had seen five, but did not approve of any enough to consider letting them share her house and place Marcus in their complete care. When the doorbell rang for applicant number six, Alexa took a deep breath and hoped for something better.

"Sean King," said the well-kept middle-aged man, holding out his hand to Alexa.

Alexa felt her stomach twist at the touch of his skin, but tried to hide it. Walking through to the front room, she sat behind her desk and asked Sean the same questions she had asked the other applicants. She tried to listen to his answers, but when he spoke the menacing voice from her dreams replied. The heavy shadow that haunted her dreams now sat before her and it took all her restraint not to run screaming from the room.

"Are you all right?" asked Sean, noticing her discomfort.

"Yes, sorry. So you can start immediately?"

"Yes, I'm between jobs at the moment."

"And you don't have any problems with it being a twenty-four hour position for at least a month, possibly longer."

"No."

"Well, thank you for your time," said Alexa, quickly concluding the interview. "I'll get back to you in the next day or two."

"Thank you. It was good to meet you – Alexa, was it?" said Sean, smiling as he left.

Alexa closed the front door, locking it as well, before rushing to the bathroom and vomiting. Her body was shaking uncontrollably. Sean was one of the more experienced candidates, and she knew her paranoia had little to do with him personally, but she hated the thought of him ever coming near her again. Her nightmares had not ceased and now she was having panic attacks while she was awake.

"Are you okay?" asked Bethany, returning home from work to find Alexa still crouched on the bathroom floor near the toilet.

"Yeah, just the last guy freaked me out," replied Alexa, steadying herself. Bethany's arrival simultaneously grounded her and stirred deep protective instincts, forcing her to her feet. "Problem is, he's probably the most qualified and I only have one guy left to see."

"You can't hire someone if they freak you out," cried Bethany, pulling Alexa through to the kitchen. "Look at you, you're shaking."

"Every guy freaks me out eventually. Not their fault I'm a mental nutcase," Alexa sighed, suddenly feeling very weary.

"You're not mental and even if you are a little screwed up, I still love you. Doesn't that count?"

"Counts a lot," smiled Alexa, hugging Bethany tight.

Bethany reciprocated, making Alexa promise she would not hire Sean no matter how dismal the next applicant was. It was a promise Alexa was thankful to give. The idea of seeing Sean again was terrifying. It made Alexa's relief at the next applicant being all but perfect profound.

Ryan Mailer impressed from the moment Alexa opened the door. Within three questions, they had gone completely off topic. As soon as Ryan mentioned he had just come back from overseas, Alexa could not stop herself from asking him about it. Half an hour later she forced herself to continue with the interview questions. Ryan answered them perfectly. He was twenty-eight and not only between jobs, but between homes. He had years of experience, more than Alexa needed, but was happy for the chance to ease back into work. His quiet, pleasant manner and good sense of humour were a good fit for the household. In fact, Alexa's only concern was how much Bethany might like him.

"Um, I'll need to check your references before I decide anything," said Alexa.

"That's not a problem," smiled Ryan, standing to shake her hand. "Just let me know if you need help arranging anything with the hospital. I know how confusing they can be. If you hire me, of course."

It was the first time Alexa understood Bethany's compulsion to hug people in random moments of excitement. She had not expressed her fears regarding securing Marcus's release, but she was glad Ryan had picked up on it.

As soon as Ryan left, Alexa called Peter, who she had updated soon after seeing Marcus in the hospital. Peter had continued her casual employment, and she had been able to increase her hours this semester with a much more condensed university timetable. He had not sounded terribly surprised by her plan, but had given her a very long list of things to consider. It had made the process more daunting than she initially conceived, but Peter thankfully volunteered to do the referee checks and finalise the contract.

"He's all yours," said Peter two hours later over the phone. "I took the liberty of calling him and requesting police and background checks. The contract has a clause that his continued employment is conditional on that coming back clean, since I know you need him to start quickly."

"Did you scare him?" asked Alexa, unsure if she wanted Ryan put on guard or not.

"He's aware of the conditions of his employment," replied Peter with a hint of laughter in his voice. "I've arranged for Ryan to come in tomorrow and sign the contact. I might reiterate a few things then, but I promise I won't scare him off. He does seem very suited to the position and he's promised to bring Marcus home to you very soon."

***

The ceiling bulged and fell, waving across the room as Marcus continued to stare at it. He had not had any visitors all day and was beginning to feel depressed. His bed felt like a cage and he wanted desperately to get out. Lucy had not been to see him for almost two weeks. She had apparently been by his side every day while he was unconscious, but as soon as he was out of medical danger, she had felt secure resuming her life and her visits had become less frequent and more sporadic. The rejection hurt; even more than Alexa's continued absence.

In the months before the accident, Marcus had thrown himself into his relationship with Lucy and found a renewed passion for her. It had made being away from Alexa bearable, but now he had nothing to make Alexa's absence tolerable. Marcus did not want to feel that way. He had tortured himself to give Alexa a chance to be free and move on from him, and promised he would never seek a way back to her. However, now Alexa had come to him, he was not sure if, in Lucy's absence, he would have the strength to refuse her friendship.

"Can I come in?" asked a soft voice from the door.

Marcus turned eagerly, hoping for Lucy, but was not disappointed to see Alexa's youthful face before him. "Sure. I'm not busy," he replied, the bitterness of his thoughts tainting his words.

"I'm sorry I haven't been back before. I've been busy organising things."

"Common theme these days," Marcus muttered.

"Have I upset you?" asked Alexa meekly.

When Marcus looked up, he was shocked to see how badly his self-pitying mood had wounded Alexa. Perhaps he had forgotten just how easily hurt she could be or maybe something happened in their months apart to make her so sensitive.

"No, it's not you," Marcus said sincerely. "I'm sorry. Lucy hasn't been for a while. I guess I just hoped you were her."

"Oh …" gasped Alexa, shuffling backwards.

"No! I'm glad you're here," Marcus said in an urgent voice. "I'm just feeling sorry for myself." Alexa did not seem convinced. She looked terrified and too scared to speak as she continued to shift away. "Alexa, are you okay?"

"You can say no if you want to," said Alexa nervously, hitting the wall in her backwards retreat. "I mean, I really didn't ask – and I should've. I'm sorry. I thought you'd want to. But you don't have to. Only if you want."

"Want what?" asked Marcus.

"I kinda hired a male nurse for you – to stay with you – twenty-four hours for now – so you don't have to stay here."

"That sounds – it'd be great – I just don't have anywhere to go. A nurse isn't much use right now. I have enough here," Marcus replied negatively, before regretting it. It was a very sweet gesture.

"I thought – maybe – you'd be okay living with me and Bethy. I realise you might not want to, but you'll have your own room and the nurse'll be with you," rambled Alexa, her words running over each other in their haste to escape her mouth. "Bethy's made ramps and everything as wheelchair-friendly as possible. You'll have to stay on the ground floor, but everything you need's there."

"Are you serious?"

"I know. I'm sorry. I should've asked. It wasn't fair to just do all that and never speak to you about it. I'm sorry."

"You think I'm upset with you?" queried Marcus, interrupting Alexa's stream of apologies.

"You can say no. It's just when you said you wanted to get out I kinda went ahead and organised it. I didn't even ask if you wanted to live with us. Sorry."

"So you made ramps, fixed up the house and hired a nurse? All for me?" Marcus questioned incredulously.

Alexa nodded meekly before apologising once more. There was something so incredibly beautiful about the way she stood there sincerely apologising for being unspeakably generous, but Marcus hated her timidness as she cowered at the door.

"It's also just – Lucy won't be able to stay over," Alexa added guiltily, though Marcus knew this was non-negotiable. "She can visit if she has to, but … I'm sorry, I really didn't think this through."

Alexa was now practically out the door.

"Good," said Marcus forcefully, halting her backwards march. "And if all your apologising doesn't mean you're rescinding your offer, then I accept. I'd love to stay with you. When do we go?"

Alexa smiled more broadly than Marcus had seen for a very long time. It was truly beautiful, though his enjoyment of the moment was destroyed by Alexa dashing from the room, leaving him alone and confused. Assuming Alexa had left, traumatised by the exchange, Marcus tempered his expectations for a quick release.

"Urgh, looks like you'll be stuck here another two days," huffed Alexa, stomping into the room half an hour later. "Some stupid inspection or something. Don't worry. It'll be fine. Bethy's done a real good job." Marcus could only stare. "Sorry."

"Alexa, please don't apologise again," said Marcus seriously. "What you've done – there's nothing to apologise for."

"But you've already been here so long," cried Alexa. "If I'd – I should've done more. I left you here."

"How did I forget how you turn everything around so it's your fault?" asked Marcus, astounded by how far Alexa was taking this. "You're doing more for me than I could ever expect and you're incessant apologising is ruining this very perfect moment for me."

Alexa smiled softly, making Marcus's heart ache. He wished he knew how to make her smile without making it about him.

"Um, I'm sorry," said Alexa tentatively, looking at her wrist.

"For what now?" asked Marcus, keeping his voice light.

"I have to go home," Alexa answered, smiling just slightly. "But I'll see you tomorrow?" Marcus loved the way she turned that statement into a question. "I'm going to send Ryan to pick you up as soon as they've cleared us. We're trying to get it done tomorrow. But if you don't like him, you have to let me know and I'll find someone else."

If Marcus thought it would have placated Alexa, he would have explained how much he would put up with just to be out of hospital, but knew a statement like that would make her worry more.

Closing his eyes, Marcus leaned back into his pillow and smiled. It was the first night he fell asleep with ease and he woke feeling more refreshed than ever. Then Alexa worked another miracle. He was being released that afternoon. When the nurse Alexa hired arrived, Marcus's regard for her became even greater.

"You must be Marcus," he said, holding out his hand. Marcus shook it, nodding and smiling. "I'm Ryan. I'll be taking care of you for the next little while, so what do you say to getting out of here?"

"I'm keen," replied Marcus happily, trying to push himself out of the bed.

"Whoa! Hang on, soldier," laughed Ryan, placing a restraining hand on Marcus's shoulder. "How about we get you showered and dressed first. They still need to finalise your discharge papers."

"Oh, clothes," stammered Marcus. "I don't think I have any."

"I've heard rumours of an escape pack," smirked Ryan.

Marcus stared as Ryan opened the cupboard by his bed and pulled out a bag. Marcus saw Rhianna bring it in two days ago, but she had only made some cryptic comment as she stashed it in the cupboard while their parents were distracted. It comprised everything he needed to leave hospital, and made him realise there had been some conspiring going on. Showering and changing into real clothes was a liberating experience. Marcus's happiness about the whole situation – particularly knowing Alexa and Rhianna had been working together – was so consuming he was grinning stupidly as he waited on his bed for his discharge to be organised. It took longer than expected, Ryan in and out trying to hurry it along. When Rhianna walked in room with a large suitcase and a smaller backpack, his prospects of escape became more concrete.

"So it's true. You're going to live with that girl again?" said his mother in a derogatory manner as she stomped in after Rhianna.

"He just wants to get of hospital, Mum. You can understand that," said Rhianna. "Sorry, they got suspicious when I started packing your stuff," she added quietly as she sat on the bed. "Be thankful you're my favourite big brother."

"I'm your only big brother," Marcus replied with a smile.

"If you're so desperate to leave, why wouldn't you come home?" asked his mother. "I've offered many times to take care of you."

"Smother him more like it," muttered Rhianna, and Marcus could not help but smile.

"Have you thought this through, son?" asked his father seriously. "You know the consequences this could have on your future."

"Oh, what consequences?" sighed Rhianna dramatically. "What exactly do you think's going to happen? Besides, Alexa's really nice – and it's pretty impressive what she's doing for him. Marc's not her teacher any more. They're both adults. It's not illegal."

Marcus wanted to fight his own battle, but Rhianna was beating him to every punch and punching much harder than he would have dared. No matter what his parents said, Rhianna had a counter. Marcus wanted to point out that he had no intention of anything happening with Alexa, but that was not Rhianna's tactic. She just kept explaining why there was nothing wrong with him and Alexa being together.

Ryan stood awkwardly near the door watching the confrontation. He had the discharge papers in his hands, but looked as though he was seriously questioning whether or not he should return them.

"Sorry, but now they've kicked you out, they want that bed," said Ryan, walking over to Marcus. "We should get going."

"Will you come home?" asked Marcus's mother, though it was more of a command than a question.

"Everything's ready for me," replied Marcus, trying not to sound defiant. He was used to being the good son. "And I can get myself around Alexa's place. How would I get up the front stairs at home?"

"We're very disappointed in you, son," said his father, stomping out of the room with his mother.

Rhianna jumped off the bed, smiling broadly. "Oh, come on, don't look so put out. That's the way they usually say goodbye to me."

It was true and Marcus suddenly felt very guilty for not standing up for Rhianna over the years.

"So, now you've made me lose my welcome, there any chance of a lift to the airport on the way to your new home?" asked Rhianna in a cheerful voice. "I think my visit is officially over."

"What about all your stuff?" asked Marcus.

"Ah, this is all my stuff," laughed Rhianna, lifting the backpack. "I travel light."

"Do you mind?" Marcus asked, looking up at Ryan.

"Not at all," replied Ryan, flashing Rhianna a pleased grin. "We're not on a deadline."

Marcus coughed over his laugh. Rhianna regularly attracted that kind of response from men. She was so lively and vibrant that it was often impossible not to go along with whatever she wanted. It was a charm she knew how to exploit, requesting pit stops along the way.

With Rhianna making all the conversation, Marcus sat back, window down, and enjoyed the fresh air blowing over him.

"Enjoy your new home, boys," smiled Rhianna when they arrived at the airport. Rhianna leaned forward and hugged Marcus's from the back seat. Marcus returned the embrace with his good arm. "Try and make the most of it this time," she added, ruffling his hair before jumping out of the car. "Nice to meet you, Ryan. Make sure you take care of him. He's my only big brother."

"I promise," smiled Ryan.

When Ryan turned the car towards Alexa's place, Marcus sighed contentedly. He was going home. The laugh escaped him before he could stop it. Home. It was what he had been trying to deny since leaving. Alexa was his home.

Chapter Three

ALEXA RUSHED AROUND tidying the house, constantly looking at her watch. She expected Marcus and Ryan to be here by now. It worried her and was why she kept cleaning despite Bethany's insistence there was nothing left to do.

Charlotte had screamed when Alexa told her what was happening. If it had not been Dylan and Mia's birthday, Alexa would not have been able to keep her away, but Mia's recovery from cancer was having a wonderful effect on the family, even allowing Charlotte to get along better with her stepmother. However, Charlotte did make Alexa promise to call that evening to report on Marcus's arrival.

"I think the house is clean," said Bethany, physically restraining Alexa. "I haven't seen you move so much in months."

"Bethy, you're insane," replied Alexa, wrestling playfully with her. "I'm no different to what I was a week ago."

Bethany tried to disagree, so Alexa let her drag them out to the front porch. Bethany's arm wrapped around her shoulders as she laid her head in Bethany's neck. It felt good not to be squabbling. They had fought so much in their months living alone together. Alexa had always envisioned them getting along so well.

"You know that no matter how much we annoy each other, I love you more than anyone in the world, right?" asked Alexa.

"I know, Lex. You're my world too, but our world's big enough for other people."

"And it's getting bigger again now," Alexa replied with an excited smile.

"I was talking about Ben," said Bethany, forcing Alexa to hold in her sigh. "You know you could've told him about Marcus."

"I assumed you'd tell him, so what's the point."

"The point is he's trying to be our father. I thought you wanted that."

Alexa closed her eyes, squeezing Bethany's hand. She did want that, more than she could ever articulate. Even after the argument over Penny, there were few things Alexa wanted more. It was just that hoping and wishing did not equal reality. Legally, they were nothing to Ben. There was nothing more than her nightmares and his guilt binding him to them. Once they were gone, he would be too, and they would become nothing more than a vague memory. Thankfully, before Bethany could extract those fears, Ryan's car pulled into the driveway.

Alexa's heart marched double-time. Her body had not had this reaction at the hospital, but the knowledge that Marcus was now home – with her – had her insides quivering. "I'm going to let them settle in while I make dinner," she said quickly. "You okay to show them where everything is?"

"Of course," replied Bethany instantly, hugging Alexa tight. "He's home, Lexie. Back where he belongs."

"Holy crap, Marc, what happened to you?" cried Bethany when Ryan opened the car door to assist Marcus into the wheelchair. Bethany rushed forward to help, but Ryan put his hand out, insisting he had it covered. As soon as Marcus was in the chair, Bethany lunged at him, throwing her arms around his neck. She liked the way his arms wrapped around her, but the feel of his cast on her skin made her jittery. Pushing away, she moved to his right side, away from his cast arm. "You okay? Your insides?" she asked, feeling his torso.

"I'm okay, Beth," nodded Marcus slowly. "What did Alexa say happened to me?"

"Say?" laughed Bethany. "She's barely spoken since hearing about the accident. She's been like a superhuman robot getting everything ready. She just told me to make the house wheelchair-friendly. I never expected this." She assumed Marcus had been paralysed, but realised just in time that he would not appreciate hearing how happy that made her. If his injuries were permanent he would have a reason to stay with them forever.

"I don't think Alexa's the only who's put in a superhuman effort this week," said Marcus, nodding towards the front door.

"It's just a ramp," Bethany replied dismissively, jumping up and heading towards the back of the car. Opening the boot, she quickly wiped away the tears burning her eyes as she grabbed their bags.

"Whoa, don't try and carry all of them," said Ryan when he saw her laden down with their bags, but Bethany could not allow herself to cry because of a simple compliment and then not be able to carry bags. Marcus already thought her weak. His dislike and distrust of her had torn him from Alexa once and she was determined not to be responsible for tearing them apart again.

"I'm right," Bethany smiled confidently. "Besides, we don't have far to go." Walking into the house first, she turned immediately into Alexa's study. "Welcome home," she smiled broadly as Ryan wheeled Marcus in. "This'll be your room. You like it?"

"It's great," replied Marcus, looking around. He used his good hand to push forward, but only turned himself in a half-circle. "You sure Alexa doesn't need it?" he asked, picking up one of the textbooks on the desk after Ryan had wheeled him across the room.

"Urgh, she's hopeless," sighed Bethany. "She cleans the whole house and forgets this. She must've been down here last night. All night, probably."

"All night?" asked Marcus, looking concerned.

"I know!" replied Bethany, hoping to finally have an ally. "It's all she does. Don't even bother trying to get her to have a life. She comes home from uni and studies. On the weekend, in the evening, this is where you'll find her. If she's not in the pool, she's here."

"Then perhaps you should put me in another room," said Marcus seriously, trying to wheel himself out.

"This is the only room that'll suit your needs. Don't worry, I'm making Lex a study upstairs. Perhaps then she'll fall asleep in her own bed." But Bethany doubted it. Something had happened to Alexa since their move. The change was not necessarily bad, but Alexa was not the carefree big sister she used to be. She was constantly anxious, and Bethany could not get her to be laid back and relaxed about anything any more.

"Where's Ryan's room?" asked Marcus.

"Here," replied Bethany. "He needs to be with you. If you just needed rest we would've brought you home straight away."

Marcus gave her a searching look. Bethany wondered if he saw through her the way he could Alexa.

"Ryan, can you give us a moment?" asked Marcus seriously.

"Sure, I think I left a couple of things in the car," replied Ryan.

"Um, Lex is in the kitchen. Don't disturb her while she's cooking dinner, okay," Bethany called anxiously to the departing Ryan.

"What's going on, Beth?" asked Marcus as soon as Ryan left. Bethany tried to be dismissive as she backed away, but Marcus was insistent. "Something's wrong. You don't trust Ryan. That much is clear. What happened? I'm telling you now, I won't stay if Alexa's not comfortable with him."

"No, it's not Ryan," replied Bethany, biting her lip. "Promise you won't tell Lex?" Marcus nodded immediately. "It was another guy. He freaked her out – real bad."

"What about Ryan?" asked Marcus firmly.

"Lex said he was great and they got on real well. I just – we don't have more spare bedrooms down here. If he's on the second floor – I'm all the way down the back and you're stuck here – she's up there and he could – we'd never know. If he's with you then …" Marcus covered his face. Kneeling in front of him, Bethany grabbed his good hand. "I know it's not great, but the daybed's real comfy. Lex sleeps on it all the time. And it's just til you get better. Once Ryan's gone you can have any room you want."

"If there's even a single second when Ryan makes Alexa uncomfortable, I'll go straight back to hospital," said Marcus firmly.

"Nah, you can stay. We'll kick Ryan out," smiled Bethany, refusing to give him any reason to leave. "We'll take care of you. I just might let Lex do the showing."

Marcus looked scandalised for a moment, before he smiled and shook his head. Bethany loved that smile, how much it betrayed, and could not stop herself from lunging forward to embrace him. Marcus immediately hugged her back, but with just his good arm this time.

"I'm sorry you got all banged up," said Bethany. "But I'm glad you're back home where you belong."

"Everything okay?" asked Ryan, standing hesitantly at the door. "Is it too late to add that I already knew we were sharing a room?"

Marcus looked up and Bethany quickly disentangled herself from him. The smile that graced her face as she swept towards the door was disarming. Alexa had been right when she told him Bethany did not wear her true emotions. "All sorted," she smiled.

Bethany's concern for Alexa should not have surprised Marcus, yet it was so easy to believe in her seemingly unconcerned façade. It would have been easy to dismiss the fearful jerks of her body as nothing more than unstable movements and it made him wonder why she was scared of casts.

"Nice girl," smiled Ryan when Bethany left. She had given him a very sweet smile and Marcus wondered if she was turning herself into a target. It was something foolish he would expect of Alexa, so could not discount the possibility. "You don't like her?"

"We have our differences," Marcus replied diplomatically, hating the way everyone fell so easily in love with Bethany's smiling exterior. "Alexa's the special one."

"Alexa, yeah," nodded Ryan seriously, closing the door. "I'm sensing history. I hope you're planning on filling me in."

"It's complex."

"Mate, we're about to get as intimate as two people get without sleeping together so you may as well tell me your complex history."

Marcus grimaced. He did not want to tell Ryan this stuff, but there was something trustworthy about him and he could see why Alexa liked him.

Ryan did not say anything as he started unpacking. Thankfully, neither of them had much, because there was only one set of drawers, which did not match the rest of the furniture.

"Apparently, Bethany didn't have time to build a wardrobe this week," said Ryan in a slightly mocking tone. "Alexa was very apologetic. However, we've been promised the situation will be rectified soon." Marcus bit his tongue, not liking Ryan's tone, but before he could think of the right words Ryan was talking again. "Now, I don't know about you, but that's about the strangest apology I've ever received," said Ryan in a normal voice. "I already realise this is an odd situation, but I'm pretty out of my depth right now. So help me out and tell me what's going on – or at least explain why anyone would apologise for not building a wardrobe."

"Like I said, it's complex."

"Sure, I'll accept that," shrugged Ryan, placing more clothes in the drawers. "Then how about I tell you what I think I know from the few hours I've been employed by Alexa and you can tell me if I'm wrong." Marcus shrugged reluctantly. "Teacher?" Marcus nodded, forcing Ryan to abandon the unpacking and sit on the daybed. "And I'm guessing Alexa was your student."

"Yes," replied Marcus. That was one thing he would never deny.

"How long ago?"

"She finished high school almost two years ago."

"So what, you guys had an affair while you were her teacher?" asked Ryan.

"NO!" Marcus cried. Ryan smiled at the strong response. "Never.

It's – it's more complex than that."

"And you think I'll disapprove?"

"I don't really care what you think," Marcus muttered.

"Mate, I'm here to take care of you, not pass judgement," said Ryan seriously. "I'm here as your nurse, not your friend, but things'll be a lot more comfortable if we can get along. And if you guys are going to keep putting me in the middle of your complex situations, then it'd be good to know what's going on occasionally. You all seem like pretty decent people and I don't need to go getting myself into stuff that doesn't concern me. Besides, you might even find I'm not as judgemental as you think."

"You'd be the first," said Marcus. Ryan smiled, but said nothing. "I love her, okay, and for very obvious reasons we can never be together, but that doesn't stop her being one of the most amazing people you'll ever meet."

"You're not exactly making this story less interesting. You realise that, right?"

"It's not just my story. I don't know you."

"Fair enough. Then why don't we get to know each other first. You can tell me all the bits of your life that don't involve Alexa."

Marcus knew that should not have been hard, but being back in Alexa's house made it feel like his life had never truly existed while they had been apart. Bethany had been right. Alexa was his life.

***

Alexa cleared the dining room table. It was at times like these that she realised how much Charlotte helped out, but she did not like missing her because of it. Charlotte's value was not her housework. However, those were the times they had spent together and Alexa never noticed how demanding the tasks were when Charlotte was around.

Bethany danced into the room as Alexa put dinner on the table. When Bethany saw the pile of cook books and the pad of paper at end of the dining table she just laughed. "Is this seriously what you did instead of going to uni today?" asked Bethany, shaking her head. "You really don't have a life, do you?"

Alexa rolled her eyes and moved one of the chairs away from the table so Marcus's wheelchair could fit. Sometimes it was useful when Bethany was so oblivious. "Just go get the guys," smiled Alexa, pushing Bethany towards the door. "Dinner's ready."

Bethany made it to the door, but did not need to go any further as Ryan appeared with Marcus.

"We smelt food," said Ryan with a grin. Ryan looked Bethany's way. It was a playful smile, but Alexa was not comfortable with it. Thankfully, Bethany's returning smile had no interest in it. It was not really fair the effect Bethany had on guys.

"Look at what you've inspired," said Bethany as they sat down, tossing the pad of paper to Marcus. "One-handed dining at its best."

Alexa felt her cheeks blush as Marcus and Ryan looked between the list and their bowls of bolognaise on spiral pasta.

"Huh, that's very practical," said Ryan, looking thoughtfully at his fork.

"Thank you," replied Alexa, sneering playfully at Bethany who was smirking behind her hand.

"This is really good, Alexa," said Marcus, eating in a much quicker manner than she remembered.

"I had a pretty good mentor when it came to this dish," Alexa replied. It was actually the first time she had cooked bolognaise since he left.

"Yeah and you've been eating hospital crap for a month," laughed Bethany. "Anything's going to taste good."

"No, I'm with Marc. This is good, Alexa," said Ryan. "I think I'm going to enjoy working here if the food's this good every night."

"Of course it's good. Lex is brilliant," retaliated Bethany, as if Ryan had insulted Alexa.

Alexa could only smile as she took Bethany's hand, eating with the other, while Ryan shot Marcus a questioning look.

No one spoke for a while, until Bethany seemed to suddenly realise there was a practical stranger at their table. "How old are you?" she asked, looking over at Ryan with a feverish glint in her eyes.

Alexa realised they were about to get Ryan's life story, whether he wanted to give it or not.

"Twenty-eight," answered Ryan compliantly.

"You married?" responded Bethany.

"No."

"Any kids?"

"No."

"Girlfriend?"

"Not at the moment."

"Boyfriend?"

"Not at the moment."

"Looking for one?"

"Which?"

"Either."

"Not at the moment," replied Ryan with a smile.

Bethany's questioning was like rapid-fire machine gunning. Ryan barely finished his short answer before Bethany asked another question. "Why'd you become a nurse?" she asked interestedly.

"I liked helping people, I guess."

"Still like it?"

"Yeah. It's a good job. Varied."

"You like Marc?"

"Oh, yeah, he's okay. Not the worst patient I've ever had," smiled Ryan. "We've been getting to know each other."

That stopped Bethany dead. It was the one problem with Marcus. To know him was to know them. It was an unavoidable consequence of having someone else in their home. Alexa tried to tell herself that Ryan was a nice guy, but she did not know that and was sure Bethany was just as wary. She would have to ask Marcus to keep an eye on Ryan and make sure he did not spend time alone with Bethany. If Alexa could have had them on the second floor, she would have been much more comfortable.

"You going out tonight?" Alexa asked Bethany, when she stood to leave the table.

"No, I have to go make you another study since you gave the other one away," sighed Bethany dramatically, though her lips were twitching as her eyes flicked Marcus's way.

"We don't really need a desk and bookshelf in our room. Why don't you take them?" asked Marcus.

Alexa almost laughed at the look that came across Bethany's face. Marcus's inability to realise that Bethany did not intend for him to leave any time soon – or at all – left her slightly incoherent. Alexa had already seen the additions to her furniture list that had resulted from Marcus's arrival.

"They go in that room," said Bethany softly before rushing off.

From the nod that followed his look of concern, Alexa knew Marcus now understood. Ryan looked confused, but that only lasted until Alexa left the room. When she returned, Marcus was whispering to Ryan and he was nodding thoughtfully.

Sitting back down at the table, Alexa scattered the cookbooks once again and grabbed the notebook.

"You really don't need to worry about more one-handed meals," said Marcus seriously. "I'll eat anything you give me."

"And I'll cut it up into little pieces if need be," added Ryan with a grin. "It is what I'm being paid for, after all."

"This isn't for you," laughed Alexa, grinning more when she saw Marcus blush. "It's for Bethy's birthday. She's eighteen this weekend. Can you believe it?"

"She's only eighteen?" asked Ryan sceptically. Alexa nodded, her eyebrows raised as she again noticed the admiration Bethany had inspired. "Wow, she looks so much older. But you – I don't – I thought you – so you're the younger sister?"

"No, older," laughed Alexa, amused by Ryan's confusion. She never realised she seemed so much younger than Bethany. Everyone always called her old for her age. "By two years."

"But you look so young."

"It happens," Alexa shrugged, putting her head down.

"So what's with all the cookbooks then?" asked Marcus quickly.

"The last birthday we celebrated together was her tenth. Did I ever tell you I used to make her a course for every year old she was?" Alexa asked. Marcus shook his head, his eyes full of sadness. "I want to do that. Our first birthday back together."

"Eighteen courses?" asked Ryan.

"Yeah," smiled Alexa. "But I need to pick all the courses, write out the shopping list, then work out how I'm going to cook it."

"And you got distracted making up a list for Marc?" Ryan asked curiously.

"No, that was consequential. I want her birthday to be perfect. I don't need dinner to be perfect. That list was easy."

"You do realise that Beth will just be happy that she's eighteen and that you're with her," said Marcus seriously. "I really don't think she has spectacularly high expectations of you or this birthday."

"It's her first birthday out and it's her eighteenth – and our first together in eight years. It means more to her than you realise."

"Must mean a lot to you too," said Ryan.

"Bethy deserves this. It has to be special," said Alexa, avoiding Ryan's comment.

"It will be," replied Marcus reassuringly.

"All right," said Ryan, clapping his hands together. "Let's break this down logically. Number of people?"

"You two will make ten."

"Well no one needs eighteen courses, so why not three courses, six dishes for each?" asked Ryan, redeeming himself with the second part of his sentence. "I'm a bit of a dessert expert – dessert lover, at least. You look like you've got mains pretty well covered, so if Marc does the entrées we should have this sorted in no time."

Alexa distributed the cookbooks and they busily chose a selection of dishes. When Ryan suggested she and Marcus compare lists, her skin flushed with the idea of moving close to him.

"What've you got?" asked Marcus as she knelt next to his chair. "Ha, apparently great minds think too much alike," he laughed. "At least we have a couple of dishes that don't double up. How about you keep those two, I'll keep these ones and we sit next to each other while we select the rest."

It was a suggestion Alexa was only too happy to comply with. It took them twenty minutes and three cookbooks to finalise their selections, after deciding to theme the dishes on Italian, Mexican and Asian-style cooking, with two each for entrée and main.

"Stick to what you know and cheat where possible," smiled Marcus.

"I don't think we'll be able to cheat our way through the next part," Alexa sighed, pulling the cookbooks closer. "Shopping list."

That was by far the longest part of the evening, because once Alexa had the individual lists, she then had to compile them. The amount of food she was required to buy was absolutely staggering and would necessitate more time off from university. Thankfully Jessica had promised to copy all the notes she missed and help her catch up. There was no way Alexa would not make an occasion out of Bethany's birthday.

"Thanks so much. Would've taken forever without you," said Alexa as she gathered up all the books.

"I'm happy to help you shop tomorrow if Marc doesn't have any prior arrangements," said Ryan casually. "You might need it with that list."

"Get me out, get me anywhere," laughed Marcus. "I've never looked forward to grocery shopping before, but this sounds fun –

although I think I might be more of a hindrance than a help."

"You can be the keeper of the list," said Alexa, refusing to give Marcus a reason not to accompany her. "You'll be responsible for making sure we have everything."

"Sounds like a plan. No better way to spend my first full day of freedom," smiled Marcus.

"You have anything you need to do?" asked Alexa. "What about work? You still have a job?"

"Can't work like this, but it was a permanent position so I'll have a job to go back to. Just not getting paid in the meantime."

"Why not?" cried Alexa, horrified they could do such a thing.

"I don't have the leave to cover it. I guess this is why they tell you to take out income protection insurance."

"You have any?" Alexa asked meekly.

"No. That's why Lucy had to move soon after the accident. It was too expensive without my in— oh shit, Lucy. I never called her. She still thinks I'm at the hospital."

"Lucy?" questioned Ryan, looking curiously over at Alexa.

Alexa went to answer, but it was too hard to speak while she tried to hide her smile.

"My girlfriend," sighed Marcus, pushing himself away from the table. "You mind taking me back to the bedroom?"

Marcus put the phone to his ear with a feeling of dread. He could not believe he had honestly forgotten to call Lucy. Thinking back over the last two days he tried to recall a moment where he thought of her at all, but there was nothing but Alexa.

"Hello?" answered Lucy in a flat voice. It was an ominous start and he guessed she already knew where he was.

Taking a deep breath, Marcus told his story to an audience of silence. "Lucy, will you say something?" he pleaded.

"I'm busy. I have to get going," replied Lucy in a detached voice.

"What's that mean?" asked Marcus. "Is this over?" He almost did not care if it was. Lucy's rejection of him had started well before Alexa came to see him.

"It means that my life didn't stop because yours did. I have to work, Marc. I have to earn a living. Not all of us can rely on our exes to take care of us," replied Lucy in an acidic tone. "If you want me to come and see you, I will, but since you're out of hospital now I don't know why you can't come to me. You have much more time on your hands than I do."

"I have two broken legs and a broken arm. I'm not exactly free to come and go as I please," snapped Marcus. "I can't even steer my own wheelchair. I've been given the chance to get out of hospital, not a miracle cure."

"Then I guess you'll have to put up with fitting into my schedule. Sorry, but my world doesn't revolve around you."

Lucy did not say goodbye. She simply hung up, leaving Marcus listening to the empty line. It took all his self-control not slam his phone on the desk.

"I didn't mean to cause problems."

Marcus looked up to see Alexa standing meekly at the door. It was a far cry from the satisfied smile he had glimpsed earlier. If she heard the conversation, she could not have possibly assumed things were going well with Lucy. Managing to turn his wheelchair towards the door, Marcus was going to push forward when Alexa started collecting her belongings from the desk.

"Me and Lucy have always been erratic," Marcus shrugged, downplaying the situation. "You saved my life bringing me here – getting me out of that hospital. I'll never be able to repay you."

"I did miss having you around," said Alexa, sitting down at the desk, her eyes firmly downcast. "But I never wanted to make things hard for you. I should've made sure you wanted to come here. It wasn't fair. I never even gave you the chance to say no."

"What happened, Alexa?" asked Marcus, reaching for her hand, but she pulled slowly away. "You never used to be this insecure."

"I was always this insecure," she replied softly.

"Not out loud," Marcus replied, knowing he could never argue differently. Yet something had definitely changed. Through every trial, Alexa always had an extraordinary level of hope and optimism. That was gone now and he hated it. "Alexa, I never wanted the chance to say no – and not just because you were getting me out of the hospital. If you'd arranged for me to live with my parents – even with Ryan – I would've wanted the chance to say no."

"You wouldn't have," said Alexa flatly.

"No, probably not, but I wouldn't have felt as free or happy. I feel more at home here – with you – than I have anywhere else."

Alexa looked up, but her eyes were instantly drawn towards the door where Ryan was standing silently. It looked like he had just appeared, but Alexa quickly gathered her books. Despite being laden down, she refused Ryan's offer of assistance. It was torturous to see her looking so small and fragile.

"Okay, I think we need to have that chat," said Ryan, walking into the room.

Marcus nodded. He barely knew Ryan, but if he did not talk about Alexa soon he felt as though he might explode. Ryan closed the bedroom door and helped Marcus out of the wheelchair.

"You want chronological or flash back?" asked Marcus, trying to think of how he could tell this story. "But just remember, this is my story, not Alexa's. You don't open that door knowing anything about her or Beth."

"Absolutely," replied Ryan solemnly. "So let's go chronological." Marcus sighed heavily. "Just start from the beginning," suggested Ryan, when Marcus opened and closed his mouth a few times with nothing coming out. "Start with where you first met."

"Then I guess we go back to my first year as a teacher and when Alexa started high school," said Marcus. Ryan drew back, jumping up off the bed. The horror on Ryan's face was comforting. It confirmed he had never believed Marcus and Alexa had had an affair, and helped Marcus believe Ryan was not here looking to take advantage of Alexa. "Don't worry, nothing ever happened then," said Marcus quickly, placating Ryan slightly, though he chose to listen from the daybed rather than sit with him. "She barely existed. That's the point. She was no one. A child. I don't understand how it got to this."

"Okay, from the very beginning then," said Ryan thoughtfully. "But I should tell you, I don't know how it got to this either, but most of us would give up a lot to just experience a point like this. I've seen the way you look at her. I've seen the way she looks at you. That's – most of us never get to know that."

"Hear the story first," replied Marcus heavily. "Loving Alexa – in the absence of everything else – is about the most magical feeling in the world. You just don't get to experience it like that. Mostly it's a lot of guilt and self-loathing. I should've never felt this way for her."

"Let's hear the story then," said Ryan settling into the daybed. "How'd you go from not seeing her to feeling like this?"

Chapter Four

CHARLOTTE BOUNCED IN her seat, her hands ready to release the buckle. Alexa tried to make sure she stopped the car before Charlotte fell out of it. She was only just successful. Bounding excitedly from the car, Charlotte raced straight to Marcus's room.

"Where is he?" asked Charlotte, emerging disappointed.

"Out?" replied Alexa. "I don't know. He's around, I promise."

"Did you tell him I was coming?" asked Charlotte, stomping to the kitchen.

"Of course I did, and he's excited to see you too, but he's not exactly independently mobile. He's kinda stuck on Ryan's schedule."

"What's Ryan like?" asked Charlotte with a smirk. "Is he cute?"

"Yeah, he's not bad," replied Alexa, grinning slightly.

It was true. Ryan was what the world would call conventionally good looking. He had tight sandy blonde curls and tanned surfer-boy skin. His light, hazel-brown eyes could be magnetic, yet Alexa was not attracted to him in the least. It made her wonder if she would have liked him more if Marcus was not around.

"Beth's out tonight, right?" asked Charlotte. "Cos there's no way we can't prepare all this tomorrow morning."

"She's staying at Sam's," smiled Alexa. "He's going to bring her over in time for the party."

"Really? She's staying the night with Sam?"

"What do you mean? Why wouldn't she?" asked Alexa, surprised by Charlotte's reaction. It seemed a natural choice to her, especially as Ben was working late. "Gran and Pop love Bethany."

"Yeah, no, I know they do. I'm just a bit surprised. I didn't think Beth and Sam were getting along that well after her relapse. He took so long to forgive her and it seemed a bit strained afterwards."

"Yeah, I know," replied Alexa solemnly. "I don't know why Sam took that so hard. It's like he never really understood that Bethy's a heroin addict. Like he never got that this is something she'll be for the rest of her life – something she'll battle for the rest of her life."

"You have to admit she hides it well," said Charlotte. "How many people decide to just give up heroin and do it? And she seems to be doing better this time going cold turkey. Makes you question if it's really as bad as you know it is."

Alexa thought hard about Charlotte's assessment. Bethany did hide things well, and in this case she had achieved what most people could never dream of. Yet few congratulated her on staying clean. Most only condemned her for suffering moments of weakness.

"Come on, first dessert," said Charlotte, as she turned on the radio. "White chocolate mousse. Yum."

The music made Alexa instantly relax. If not for Charlotte, Alexa was sure she would have lost music from her life forever after her meltdown earlier that year. However, after months of a music-free home, Charlotte politely queried if she had ever had problems with music that was not from her childhood. The answer was an emphatic no. Bethany immediately and enthusiastically disposed of all the music that had been recorded prior to Alexa starting high school, which constituted a large chunk of her music collection. Alexa thought Bethany would be upset about discarding so many newly acquired possessions, but Bethany just wanted to listen to music again too.

With the mousse setting, they started on the cheesecake. Ryan's selection of easy-to-make desserts and Charlotte's cooking prowess allowed them to quickly prepare the desserts. Alexa let Charlotte take charge. She had natural talent when it came to running a kitchen and even had their schedule for the next morning planned out by the time they placed the last dessert in the fridge.

"Dinner," said Charlotte, skipping over to the list of one-handed meals Alexa had compiled. "You know some of these are really borderline two-handed meals."

"Not if you serve it in a bowl," retorted Alexa.

Charlotte chuckled and strategically pulled food out of the fridge. Music blaring, they danced around the kitchen, not missing Bethany's rhythm, which always made them feel ridiculously uncoordinated.

"Aha, the dance troupe returns."

Charlotte squealed at the sound of Marcus's voice, rushing to hug him. Alexa dived between them, grabbing the large knife from Charlotte's hand. "Whoops," smiled Charlotte, giggling nervously as she hugged Marcus with slightly more caution.

Marcus reciprocated with a one-armed hug, his cast in his lap. Charlotte pulled back and grabbed his cast. "There's nothing written on it," she said. "You'll have to let us decorate it for you."

"You going to put flowers on it to make it look less fearsome?" asked Marcus with a smile, though it faded when Charlotte turned Alexa's way. Alexa had hoped he had not noticed her and Bethany's discomfort around his cast.

"You look terrible, Marc," said Charlotte, astutely assessing him.

"Gee, thanks. It's nice to see you too," laughed Marcus. "It's not exactly the best I've seen you look either," he retaliated, waving his hand at Charlotte's food-splatted clothes.

"I can wash this off. You're all messed up. And Beth said this was you looking good, so you must've been pretty bad. She was in tears describing what you looked like."

"Looks worse than it is now," replied Marcus earnestly.

"Looks like two broken legs and a broken arm. Is it really better than that? You faking so you could come home?"

"Yeah, okay, it looks as bad as it is, but it's better than it was. Definitely not faking it."

"But maybe worth it to come home again?" asked Charlotte with a sly smile. She did not wait for an answer before introducing herself to Ryan.

"Oh, yeah, sorry. Ryan, Charlotte's our – um – friend, I guess. She lived near to our old place," said Alexa.

"What Alexa really means is that Charlotte's pretty much family in every way but blood, but if she introduced her to you as her little sister you'd get confused and ask lots of questions she couldn't easily answer," clarified Marcus.

"Yeah, something like that," said Alexa with an unsure smile, but Charlotte appeared quite chuffed by the explanation.

"You guys need any help?" asked Ryan composedly.

Alexa guessed he was getting used to their strange situations by his calm response, and that Marcus was keeping him clued in. It was inevitable Ryan would find out a lot about them given the intimate contact he had to their lives, but Alexa did not necessarily believe he needed to know more than what he would find out by chance.

"We're good," smiled Charlotte. "We'll call you when it's ready."

Ryan did not argue, but they did not have much time to relax, with dinner on the table fifteen minutes later.

"I confess I feel as if I'm taking advantage of the situation," said Ryan as he sat at the dining table next to Marcus. "You're paying me very well to live in your house, eat your food and take care of a pretty good patient. If I get too used to this lifestyle you might find Marc has another accident."

"You realise Alexa's only paying you for the privilege of wiping shit from his arse, right?" asked Charlotte seriously. "The rest we could handle."

Food flew out of Marcus's mouth and across the table. Alexa covered her mouth to prevent a similar display, while Ryan spat his food back on to his plate.

"What? It's true," said Charlotte with a meek shrug.

"Yeah, I know," laughed Alexa, struggling to compose herself. "We just don't always need to vocalise those truths."

When Alexa looked up, she noticed Marcus had a strange look in his eyes. Though he smiled, she wondered if he thought less of her because she admitted she was not competent enough to care for him. Thankfully, Charlotte decided to get to know Ryan, with the talk soon turning to Ryan's recent travels. Charlotte was fascinated. Alexa could see her mentally listing all the places she wanted to go. It was not long before Alexa realised she was doing the same thing. She wanted to take Bethany to all these places, but had never dared to mention it for fear Bethany would not want the same thing. They were not as similar as she had always assumed and she wondered if it would be Charlotte who she ended up sharing those experiences with.

"Hey, Budapest, isn't that where you met that guy?" asked Charlotte with a sly smile, causing all eyes to turn on Alexa.

"Um, what? No. I've never been there," replied Alexa, her eyes down and shaking her head in Charlotte's direction.

"What guy?" asked Ryan, turning his grin Charlotte's way, as though they were both in on the joke.

"I don't know, but Sam goes on about him as though Alexa was a step away from running off and marrying him," replied Charlotte.

Alexa could not help but laugh. That was so typically Sam. She had no idea he ever thought about that. She had not thought about that guy for ages. There was honestly not that much to think about.

"My best friend Sam," said Alexa, looking over to Ryan. "Thinks there're hordes of guys just hanging around, desperate to marry me and I'm actively choosing to deny their existence. According to him I'm all but walking around with my eyes closed." Ryan laughed, but said nothing. "I don't even know what his issue is. He's liked this one girl for ages and I don't think he's even asked her out yet," Alexa continued, surprised she had never realised that before. She would have to keep it in mind when she next had to defend herself.

"So never been to Budapest, then?" said Ryan, looking bemused by the turn in the conversation.

"No," smiled Alexa.

***

Marcus shifted agitatedly on the lounge. It was annoying to be so useless. Alexa and Charlotte were in the kitchen cleaning up after dinner and preparing for Bethany's party tomorrow. Even Ryan was cleaning the lounge room. It was only him who was incapable of helping.

"Would you stop being so restless," sighed Ryan. "No one expects you to do anything in your state. If you were still in hospital you wouldn't be doing this much."

"I don't like Alexa taking on so much," Marcus sighed heavily. "The only good thing I did when I lived with her before was take some household duties off her hands. You could see how grateful she was when she came home and didn't have to cook or found the cupboards already full. I should be helping, not sponging off her. It annoys me. I want to do more."

"She's a different girl with Charlotte around," said Ryan, ignoring Marcus's self-pitying rant.

"I often think Alexa and Beth love each other too much," nodded Marcus. "It makes them do stupid things. Charlotte, she's been good for both of them – and they've been good for her. "

Ryan collapsed on the other end of the lounge with Marcus. "I officially think you're insane," said Ryan. "And it's taken me – what – two days to come to that very firm conclusion."

"You don't know what you're talking about," muttered Marcus.

"Personally, I'd take Beth," smiled Ryan. Of course he would, thought Marcus in disgust, and see the situation through ridiculously romantic eyes as well, no doubt. "She's a free spirit, beautiful and just so fun – if a little rough," continued Ryan as Marcus scowled. "But Alexa, she's amazing. You just don't come across girls like her."

"I already know that," replied Marcus, choosing to ignore the complimentary comments about Bethany, unsure what it was about her that inspired so much adoration.

"Yeah, but you're too guilt-ridden to do anything. And I can't work out why. I haven't met Lucy, but I've seen enough to know you don't love her even a fraction of what you do Alexa. Add to that everyone's stoked you got yourself all banged up. They all keep welcoming you home. I don't get it. Why are you and Alexa so determined to let this chance pass you by?"

"Were you listening last night?" asked Marcus incredulously.

"Yeah. Were you? Alexa might not be all the things I think Beth is, but she's amazing in the most inspirational way. She's paying me a lot of money to take care of you and … look, I've seen her budget," added Ryan guiltily. Marcus's head snapped up, his eyes scathing. "Her laptop was open. I didn't mean to see it, but for someone who has so much money, she's amazingly diligent. All the money's strictly assigned and not a cent goes to luxuries."

"She's not that kind of girl," replied Marcus in a growling voice, still not convinced by Ryan's explanation. He had lived with Alexa for months and never seen that kind of information. If her laptop had been open, he had not once snuck a look at her private information.

"No one is, mate. No one has that kind of restraint. Seriously, who do you know who could do that?" asked Ryan. No one was Marcus's answer. He could not have done it and would not have wanted to. The stories he heard from Nick and Alan about Bianca's exploits only served to highlight how remarkable Alexa was. "When I turned up here, I assumed rich parents," said Ryan candidly. "Then it became clear it was just Alexa and Beth, so I thought maybe an inheritance. Even that was impressive, being so together when they're so young and alone. Until you told me, I never would've guessed what they'd been through. Then to go from nothing – less than nothing – be given all that money and not go crazy, that's something else altogether."

"Don't ever mention what you know to them," said Marcus in a low voice, looking behind him. "If she thought about it, I'm sure she'd realise I know. She's let stuff slip, but she's never told me and thinks I only know about the payout from the school. She's complex that way. You need to not know anything about this – not ever. Doesn't matter what she lets slip, doesn't matter what your curiosity wants to know. You never, ever speak to her about any of it. None of that – it doesn't define her."

"See that's where we disagree," said Ryan. "All those things, they make her the amazing person she is. If she was just her after having a normal life, you'd say she's a nice girl, but fairly unremarkable. You would've met a thousand girls like that and never looked twice. You know as well as I do it's the rest of it that makes her special – that draws you in."

Marcus did not answer. He had never thought of Alexa that way – never considered if he would have liked her if her circumstances had been similar to the other girls he taught. The reason why was obvious; he did not like to think that Alexa's main attraction was her vulnerability, but there was no way to divorce the person Alexa was from the things she had been through.

"I'm going to tell you something you should've realised yourself. What you and Alexa have is too special to let pass by. I get why you never considered being with her before now. When she was your student – right out of high school – both good calls. The thing is, Alexa's twenty now. She's an adult and a pretty competent one."

"You don't know what you're talking about. You've only seen her when she's strong," replied Marcus. "You haven't seen her weak and vulnerable. You haven't seen what the world has done to her. What right do I have to take advantage her? She may be twenty, but she's barely more than a child."

"Take advantage of her? What are you planning to do? You plan to screw her and toss her away?" asked Ryan. Marcus glared at him hatefully. "No, seriously, I'm trying to work this out. You've never taken advantage of her. When she's been most vulnerable, you've protected her. You're not her teacher any more. You never will be again. You're older than her, but she's very mature for her age. Screw what the rest of the world thinks. Don't ever throw love like this back. Most people never get this lucky."

"She deserves more than me."

"More than a man who loves her more than life itself?"

"You and Beth sound exactly the same."

"Me and Bethany might just know what we're talking about," said Ryan seriously, before continuing to clean the room.

Marcus laid back and closed his eyes. Bethany, Rhianna and now Ryan, all telling him to take a chance. It was a strange counter to the pressures Marcus was usually under when it came to Alexa. It made it harder to supress his natural desires. He did love Alexa more than life itself. That love burned through his veins, becoming a part of him, but until she reached out for him, he could not consider being more than her friend.

***

Charlotte and Alexa were up early, cooking from first light. Maria arrived soon after, immediately submitting to Charlotte's plan to ensure everything was cooked in time.

"It's good to see her so confident," said Maria in a quiet voice as Charlotte flitted around the kitchen doing a million things at once. "She's really come out of her shell recently."

"Can you believe Bethy's upset things are going so well for her at home?" laughed Alexa softly. "She really thought Charlotte'd be living with us by now. I miss her, but I'm glad she's not. It's not fair for her life to get all screwed up. She has so much potential. She could really be something."

"You and Beth have potential too," said Maria kindly, though there was a deep forcefulness to her voice.

"Bethy does," agreed Alexa. "Her furniture's amazing. I can't believe how easy it seems to be for her to make it."

"Alexa, why do you make it so difficult?" asked Maria with a sigh. "You know I won't stop telling you how wonderful you are just because you want to deny it. I also won't stop if you happen to accept the odd compliment, either. I'll think you're tremendous whether you agree or not."

Alexa hugged Maria warmly. It never stopped astounding her how amazing Maria was. She was such a wonderful influence in their lives, yet Alexa still struggled to classify her place in their world. Not quite a mother, not really a grandmother.

"Can you guys hug later," said Charlotte with mock seriousness. "You're messing up my schedule."

Alexa laughed, but she was thankful for the interruption. She hated thinking about Maria's place in her life. Maria was like Ben; mysteriously wonderful for being in their lives in the first place, but just as likely to leave when she realised they were not worth staying for.

With Charlotte and Maria handling the kitchen, and only a couple of hours until guests arrived, Alexa began decorating the house.

"Need help?" asked a voice as Alexa tried to hang streamers across the lounge room.

Alexa stumbled off the chair she was standing on. Ben grabbed her to stop her from falling, but she flinched away from him and he instantly moved back.

"You're still upset," said Ben forlornly.

"No, I'm fine," replied Alexa dismissively, waving her hand as she moved around him to grab some balloons.

"Please, Alexa, talk to me."

"There's nothing to say."

"You won't let me near you."

Alexa tried to walk away, but Ben followed her to the dining room. Charlotte walked in at that moment with another large dish of food. Alexa hoped to escape with Charlotte back to the kitchen, but Ben had other ideas. "Charlotte, a moment, please," he said firmly. Charlotte did not leave until Alexa nodded. "Now, please talk to me. I can't sleep thinking you believe I'd ever touch you inappropriately or that I want you like that."

"I don't, okay, Ben. I believed you."

"You think I believe you want me that way?" asked Ben.

"No," replied Alexa defensively, wanting that to be the truth.

"Then what, Alexa?" questioned Ben, his arms out in pained desperation. That look took Alexa back to the face of her saviour who had always tried to keep her safe through the worst her nightmares threw at her. It made it difficult to reconcile the feelings swirling in her. "Why are you afraid of me? Why won't you talk to me any more?" asked Ben in a broken voice. "What is it you think I'll do?"

Tears began to sting the corners of Alexa's eyes as the answer stirred painfully in her chest. "Leave," she eventually replied, though her voice was hardly above a whisper as she rushed towards the lounge room.

"Sam called," said Charlotte, walking into the room from near the front door. Alexa looked up and Charlotte immediately pulled her close. "They'll be here in half an hour." Alexa nodded, feeling her heart strain with the look on Ben's face. "Let's get dressed."

"I haven't finished decorating," whispered Alexa.

"I can finish it," said Ben immediately. "Go get ready. This'll be done by the time you get back down."

Alexa was shaking as she stood trying to find something to wear. It was something she should have prepared beforehand, because the decision now had her close to tears. Charlotte once again came to the rescue. She walked into Alexa's wardrobe and picked an outfit in less than a minute. Alexa did not even care if she liked it or not. She was just thankful that she did not have to choose herself.

"Very nice," smiled Charlotte slyly when Alexa was dressed.

Alexa did not get the chance to understand the comment, because Charlotte was dragging her downstairs before she could glance at a mirror. However, when Alexa saw Marcus's eyes appraising her as she entered the lounge room, she realised Charlotte had been very strategic in her clothing selection.

Everyone gathered near the lounge room door to await Bethany's arrival. Alexa moved to the front and Ben positioned himself behind her, putting his hands on her shoulders and kissing her hair. She shivered slightly, but Ben just rubbed her arms gently. It made Alexa step back against his chest, and she felt him sigh heavily as he kissed her hair again.

The gravel crackled outside. Footsteps drew closer to the front door before hesitating. Alexa felt her heart stick in her chest. This party was not a surprise, so she could not understand Bethany's hesitation. Even Ben's grasp on Alexa's shoulders became more fidgety. However, when Bethany crept slowly into view, tears already in her eyes, Alexa understood completely. The cry of 'Happy Birthday' was deafening, but Alexa could not join in as she rushed to embrace Bethany, her own tears stinging her eyes.

"Happy Birthday, Angel," squeaked Alexa, squeezing Bethany tighter.

"This is the best, Lex," choked Bethany. "I can't believe you did all this. You're so good to me."

"It's your eighteenth birthday. I had to make a fuss. I had to. You're worth every bit."

"Thank you, Lex, thank you. I love you so much." Bethany was crying now, but she tried to master her voice as she spoke again. "Are there really eighteen dishes? Just like before."

"Yeah, just like old times," gasped Alexa, just able to squeeze out the words. It had been their tradition once upon a time, but being able to do it again – even just this once – was like finally closing a circle, fusing their lives back together.

"I love you so much, Lexie."

"I love you too, Angel."

When they both began openly weeping, Ben stepped in. He held them tight in his arms, reminding them tenderly that this was a happy day. Alexa and Bethany both nodded, finally stepping apart to allow everyone else to wish Bethany a happy birthday. Charlotte took Alexa's hand, but somehow when Alexa looked around, it was

Marcus who was next to her. He rubbed her forearm tenderly before pushing himself forward to embrace Bethany.

With the morning clouds burning off, everyone decided to move the party to the backyard. Filling their plates on the way out, they sat on the grass in the sunshine, revelling in the joy of the day. Sam was testing the limits of his digestive system, insisting on trying every dish. Bethany joined him in the challenge, along with Ryan, though she was the only one of them to succeed. Eating in a more sedate manner, Bethany was not even ill at the end of it. Sam looked on the verge of vomiting as he tried to ingest the last three desserts, while Ryan gave up well before then. The sight of Bethany's smug smile as she walked back out from the house, Sam nowhere to be seen, was very satisfying for Alexa, and she made no attempt to go easy on him when he emerged looking very worse for wear.

"You should be praising me for trying to help you get through all this food, not punishing me," said Sam uneasily, pushing away the cake Alexa was waving under his nose. "Such a waste otherwise."

"That's your problem. You assume it'll go to waste. It'll all get eaten. I just don't feel the need to eat it all today," Alexa laughed.

"I think this deserves a toast," said Pop loudly, shaking his head indulgently in Alexa's direction as he raised his glass of non-alcoholic wine. Bethany was next to him and Alexa knew she had intervened to save Sam, though by the blush of her cheeks did not realise what Pop had planned to say. "To Bethany. Happy eighteenth birthday. Welcome to adulthood."

"To Bethany," cried the group, lifting their glasses of non-alcoholic wine, while Bethany bowed her head. Alexa understood. It seemed strange Bethany would only now be classified an adult, when it felt like they had lived most of their childhood in the adult world. All the rites of passage others saw as an adventure had been more a form of torture to them. Yet it was a milestone. There was no longer any danger of them being split apart, of another person having rule over what Bethany could do. It made Alexa feel ungrateful to think such a thing, but it now also meant the end of Ben's guardianship of Bethany. Once more, they would belong to no one else but each other.

The party continued through the afternoon in a leisurely manner. It was a beautiful day and Bethany was having a wonderful time. When it was time to give presents, Bethany sat with Sam absolutely beaming. However, the generosity of the gifts quickly overwhelmed her. Gran and Pop gave her a beautiful silver watch. Bethany put it on her wrist with shaking hands, before crawling over to them to give them a teary hug of thanks. Ben and Sam's presents of matching bracelet and earrings made Alexa realise there had been a lot of collaboration in the present buying, and dampened her confidence in her and Charlotte's gift. However, Bethany's reaction dissolved her fears.

"It's us," gasped Bethany. "The three of us."

Alexa nodded, unable to speak, as Bethany ran her fingers over the interlocked, three-circle pendant made of three different types of gold. Charlotte appeared just as touched by Bethany's instant recognition of the symbolism, especially since it had been her who came up with the idea.

"Well I advise you, don't go looking for more jewellery in my present," said Maria happily, as she moved over to Bethany with her present in one hand and a box of tissues in the other. "Dry the tears first. Don't want to get this one wet."

It was a wasted effort. Bethany was in tears again as soon as she opened the large card. Enclosed were four gift vouchers for a dinner cruise on the harbour. Alexa still remembered the off-hand comment Bethany once made while at Maria's, wistfully imagining being sophisticated enough to dress up and go on one of those boats.

"Girls night?" asked Bethany tearfully.

"Any kind of night you like," replied Maria kindly. "It's not so expensive that we couldn't buy more tickets and take everyone."

Bethany just nodded, trying hard to compose herself, though it did take almost half a box of tissues to do so. "Thank you, everyone," she said, as more tears slipped down her cheeks. "This is so much – too much – but I love it."

"Whoa, it's not quite over yet," cried Marcus, pushing his chair forward as he reached behind him. Ryan was rushing towards him from the house, but disregarded his outstretched hand and placed the large present in his lap. "Don't discount me just because I don't move as quick as I used to."

"But you're hurt," said Bethany with wide, confused eyes, and Alexa knew she had never expected anything from Marcus.

"Yes, but I have a chauffeur now and he took me shopping," smiled Marcus brightly, trying to lift the present with one hand. "You'll have to come and get it."

Bethany ignored the present. She lunged at Marcus and hugged him tight, her chest convulsing with sobs. Marcus reciprocated with his good arm, comforting Bethany until she composed herself enough to take the present. Once unwrapped, Bethany just stared. Marcus turned, catching Alexa eye, silently questioning if he had done something wrong, but all Alexa could think about was how he could have possibly known.

"I – ah – there was just this one time. Alexa said – mentioned – I thought maybe you didn't have enough room in the apartment." Marcus obviously felt as though he had heard something he should not have, but Alexa could truly not recall ever speaking to him about Bethany painting. "I can take it back, buy you something you really want," said Marcus sincerely, but Bethany was shaking her head before he had even finished.

Bethany took a stuttering breath before calming herself and giving Marcus her thanks. It was very controlled and measured, almost cold, and Alexa hoped Marcus understood why. Collecting all her presents, Bethany walked inside. Sam signalled that he would go after her.

"Alexa," called Sam from the back door minutes later. He did not speak, but just motioned for her. When she drew up next to him, he explained that Bethany wanted to speak to her.

Bethany was sitting on her bed shaking. Alexa sat behind her and hugged her tight.

"I don't remember it being like this."

"That's because it never was," said Alexa, her voice breaking.

"I didn't ask for all this, did I? I didn't demand it, right? It's so much, Lex. I know I always wanted so much more than you, but this is way too much."

"Oh, Angel, you didn't demand anything," said Alexa truthfully. "You wanted a party, but everything else, that's what we wanted to give you. I know I didn't have to make eighteen courses, but I wanted to. For us. You don't like that I don't celebrate my birthday and don't understand why, but I can't. I love this day. I love you."

"I have to go," gasped Bethany, turning and hugging Alexa fiercely. "I'll come back before midnight, but I can't stay – can't have any more – not today."

"It's okay. I understand," Alexa replied. If she could have told Bethany about the last Christmas she spent with the Whites and the gifts they showered her with, she would have been able to make

Bethany realise how deeply she understood, but they never spoke about the Whites.

By the time Alexa walked back out to the backyard, the party was all but packed up. Sam agreed to take Charlotte home at the same time as whisking Bethany away. It looked like the right decision, Bethany clinging to Charlotte as they sat together on the backseat. With Maria engaged in conversation with Marcus and Ryan, the clean-up was left to Alexa and Ben.

"It was a good day," said Ben, drying the dishes as Alexa washed. Alexa felt as though he was sticking to safe topics, and deliberately choosing not to elaborate.

"Yeah, but I'm glad it's over. I've missed so much uni with this and Marcus," said Alexa, hoping she would not receive a parental reprimand in return.

"How's Marcus settling in?"

"Okay, I guess," answered Alexa, unsure if that was Ben's real question. "I haven't had much of a chance to chat to him. I can see he gets frustrated not being able to do things, but I know he likes being out of the hospital."

"Ryan seems nice," said Ben, again sounding as though there was something more to the question.

"Yeah, he's really good and he and Marcus get on really well."

"He's not the one that scared you, was he?" Ben asked more pointedly.

Alexa shook her head, wondering what Ben did not know. "No, but you can't hold that against the guy," sighed Alexa. "I managed to do the same thing to you once."

"I know. I'm glad things are working out. You and Beth have done really well with this place. I'm proud of you," smiled Ben, moving his arm towards Alexa's shoulders. Alexa shied away from his hug, feeling her heart stammer uncomfortably. "It's okay. I understand."

"How's that possible? I don't understand," cried Alexa.

"Things between us – they'll get better. Trust takes time to build and I've ruined that a couple of times. You don't know the torture I feel when I look at you."

"Great," muttered Alexa.

"You deserve more than you have. If I'd done the right thing all those years ago, you wouldn't be in this position. I imagine what our lives would've been like – you and Beth as carefree teenagers."

"I'm not a teenager."

"No. Alexa, I'm not leaving and in time I'll earn your trust. Please, just don't push me away. Let me be a part of your life."

"I'm trying."

It was the best Alexa could offer. She wanted more, but having Ben around, unable to connect with him, felt like the world taunting her with all she could never have. It made her thankful for her looming exams, giving her a legitimate excuse to withdraw from everything.

Up early each morning, Alexa was out swimming before the rest of the household had even risen. Breakfast was then prepared, but Alexa did not stay to eat with everyone. Quickly throwing down her food, she retreated up to her new study until it was time to leave for class. When she returned home, a swim preceded dinner, then straight after dinner she returned to her study.

"I'm going shopping on the weekend. You want to take a short break and join me?" asked Bethany as they all ate dinner together.

"No, I shouldn't," replied Alexa, not looking up to see Bethany's disappointment. They had had this conversation too many times.

"Taking a break might do you good," said Marcus, winning him a smile from Bethany.

"Thank you," nodded Bethany, pointing at Marcus. "Come on, you need a break and you need new clothes. Do you realise you've barely bought any clothes and most of them are way too big?"

Alexa looked down at the clothes she was wearing. They were old and too big, but they had been given to her by the Whites – something she had never told Bethany – and she treasured them too much to give up or replace.

"I really need to study, Bethy," replied Alexa. Bethany rolled her eyes. "And I don't really have the money, either."

"That's crap. How can you not have money?" cried Bethany.

"I don't work, Bethy. There's no money coming into the house. You're the only one working."

"But you get the same amount from the trust as I do. Where's it all go?"

"Boring stuff," smiled Alexa with a shrug. "Groceries, bills, Ryan. There's not a lot spare at the moment."

"You're paying Ryan out of your allowance?" gasped Bethany.

"Not fully," muttered Alexa, not keen to have this conversation in front of Ryan and Marcus. "I can't afford that, but as much as I can, yes." Bethany did not respond. She just put her head down, her eyes occasionally flicking Ryan's way. "Just give me a couple of months to get my savings back," smiled Alexa. "Then we'll go shopping, okay."

Alexa took Bethany's hand and squeezed it. Bethany did not look completely appeased, but she was slowly starting to smile when the sound of cutlery and crockery clanging angrily against each other turned their eyes across the table. Marcus was pushing away his dinner in disgust and glaring at Bethany.

"You've got a problem?" asked Bethany in a hard voice. Marcus did not answer, just stared, refusing to catch Alexa's disapproving eye. "Oh, right. Me. You think I'm a selfish, self-centred bitch?"

"You said it," replied Marcus, with a would-be casual wave of his hand.

"Do you think that about me?" Bethany asked Alexa balefully.

"Of course not, Bethy," Alexa replied softly, stubbornly avoiding Marcus's gaze.

"No, of course not," muttered Marcus under his breath. "She expects the world, but doesn't appreciate it when it's given to her – but, no, she's not selfish."

"You've always made it clear what you think of me," said Bethany in a shaky voice as she rose from the table. "That's never going to change no matter what I do. If not for Lex —" Bethany stalked off, the sound of the backdoor slamming indicating she had retreated to the sanctuary of her workshop.

"Was that really necessary?" snapped Alexa, turning on Marcus. "It's not up to her to know about the cost of running this place."

"Why the hell not?" cried Marcus, clearly as agitated as she was.

"Because it's her time to live. She's never had an easy moment in her life," explained Alexa, hating that Marcus did not understand this already. "This is her chance to get used to living. She doesn't need all the pressures of bills and everything else on top of that."

"And how's she ever going to learn to live independently when she's had you taking care of her the whole time?" countered Marcus.

"She'll figure it all out when she moves out. Until then, no, I'm not going to force her into growing up. She needs a life."

"And what about you? What about your life?" asked Marcus passionately.

"This is my life," muttered Alexa, not wanting Marcus to continue talking like that. "I don't need new clothes. I need to look after her and make sure she's okay."

"And who takes care of you?"

"I don't need anyone to take care of me. No matter what happens, I can take care of myself," said Alexa forcefully.

"Right, I forgot," snapped Marcus. "I bet if someone smashed three-quarters of your limbs you'd still be getting around doing everything for yourself as well."

Marcus tried to push himself away from the table and, with his one good hand, wheel himself out of the room, but got stuck on the table leg. Getting more and more frustrated, he angrily conceded defeat before Ryan tugged his wheelchair and whisked him away.

Marcus cursed himself. He was making all the old mistakes and losing the gains he had made with Alexa in the first half of the year. It was stupid, but the recession in Alexa over the last few months was so marked he could not help but wonder what had caused it.

"So Beth's a protected species in this house?" asked Ryan, sitting down at the desk as Marcus sat on the other side in his chair.

"You'd better believe it," snarled Marcus.

"Then don't attack her," sighed Ryan. "If you want Alexa, you're going to have to accept the concessions she gives Beth. And perhaps consider the allowances she gives you. I bet there're others who disagree with her there."

Ryan was right. Ben and Sam had not made a scene at Bethany's birthday, but there had been no warm welcome either. Sam barely spoke two words to him and Ben had been little more than civil.

"Besides," said Ryan. "Beth's on your side. She's already been in my ear about the two of you. All she wants is for Alexa to be happy and thinks you're the one who can make that happen. Don't get Beth offside. I think she might be as great as Alexa. Just give her a chance to prove it to you."

Marcus took the advice on board, and intended to show that he was the bigger person and apologise first, but never got the chance. Bethany had left by the time he emerged from his morning shower. When she did come home, she fell instantly to her knees, apologising and hugging him tight. Marcus looked into Bethany's eyes. She was harder to read than Alexa, but this was not a girl truly comfortable with her actions. Marcus could see her fear, as though waiting to be rebuffed, and when he shifted his cast arm, she flinched badly.

"So where've you been today?" asked Marcus, releasing Bethany.

"Shopping," Bethany replied sombrely. "For Lex," she quickly clarified. "Took Charlotte so I could get the size right."

Marcus's smile was tight-lipped. It was very sweet and there was nothing not to love about Alexa's heartfelt reaction. It was just that he also believed the money would have been better spent on a utility bill. However, even he had to admit that it was nice seeing Alexa in clothes that fit.

***

As the last week of classes rolled in, Alexa took some comfort in the return of household harmony. However, she was finding Marcus's presence strangely distracting. It was odd, because they had virtually lived in each other's pockets in the apartment, yet she had found him more of a comfort during her last exam period. If Alexa had not found being in his company so challenging, she would have occasionally moved her study down from the third floor. It was just that the few moments they got together now always involved something deeper than general conversation. Marcus's sincere apology for starting the fight with Bethany was genuinely touching. It made Alexa's heart ache for him in a way she did not want it to.

However, the enticements of Marcus's company did mean Alexa put aside the occasional hour to sit with him, Bethany and Ryan after dinner. Despite having a textbook with her, much of the time she found herself stealing glances Marcus's way. She tried not to let him see, but when he did, she liked that he just returned her gaze. He did not always smile or acknowledge the contact, just quietly held it.

"The eighteen-year-old driver led police on a high-speed chase across three suburbs last night before losing control of the stolen car and slamming into a telegraph pole," said the grim-faced newsreader. Marcus turned away, diverting Alexa's attention to the television. The scene looked familiar so she watched the continuing story. "The driver then jumped out of the car with his fifteen-year-old sister, who had been travelling in the front passenger seat, leaving the two injured backseat passengers. When confronted, the driver pulled out what was later determined to be a replica handgun and held it to his sister's head. When the man threatened police, an officer opened fire, hitting him in the chest. He was attended to at the scene, but was pronounced dead on arrival at hospital. Both backseat passengers, aged fourteen and eight, were released from hospital after being treated for minor injuries."

"Wow. Imagine that," said Ryan, running his hand through his hair. "Imagine pretending to shoot – threatening to shoot – your sister just to get away from the cops. Poor kid. She must've been terrified. You gotta hope she knew the gun was fake."

Bethany's face paled instantly. With a glance at Alexa, she dashed from the room. Alexa did not look Marcus's way as she raced after her, but caught sight of Ryan from the corner of her eye. His hand over his mouth confirmed he knew that story too.

"Angel," said Alexa tenderly, walking into Bethany's bedroom and closing the door behind her. Bethany was standing in an unsure manner. Her body was shaking and her eyes were darting around the room, as if looking for an escape. When Alexa moved forward, Bethany skipped away with her hands up. Bethany started pacing. Alexa remained close, but did not try to hug her again.

"He didn't mean anything by it. He doesn't know about you."

"Right, Marcus's told him nearly everything about you, but he wouldn't know anything about me!" cried Bethany savagely, before her body crumpled. "Doesn't matter though, does it? He's right. What kind of a person holds a gun to their sister's head and threatens to shoot them?"

"In your case, a very scared and troubled girl, so affected by drugs she didn't know what she was doing," replied Alexa gently.

"You think I don't remember that day? I remember everything," spat Bethany, making Alexa's heart stammer. They had never spoken about that day before. "Finding out Leo got arrested, knowing he really raped and beat you and tried to kill you. It was my fault. I just didn't know how to fix a mistake that big. I thought you'd never want to see me again and I really wanted to die, but we made a pact."

"I know we did. It kept me alive – all those years, that's what kept me here – what saved me. I never wanted you to die, so I knew I could never kill myself."

"But I could kill you! What does that say about me?"

"You didn't. Angel, you had all the time in the world to shoot me. I even forgave you. Gave you my blessing. You don't know how sorry – in the days after – on all the bad days – sometimes all I ever wanted … you're not the only one who wanted to die that day," confessed Alexa. She hated admitting that, hated the feelings swirling in her body, drawing her back to that place and desire. It took longer than it should have to remind herself that that was no longer her life and she no longer lived every day hoping the next would never come. "If you could've killed me, you would've," said Alexa solemnly. "Even if the cops didn't arrive right then, I know you wouldn't have pulled the trigger. Whether we wanted it to or not, that pact saved us, and that day probably saved you. I know you hated being locked up and I hated it too, but it probably saved you, being arrested that day."

Bethany looked up and collapsed in tears. "I just don't want to be that person any more," she sobbed.

"You aren't," said Alexa soothingly, instantly embracing Bethany and gently smoothing her hair. "You're so different now, so much better. You, when you're clean, you're the best person in the world and I'm so glad you're my sister."

"Really? You don't wish …"

"What I wanted was to be free with you. You're what I wanted. I have that now. I don't ever wish for anything but what I have now. Angel, you're my life. You've done bad things, but so have I. We're building new lives. Our pasts are behind us. I'm in this for the future. You with me?"

Bethany gave a soggy nod in Alexa's shoulder. Alexa hugged her tight, squeezing hard as Bethany reciprocated. They stayed like that for a long time. When they moved, it was only to the bed. They did not sleep. They stayed awake, talking and crying, but despite her best efforts Alexa was unable to convince Bethany she was no longer the troubled girl who had been forced to such desperate measures. It meant they each rose the next morning feeling tired and depressed.

"I know you didn't believe anything I said last night, but I love you, Angel," said Alexa tenderly.

Bethany kept her head down, focused on the toaster, but when Alexa wrapped her arms around Bethany's waist, Bethany grabbed them and held them to her. With a final squeeze, Alexa pulled away to get ready, but stopped when she saw Ryan wheeling Marcus into the kitchen.

"I'm sorry about last night," said Ryan, standing awkwardly behind Marcus. "I – I wasn't thinking. I never meant it like that."

"See," said Bethany, turning her head slightly Alexa's way. "I told you Marcus told him everything."

"I wasn't telling him everything about you, if that helps," said Marcus. Alexa noticed he would not look at her.

"No, you were telling him all about Lex."

"No," countered Marcus. "I told him about me. The only reason he said what he did was because he's never met the girl I described." Bethany said nothing. "You know I was terrified of meeting you – meeting that girl. Instead, I met the girl I believed was a figment of Alexa's imagination – the one she used to tell me about and fight for and insist was the best person in the world."

"You don't have to say this," said Bethany, tears rolling softly down her cheeks as she turned around. "You hate me."

"I hate the memory of you," said Marcus feelingly.

"I hate me," Alexa heard Bethany whisper before Bethany walked out of the kitchen. Minutes later the front door slammed shut.

"I am sorry," said Ryan sincerely.

"I know she's not what you want her to be and she doesn't do as much as you think she should, but she's not heartless," said Alexa passionately, though she could not quite meet Marcus's eyes.

"I never said she was," argued Marcus.

"I know," Alexa whispered, falling to her knees in front of Marcus and taking his hands in hers. "I know, but she needs you to believe in her. We don't have fathers or brothers or uncles or anyone to tell us we're not complete stuff-ups, that we're worth something. She's trying and she loves you."

"Beth's interested in matchmaking," Marcus sighed. "She ... if it wasn't for you ..."

"Bethy loves people. That's what she does. She makes people love her. You're just one of the few people who can resist her charms. Give her a chance. Forget the memory. We all have our demons. You've seen mine and never walked away."

"Because I know the other side."

"Then get to know her other side. Please, for Bethy. Everyone can use another friend."

"Beth doesn't want me as friend. She wants me as a brother."

"Then be our brother," replied Alexa, feeling her heart twist. She was suddenly very aware of Marcus's hands squeezing hers. As he closed his eyes and nodded, she wondered if it hurt him as much to hear those words as it had for her to speak them.

It was a very quiet day at university. Jessica seemed to know not to ask questions, and just spoke about their upcoming exams. It was distracting in the only way that mattered, and gave Alexa the clarity of mind to focus on her work rather than the empty feeling in her chest. This situation would not blow over quickly, no matter how soon Bethany's smile returned.

Walking back into the house at the end of the day, Alexa was greeted by the smell of smoke and the sound of panicked voices. Dropping her bag and running through the lounge, she was horrified by how dense the smoke was in the dining room. Knowing the voices were coming from the kitchen, she raced into the room without a moment of hesitation.

"Bethy!" Alexa cried, before slamming into her. "Are you okay?" she asked frantically, checking Bethany over. "Is everyone all right?"

No one answered immediately. Through the thick smoke, Alexa could see Ryan frantically dousing something with water in the sink. Alexa could not see any flames so moved forward to see the remains of the curtains in a charred and watery heap. Turning around, she noticed Marcus was next to Bethany, quietly comforting her as tears streamed down her face.

"What happened?" asked Alexa, looking around the room. There were smoke marks from the stove across to the sink, and her first thought was that it could have been much worse.

"I just wanted to do something nice," sniffed Bethany in a broken voice. "I know I don't help out enough, so I wanted to cook dinner."

"What were you cooking?" asked Alexa, trying to keep her voice from a sigh, thinking that Marcus was to blame for this.

"I thought simple would be best," explained Bethany softly. "I talked to Maria and she told me how to make fish and chips."

Alexa moved over to the bench. It looked as though Bethany had done a fairly good job at crumbing the fish and cutting up the potato. It was just not clear how it got from that to catastrophe without any food being cooked.

"It looks good, Bethy," said Alexa encouragingly. "What went wrong?"

"I was going to cook it all together, but then remembered I had to do it separate. But I didn't want to waste oil because I know we don't have heaps of money spare at the moment so I tried to pour half in the other saucepan. Just some spilt." Alexa nodded. She could imagine how quickly the fire would have taken hold on the stove. How the fire spread was still a mystery. The curtains were purposely kept a safe distance from the stove. "When I went to chuck it in the sink to stop the fire, it just went everywhere," Bethany explained meekly.

"It was pretty well alight when we came in," explained Ryan. "It's a good thing you had that little fire extinguisher in here."

It was a more than that. Alexa had not put it in the kitchen. It had been there when they moved in, but she would buy a dozen more.

"Wait a minute – you brought him in here – into a burning kitchen!" cried Alexa, staring at Ryan in disbelief as she pointed at Marcus.

"I brought myself, thank you," responded Marcus firmly, and Alexa could see he had not forgiven her for her previous comments.

"You might want to thank him for that, too," added Ryan seriously. "No offence to Beth, but her actions trying to put the fire out nearly burnt the whole place down and she seemed determined to stay in the middle of it to fix her mistakes – or die trying."

Alexa rushed back over to Bethany, checking her over once more. There were a number of burns on her hands and arms. They did not look serious, but she would have to make sure Bethany saw a doctor.

"I'm okay, Lex. It's nothing," muttered Bethany softly.

"Marc," said Alexa, turning to face him. "You have no idea —" The doorbell clanged loudly. Alexa was prepared to ignore it, but it clanged again straight away. "Perhaps the neighbours smelt the smoke and called the fire brigade."

The doorbell clanged again, then again, and again, impatiently dragging Alexa forward.

"Okay, I'm coming," cried Alexa, wondering if the fire brigade were always this insistent. "Charlotte, what are you doing here?" asked Alexa slowly, confused by the sight of Charlotte's distraught face as she stood flanked by her parents at the front door. "Mr and Mrs Jammel, what's going on?"

Mrs Jammel reefed Charlotte from her father's arms and pushed her into the house.

"She's all yours."

Chapter Five

ALEXA INSTINCTIVELY GRABBED Charlotte and wrapped an arm around her shaking body. Then she spotted the large bruise across the right side of Charlotte's face. "What's this?" Alexa cried angrily. Charlotte turned away as Alexa tried to inspect her. "What the fuck's going on. If you've hit her, I swear —"

"I've never laid a hand on her – and not because she doesn't deserve it – so don't get all high and mighty on me," yelled Mrs Jammel. "I'm sure you saw the news last night. Charlotte decided to take our daughter on a joyride in a stolen car and nearly got Mia killed. She's still recovering from cancer, but Charlotte couldn't stay out of trouble. I won't have my children corrupted by her. I'll never let my children's lives be put at risk because of her ever again."

"Dad, please believe me. I didn't know the car was stolen," cried Charlotte, tears streaming down her face.

"Don't you dare call him that! You know full well that's not what he is. You're nothing to us and I'm not going to keep you under my roof so you can keep endangering my children's lives."

"What are you talking about?" asked Alexa. "Mr Jammel?"

"David's not Charlotte's father," said Mrs Jammel callously. "Charlotte's known that for some time now, but chose to remain in our house. And still that wasn't enough for her to respect the man who raised her and ensure the safety of his child."

"Dad, I'm sorry. Please."

Mr Jammel could not tear his eyes away from Charlotte, but did not reach out for her.

"Don't do this, Mr Jammel. Charlotte's your daughter in every way that counts. No child's perfect. Don't kick her out of your life for one mistake," pleaded Alexa.

Mr Jammel's eyes filled with tears, but he remained unmoved. Alexa could not fathom what was holding him back.

"It's too late for that," said Mrs Jammel savagely. "We don't want her."

"Well I do," gasped Alexa, holding Charlotte tighter.

"Then have her."

Mrs Jammel grabbed her husband's arm and dragged him away. Alexa watched them leave, feeling heavy tears fall on to her arms that still held Charlotte to her chest. When the sounds of the car drifted away, Alexa pulled Charlotte inside and closed the door. Bethany, Marcus and Ryan were behind them. Charlotte did not acknowledge them. Alexa led Charlotte into the lounge room, but only Bethany followed.

"What happened?" asked Alexa, sitting Charlotte on the lounge. "Why'd they suddenly kick you out?"

"You heard," spat Charlotte, before her head dropped and her voice became much meeker. "Because of what happened last night. I swear I didn't know the car was stolen. Me and my friend were going to the movies. Mia wanted to come. They said she could. Clare's brother was going to give us a lift home. She didn't know the car was stolen. She kept yelling at him. Then the cops saw us and we thought we were going to die. He was driving so fast."

"Then you crashed?" asked Bethany.

"Eventually," answered Charlotte, her voice shuddering. "I was almost glad when he did. I wanted it to be over. He lost control and the back hit a pole. It hurt so much and Mia was crying. I held her. I saw her arm was broken, but my head hurt so much. When I looked up I saw him dragging Clare out of the car. He had a gun. I tried to get us out, but the door was stuck and I didn't want to get out where he was. I kept Mia's head down. They shouted and shouted. Clare was crying. Then I heard the bangs. He fell and Clare just stood there screaming. Mia was crying – holding her arm and burying her head. I just sat there until the police got us out."

There was silence for a while, Alexa and Bethany exchanging looks, wondering what was best to say.

"But why'd your stepmother say that you weren't your dad's daughter?" asked Bethany delicately.

"He isn't my dad," said Charlotte firmly, forcing Alexa to recall her previous distress at her family somehow finding out they no longer had to love her. "I wanted to find my mum. Things were real bad at home so I thought maybe if I found her she'd want me. I sent her a letter, but when she wrote back she told me she left because she didn't want me any more and my real dad never wanted me. Left before I was born. Said I should be grateful cos my dad was the only one who ever wanted me."

"Did your dad – I mean, Mr Jammel – know he wasn't your father?" asked Alexa.

"I think he had an idea, but we'd been getting on so well. I was real happy at home and he was finally proud of me."

"Then why now?" asked Bethany with a hard edge to her voice. Even though she had always wanted Charlotte to live with them, it was clear she took issue with parents – biological or not – rejecting their child.

"Because Carla never knew. Dad never told her. She found the letter from my mother today. She was packing my stuff anyway, but my dad was saying I should stay. When she found that – they had the hugest fight – didn't matter in the end. It was the excuse she'd been looking for. When Dad stopped arguing, she finished packing and forced me into the car. Dad didn't say anything. He wouldn't even look at me. They never even let me say goodbye to Mia and Dylan."

"I know it's not much of a consolation right now, but you're more than welcome to stay here," said Alexa sincerely. "We have plenty of room and we missed you."

Those words allowed a tiny shadow of a smile to reach Charlotte's lips, but it was short-lived. "I don't want to be somewhere I'm not wanted," she muttered, not looking up.

"You're wanted here," said Bethany so firmly it sounded angry. "You're our sister and we'll adopt you if that's what you need to convince you that we want you."

The doorbell stole Charlotte's chance to argue further. Her eyes lit up hopefully as she trailed hesitantly behind Alexa to the door, but when they were greeted by Ryan and a stack of pizzas, Charlotte rushed up the stairs.

"Sorry, I just thought no one would feel like cooking," said Ryan apologetically.

"You must be regretting this job about now, huh," sighed Alexa.

"You guys certainly know how to do complicated," smiled Ryan.

Alexa took the pizzas so Ryan could push Marcus. They ate in the lounge room, not bothering with plates, chatting half-heartedly. No one mentioned the disaster in the kitchen or Charlotte's arrival. When Ryan offered to clear away dinner, Alexa did not object.

Bethany followed Alexa up the stairs. They did not speak. Alexa knocked quietly at Charlotte's usual room, but received no answer. Bethany pushed the door open just slightly and peered in, before opening the door further to show Charlotte asleep on the bed. She was curled up in a ball in the middle of the bed, still dressed in her clothes. Bethany gently closed the door again.

"She's ours now. They can't have her back," said Bethany angrily. "We want her."

"Yes we do," nodded Alexa, rubbing Bethany's arm consolingly.

"You won't give her back?"

"I'll fight anyone who tries to take her from us for as long as this is where she wants to live. I promise."

Unfortunately, the situation was not as simple as that. Charlotte was not yet sixteen and Alexa could never be described as a model citizen. If they went to the authorities to sanction their situation, there was the chance they would forcibly remove Charlotte – just as they had done to them so many times. That thought kept Alexa awake much of the night. She was trying hard to live a normal, law-abiding life. Previously she would have had no hesitation keeping Charlotte's living arrangements secret, but that was not the life she wanted to set up for her. She wanted Charlotte to have everything she and Bethany had only ever dreamed of.

Waking early, Alexa decided she would deal with the simplest problem first, so headed down to the kitchen. Prepared to face the full extent of the damage, she was confused by the sight of a generally unharmed-looking kitchen. It was only four-thirty in the morning. It made Alexa wonder when Charlotte had been there and if she had been feigning sleep when they had come to her room. Trekking up the stairs, Alexa found Charlotte sitting on her bed, looking out the window at the pre-dawn sky.

"You happy with this room?" asked Alexa, stepping tentatively into the room.

"Why wouldn't I be?" replied Charlotte softly.

"It's just that this is your home now and no one really makes use of this floor. You can have whatever room you want."

"This one's set up for me."

"I know, but that was Bethany's choice, not yours. Come have a look." Alexa took Charlotte's hand and led her to the room in the back left corner. It was one of the largest rooms on the floor and had a balcony that overlooked the backyard. "What about this room?"

"But it's huge."

"The whole house is huge," countered Alexa.

"Beth has all the furniture set up in the other room," said Charlotte softly.

"It mightn't be as bad as I made out to pull apart and reassemble," said Bethany from the door. She was smiling slightly, but she looked as tired as Alexa felt. "I can have it ready for you by the end of today."

Charlotte nodded and Bethany walked over and hugged her fiercely. It was not a celebratory hug, and Alexa wondered if Bethany felt guilty for wishing for something that had now happened, but not without the destruction of Charlotte's family.

They began moving everything immediately. It did not take long and was when Alexa realised Charlotte had no belongings. Charlotte had spoken about her stepmother packing her bags, but they had left nothing but her on their doorstep.

"You want me to go and pick your stuff up? They can't keep it," said Alexa, dreading the idea of confronting them.

"No, I don't want anything to do with them," replied Charlotte in a soft, but firm voice. "They made their choice."

"Okay, but you need essentials, you know, personal stuff – so I'll give you money to buy that," said Alexa, trying to think through all Charlotte would need. "You can also raid my closet for now."

"And mine," interjected Bethany. "Just take whatever you want. If I need it, I can just come get it. It's all yours."

It was a very generous offer. While Bethany was very kind-hearted, she did not always share well. However, in moments of genuine need, Alexa knew Bethany would give away her very last possession if she truly loved the person who needed it. It was then Alexa realised just how deeply Bethany cared for Charlotte and that she did truly see her as their sister.

"After my exams, we'll go shopping to sort the rest out," nodded Alexa.

"I don't want your money," said Charlotte defensively. "I can get things for myself. I'm going to get a job. I'll pay you rent and for food and stuff. I'm going to pay my way here."

"We can negotiate that, but you're just fourteen. You need to finish school. You're not even allowed to leave yet," noted Alexa, glad she could win that argument on a technicality. "You can get a part-time job if you can find one and pay rent if you really want to, but I'm not going to ask for it – cos I'll spend it all on you anyway."

"I have no right to be here," huffed Charlotte. "I'm going to pay my way."

"You belong here," cried Bethany, as though Charlotte's words had been a rejection of her.

"This is your home," added Alexa sincerely, though she could also see that was no longer an issue. Charlotte was already squeezing Bethany's hand comfortingly. "But while you live here, you still have to fit with my rules."

"You're not my mother," Charlotte retorted, reminding Alexa of the girl Charlotte had been a year ago.

"No, I'm not, but I'm going to be responsible for you from now on and I'll make sure you don't miss out on the best in life because you're too stubborn to take the chances that come up."

"Like you can talk."

"Yeah, I can. I'm not going to let you make all of my mistakes!" cried Alexa, finally losing her composure. "I know where they led me and I don't ever want you to go through that. There's no reason for you to fuck up your life the way I did mine."

Charlotte did not argue any further, and Bethany insisted she could get her settled in. It was an offer Alexa could not afford to refuse. Her first exam was in a week and she was nowhere near ready. It did not help that she spent much of that week going to appointments for Charlotte. The process of becoming her guardian was both easier and more complicated than Alexa expected. Charlotte's parents' willingness to openly state that they no longer wanted her to live with them, and Alexa's open desire to look after her, resulted in little opposition to the change in living arrangements. Yet the number of forms and meetings to formalise it seemed excessive in the extreme.

When Charlotte received all the finalised documentation, she went straight to the local high school and enrolled herself. When she came back home that day, Alexa was surprised by the announcement that she also had a job at the local supermarket.

From that day on, Charlotte said nothing of her former family life. If anyone asked her how she was going, her answers were always framed in a way that made it sound like she had been living with them the entire time. Alexa wished she could have spent more time with Charlotte outside the meetings, not to crack her façade, but to ease her back to the girl she had been before they moved. However, there was one thing that had not changed about Charlotte – her immense helpfulness.

As Alexa's exams began, there was so much housework that Charlotte took off her hands. Charlotte cooked. She cleaned and did the laundry. Then, on top of that, Charlotte started paying board. The sight of the envelope on her desk annoyed Alexa, but she knew better than to give it back. Putting it to the side, she concentrated on studying for her next exam, comforted only by the knowledge that she would soon have three uni-free months to sort out the situation.

The exams were much harder than Alexa anticipated. While her study habits prior to Marcus and Charlotte's arrivals helped to keep her ahead, with all the disruptions she had struggled to gain more than a basic overview of the coursework. It was disappointing, but it was not a sentiment she could share with the household. Thankfully, Jessica was sympathetic, so when Alexa walked out of her last exam barely able to contain her tears, Jessica took her by the hand and insisted they go shopping.

"I think you might need new swimmers," smirked Jessica.

"Nothing's changed," sighed Alexa. "He still has a girlfriend."

"And that's my point," laughed Jessica. "I think you could change that with the right pair of swimmers."

Alexa refused to agree, but did not object to the shopping expedition. It was pleasantly distracting and Alexa thought Bethany might be happy if she came home with something new. However, her contentment with the plan came unstuck when she saw Jessica smirking behind her hand.

"What?"

"Hey, don't get defensive," laughed Jessica. "I was just noticing the difference between this trip and the last one – the types of swimmers you're voluntarily looking at compared to the ones I had to force you to consider before. I think Marcus might be in trouble."

"Shut up," smiled Alexa, but the comment got her thinking. As they offered opinions on each other's selections, Alexa realised she was no longer so shy of showing off her body. She was not even terrified of presenting it in front of Marcus, hoping he might admire it. Yet darker thoughts swirled behind that realisation.

"What's going on? You've gone all gloomy on me," said Jessica as they left the store. "Seriously, I'm sure you passed. I know you want to do better than that, but sometimes life lets you down."

"Jess, have you ever been raped?"

"Oh, shit, Alexa – what – not Damien."

Alexa shook her head. "Before him."

Jessica did not say anything else. She just wrapped her arm around Alexa's shoulders as they walked. It took Alexa a while to realise Jessica had brought her to a quiet booth in a coffee shop.

"I know you don't like questions, so you just tell me whatever you need," said Jessica kindly once their coffees arrived.

"It's just what you said – you know – the swimmers – showing off – just don't want anyone to think I'm asking …"

"I really didn't mean it like that," said Jessica softly. Alexa nodded, already knowing that was the truth. "And no one's ever asking for it."

"But you've never …"

"Every girl has their story – guys pushing them too far," shrugged Jessica. "But not that far for me. You know, groping, talking shit – my ex – sometimes I'd do stuff I didn't really want to just to get him to back off."

"Damien was like that," said Alexa softly.

"You scared Marcus would be? Ever think he would?"

"No," replied Alexa honestly. "He knows about – he's always been real proper."

"Then maybe you can just wear them for him," smiled Jessica supportively, reaching out and squeezing Alexa's hand. Alexa could not reply. "No one ever asks for it. I reckon you already know that – and anyone who's told you different is a disgrace to the human race."

Alexa almost wished she could have said more, but what she had confessed already was more than she had ever revealed to anyone unconnected to those events. Jessica seemed to understand and did not push for details, but in contrast to everyone else, she also did not avoid the topic either. It was nice, because Alexa felt like she could slowly confront the issue without delving into specifics.

"I just feel really exposed in a two-piece," said Alexa. "And – I know what you said – and that it's true – but – sometimes I look in the mirror and I like – you know, I think it looks okay, but then I feel wrong for feeling like that."

"Think someone'll call you a slut?" asked Jessica. Alexa shrugged. "It's ironic, you know. The only times I've been called a slut is when I've knocked a guy back. It's like they don't get the meaning of the word."

Alexa could not help but laugh. It was a relief to find out that other girls had similar, though thankfully milder, experiences at the hands of guys. It started to lessen the fear that it was something innate inside of her that drew those events into to her life. When she expressed that, Jessica could not help but point out how strange it was for any woman to take comfort in the knowledge that sexism was such an entrenched problem in society.

It was a good afternoon and the second time Jessica had allowed Alexa to go home after her last exam feeling a thousand times better than when she finished it. The day only improved when Alexa arrived home to find dinner on the table. Everyone was waiting for her, their moods subdued, as if they knew she was unlikely to be cheerful.

"Half-way, Lexie," smiled Bethany sweetly.

"And we're sorry for screwing up your marks," said Charlotte.

"Grateful," added Marcus. "But sorry."

Alexa waved her hand dismissively, unable to speak as her throat constricted and her tears burned her eyes. Bethany saw and threw her arms around Alexa, pushing her forward so they could sit on the same seat. And that was the way they stayed right through dinner, eating off the same plate, Alexa leaning back softly against Bethany as she leaned forward and rested her head on Alexa's shoulder. Charlotte excelled herself with dinner, though it was her chocolate lava cake that had everyone in raptures.

It was a really lovely night, and Alexa woke the next morning feeling more at ease with her current situation. Jessica was right, if she could improve her marks in the following semesters, it probably would not matter what she got now, as long as she passed.

"Alexa, you know I – it's not cos I don't want to live – I –"

Alexa turned to see Charlotte standing in the doorway of the kitchen in her school uniform. There was genuine shame in her face.

"Char, you don't need to explain anything," said Alexa. "Me and Bethy, we get it."

As if to prove that point, Bethany appeared and hugged Charlotte from behind. "Can you believe it?" asked Bethany cheerfully, walking Charlotte into the kitchen as she continued to hug her. "It's the first day of her holidays and she gets up early for a swim."

"And makes your lunch," added Alexa, handing Bethany a lunch box.

Bethany squealed, eagerly peering inside. If not for that reaction, Alexa would never bother, but it was one of the deprivations they had felt keenly in their childhood. That someone making her lunch now could make Bethany feel so special tore at Alexa's heart.

"You're awesome, Lex. But I'm late, so I gotta run. Be home late. Going out after work with friends. See you when I get home. Love you lots. So glad you're here, Char," Bethany smiled, dancing out of the room.

"We can take turns making her lunch, if you like," said Charlotte.

"You don't have to," replied Alexa. "She doesn't expect it and I don't want her to."

"Yeah, but look at the mood it puts her in. You could've shared that secret with me earlier. We could've been friends from the start."

The ease in Charlotte's voice was not quite enough to cover the deep sadness in her eyes, but it was good to see a bit of her vibrancy re-emerging. It gave Alexa hope Charlotte would recover from this rejection and fulfil the dreams they all had for her, though it would not be without scars.

When Charlotte left for school, Alexa realised it would be the first time she would be practically alone with Marcus without the need to lock herself away and study. She had the feeling Marcus realised that too, because moments after they all sat down together for breakfast, Ryan excused himself.

"How are you?" asked Marcus as soon as they were alone.

"I'm okay," nodded Alexa. "Glad I have some time to breathe. It doesn't seem real that you came here only five weeks ago."

"What you've done – you know you're the – what do you have planned for your lazy summer days now you're a free woman?" asked Marcus, abandoning whatever he intended to say.

"Get organised," said Alexa. "Make sure Charlotte's really okay."

"You sure you're okay with me being here – taking up room, eating all your food and costing you lots of money?"

"Got somewhere better to go?" asked Alexa with a slight smile and raised eyebrows. Marcus laughed and shook his head. "Then you can stay."

"Thank you. I know you haven't been around for me to say that to, and I feel awful knowing how stressful these last few weeks have been for you, but they've been some of the best of my life. You're responsible for that, and I'm very grateful," said Marcus softly, his eyes locking on to her.

It was hard for Alexa to look away. There was something truly calming about Marcus's presence, and she was disappointed by

Ryan's return. However, when they went out, Alexa felt her freedom hit with greater force. It was joyful and liberating, and she skipped out of the house with a lighter heart than she had had in a long time.

It was a good day. She spent the morning with Maria, before working with Peter in the afternoon. She had not done any work for him for a number of weeks and felt guilty about abandoning her duties, but Peter was not fazed. He was more understanding than Alexa could comprehend, but she was glad he had no problem with her haphazard offering of hours. It was still too important to keep it a secret, though even she did not understand why.

When Alexa arrived home, Bethany was still out. It made Alexa uneasy despite Bethany telling her she would be late. However, those concerns faded to nothing when Marcus wheeled himself into the room. "Two hands!" she cried.

"Yep, back to two hands and some semblance of independence," smiled Marcus, clearly relieved by the improvement.

Bethany was somewhat less enthused by the sight, cautiously asking when the casts on his legs would be removed.

"Not for another two weeks," replied Marcus with a bemused smile. "But when they found out I had access to a pool, they changed them to waterproof casts so I can do some exercise."

"You can swim with me," smiled Alexa, thinking about her new swimming costumes. "I'm not even swimming early any more – not til seven."

"You know that's most people's idea of early, right?" said Ryan.

"Yeah, but you're going to need to stay after your casts come off, right," interjected Bethany. "You'll need to recuperate. Ryan might need to still take care of you."

"No, no, he'll be completely fine to come and go as he needs," replied Ryan reassuringly, clearly misinterpreting Bethany's fear.

"I won't need Ryan once the casts come off," Marcus said firmly. "He costs Alexa too much. But by the time I get these things off me, it'll be pretty close to Christmas. My life's a bit of a mess right now. I'll need time to sort myself out. You'll be stuck with me for a while."

"Good," smiled Bethany, turning and hugging Charlotte who was sitting next to her, while Ryan just shook his head.

***

Marcus had not set an alarm in such a long time that he had forgotten what a disturbing effect it had on his body. It was horrible the way it tore him from his sleep, but as soon as his conscious mind woke up, he forgot all of his bodily discomforts.

"Now you don't need me to actually get in that water with you, do you?" asked Ryan with tired distrust. "I know I'm being paid enough to, but I don't think I can pretend to enjoy the experience."

"Just pull me out if it looks like I'm drowning," said Marcus, not wanting Ryan with him at all.

"Okay, let's go engage in this insanity," Ryan sighed, wheeling Marcus out to the backyard.

Alexa was already swimming when they arrived. Marcus watched the rhythmic flow of her body through the water, loving the way it moved. She stopped when she noticed their presence, standing and holding her hand up as a greeting. Marcus smiled, but noticed Alexa suddenly looked embarrassed, her hand slipping back underwater. The scars on her arms and wrist were more visible in this light and they had obviously caught Ryan's eye.

"Let's get you in there," said Ryan, sounding flustered.

It took a moment for the cold to register as Marcus slipped his cast legs into the water. "Oh crap, Alexa, it's cold. How do you do this?"

"I swim. Makes me warmer," she replied as though he was daft.

Remembering why he was here in the first place, Marcus slid the rest of his body into the water. He immediately tried to swim but the clumsiness of his broken limbs almost drowned him. Alexa left him in that pitiful state, jumping out of the water and rushing inside. Marcus felt like a failure until she jumped back into the water with a kickboard.

"Someone told me it'd be good for pool work. I hate it," said Alexa, annoyance in her voice.

Marcus smiled, wondering just how much it grated her that she spent money on the advice of someone else on something she did not use – and if she used it occasionally just to prove it had not been a waste of money.

Using the kickboard to keep his head above water, Marcus kicked in a slightly more coordinated fashion to the other end of the pool. That was where he met his next dilemma. He managed to turn around without hitting Alexa with his cast, but only just. Thankfully she chose to be amused rather than annoyed, although she did swim further away from him after that.

Marcus only managed a few laps. He was exhausted by the end of each one and struggled to push himself to continue. It was a far cry from the graceful movement of Alexa's body. Lifting himself out of the water, Marcus sat on the edge of the pool until Alexa noticed him.

"How'd you go?" she asked, wading next to him.

Marcus was almost ashamed of his view, but was mesmerised by the drops of water slipping from her hair down her chest. "Possibly the worst swim ever," he laughed, looking into Alexa's eyes.

"So not coming back?"

"I don't think I'm supposed to give up so easily," replied Marcus, not looking for any excuse to miss time alone with Alexa. "And I can only get better from this point, so I might feel like I've achieved something if I come back."

"Marc, you're freezing," cried Alexa suddenly. "You need to go inside. Where's Ryan?"

"He's just using the bathroom. It's fine, really," replied Marcus.

"No, look at you. You're covered in goose bumps."

Alexa suddenly moved forward, her hands rubbing the tops of his arms. Marcus had been slightly chilled by the unseasonably cold morning air, but that was nothing to the shiver that burst through his body at Alexa's touch. Nearly every hair stood on end as if excited by static electricity. Seconds later, Alexa jumped out of the pool. Her concern was touching, but seemed a little extreme and he wondered if she just wanted him to leave.

"Do you need help getting out of the pool?" asked Alexa.

Marcus noticed she was also shivering, making him smile. He wanted to get her in and warm too. "No. If you can just bring the chair close, I should be able to pull myself up."

Alexa did as he asked and set the brakes. This was a manoeuvre Marcus had been working on with Ryan even before the cast came off his arm. He wanted to be as self-sufficient as possible, as well as give himself some privacy and dignity. Positioning his hands on the arms of the wheelchair, Marcus lifted himself up slowly. He was almost seated when his grip slipped.

It took a moment for Marcus to realise he was not flailing in the water. His heart was beating erratically, and yet he had not fallen. That was when he noticed Alexa holding him. She had caught him in time.

"Shit!" cried Ryan, racing towards them. "Just keep hold of him."

Alexa's grip on Marcus's chest tightened. She was surprisingly strong, but Marcus could not enjoy the intimacy of her touch as his fear of falling gripped him as tightly as she did. Ryan pulled Marcus's legs closer to the chair. Marcus managed to shift his weight backwards and into the chair, his chest shuddering.

"It's okay," said Marcus softly, touching Alexa's shaking arm.

"You're lucky it is," said Ryan in an agitated voice. "I don't know what you were trying to do besides kill yourself. If you're going to move yourself around, then you do it with dry hands."

"I'm sorry," said Alexa before Marcus could speak.

"Not you, him," retorted Ryan, though he had a smile on his face. "Um, but I should get you inside. You have a visitor."

"Who me?" asked Alexa confusedly.

"No, Marc."

"Who?" asked Marcus, as perplexed as Alexa. He had not had any visitors since leaving hospital. His parents had not even spoken to him.

"Your girlfriend," replied Ryan, his voice somewhere between amusement and concern.

Marcus could not respond. The change in Alexa's demeanour worried him too much.

Alexa had her towel caped around her body as she looked around frantically. "Where is she?"

"Marc's room. I asked her to wait there," replied Ryan cautiously. "That okay?"

"Um, yeah, that's fine – yeah – no – okay."

And with that Alexa dashed inside, turning towards Bethany's room rather than the staircase. Her reaction made Marcus sick. It was so ridiculously selfish to allow Lucy anywhere near Alexa's life. As Ryan showered and dressed him, all Marcus could think about was how deeply it must have hurt Alexa to have Lucy accuse her – indirectly though it was – of stealing, and for him to have taken Lucy's side. If Lucy did not have a good excuse for her recent absence, Marcus decided he would just call the whole thing off.

"I'll let you guys catch up," said Ryan, pushing Marcus into his room.

Marcus had never appreciated how tall Lucy was until now. He never felt dwarfed by Alexa when she stood next to his chair, but Lucy towered over him and refused to come down to his level the way Bethany always did.

"So that's all the greeting I'm going to get? Silence?" asked Lucy haughtily.

"That's all I've had from you," countered Marcus.

"And what exactly did you expect me to say when you told me you were shacking back up with your ex?"

"What you told me was to come to you since I had all the time in the world. I tried," said Marcus. "You haven't responded to a single call or text or message in the last five weeks."

"I was at your bedside every day after the accident, which is more than you can say for that girl," snarled Lucy, holding herself tall.

"That girl had no idea I was even in hospital, something you made very sure of. What I'm curious about is why you decided I wasn't worth visiting – even every second day – after I woke up."

"My life couldn't stay on hold forever," retorted Lucy. "You were going to be fine, so I thought I could finally take a breath – get my life back in order. In case you've forgotten, your little accident wasn't without impact on me. I had to move – pack up all your things, never knowing if I was ever going to unpack them. Just because I don't do everything the way you want doesn't make me heartless."

Perhaps it was habit, or the ingrained need to have a girlfriend who was not Alexa, but before Marcus could think about stopping himself, he was smoothing things over and taking Lucy back. Ignoring Lucy's taunting comments and assuming blame for what remained quickly diluted the tension. Lucy's smile as she moved forward made Marcus feel manipulated.

"I'm sorry too," said Lucy sweetly, kneeling in front of him, her hands on his thighs. "I shouldn't have been so petty, but I truly have been very busy. Things have calmed down a bit, so if you're serious about giving us another go, I'll make everything up to you."

Lucy's hands moved seductively over Marcus's thighs. He wished he could have controlled his body's reaction, but it had been a long time since he had been intimate with anyone and Alexa's proximity this morning had him on edge. Lucy smiled triumphantly. When she climbed on to his wheelchair, Marcus's hands immediately stripped off her shirt. Lucy reciprocated, and they fumbled with their clothes as they kissed passionately. Marcus felt his chair slide backwards, making his heart jolt. Thankfully, they hit the end of the bed, not the floor, but it had the effect of sobering him up from his lustful state.

"Perhaps we should leave this until I get full use of all my limbs," he said, pushing Lucy off him.

"I don't need any of your limbs for what I had in mind," replied Lucy with a seductive smirk. "Now, can you get on the bed yourself or do I need your man-hand to come and help?"

Alexa walked down the stairs, trying not to hear the noises drifting from Marcus's room. It was difficult, because Lucy clearly intended to be heard. Ryan was sitting in the lounge room, and when his eyes flicked up towards her, she felt something searching in his gaze. Charlotte and Bethany soon arrived in the room. Bethany was dressed to go out – again. It was something Alexa had only just picked up on. The hectic nature of the move, followed by settling in, then the recent upheavals, meant Alexa had not noticed the increasing amounts of time Bethany was out. What was more disconcerting was the details that used to be given freely about her activities were now withheld – sometimes angrily. It made Alexa uneasy. The behaviour was not like the clean Bethany. Yet it was not addict Bethany either. Something was not ringing true, but Alexa could not work out what it was.

"You can hear them halfway across the house," said Bethany in a disgusted voice.

"Then how about we move all the way across the house," Alexa suggested, not keen to hear any more either. "You can help me make breakfast." Bethany followed Alexa and Charlotte, but insisted she could not eat because she was going out soon. "Where are you going?" asked Alexa, trying to keep her voice casual.

"Just out for breakfast – well, late breakfast," smiled Bethany, but there was something forced about her answer.

"Sounds good," smiled Alexa. "Who you going with?"

"Just friends. What's with all the questions?"

"I'm hardly grilling you, Bethy," said Alexa, concerned not only by Bethany's reaction, but by Charlotte staying completely out of the conversation.

"Can't you just trust me and let me have a life?" snapped Bethany. She was about to storm out of the kitchen when Lucy swanned in, dressed only in one of Marcus's t-shirts.

"Oh, excuse me. Didn't mean to interrupt. I just need a drink of water," smiled Lucy pleasantly, before standing and waiting in the middle of the kitchen.

"Cups are up there and tap's over there," said Charlotte derisively, flicking her finger across the kitchen as direction.

Alexa had to hide her smile as she walked over to Charlotte and placed a comforting arm around her chest.

"Look, I realise I made a mistake about the wallet," said Lucy in a lofty voice, pulling herself to full height. "What can I say? I'm sorry."

Alexa was not sure she had ever heard a less sincere apology in her life, and she had been the giver of many.

"Like sorry makes up for what you said about us," snapped Charlotte.

"It's okay," whispered Alexa in Charlotte's ear.

Bethany stood silently on the other side of the kitchen, unable to disguise the look of pure loathing on her face.

"Alexa, can I talk to you a minute?" asked Lucy, looking around the room. "Alone."

"Whatever you have to say, you can say in front of us," said Bethany, breaking her silence with a tone of pure hatred.

Alexa turned to Bethany and shook her head just slightly, before inviting Lucy out to the backyard. Standing just to the side of the open kitchen window, Alexa waited for Lucy to join her and make her demands.

"I understand you're angry about the wallet situation, but Marc's my boyfriend and you don't have the right to say I can't spend the night with him," said Lucy firmly.

"I never said you couldn't spend the night with him," clarified Alexa. "I said you couldn't stay the night in this house. Marc's free to come and go as he pleases."

"No, he's not. Both his legs are in plaster. He can barely get around his bedroom."

"He has a full-time nurse. You want to go anywhere, just take Ryan with you," replied Alexa, refusing to back down.

"I don't want Ryan with us," snapped Lucy. "Just because you're happy to have strange men in your house, doesn't mean I am. And I don't have a spare bed for Ryan, so he couldn't stay anyway."

"Then take care of Marcus yourself," suggested Alexa. Lucy just scoffed. Alexa shrugged unaffectedly. "This isn't my problem," Alexa said. "My preference is that you never step foot in my house again. My concession is that you may visit. Besides, the casts on his legs'll be off in a couple of weeks. Then all of your problems will be solved."

Lucy pulled her body to full height and crossed her arms. "I'm asking you to reconsider your position," she said forcefully. "I've apologised. What more can I do to rectify the situation?"

"Nothing," replied Alexa in a cold voice, refusing to give Lucy any more than she had. "It's too late for that."

"Fine," snapped Lucy, storming back into the house.

Alexa followed at a subdued pace to see Bethany and Charlotte smiling happily in the kitchen.

Lucy did not leave until late that night and was back early the next morning. The sounds coming from the bedroom also did not alter. It was more than Alexa could handle and was made worse by Bethany's continued absence. After going out for breakfast the day before, she had not arrived home until dinner time. Today she had gone out before lunch and it was now late in the night.

"You okay?" Alexa looked up to see Marcus wheeling himself into the lounge room. "Lucy just left," he explained, looking ashamed.

Alexa wished she could have lied, but tears were burning the sides of her eyes, and the truth was she was very far from okay.

"Oh, shit, hey, I'm sorry," said Marcus frantically, pushing forward and grabbing Alexa's hands.

"It's not you," said Alexa quickly.

"Beth?" asked Marcus. Alexa nodded. "Her being out so much?" Alexa nodded again, unable to speak. "Yeah, I was surprised you were so cool with it when I arrived, but I'm guessing you were so overwhelmed you never noticed."

"It's getting worse," gasped Alexa.

"But I don't think it's drugs," replied Marcus. "I know I don't have the experience you do, but it doesn't feel like last time."

"I know," admitted Alexa. It did not feel like drugs to her either. "I just don't know what else it could be. Maybe she's just gotten better at hiding it."

Marcus did not answer, and Alexa let her head drop into her hands. The feeling of Marcus's hand on her head was warming. He said nothing, but stayed close.

"Well this looks cosy."

Alexa's head snapped up. Bethany was standing in the doorway, smiling broadly.

"Where have you been?" asked Alexa forcefully.

"Not this again," sighed Bethany. "I'm going to bed." Bethany walked away, but Alexa followed, demanding to know where she had been. "It's none of your business," snapped Bethany. "I never thought

I'd wish you'd go back to studying. At least then I got some peace. Never cared before that I went out."

"Because I don't want to track you," cried Alexa. "But you're never home any more and when you are you won't talk to me."

"Then I've got nothing to tell you!" yelled Bethany, slamming her bedroom door in Alexa's face.

Alexa did not sleep. The entire night was spent sitting on her bed with her knees curled up into her chest, trying to deny this return to her old reality. That world she thought she had left behind was one she did not want to face again. Worse, she was not sure she could face it again. This peaceful life had weakened her so badly she feared she would not be able to save Bethany if she wanted to. Waiting in the lounge room for Bethany to emerge the next morning, Alexa was glad Bethany appeared to have had a sleepless night too. Yet there was no peace offering. After previous fights, they had always made up, but each of them was standing their ground.

"What time are you going to be home tonight?" asked Alexa.

"Late," replied Bethany petulantly.

"Where are you going?"

"Out!"

"With who?" continued Alexa.

"It doesn't matter," cried Bethany defensively.

"Yes, it does. If you don't tell me where you're going or who you're going with, then you can't go," said Alexa firmly.

"You can't tell me what to do! I'm eighteen. I don't need anyone dictating to me."

"You do if you're sneaking around taking drugs again," replied Alexa, her voice shaking badly.

"I'm not taking drugs!" gasped Bethany in a high-pitched voice, her eyes wide.

Their arguing had drawn Charlotte and Marcus out of their rooms, but neither Alexa nor Bethany paid them any attention.

"I don't believe you. You've been lying to me. You're never home and won't tell me where you're going. You used to tell me stuff. We used to talk," cried Alexa, hoping Bethany would provide another explanation, but all she got was more denials. "You go out tonight, then don't bother coming back," said Alexa, her mind made up.

"What?"

"Alexa," cried Marcus, wheeling himself closer. "Don't do this."

"It's none of your business," Alexa hissed at him, before turning back to Bethany. "I won't have you lying to me. You want to live your own life, take drugs, do whatever you like, you can do it in your own place. I'm not going to lose you like this."

"Just let me go," pleaded Bethany.

"I am," replied Alexa coldly. "Just don't bother coming back."

Chapter Six

ALEXA PUSHED PAST Marcus and Charlotte and rushed into her room, tears gushing down her face as the front door slammed shut. After crying so long and forcefully she retched several times, Alexa sat up with a bright, clean razor in her hand. She had not truly considered cutting herself in many months, but now it was all she wanted.

Bethany was lost.

Alexa was not sure how long she sat there contemplating the harm she could do herself, or when exhaustion took over and she collapsed on her bed. All she knew was the world only looked bleaker when she woke. A knock eventually pulled Alexa from her stupor, but she did not move. It was all too hard.

"Can I come in?" asked Sam, slowly pushing open the door.

Alexa rushed at him, throwing her sorrowful arms around his neck, and sobbed against his chest. Sam sighed heavily as he embraced her, holding her tight as he tried to soothe her, but his words could not ease her fears. "She's taking drugs again. I'm losing her, Sam. I'm losing her," Alexa cried. "I don't know how to stop it."

"It's okay. She's not taking drugs. I swear," said Sam confidently.

"She won't talk to me any more, she barely even looks at me and she's lying to me," explained Alexa in a broken voice, trying to make him see the truth. "I don't know what else it could be."

"I do," said Sam slowly, sitting Alexa on the bed.

"You do?" asked Alexa sceptically.

"I'm sorry. I should've come to you earlier. I guess – we thought you kinda knew. We should've told you, but I guess we didn't think you were ready," said Sam cryptically.

"Ready for what?" snarled Alexa, anger replacing her fear as Sam knelt in front of her. He had been hanging out with Bethany, had known what was wrong, and kept it from her.

"Beth met someone. She's fallen in love and he loves her just as much," said Sam, speaking carefully.

"Why would she hide that from me? I want her to be happy. That's not it! She wouldn't keep something that good from me."

"Yes, she would. She would if she was worried how you'd react to the guy."

A spike of fear shot through Alexa as she realised why Bethany had been so secretive. Leo. She had hooked back up with Leo; the sadistic paedophile drug dealer who had tortured and raped her.

"It's not that bad," said Sam anxiously.

"How can you say that?" Alexa gasped. "She's going to die."

"That'd never happen. I'd never let it," replied Sam forcefully.

"How could you stop it?"

"Because I'm the one that loves her."

Sam's sigh of release was the only sound in the room. Alexa's head was spinning. It suddenly made sense – all of it – and she too wondered why she had not noticed sooner. However, the relief was short-lived. "No, you're not in love with her," she said, shaking her head as she backed away from Sam. "You're in love with me and because you can't have me you transferred your feelings to Bethy."

"I thought that was the case too, but it's not," said Sam firmly, looking in Alexa's eyes. "I don't love you, not like that. I haven't since that week we spent together. That week confirmed everything I felt for Beth was real and wasn't for you."

"This's been going on since then?" cried Alexa, feeling betrayed.

"No! I mean, I started liking her while she was in gaol, but knew we'd have to wait until she was released to see if those feelings stood up to the real world and they did – until she relapsed," said Sam, suddenly reframing all those events in Alexa's mind. "It took us a long time to recover from that, but we're in love."

"So you've been fucking my sister behind my back and didn't even have the guts to come and tell me."

"I've only kissed her once!" cried Sam indignantly. "I wouldn't do that to you. We knew we'd have to tell you soon and if you say I can't see her then I'll walk away, but neither of you'll see me again, because I can't just be her friend any more."

"You could with me," noted Alexa.

"Yeah, cos I always hoped we'd get back together. But that's nothing. What I felt for you is only a fraction of what I feel for Beth."

Sam looked ashamed of his revelation. If Alexa had not been a giant swirl of emotions, she might have reassured him. They did not want to be together, but this was not just any girl Sam was talking about. It was Bethany, and that changed everything.

"Look, I know it's a shock," Sam said, taking Alexa's hand. "We should've told you, but we wanted to be sure about our feelings first. I never understood how you could imagine a life with anyone but me until I met Beth. Suddenly I realised how you must've felt about Marcus."

"What if you still love me?" asked Alexa cautiously. "I can't have her hurt like that. She deserves so much more."

"She does and I'll give it to her," answered Sam sincerely. "Since I started falling in love with Beth, I've loved you more and more. She's so amazing, capable of so much love and joy, so much more than you, and it's because of you."

"Is that why you chose her and not me?"

"This wasn't a choice! I never chose her over you. We were never going to be together. I didn't want you and you don't want me," sighed Sam. "What I'm saying is you're the reason Beth's such an amazing person and I love you for it. You put her first your whole life and you've paid dearly. You were more of a mother to her than anyone and you're only two years older than her. I love you. I always will. What we had can never be taken from us and I'll treasure it forever, but that's our past. I want my future with Beth and I want your blessing."

Alexa felt like a spinning top. She made her way to the balcony door. "Is Bethy here?"

"She came straight home after work. She called me and I came over. She doesn't want to hurt you."

"I need to talk to her."

The room went silent. Alexa waited, wondering what she would do next.

"Lex?"

Alexa turned to see Bethany's terrified, tear-stained face. Without a word, she crossed the room and took Bethany's face in her hands. Bethany did not resist and looked back at her with open eyes. Bethany stayed silent for many moments before the words blurted out. "I couldn't talk to you," she gasped, her body shaking. "I thought if I did, even about the weather, you'd find out how I felt about Sam and you'd hate me. I didn't mean to fall in love with him, I promise. I'm so sorry, Lex. Please don't hate me."

"Shh," hushed Alexa, dragging Bethany's head down into her shoulder. "It's okay. I don't hate you. I just don't want you to get hurt. I can't stand the idea of losing you."

"I love him, Lex. I wish I could love someone else," Bethany confessed, though it looked like her heart broke to speak such words. "I know I shouldn't love him and I'll stop if I have to, to keep you."

The pain Bethany was in trying to deny herself the happiness Alexa had always wanted for her was too much. "It's okay. I don't want you to stop. I want you to be happy," said Alexa quickly, looking straight into Bethany's eyes. "You can't help who you fall in love with."

"So I can see him?" asked Bethany with constrained excitement.

"Yes, but on one condition," said Alexa sternly.

"What's that?" asked Bethany tentatively, biting her lip.

"That I get my sister back." Alexa could not speak those words without her voice breaking.

"I promise, Lexie. I promise."

Bethany's hug made Alexa gasp for air, it was so tight, but Alexa refused to push her away. In so many ways Bethany was still her life and she never wanted to push her away again. However, that did not make Alexa easy about the situation. Following Bethany down the stairs, Alexa felt her stomach tie in knots at the sound of the excited squeals that drifted up to her. Alexa made it to the lounge room in time to see Bethany bounding off to her room, while Sam stood beaming.

"We're going out for dinner – to celebrate – if that's okay with you," said Sam excitedly. Alexa felt suddenly exhausted. She really hoped Sam was not going to ask her permission for everything they did together. "I'll bring her back early," he said. "But I was just wondering, if it's all right if I stay the night here?"

Alexa sighed. Apparently he was. That at least gave her one point of advantage. She grabbed his arm, forcing his eyes to hers. "I swear, Sam, if you ever hurt her, screw her over or hit her —"

"Lex!"

"I'll kill you with my bare hands," she continued unrepentant.

"I wouldn't have it any other way," replied Sam, pulling Alexa into a tight embrace. "I love Beth. I won't hurt her, I promise."

Alexa pushed Sam away before he could see her tears. It was not that she did not want them to be together, but the knowledge of how happy and in love they were only made her remember how alone she was. It left her collapsed on the lounge when they went out.

"All sorted?" asked Marcus, wheeling himself into the room.

"Yeah," sighed Alexa, not moving. "Did you know?" she asked, slowly turning to face him. He was smiling slightly.

"I had my suspicions. I mean, not so much recently – before – when we were all living together. I just assumed you would've seen it too."

"I guess I did in a way. It's just hard with Sam. When I saw them together I didn't see anything different to the way me and him used to be when we were younger – you know, after we broke up."

Marcus was smiling more broadly now, almost laughing. "Yeah, I know. That's what tipped me off."

Alexa did not laugh. Marcus moved closer and took her hand. He was about to speak when the doorbell rang. It was Lucy. This day was far too long already, and this was one step too far. Retreating quickly, Alexa hid until Lucy was safely in Marcus's room then dashed upstairs. Locking the door behind her, she collapsed on the bed and hoped for a better day tomorrow.

***

It was an anxious morning. Peter had called and asked Alexa if she wanted to spend the day out and about rather than in the office. They had never really gone out together, and Alexa was worried he did not want her back in the office. Not wanting to be late, Alexa waited on the front step for Peter to arrive. When he pulled up in the drive, she jumped straight in the car.

"Glad you could join me today," said Peter as they pulled back on to the road. "I had a few things to talk to you about and thought it might be nice to do that away from the office."

"Because I stuffed something up?" asked Alexa tentatively.

"Ha, no, not at all. I find you very useful. However, my work situation is – changing – well, it's going to be very different for the next couple of months."

"Oh," said Alexa softly.

"I'm going away with my family just before Christmas until the end of January – my wife has finally won that battle and is making me take some time off."

"But that'll be real nice," said Alexa, confused by Peter's attitude.

"Yes, it will, but it's going to leave me very busy and essentially unavailable until I return. While I'm very happy for you to continue working in the office, I would have had to hand you over to another colleague and I wanted to see if you're ready for that." Alexa felt her heart begin pounding erratically. It shocked her how forceful her physiological response to that proposition was when the theory should have been so straightforward. "Okay, that's all the answer I need," said Peter quickly.

"I'm sorry," replied Alexa meekly, not even able to refute Peter's assessment. "I don't know what's – I don't know why."

"I do," replied Peter solemnly. "I probably understand better than you at times, and you don't need to apologise. I actually think what you can do is much more remarkable than anything you can't."

"So what's today, then?"

"I guess that makes today our Christmas party," smiled Peter.

"Just me and you?" asked Alexa confusedly. She had never been to an office Christmas party before, but had always assumed more people would be involved.

"If that's okay. I thought I would keep a promise to you."

Alexa just stared uncomprehendingly. Peter started running his hand over the steering wheel, then the dashboard. He kept looking at her, clearly waiting for her to understand.

"No!" she cried with a mixture of disbelief and longing.

Peter was not joking. He took them to a racetrack where he had booked a session for them to drive his car around it. When Peter got out of the car and invited Alexa around to the driver's side, she suddenly felt very sick. Peter just laughed at her anxiety as he sat next to her, guiding her through the gears.

"First lap as slow as you want."

It was very slow. Alexa struggled with the gears and was so scared that the whole thing was nowhere near as fun as she imagined. The next lap was slightly better. Peter was so encouraging, joking when she made mistakes, that it soon became almost enjoyable. By the end of their hour, Alexa was driving at street speed. On the last lap down the straight, Peter told her to floor it. "Last chance," he smiled.

Alexa nodded and put her foot down. The acceleration, minus the clunky gear changes, was phenomenal. The thrill was so great she could not stop smiling during lunch and was excited by Peter's suggestion they do it again one day.

"I think I'll go for lessons in a manual car before next time," she grinned.

"I'll make sure we schedule it in ahead of time then," replied Peter happily.

"Do you do this with all your clients?" asked Alexa sceptically.

"No, but you are also my employee," answered Peter, but Alexa only scowled. "I know what you're asking," he said seriously. "You already know I view you and Bethany differently to my other clients, and it's rare that I have the privilege of watching one of my clients grow from a very troubled and disadvantaged child into a fine example of a woman."

"Does your wife know you spend time with me?" asked Alexa nervously, not daring to look up. "Doesn't she worry that …"

"What? Alexa, you don't think I see you – you are just my client," said Peter in a voice that betrayed more than a little concern. "You're a very nice person, and as we have this long-standing professional relationship, I do enjoy being able to see you under more favourable circumstances than history has previously allowed. Your existence and circumstances are no mystery to my wife, though your identity is. And I can honestly say my wife has no concerns about me having an affair – with anyone – let alone someone I have been representing since they were a child."

"Might be different if you were getting a divorce," replied Alexa.

Peter pursed his lips, taking a long, slow breath. He started eating again, but Alexa could only watch him, waiting for him to say it was better they never saw each other again.

"How's everything going at home?" asked Peter after another silent minute. "I'd been hoping I might get to sneak a look inside – see what you'd done to the place." Alexa's heart dropped. "But I wanted to get on the road this morning. Perhaps if we get a good run back. If you're happy to invite me in."

"Yeah, that sounds good," replied Alexa timidly.

"Will also give me a chance to see Ryan again. The contract should be coming to an end soon, shouldn't it? You don't think he'll give you any problems? Not leave?" asked Peter.

"No. He's been great. He has a job lined up and a place to move into," said Alexa, deciding not to mention that Ryan had joked a couple of times that he would not want to outstay his welcome given how lawyered-up she was. "It'll be strange, not having him around. You get used to it."

"What about Marcus? He have a place lined up too?" asked Peter casually. Alexa just shook her head, her eyes not meeting his. "No, I guess it'll take him a while to get back on his feet, metaphorically speaking. Probably a good thing he can stay with you."

"You don't think it's wrong?" asked Alexa tentatively. Peter had not previously raised many concerns about Marcus living with her, but she could never trust that silence. Everyone had an opinion when it came to Marcus.

"I don't make a habit of having opinions about other people's relationships. But I can tell you that Marcus Knight living in your house gives me little cause for concern."

Alexa smiled happily, glad there was one person who could be un-opinionated on that issue. It made her willing to talk about how Bethany and Charlotte were going. Peter appeared impressed by Bethany's carpentry skills and was looking forward to seeing her wares. He even hinted he could be a potential client if Bethany was willing to do custom builds. When they spoke about Charlotte, Peter was more concerned about the situation than Alexa anticipated.

"No, don't go getting that look on your face," said Peter. "I never said Charlotte should not live with you. What you've done for her – like what you did for Marcus – is very generous and kind-hearted. But the fact remains that Charlotte is just fourteen and has no parental influence in her life."

"I don't understand why her father decided to kick her out then," said Alexa. "I mean, if he'd always known – it's not like they'd always gotten along. Why then? Why when everything had been going well for so long? I think Charlotte would've expected it last year, but not then – not like that."

"I don't think there are always acceptable answers to questions like that," said Peter solemnly. "Life doesn't always bring out the best in people, but people like you restore our faith. Charlotte seems like a nice girl with a lot of potential. It's good she has you and Beth." Alexa did not respond. She found it difficult to believe Peter thought as highly of her as he professed to. "Ah, I almost forgot," said Peter, drawing Alexa's eyes up. "The invoice for the employment contract I wrote up for you. I'm glad there've been no problems."

"I'll pay it by the end of the week," nodded Alexa fervently.

"If only all my clients were so diligent," Peter laughed. "And that's why you get a free lunch. I keep clients that pay on time."

Alexa could not help but smile. When Peter went to pay for lunch, she quickly phoned Charlotte to alert her to his imminent visit. Charlotte did not disappoint, having carrot cake and pot of tea waiting on the dining room table on their arrival. Peter joked that Alexa could pay her entire invoice in cakes. Charlotte enjoyed the indirect compliment, smiling shyly. She had only just started to open up when Marcus and Ryan arrived home. Peter greeted them warmly, but did not stay beyond fifteen minutes – long enough to thoroughly quiz Ryan on his departure plans and establish there was no chance he was going to outstay his contract.

When the day of Marcus's release from his medical constraints came, Alexa found herself so anxious she could not sit still. Although Lucy had not been over for a few days – after practically camping out at the house for over a week – Alexa could not help but fear her arrival. And Marcus's departure. While he had not said anything about leaving, Alexa knew there was little to keep him with them. Despite the arguments against them being together diminishing over time, Alexa was still not sure she could be what Marcus wanted and feared his rejection more than never being with him.

The only way Alexa knew to pass the time as she waited for Marcus to come home a physically free man was to swim. Even when she got out of the pool, she just towelled down and threw on clothes until she could stand it no longer and dived back in the water. The mixture of water and Marcus on her mind kept Alexa's thoughts drifting back to their stolen day at the beach. More than once, she had examined maps of the coastline, trying to find where that little inlet had been. If she had not been so terrified of his motives, she might have been able to take in her surrounds a little better. That place, like most of the good experiences in her life, was like an abstract mystery. It sat to the side, a pocket of unreality that sometimes enticed, and other times taunted, her. That was probably why she had never made the concerted effort of travelling to any of the places she had identified on the map.

Needing to yet again divert her thoughts, Alexa jumped out of the pool and headed to the kitchen. Making lunch would not take long, but by putting conscious thought into meaningless decisions, she found herself effectively diverted – so much so that the sight of Marcus walking in the front door took her completely by surprise. Marcus smiled as she continued to stare. He was so much taller than she remembered.

"What do you think?" Marcus asked, stepping forward and giving an unsteady twirl.

"I think you need more practice," Alexa laughed, quickly grabbing him to keep him from hitting the wall. "Where's Ryan?"

"Had to head off. He needs to get his new place organised. Nice place, actually."

"You've seen it?" asked Alexa.

"Oh yeah, that and about a hundred others. We did a lot of house hunting together in the last month. We did a lot of everything together," said Marcus with a slight smile on his face. "It'll be strange not having him around, but I have to admit, I'm looking forward to showering alone. Just me and my own hands."

Alexa almost choked trying to hold back her laugh. Marcus smiled and shook his head, looking at her as though she was very immature.

Marcus walked into his room and sat down on the bed, his smile very content.

"So what are your plans now you're free?" asked Alexa brightly.

"Asking me to leave?" Alexa frowned for a second, confused by the question, before realising what Marcus thought she was asking. She just smiled and shook her head. "Want your study back?"

"I do like this room," smiled Alexa. "But you can have it. It's what Bethy would want."

"Beth made all the furniture?" asked Marcus, looking around. "It's really good. She's talented. I can't wait to see Charlotte's room. She's been trying to describe everything to me." Alexa grimaced, her heart pounding. "Charlotte mentioned Bethany had to make this bed specifically for you – that there was a problem with hers," he said softly. "What was wrong with it?"

Alexa ran her hand along the headboard. She tried to keep her mind blank, focused only on the wood. "Flat," she said in a shaky voice. "This one – flat – nowhere you can – nothing to tie —"

Alexa found herself suddenly engulfed in warmth. It took her a moment to realise Marcus was hugging her. He must have felt her tears soaking into his top as she curled up against his chest, because he held her tighter. One of his hands stroked her hair, comforting her until she composed herself.

Marcus stepped back just slightly. Alexa refused to meet his eyes, but his hand cupped her cheek, his thumb wiping away the tears that stained it. That was when she looked up. Her heart stopped. Even her lungs felt like they had ceased working. Marcus shifted, his lips moving to hers. Alexa was about to lift her body when he hesitated.

Marcus smiled, his right hand cupping the other side of her face. Their lips were so close she could taste the coffee on his breath.

The front door creaked open, ripping Alexa away from Marcus as though she was tethered to it. By the time Bethany bounded to the bedroom door Alexa was leaning near the door frame as Marcus sat innocently on the bed.

"Hey! Back on two legs!" cried Bethany, walking straight in and pulling Marcus to his feet. "Hmmm, still a bit unsteady. You'd better stick around so we can take care of you."

"We? You including yourself in that?" asked Marcus playfully. "I'd like to see that. Now what can I get you to do for me?"

"As long as I don't have to cook it, I'll be fine," replied Bethany jokingly, causing Alexa to step forward and hug her. It was the first time she could remember Bethany poking fun at herself over such a catastrophic failure.

"I could do with a tea. Reckon you could survive boiling water?"

"For you, I'll risk it," replied Bethany, literally bouncing forward to hug Marcus. He reciprocated, looking over her shoulder to Alexa. The look he gave her tore her heart and she could do nothing but dive back into the pool to try and outswim her emotions.

It did not help. Dinner that night was tantamount to torture. Alexa could barely even look at Marcus without her body flushing with the memory of his touch. Lying awake that night, Alexa pondered if there were any good arguments left against them being together. Surely she was old enough to prove she had not been lured and manipulated into a relationship. Marcus was no longer her teacher and never would be again. He was older than her, but it did not feel like ten years. In many ways, Alexa felt a greater age disparity when she was with people her own age.

There was Lucy. Alexa knew she should have more respect for Marcus's relationship, but it was difficult to feel anything close to respect for Lucy. Alexa was positive Marcus's relationship with Lucy was as flawed and taxing as her relationship with Damien had been. If Marcus was willing to leave Lucy for her, Alexa was not going to stop him – and as the night wore on she found herself considering how she could entice him. She did not want that to be the last time she felt Marcus's arms around her, and she did not want him to only be there in her moments of distress.

The resolution made Alexa fidgety. Though she rose with the

household, she was quiet at breakfast. Bethany was clearly concerned by her mood, because she hugged her from behind as Alexa washed up, squeezing her tight. "He's not going to leave us," Bethany whispered in Alexa's ear. "It's just Ryan who's going. He's going to stay. He is. He is."

Alexa could not help it. She turned and hugged Bethany tight. If things went well today, maybe she could give Bethany a reason to hold on to that faith. Charlotte left soon after Bethany, and then it was time for Ryan's departure. Alexa left Marcus and Ryan alone for much of the goodbyes. It appeared they had become quite close over the seven weeks they have been together. It was nice to see, but it did not come close to the realisation that she and Marcus were truly alone together for the first time in what felt like a lifetime.

"You want another coffee?" asked Alexa, hoping Marcus did not have somewhere else he needed to be.

"No, but I could go for a juice. I think it's going to be a hot one today," smiled Marcus.

They sat in the backyard. Their lack of gardening skills keeping it very wilderness-like. Alexa liked it, feeling as if it kept the world out, making their house a sanctuary from the horrors lurking beyond their walls.

"You sure you don't mind me staying?" asked Marcus seriously. "Now things have settled down."

"Do you mind me asking why you want to stay?" asked Alexa, her thoughts returning to the plans she had conjured last night. "I would've thought you'd be itching to move back in with Lucy." Alexa could not help but smirk. Her comment sounded so clumsy it had to be obvious she was fishing.

"I don't think Lucy wants to move again," replied Marcus. "She was pretty annoyed at me for having to move in the first place."

"Even though you almost died?" asked Alexa incredulously, all but making up her mind.

"Things have cooled off a bit anyway," shrugged Marcus. "I haven't heard from her since her last visit."

"Maybe not a bad thing," smiled Alexa, buoyed by his answer. "We were starting to get noise complaints from the neighbours."

"I'm sorry about that."

"I was joking," replied Alexa, seeing Marcus's guilty look. "But if you've got nowhere to go, you can stay as long as you like. I just need you to start paying rent – even just a bit. I can't have Charlotte paying and you not."

"How much do you want?" asked Marcus immediately.

"More than Charlotte," answered Alexa seriously. "I'm sorry, but I have to. I wish she wouldn't pay, but she insists."

"You're apologising for making me pay more rent than a fourteen-year-old?" laughed Marcus. "You're something, you know that."

Alexa smiled, feeling jubilantly reckless. "I want to go to the beach today," she said, leaning forward with a mischievous smile. "Want to come? I want to go somewhere quiet – away from lots of people." Marcus shifted forward as she spoke. "Remember that beach you took me to? I don't know how to get there. Will you show me?"

"You've never been back there? But it was so close to your apartment," said Marcus, sounding genuinely surprised.

"What?"

"I always wondered if that was part of the reason you chose to live around there."

Alexa could only shake her head. "It was why I wanted to live by the beach though."

"Then let me show you where our bay is," grinned Marcus, making Alexa's heart beat erratically.

The idea of swimming with Marcus in that peaceful inlet brought all sorts of strange twinges to Alexa's stomach. She wondered if she made a move whether he would push her away, but there was something in his eyes that told her he wanted the same things she did.

"Shall we go?" asked Alexa.

"Absolutely."

Alexa jumped up with more enthusiasm than she knew she had a right to. Marcus was technically still a taken man, but she did not care. This was the time to be daring and she was suddenly very thankful for her recent shopping trip.

There was a knock at the door as they walked inside. Alexa smiled at Marcus and started up the stairs. "You can get that," she said. "Probably Ryan. Forgotten something already."

Alexa hoped Marcus got the hint that her mind was already at the beach and she was desperate for their bodies to catch up. The thought of Marcus's body close to hers was so enticing, and she was not interested in being polite to an unexpected visitor, even one as nice as Ryan.

"I'm here to see Caitlin King."

Alexa stopped dead, her body trembling at the sound of that voice.

"Caitlin King? No one by that name lives here," said Marcus, in a confused voice before suddenly looking up at Alexa. Panic surged across his face. "Run, Alexa, run," cried Marcus, wrestling with Sean King, who was trying to force his way into the house.

Alexa watched, frozen, as the man she interviewed for the job as Marcus's nurse, the man who had filled her with so much fear, knocked Marcus to the ground with a sickening thud.

"Caitlin," called Sean, standing at the base of the stairs. "I've been waiting for this day for a long time. Why don't you come down here?"

Alexa found her feet and fled up the stairs into the second floor lounge room, locking the door behind her. Diving for the phone sitting in the corner, she dialled frantically, waiting an impossibly long time for an answer.

"Detective B—"

"Ben, please help me," cried Alexa, her voice shaking.

"Alexa?"

"Sean King, he's here. He hurt Marcus," gasped Alexa, terrified Marcus was dead because of her. "I'm upstairs, but he's trying to get in." Alexa shook violently as Sean tried to break down the door.

"What? Sean King? Are you sure?" asked Ben frantically.

"Yes! He's the man from the interview. The one that scared me. Please come quick. Please —"

Alexa's pleas were cut short as the door gave way. Ben was yelling at her, but she was too frightened to speak. Sean twirled a knife in front of him, walking casually across the room and cutting the phone cord. Ben's panicked voice went silent. Alexa wanted to run, but was so frightened she could not move. Sean took her hand and led her to the lounge. She complied, feeling completely unable to do anything but. Sean's hand gently stroked her face. It was sickeningly familiar and Alexa knew what was about to happen.

"I've missed you, Caitlin," cooed Sean, his hand continuing to move over Alexa's body.

"My name's Alexa," she whispered.

"Okay, I'll call you Alexa, but I always liked Caitlin more," said Sean, his voice menacing and possessive. "You hurt me when you went away. You were mine and I wanted you back. You and me were special together. We loved each other."

Alexa's heart sank. He was insane. He was going to rape her and she was not even the girl he was looking for. Sean cupped her face, pulling her to him. Alexa trembled with fear. The moment his lips touched hers, her stomach lurched. She turned and vomit splashed across the floor.

"It's okay, sweetie," said Sean tenderly, comforting her with groping hands.

"I'm scared," Alexa whispered, feeling like a helpless child.

"You don't have to be scared. I'll be gentle. I won't hurt you."

"I don't want to," cried Alexa, knowing he was lying.

"I told you I'll be gentle," Sean snarled, shaking Alexa violently. "You owe me this much after all the trouble you caused. We were happy, Caitlin." Alexa flinched at that name. Sean's face softened, his hands resuming their exploration of her body. "Sorry. Alexa. We were happy and you ruined things. I just want things to be as they were."

Alexa looked desperately towards the door, wondering if she could escape before Sean caught her. The image of Marcus's lifeless body floated in front of her eyes. She had lured Marcus into the disaster of her life and now he might die because of her. She had to get out – get Marcus out – and away from Sean. Knowing Sean was never going to give her a chance to leave, Alexa shoved him away and ran as fast as she could. Marcus was lying at the base of the stairs. She tried to pull him to his feet, but he could not support his own weight.

"Alexa, run," Marcus slurred, his arm grasping hopelessly to the banister.

Alexa refused to listen and had Marcus to his knees when she saw Sean standing over them. With a vicious swing, Sean felled Marcus. The thud of Marcus's head against the floor made Alexa's heart stop. Alexa searched for some sign of life as Sean dragged her easily up the stairs, but there was nothing.

Sean hauled Alexa back into the second lounge room, her heart screaming with fear. "No, no, no," said Sean angrily, shoving her roughly. "I wanted this to be nice. I can only be gentle if you let me, otherwise it'll hurt and we don't want that, do we?"

A chill ran across Alexa's neck as Sean laid her face down on the lounge. The stinging pain of the knife cutting into her throat tingled her skin. Alexa focused on that, the burn of the cuts, to block out what Sean was doing to her body, but she could still feel his weight on her legs, pinning her to the lounge. Sean used his free hand to violently tear off her top and yank up her skirt. Alexa could feel his excitement. She knew what came next and did not want to live through it.

"Get off her, Sean!"

Alexa tried to look towards the voice, but was hauled off the lounge, Sean crying out angrily. The knife dragged along Alexa's throat before being pressed back harder into it, making it difficult for her to breathe.

"Let her go, Sean," growled Ben, his gun pointed straight at Sean. Ben's partner, Shane Parker, stood next to him, just inside the door. He looked equally stern, his gun pointed in the same direction.

Alexa waited for them to shoot Sean and release her from this terror, but they just stood there.

"She's mine. You can't take her away from me!" snarled Sean, stroking Alexa's hair and body with his free hand as he held her in front of him, pressed against his body.

"She's nobody's, least of all yours and I'll take her away from you again and again," cried Ben. "Now let her go!"

"We love each other. Nothing can change that."

"Love? How can you call this love? You have a knife to her throat."

"She loves me. I need to remind her. You made her forget how much she loves me!" screamed Sean, pulling Alexa into him.

"She never loved you!"

Alexa was annoyed with the back and forth argument and could not understand why Ben was indulging in Sean's insane fantasy that she was Caitlin King instead of getting her away from him.

"Lex!" screamed Bethany, racing into the room, pushing between Ben and Parker, who tried to keep her back.

"Well, well, well. Becky, haven't you grown. You look just like your mother," snarled Sean with great disgust.

Alexa turned to Bethany, willing her to run. There was one thing Alexa knew with every fibre of her being, and that was Bethany would die if she stayed. All Alexa wanted was to get away from Sean and drag Bethany to safety. Ben and Parker had guns and Alexa hoped that would be enough to clear their passage. Shifting slightly to the side, Alexa tried to give Ben and Parker a clear shot, but Sean grabbed her, wrestling her back into position. Parker took half a step forward, giving Alexa the courage to keep struggling. Sean was strong, somehow managing to restrain and grope her at the same time, but Alexa eventually got an arm free and with all the leverage she could muster, swung it into Sean's crotch. Sean's grip loosened slightly. Alexa pushed away from him at the same moment a loud explosion tore through the room.

Pain seared through Alexa's neck as she stumbled away from Sean, struggling on her hands and knees. Her body weakened quickly and, without being able to control it, she fell to the floor. Clattering noises filled the air as footsteps raced towards her. Large hands wrapped around her neck. Bethany was screaming her name. Alexa could not believe it. They had shot her instead of Sean.

"Where's the ambulance?" asked Parker.

Alexa tried to talk, but Ben's hands were too tight. Her head swirled when she moved it. There was a strange sensation in her arm. Then Bethany came into sight and Alexa realised Bethany was holding her hand. Bethany was screaming, but Alexa could not make the words stick in her head long enough to understand them.

"Marc," gurgled Alexa, pushing the words from her throat. She was feeling fainter by the second, Bethany swirling in and out of focus, but she had to know that Marcus would not die because of her.

Alexa watched her hand fall from Bethany's grasp. Scuffling noises filled the room, jostling Alexa in an abstract way. The movement swirled inside of her even though she could not see what was happening.

"No!" screamed Sam.

Bethany returned to Alexa's side, shoved against her as though she had been forced. Alexa saw her hand return to Bethany's. Bethany was hugging it to her chest as she rocked back and forth. Alexa tried to squeeze Bethany's hand, but could not tell if she was. One of Bethany's hands moved to Alexa's head. Everything around Bethany started to fade away. Only Bethany remained. Alexa wondered how Bethany was being dragged with her into death and if Bethany was in pain. All Alexa knew was that their pact had held. In life and death, they could not be torn apart.

Chapter Seven

LIGHT AND COLOURS danced across Alexa's eyes like a psychotic symphony. It was strangely hypnotic, but Alexa was glad it finally subdued into a peaceful swirl that reminded her of waves crashing on the beach. Perhaps dying would not be so bad if this was all it was. Watching the colours move, random shapes began to form, making Alexa wonder how the afterlife worked. Perhaps she was transiting through to her next life, whipping past the possibilities before finally being flung into a new, tiny body. Or maybe whoever presided over death was deciding whether she should be sent to heaven or hell.

When Pam and Karl White materialised in front of her, Alexa knew she could not be in hell. People like them would never be sent to hell. But if they were in heaven, they must have died too. Pain shot through Alexa's body as she tried to scream, but then she realised she no longer had a body.

"It's okay," said Pam. "Just rest. We'll stay with you."

Alexa did not understand. She was dead. She never needed to rest again. Pam continued to soothe her. She was speaking tenderly, but her voice was jittery, and another possibility crossed Alexa's mind. Perhaps she was a ghost and she had gone to find them now she could no longer bring harm upon them. The answers would not come and Alexa realised that, dead or not, she did need to rest. Closing the eyes she was not sure she had, Alexa was thankful the colours quickly dissolved into blackness.

Bright light tore across Alexa's view like a comet, tearing her from the peaceful darkness. The colours of before erupted, but they were darker now, denser. Pain stabbed through what was left of her being. Alexa knew the decision had been made. She had been sent to hell. The horrid visions of her past returned, tumbling over each other, one after the other, without end. This was her punishment. Her eternal damnation.

Alexa felt like she had lived another lifetime when the light streaked past her once more. She wondered what the next round of torture would be. The colours leeched away with the light, leaving just swirls of black and white. They started to solidify into shapes before

108

slipping back into nothingness, then reforming once more. The black and white shifting back and forth was so disorientating it made Alexa want to vomit.

It took forever, but the darkness finally found the strength to hold its shape. Images formed, solid and life-like, but Alexa could not work out what picture they painted as pain tore through her. Starting in her throat, it streaked down her chest, making it hard to breathe. A body. She was connected to her body. She was not dead. It made no sense. She tried to remember the images that had swirled before her, but they dissolved into confusion, leaving behind only panic.

"Alexa? Are you awake? Alexa?"

Alexa could not see anything, but she knew that voice and if she was not dead then she feared they soon would be.

Needing to know what was happening, Alexa focused everything on making sense of this strange situation. Slowly at first, then suddenly all at once, the world snapped into sharp focus. The sight that greeted her was the nightmare she had always wanted to avoid. Her body recoiled as though she could somehow crawl away from this mistake, but she knew there was no escape and tears slipped down her face over the loss she would have to face.

"No, please," Alexa gasped, pain ripping through her throat as she spoke. "Please, go away. I don't want you hurt. I don't want you to die. Please, you have to leave me."

"Calm down, Alexa," said Karl, gently restraining her.

"No, please. It's not safe. I'm not safe. Please."

"It's okay. We're okay. We're safe. You made sure of that," said Pam, grasping Alexa's hand until she stopped trying to move away. "We saw what happened on the news. We couldn't stay away any longer, not when we knew where you were." Alexa could not reply, the pain in her throat now too severe. They knew what happened to her and why she was in pain. Alexa waited for an explanation, but they said nothing about that, leaving her in ignorance. "We wouldn't be here if we thought we or Brett or Hayley were in any danger," said Pam kindly. More tears slipped down Alexa's face at the mention of Hayley's name. "They're fine. Hayley's fine. She's worried about you. We all are."

It took a while for Pam and Karl to calm Alexa down, by which time a nurse had realised she was awake and ordered them out so they could examine her.

"We have to go now," said Karl, rubbing Alexa's hand. "But we'll come back tomorrow."

In the absence of guests, Alexa realised she was in a hospital, yet did not know why. Something had happened to her. Perhaps it was just a car accident or a fall down the stairs, but something darker lurked in her mind, telling her things were never that simple. Trying to piece together the last thing she remembered, Alexa bounced back and forth between memories over the last three months. They slowly started to filter down to the last week. Alexa remembered having breakfast alone with Marcus. That faded, shifting to her trapped in the second lounge room with Sean King. Alexa could not work out why Sean had been in her house. When the memory of Marcus's lifeless body at the bottom of the stair flashed across her mind, Alexa realised Sean had hurt Marcus. Perhaps killed him. Then Alexa remembered Ben's gun pointed towards her and wished now it had killed her.

A noise turned Alexa's eyes to the door. Bethany, Ben, Sam, Maria and Charlotte crept slowly to her bedside. It only then struck Alexa as strange that it was the Whites who were by her side when she woke and not Bethany. Even now no one spoke. They all just stood there and looked at her. Bethany did not approach. She looked timid and frightened. Tears fell down her cheeks, but she stayed out of reach.

Alexa did not understand. Any of it. No one said anything. No one explained what happened. Why Ben had shot her and why they had not always been by her side.

"How are you?" asked Maria tenderly, taking Alexa's hand and sitting beside her.

That seemed to be the cue for everyone else to move. Charlotte took Bethany's hand and pulled her to the bedside. Bethany lunged forward and hugged Alexa, sobbing uncontrollably as she apologised over and over. This only confused Alexa more. There was no reason for Bethany to be sorry. She had never met Sean King. She had not been the one to drag this terror into their lives. It was her. It was always her. It made Alexa want to disentangle herself from her life – hide away from it and the horrors she attracted.

"Marc's okay," said Charlotte eventually. "He's just a few rooms away, actually. He should be released in a few days."

Alexa's mind swirled back to Marcus lying unconscious on the floor. He had been hurt because of her, but he was not dead. Yet he was still in hospital. Not to be released for several more days. It had to be bad, but how bad, she did not know because no one said anything else about Marcus or the situation that had put them both in hospital.

Looking over at Ben, Alexa noticed he would not meet her eyes. Perhaps he felt guilty for shooting her. She would have forgiven him if he just spoke to her. She and Ben had not been on good terms for months, but he had come when she needed him and she wanted to say thank you, but could not face speaking that much.

It quickly became overwhelming. Rolling over towards Bethany, Alexa clung to Bethany's hands and closed her eyes, willing the world to make more sense when they opened again.

"Hey, you awake?"

Alexa opened her eyes slowly. There was nothing in front of her, but was sure she had heard someone speak. Just that tiny mystery was enough for her to wish her life would dissolve into nothingness. Closing her eyes again, she willed them to never reopen, but barely a minute had gone by before a hand touched her shoulder, pulling her back to the life she detested. Rolling over, Alexa was not comforted by the sight of Marcus sitting by her bedside. He did not look well and part of his head had been shaved.

"Blood on the brain," Marcus explained, touching the side of his head as she continued to stare. "They had to drain me to relieve the pressure. You'd think they'd just shave it all off instead of making a patchwork of my head," he said light-heartedly. "I'll fix it up when I get out of here." Alexa said nothing, hating herself even more, seeing what her life had done to Marcus – all because of her selfishness. "You know when they're releasing you?"

Alexa shook her head, tears building in her eyes as the memories of that morning returned. "When I heard your head hit the floor ... I thought you were dead," rasped Alexa, talking through the pain.

"I thought you were dead," replied Marcus, his voice breaking. "He didn't – they got him before he could hurt you, right?" Alexa nodded. Whatever happened, she knew she had not been raped. "Except for your throat," said Marcus shakily. Alexa put her hand to her throat. "He slit your throat."

"Wasn't shot?" she asked.

Marcus shook his head, triggering more memories. The cold, sharp blade against her throat. The sting as the room exploded. Alexa looked back at Marcus, suddenly understanding why all this had happened.

He reached out for her hand, but she quickly pulled it away to cover the guilty tears streaming down her face.

"You're not being punished," said Marcus. "You did nothing wrong. It was just a random, horrible thing."

Neither idea was comforting. Either Marcus was wrong and she was being punished for what she had planned that day, or he was right and she attracted trouble like a super-charged magnet.

Those thoughts left Alexa deeply depressed as she lay alone in her room contemplating what had happened. This was the life she did not want to live. The life she thought she had escaped. Once more she had been lulled into a false sense of security, then punished for believing she deserved more than she had been born into. Determined not to face this pain any longer, Alexa looked around for anything that would bring her life to a swift end.

"Hi, Alexa. How are you feeling?" asked Peter solemnly, walking into her room right at the moment her eyes spied a stash of medical supplies, including what looked like a sterile blade. When their eyes met, Peter was instantly by her side, his hand grasping hers in a way that felt more restraining than comforting. "What's going on?"

"I need to break my promise," replied Alexa, tears slipping down her cheeks.

Peter did not need further explanation. He looked straight down at the scar on her wrist. "I'm never going to give you permission to do that," he said firmly. "You do anything and you'll be breaking that promise. But I will do anything else I can to help you. Anything. What do you need? You want to get out of here?"

"Can't go back there," gasped Alexa, her throat burning.

"No, that's fine," replied Peter. "What about somewhere else? Somewhere safe. Just say the word, Alexa, and I'll get you out of here. I just can't let you break that promise."

Alexa nodded, curling her body up into a ball and tucking her arms into her chest. Closing her eyes, she cleared her mind. It was as close to a non-living state as she could get. She paid no attention to anything. Even when the doctors and nurses came to discuss her discharge, she did not respond.

"Okay, we're out of here," said Peter some time later.

Alexa did not know if it had been a minute, hour, day or week since he was there last. Throwing on the clothes he gave her, not knowing who they belonged to, she followed him out of the hospital.

She wondered if Peter was taking her home with him, but did not ask. She did not care. Even if he dumped her on the side of the road, she would just curl up in a ball and wait to die.

"I just need to call ahead to get access," said Peter quietly.

Alexa did not respond. She did not even look up when Peter parked the car in a garage. He walked around to her door and led her into the house. That was when she stopped dead.

"Welcome home, Alexa," said Pam tenderly.

Peter held Alexa's shaking body, quietly reassuring her, but nothing could.

"It's okay, Alexa," said Karl. "You're safe here."

"But you," Alexa gasped.

"We're all very safe here," Karl reassured her, moving forward and taking her hand. "I'll show you to your room."

Alexa did not move, her eyes darting around. She did not have to verbalise what she was looking for. "They're out at the moment," said Pam softly. "Let's get you settled in before they get back."

Alexa looked up at Peter, who nodded reassuringly. "You want me to come with you?"

Alexa nodded, and Peter walked with her as they followed Pam and Karl up the stairs. The bedroom they took her to disoriented Alexa. They had not put her in a spare room. They had taken her to her room. Little things she had left behind, always expecting to come back to, sat on the bedside and dressing tables.

Peter sat Alexa on the bed, stroking her hair paternally as he squeezed her hand. "You call me anytime you need to," he said kindly. "And stay here as long as you need."

"They won't get hurt?" whispered Alexa, tears slipping down her cheeks.

"No, I promise. You're safe here and so are they. Did you see the security when we came in?" asked Peter. Alexa shook her head. "This is the safest place you could possibly be. You just find some peace."

"What if I never find peace? Will you let me break my promise?"

"If you don't find peace here, I'll come back for you. You can come with me and my family on our trip away – you don't have to stay with us, but you can have time away. After that, if you still have to – we can talk about it then. Okay?"

Alexa nodded. Peter sighed heavily and squeezed her hands once more. With a quick word to Karl, Peter said his goodbyes. Through the open door, Alexa saw Hayley's room across the hall. The world was spinning. Nothing seemed real. Never had Alexa allowed herself to believe she would see the Whites again, let alone be in their home.

"Let's get you settled in," said Pam softly, as Karl slipped out of the room. "Your clothes are in the drawers. They're all clean. But you can have a bath first – get refreshed. I'll run it for you now and you come down when you're ready and we'll have dinner."

Pam tended to Alexa in a way she had never been cared for before. If Alexa had had the strength of a will to live, she would have made her stop, but she could not even manage that. Sitting in the scented bath, Alexa knew she did not even have the strength to hold her head under the water until her lungs gave out. The best she could do was naively will the water to drain out of her whatever continued to draw disaster into her life.

When the water was stone cold, Alexa pulled herself out of it. She shivered as she dressed in her clothes from three years ago. They were too large, but she did not care. Her actions now were as reckless as those that had caused this latest trauma, but she would enjoy this moment before ending her life.

Darkness had begun to engulf the house, but Alexa could make out the small figure that sat on the end of her bed. The eyes that stared out at her were not the childish and innocent ones she remembered. Puberty had taken hold of Hayley's body and, closing in on fourteen, she was much more woman-like than the child Alexa had walked away from.

"Do you still hate me?" croaked Hayley, after a minute of painful silence.

Alexa felt the rush of hot tears and fell to her knees in front of Hayley. "I never hated you. I loved you," gasped Alexa, speaking through the pain. "I had to go. I had to make sure you'd be safe."

"I thought maybe you hated me for having to go with that man, for having to protect me and all they did to you." Tears streamed down Alexa's face as she shook her head. "Promise you don't hate me?"

"I could never hate you," sobbed Alexa, every word a painful torture. "I was scared you'd hate me."

"How could I? You saved my life. You stopped them from – you almost died for me!"

Alexa could not answer. Hayley's guilt did not assuage her own.

What happened was her fault. She just could not speak to explain how greed got the better of her.

"I'm glad you're home," said Hayley softly after many moments of silence. "Do you want dinner? It's ready."

Alexa nodded, following Hayley downstairs. Walking into the dining room, Alexa felt arms embracing her before she knew who it was and was shocked by the warmth of Brett's hug. He was the only one who had understood how inherently dangerous she was, who had not begged her to return to live with them. And now she was here, putting them in danger all over again. But before Alexa could react, she was pulled to the dining table where their dinner was waiting.

"Discharge papers said soft foods for at least a week," said Pam, gesturing towards the soup that sat in front of Alexa. "The cut to the windpipe will take a while to heal, so you need to take it easy with eating and drinking. And don't push yourself with talking."

An awkward silence fell over them. Alexa was not sure if Pam meant they did not want her to speak. Alexa did not know what she would have said anyway.

Everyone started slowly eating, their eyes roving tentatively around the table. It was uncomfortable, but Alexa found herself strangely at ease.

"I can't – I can't do this," cried Brett suddenly, pushing away from the table in an agitated manner. "I can't sit here pretending nothing happened."

Alexa's heart sank. She knew this had been coming, but had hoped they could have pretended for a little while longer.

"Brett, it's not the time," said Karl. "She's just out of hospital."

"No, it's okay," said Alexa, holding her throat through the pain. "I'm really glad I got to see you all again. I can go."

"We don't want you to go," cried Brett, grabbing her hand.

"But you didn't want me to come back," gasped Alexa. "You said so. You knew – you understood how dangerous I was. Am."

Tears slipped down Brett's face as he slowly shook his head. Alexa had never seen him cry before and was distressed by the sight. "I knew you wouldn't come back. Knew you'd blame yourself for what happened," said Brett, mastering his voice. "I told Dad, but they wanted to convince you to come back. I only said that – I wanted Dad to say you couldn't come back, but we'd visit you. Thought that if we stayed in contact then you'd come back after a while."

Alexa tried to stop herself from sobbing as she held Brett's hand tighter.

"Would you've wanted that? Accepted that?" asked Karl.

Alexa nodded, her whole body shaking.

"Brett's always been very good at working people out," said Pam. "It wasn't that we – we couldn't do it. You'd just given your life for us. It felt like the height of cruelty to offer you anything less than full inclusion in our family."

"We fought a lot after that day," said Karl gravely. "Particularly Brett. He was so angry – with us – those men – himself. He was right. We never should've let you go with those men. We should've done more to protect you. I should've fought for you."

"If anyone of us – it should've been me they took," said Pam in a wavering voice.

Alexa fell to her knees next to Pam's chair, tears streaming down her face at the thought of Pam in that place, beaten and raped. "No, no," Alexa gasped. "Not you. Not ever. I could never live with myself – I was the only one – no one else could've survived that place. That's my world. I couldn't let it touch any of you."

"You're so young," said Pam in a shaky voice, stroking Alexa's face. "You never should've experienced all the things you have."

"We should've been able to spare you," said Karl solemnly. "We wish we'd been able to spare you."

Dinner became an afterthought as they sat around discussing the events of that night two and a half years ago and the fallout that had followed. It was not a conversation Alexa wanted to have, but it was clear this was something they had kept bottled up for a long time.

"Hayley didn't speak – after that night we went to see you – she didn't speak for about a month," explained Pam sombrely. "And since then she's been very quiet – not the girl she was."

Alexa turned to Hayley, but Hayley would not meet her eyes. "I felt like I ruined everything," said Hayley, her voice barely above a whisper. "I wanted to take it all back – not have presents or birthdays or any of that stuff. I just wanted you not to hate me any more."

"I didn't hate any of you," replied Alexa. "What happened – that was all my fault. You should hate me, not each other or yourselves."

"What we decided," said Karl in a firm voice. "Was we wouldn't hate anyone who wasn't to blame for that night – including ourselves. You can see we're still struggling to put that into practice, but the reality is the only people to blame are those thugs who barged into our house and destroyed our family. That doesn't include us, you or your sister. We need you to know that."

"You don't blame me and Bethy?" squeaked Alexa.

"You're sister was just fifteen – a child living on the streets. No family. No parents. No guidance," said Karl. "There's no way to untie her from the things that happened, but it doesn't make them her fault. We know and we believe that. We just also know that passion and pain sometimes cause us to lash out at the easiest target. We're not healed, but we know who's to blame for what happened."

"We've been through a lot of counselling," said Brett, looking over at Alexa with a shadow of a smile. "Dad and Hales, they're the best for it. Me and Mum – takes more for us to let go of our anger."

Although they did not continue to dwell on the event that tore their family apart, it was difficult to avoid it completely. Alexa was surprised she did not feel the worse for it. Though her throat burned from the use, and her heart was heavy with guilt, she felt like poison had been sucked from her blood.

"You should head to bed," said Pam, when they started clearing their half-eaten dinners from the table. "You need to rest."

Alexa would have argued if she had not been suddenly swamped by the fatigue the reunion had kept at bay. Hayley took Alexa's hand and led her to her room. It was strange, feeling so at home in a place she had never been before, but things were so similar to the way she had left them that she could have almost willed the years apart out of her life.

"Alexa," said Hayley once Alexa was dressed in her pyjamas. "Would it be okay to stay with you tonight? Like before. I know things have changed, but —"

"Nothing's changed, Hales," said Alexa quickly. "We've spent lots of time apart, but nothing's changed."

Hayley returned ten minutes later. Alexa sighed heavily as Hayley crawled into the bed next to her. Hayley's hug was tentative, but sweet, and caused yet more tears to slip down their cheeks. "I really am sorry for everything, Hales," said Alexa. "I never meant for you to get hurt."

"I never wanted you to get hurt either," sniffed Hayley, hugging Alexa tighter. "Next time, we'll kill them before they hurt you – before they hurt any of us."

"Don't talk like that, Hales," gasped Alexa.

"Me and Brett, we started martial arts. Brett's real good. We only wish we'd been around so that other guy couldn't hurt you either."

Alexa held Hayley tight as her body shivered. She hated the idea of Hayley being anywhere near Sean. It seemed impossible that her little frame could have fought him off. The memory of Marcus being so easily felled made her doubt Brett would have stood a chance. It only reminded Alexa of how reckless and selfish it was for her to be here. She would stay tonight, but would have to find the strength to leave tomorrow.

When morning arrived, Alexa tried to gather her resolve, but as she sat down at breakfast, she saw a pad of paper and pen sitting on the table.

"We don't want you straining yourself," said Karl. "You were holding your throat a lot last night. You need to take it easy."

Alexa nodded. She would not have been able to speak anyway. Her throat was constricted with emotion at the kindness the Whites were showing her.

Pam and Brett made breakfast smoothies for the family. They sat out in the backyard in the morning sun, relaxing in a way Alexa had never been able to before. There was nothing she had to worry about. Cooking, cleaning, planning. It was all being done for her. It was so comforting she forgot all about her need to leave – until the intercom at the front gate buzzed angrily.

Brett immediately grabbed Alexa and Hayley, pulling them to the lounge room as Karl and Pam headed towards the front door. Alexa tried to stop them, but her whole body was shaking. Brett held her tight, restraining her as she wrestled anxiously against him.

"No one can get in," said Brett in her ear. "We can see who's at the gate. Look."

Alexa looked up at the television screen that was now showing security camera footage. Hayley was using a remote to flick through images and camera angles.

"Ben," gasped Alexa, her body collapsing as she watched Ben and his partner, Shane Parker, hold up their badges to the camera. "Don't want to go home. Can't go back there yet."

When Pam walked into the room, Brett relinquished Alexa into her arms and rushed out of the room. Pam soothed Alexa as Hayley held her hand. Brett and Karl joined them minutes later. Alexa buried her head, unsure how she would face Ben.

"They're gone," said Karl softly.

"Coming back?" whispered Alexa, her body shaking with the conflict of not knowing what she wanted the answer to be.

"Only when you're ready," answered Karl, stroking her hair.

No one spoke again for a long time. When Alexa finally looked up, she found herself on the lounge. There was food on the coffee table and the television on in the background. Everyone was chatting quietly, and when Alexa uncurled her body, they handed her a drink as though nothing strange had happened.

"Sorry about before," said Alexa meekly.

"We've all had our moments the last couple of years," replied Karl calmly.

"Was Ben mad?" asked Alexa tentatively.

"No. Just very worried. It was a surprise, you being here. He just wanted to know that you were okay." Karl paused, making Alexa's heart stammer. "He wanted to let you know that Sean King – the man who attacked you – died overnight. Complications following surgery."

Alexa did not respond. She was relieved Sean was dead, but was not sure it would do much to dent the population of psychopaths she attracted. Knowing there was no reason for Sean's attack – that it had been as random as it was violent – made her realise how dangerous she was. It snapped her out of inactive state, forcing her from the lounge, but her determination must have shown on her face, because Karl was instantly blocking her path.

"You just had a panic attack at the thought of going home," he said firmly. "You can stay here. We want you to stay here."

"But you'll die," Alexa gasped.

"We're not in danger now," said Pam, rising and placing comforting arms around Alexa's shoulders. "You're safe and we're safe. You need to stay and rest. We're not holding you hostage, but you're not ready to go home yet. As soon as you are, we'll take you there. Until then, you just need to get better."

Alexa could not fight them. She did not have the strength or the desire. As she laid back down on the lounge, noticing Brett's slight smirk, Alexa realised that Pam and Karl had subtly changed the way they dealt with her. Where they had previously just left her – too scared to confront her – they now took her on, telling her how things would be. It was strange how effective their new approach was. The last thing Alexa would have guessed she needed was more people telling her what to do.

The rest of the day passed quietly, but serenely. The way the Whites drew Alexa into their peaceful existence was magical, but she knew this could not last. No matter what they said, she could not let herself believe this could continue. As soon as she was well enough to go home, she would have to cut ties with them once more. Cultivating that reality was difficult. The only way Alexa could face it was to remind herself of what would have happened to Hayley if she had not been able to convince Leo to take her instead.

The result was the dissection of Alexa's days into two stark experiences. During the day, her life was light, joyful and serene. She did not ask why none of the family left the house. She was not sure if they were supposed to be at work or school, and did not want to know. Their time together was too precious to question. They did not do much. They watched television and even played board games. Sometimes they chatted, but just as often they hung out in silence. It was relaxing and liberating in a way Alexa had never known. Then, when evening came and Alexa retreated to her room, the darkness descended.

Each night, Alexa took herself back to those horrid days, locked in Leo's filthy apartment, except in her mind it was not her tied to that bed. It was Hayley. Through the night, it was Hayley's screams that tortured her. She dwelled on it so much that even when she did fall asleep, her dreams continued the torment. Without fail, the images brought Alexa to tears. When Pam and Karl came to see what was wrong, Alexa could not even lie about the cause of her distress.

"Hayley, Hayley, Hayley," Alexa sobbed, hugging her pillow.

"Shh, she's safe," said Pam soothingly, but Alexa could only shake her head.

"Not if I stay," replied Alexa, clasping the pillow tighter.

The kindness and understanding that Pam and Karl showed her at these times only reinforced the danger she posed. It was a vicious cycle that continued on for many days before Karl finally found an end to his patience.

"No, Alexa, no more of this," hissed Karl, as he stormed into her bedroom in the middle of the night. Alexa was curled up on her bed, clutching her pillow and crying so violently she was almost vomiting. "You're torturing yourself for nothing – torturing us for nothing."

"I can't let he die because of me."

"Alexa," said Karl gravely, taking her face in his hands to turn her eyes to his. "Hayley is alive because of you. There was no one there to protect you and your sister from that man, and I'm so sorry for that, but you need to stop blaming yourself. You are not to blame. Your sister is not to blame. You must believe that." Alexa could only shake her head forlornly. Karl sighed heavily and walked out of the room. He returned minutes later with a book and switched on the lamp. "You need to read this," he said sadly, opening the book to a page near the middle.

It was a journal, but it was not his writing. It was rounder and neater, and Alexa knew immediately it belonged to Hayley. The entry was dated a day ago.

I always knew she hated me. Saw it in her eyes the night she told me she would never come home with us again. She hides it better now. Waits until she goes to bed. I hear her crying every night. I remind her of what they did to her and how much they hurt her. I wish I was as strong as her. Then they could have taken me. Next time I'll make sure they do.

Alexa closed the book, refusing to read any more.

"Our family lost two daughters that night," said Karl, his voice cracking as tears filled his eyes. "We tried to convince ourselves that we could say goodbye to you with few consequences – that the word foster would spare us most of the pain. You won't believe how wrong we were, and we've all lived with your loss.

"Losing Hayley – I sometimes found myself wishing she'd just grow up – understand the world for what it was. Her childishness – I was wrong about that too," gasped Karl, his tears finally spilling over. "The girl Hayley was died that night – probably about the same time the girl you were – the girl you were becoming – died."

Karl took a deep breath and wiped his eyes. Alexa wished she could have hugged him.

"Blaming ourselves won't make this situation better, because we aren't to blame. I know how hard this is for you, but we need you to be okay – we need you to show Hayley that life goes on. We need more than we have the right to expect. You're barely more than a child yourself, but we need Hayley to believe you love her, that you don't blame her – or yourself – and that as terrible as that night was, we can all have a happy life after it. Together."

Alexa was thankful that Karl understood just how much she would need to pretend to achieve all that. For Hayley, she would do much more, so slowly nodded as she handed back Hayley's diary.

"And when we say together, we do include your sister in that," added Karl in a gravelly voice. "We know the two of you are a package deal. You don't have to choose between us. That has kept us apart these last couple of years, but we're all adults now. It doesn't have to keep us apart any longer."

It was a beautiful gesture. The problem was that Alexa was caught in a strange limbo of not quite living. Life with the Whites was so easy that it did not seem real. It was nothing like her normal life – even the relatively stable life of the last two years. The lack of responsibility was disorientating, but appealing. And despite her separation from Bethany, Alexa could not find the strength to return to her life. However, as the days accumulated into a week, Alexa noticed her brain starting to function more clearly. She stopped being a ball of ungovernable emotions. Small things no longer overwhelmed her, and she found herself wishing to involve Bethany and Charlotte in her activities. Alexa even found herself able to talk to Hayley and it was not long before Alexa felt their sisterly bond rebuild. And that, more than anything else, was what made Alexa want to return home.

The only problem Alexa had was how to tell the Whites she needed to return to Bethany, now the time away from her was starting to hurt more than their love could heal.

"You don't need to look like that just because you've decided to go home," said Brett as they sat eating breakfast.

"What?" cried Alexa.

"Oh, sorry – I – so you weren't – I just thought – don't worry," waved Brett, quickly backtracking.

"No, I was – I mean, I was going to talk to you – tell you – how did you —?"

"Just the look you get when you want to say something, but don't know how we're going to react," explained Brett. "Figured that'd be the only thing you'd be scared of talking to us about."

The table went silent. Alexa turned to Hayley to see tears slipping down her cheeks.

"Will we see you again?" asked Hayley, her voice breaking.

"Yes," answered Karl firmly. "We're not letting her go this time."

"You know I love you guys," said Alexa.

"So it's decided then," said Pam over the top of her.

"No, I'm better now – thinking straighter – the danger – it's too much," replied Alexa, struggling to fight against their arguments.

"We're not going to listen to that," said Brett. "You know we think that's all crap. Besides, we're driving you home. So we're going to know where you live. You'll never be able to escape us."

"But …" said Alexa, not able to construct another objection.

"You can't beat us on this one," said Karl. "But we are very glad you're feeling up to going home. We'll miss you – not having you around every day – but getting used to you living out of home will help prepare us for when Brett moves out."

"When are you moving out?" asked Alexa, turning to Brett. "You only just finished school, didn't you?"

"Like you can talk, Miss Independent," replied Brett with a smile. "Not yet. Have to go to uni first, but after that I'm going to be a cop. I want to be the person putting scum behind bars and stopping them from hurting people like us – like you and your sister. No one should ever have the lives you guys did. I want to be a part of changing that for other people."

Alexa was proud of Brett's decision, but the thought of him being a police officer still sent a chill through her heart. She could not stop herself from seeing his body lying at the end of the pipe, his glassy eyes looking out lifelessly as she cowered in fear. Thankfully, no one let Alexa's mind dwell. Once they tidied up after breakfast, they started to organise her return home. It was then Alexa realised there was something else she had never told the Whites.

"Um, I should probably explain one thing that happened," said Alexa tentatively. "I mean, it kinda happened while I was living with you guys, but not really til after."

"Are we going to have to guess?" asked Brett with an exaggerated sigh.

Alexa shook her head, then just blurted it out.

"Ah, what?" gasped Brett. "Seriously? You won the lottery? No. Really? No."

Looking over at Pam and Karl, Alexa realised they did not look very surprised.

"We knew the money came from you," said Pam in a soft voice, nodding as Karl held her tighter. "Peter refused to confirm anything, but we knew. He kept in touch with us."

"Probably more accurate to say that we kept in touch with him," said Karl. "Paid off. He told us about you being in hospital – helped us see you without anyone seeing us. We weren't sure how you or your family would react to our presence."

"He kept Bethy away from me?" asked Alexa angrily.

"No, he just let us know when everyone had left," replied Pam, though she looked cautious about her answer.

"Come on, let's get you home to your sister," said Karl kindly, stroking Alexa's hair gently and tucking it behind her ear. "We'll see you again soon."

Alexa nodded, her stomach fluttering with nerves. It made her sick. She had never wanted to be scared of her own home again. When she was finally ready to face it, she was not allowed to leave without giving Hayley her address and phone numbers.

"I won't pester you, I promise," said Hayley solemnly.

"It's okay, Hales," replied Alexa, hugging her tight. "I want you to pester me. I've always wanted that."

"You're the best big sister ever," Hayley whispered in Alexa's ear as her body shook. Alexa could only hold her tighter, willing the tears to stay at bay.

Pam hugged Alexa next, before Brett wrapped a very brotherly arm around Alexa's shoulders and led her out to the car. Alexa was surprised that he hopped in the back seat with her, but she had to admit that he was very good at distracting her.

"I don't get it, Brett," Alexa eventually said. "How do you know me so well?"

Brett smirked, but did not answer straight away. "Okay, don't get mad. It's just, well, you're really predictable."

"What?" cried Alexa.

"See," Brett laughed. "You like to act all woman of mystery, but – it's not as bad as you think. You're not completely transparent, but certain things, you always react the same way. You always take the blame and never think you're worthy of stuff. That's why Mum and Dad couldn't go along with my plan. It involved allowing you to take the blame for what happened. On principle, they couldn't."

"We still won't," said Karl firmly from the front seat. "And when we meet your sister, we won't let her blame herself either."

Alexa bit her lip. She and Bethany had still never really spoken about that night. Even Alexa was not sure she could approach such a conversation and truthfully state that she did not blame Bethany. That was probably the real reason why she still blamed herself.

"You know there's a bus that goes pretty much from the end of your street to our house," said Brett, pointing to a bus that pulled out from the bus stop in front of them as they turned the corner. "Never keep us away now."

It was a reassuring threat, and helped to ease the tension swirling in Alexa's stomach as they pulled into her driveway. Taking a deep breath, she waited for the inevitable panic attack, but it did not come. This was still her home – more than it was the place where she was randomly attacked.

"Come on, you can do it."

It took a moment for Alexa to realise what Karl meant as he stood at her door, holding out his hand. Brett was already lingering near the front door. Alexa nodded and stepped out of the car. Karl placed a gentle hand on her back and walked her to the front door.

It felt strange for Brett to be knocking on her front door for her to gain access to her own house. The door opened slowly. Ben looked like a bodyguard – until his eyes met Alexa's. His whole body slumped in relieved exhaustion, and Alexa felt like he aged a decade in a second as he pulled her into a heartfelt embrace. "Alexa," he sighed, cupping her head and holding her to his chest. "Thank you," he said over the top of her, before she felt his arm reach out behind her and shake two hands.

Ben released Alexa and turned her slowly back to face Karl and Brett. Karl stroked her cheek, then held out an envelope. "Our address, your security code and key," he said with a soft smile. "You don't have to call. Come by whenever you want and stay for a minute, an hour or a lifetime. It's up to you. Our home is your home. You're welcome anytime. So are Bethany and Charlotte. Anytime."

Alexa could not respond. Her heart was almost bursting with the kindness the Whites were showing her. It went well beyond reason, but her capacity to reject it has been destroyed. Karl and Brett both smiled and made their way back to their car. It was surreal watching them leave. What was more real was the touch of Ben's hand on her shoulder turning her back to the life she had fled in fear of.

As soon as the front door closed, Alexa heard footsteps rushing from the lounge room. Bethany did not embrace her as she expected. She stopped a few metres away, her eyes full of tears and remorse.

Alexa rushed forward and hugged Bethany tight as Bethany sobbed into her neck.

"I'm sorry, Lex. I'm so sorry. I should've told them – should've let them know," said Bethany, confusing Alexa. "There was so much blood and you closed your eyes. I was sure you were going to die. I don't know what I would've done without you. I'm not strong enough to live without you."

The comforting words Alexa intended to speak dissolved before they could find their way to her mouth. All Alexa could do was stroke Bethany's hair and wipe the tears from her cheeks. In her week with the Whites, they had barely spoken to her about this attack. For them, the pain was set further back, all tied up with Leo's invasion. It had diverted Alexa's mind so effectively from the present that Sean's attack had been almost non-existent. In many ways, it had felt like she had been with the Whites recovering from Leo's attack and Alexa had not realised how hard it would be to confront Sean's memory.

Despite Alexa genuinely wanting to come home when she had left the Whites, there was no getting around the fact that this attack had been so different to all the other terrible experience in her life. There had always been reasons before. This was just so random. There was no explanation why a man she interviewed for a job should mistake her for someone else. There was no justification for his conviction that they had once known each other. All Alexa wanted was answers, but she did not have the strength to search for things that did not exist.

Bethany took Alexa's hand and walked her to the lounge room. Everyone was there, despite the fact that Alexa had not told anyone she was coming home. They turned as one at her entrance. The sight simultaneously annoyed and warmed her.

"I think I'd better find something to feed us all with," said Maria, smiling at Alexa as she made her way to the kitchen.

Alexa wanted to smile back, especially when Maria's exit pulled Gran and Pop out of the room. There suddenly seemed to be more air to breathe. However, the people who remained just sat and stared. Alexa knew they were waiting for her to talk, but she could not comprehend what they expected her to say. It was too much and the best Alexa could do was curl up on the lounge, her head in Bethany's lap, and close her eyes. At the sound of footsteps, Alexa opened her eyes briefly to see Marcus leaving, and she knew he understood. Maria returned some time later with plates of food. It smelt good, but

Alexa did not eat. They all encouraged her to try something, but Alexa just closed her eyes and ignored them. When everyone finished eating, there was nothing left to distract them from their staring.

Knowing no one would leave until she did, Alexa made her way up to her bedroom, closing her eyes as she walked past the second floor. The one consolation was Alexa felt safe in her room. It was just very lonely after a week of being surrounded by people. But though she craved company, Alexa could not face the prospect of returning to so many sets of eyes. What she really wanted was to curl up with Bethany.

Waiting until the house became dark and silent, Alexa crept down the stairs. The sound of Sam's voice as she put her hand on Bethany's door made Alexa freeze with fear. Sam had always been one of the few people she could turn to in moments like these, but his relationship with Bethany had changed all that. Backing away, Alexa consoled herself with the knowledge that Bethany would find comfort tonight. Alexa just wished that that did not leave her so terribly alone.

Chapter Eight

MARCUS TRIED HARD to focus his eyes. He was tired, but the constant inactivity of his mind left him too mentally alert to sleep. It was keeping him in a strange state of jetlag he had not experienced before – even when travelling. It was not assisted by how difficult the last week had been. Although he had been home only a couple of days, living in the house without Alexa was an experience he did not enjoy. It should not have felt as awkward as it had, particularly as Bethany and Charlotte had spent a lot of time at his bedside in hospital.

Bethany had all but gone to pieces after Sean's attack, and it still disturbed Marcus how much blame had been laid on her. Ben and Sam's reactions seemed to lack all manner of reason. The fight that erupted at the hospital when Peter informed Ben of Alexa's whereabouts was completely inexcusable. Peter's explanation of why Alexa was better off with the Whites should never have been necessary, nor his vehement defence of Bethany. It was not as though Marcus could not see how much Ben cared. His love of Alexa and Bethany was boundless, but Marcus could not help but think it misdirected.

Now Alexa was home, things just felt confused. Alexa was not the girl she had been a fortnight ago. It was horrible to know that yet another piece of her had been torn away. It made Marcus's heart ache for the possibilities that had been ripped away from her. Refusing to let himself dwell on those painful what ifs, Marcus turned his eyes back to his book. Nothing was sinking in, but the effort was helping to tire his mind.

The sound of the door creaking open made Marcus jump. He turned to see Alexa slipping through a small gap into his room. She did not look over at him as she stole in and curled up on the daybed. Seeing Alexa shivering, Marcus pushed away from the desk and walked over to his bed. He grabbed the blanket and laid it gently over her. Kneeling next to her, he could not stop himself from stroking her hair and brushing her cheek. Her eyes were so haunted. Alexa's hand reached out and rubbed his shaved head. Marcus missed his hair and had the feeling she might as well.

"I was just reading – trying to tire myself enough to sleep."

Marcus smiled at the expression in Alexa's eyes. When she wanted to be, she was like an open book. He grabbed his book, settled himself on the floor near Alexa's head and began to read out loud. Fifteen minutes later she was asleep. The sight was enchanting. All the pain dropped from her face. It made her look incredibly young, a realisation that panged at Marcus's heart, but Alexa's age was not the concern it used to be.

Ben had assured Marcus soon after he first woke that he had arranged officers to inform Lucy and his family of his situation. His parents had visited him regularly in the hospital – until their crude comments about Alexa had become too obscene to ignore and he asked them to leave and not return. Lucy, on the other hand, visited only once – the day before his discharge. Marcus waited only five minutes before breaking up with her.

The spark in Alexa's eyes that morning as she had spoken about their cove was so enticing that Marcus still felt bewitched. He was not sure what would have happened that day. All he knew was that if that moment ever arose again, he wanted to be able to give any and every part of him Alexa desired. He knew now more than ever that he was hers – whether she took him or not.

If Alexa ever did choose to be with him, he knew it would not happen any time soon. Although he refused to believe Sean's attack was punishment for their desire to be together, Alexa did not feel that way. However, Marcus did not need things to happen quickly. He was content to remain by Alexa's side and comfort her through this latest attack on her life and liberty. When she was ready, when she had the desire to reach out for something more, he would be there waiting for her. If there were consequences that followed, he would deal with them as they came. It made Marcus smile, hearing Ryan and Rhianna's words run through his head. They would be happy to know how great an impact they had had on the evolution of his feelings.

"How are you feeling?" asked Marcus, pushing himself up groggily to see Alexa sitting on the daybed with her legs tucked into her chest. He did not remember falling asleep, but he had slept well. Looking over at the clock, he was surprised to see that it was after ten. Alexa just shrugged a reply. "Why don't you go and sit in the sun. It'll make you feel better and I'll get you some breakfast."

Alexa rubbed her hair and jerked her head towards the ceiling.

Marcus nodded, following suit. Showers were much shorter now without his hair, so he had Alexa's breakfast ready by the time she came back downstairs.

"Can I take it out to her?" asked Bethany meekly. "It's selfish, I know, but I need to be with her."

"I think she needs to be with you too," said Marcus, placing a consoling hand on Bethany's shoulder. This last week had aged Bethany, and Marcus found himself sad about it. As much as he often argued that she needed to grow up and be more responsible, he did not want her maturing the same way Alexa had.

Marcus watched from the kitchen window as Bethany sat down behind Alexa on the grass. Bethany hugged Alexa tight before handing her the food. Alexa ate, but not much, preferring instead to rest her head on Bethany's shoulder. Charlotte joined them a few minutes later. Marcus was sure Bethany would be jealous or angry at the invasion, but she welcomed Charlotte with a kind smile and pulled her down with them. Marcus did not want to interrupt, but when he noticed each of them wiping their eyes, he carried out a tray of waters and tissues before going back inside and giving them privacy.

As the days wore on, Alexa found the house becoming progressively fuller. Sam and Ben practically moved in. It was very similar to the days after her one-week disappearance earlier in the year, although Alexa was somewhat more sympathetic to their presence now. Ben nearly always wore his gun in the house, something he had never done before. When he dozed off in the common areas, Alexa noticed that he did so with his hand on the gun. It was equal parts disturbing and reassuring.

Alexa also found she was never left alone. Someone was always nearby. If it was Marcus or Charlotte, the supervision felt more like company. Bethany's presence could never be called passive. Every time Bethany returned from work, she rushed straight up to Alexa and hugged her tight. They would then spend as much time as they could on the lounge together with their limbs entwined. They rarely spoke, and if they did it was only Bethany talking. Sam, Ben and Maria were much less inclined to accept Alexa's silent state. Maria chatted on, as though she might talk a conversation out of Alexa, but did not get upset when there were inevitably no verbal replies. Sam and Ben were having none of it. They all but demanded that Alexa speak. Alexa found it infuriating, but the hurt in their eyes kept her from silently expressing her annoyance.

It did not matter that Alexa knew her behaviour was not normal, and that everyone just wanted her to get better, things had gone too far this time. Her continued existence was about all she could manage. The situation was not made any better by Christmas hurtling towards them. Even away from the outside world and in the absence of a single decoration, Alexa could still feel it lurking, creeping ever closer, like a dark storm cloud she could not outrun.

"You don't mind me working so much, do you?" asked Charlotte as they prepared dinner. Alexa had snuck into help, hoping no one saw her and ordered her out to rest. "It's just been a bit crowded here lately," Charlotte added tentatively. "And it's busy at work – people buying up a storm. You'd think the population doubled at Christmas time. It's crazy. And they all go mental if you run out of something – as if they're the only person cooking a Christmas lunch."

Charlotte looked at the food in the fridge for a second before moving over to the cupboard. The kitchen was a little bare, but inspiration must have struck, because Charlotte suddenly danced back to the fridge and started pulling out a collection of foods.

"This is going to be a bit experimental," said Charlotte with a half-smile–half-grimace as she collected more ingredients. Alexa could only nod, thankful Charlotte believed she could create anything out of the food in front of her. "I called my dad yesterday. Thought maybe things might've cooled down after I moved here and … since I'm never moving back there … I asked if maybe I could still see them for Christmas – give the twins their presents." Charlotte said nothing as she started to cook. Alexa moved next to her and saw tears in her eyes. When Alexa rubbed her shoulder, Charlotte's lip quivered, but when Charlotte spoke, her voice was even. "Dad said he'd meet me somewhere, but Carla won't have me back in the house. Not a real surprise, but … you think I should meet him? Think it's worth it? I know he's not my dad, but he kinda is." Alexa hugged Charlotte tight. "Yeah, I don't know either."

Bethany walked in while Alexa was still hugging Charlotte and her arms immediately joined the mix. It was heartfelt, and while Alexa loved the tenderness of it, she could not help but miss the joyous bear-hugs she usually received from Bethany.

Dinner was a crowded affair. Ben and Sam forced conversation and Bethany played along dutifully. Alexa was surprised how compliant Bethany was. She was so much more pleasing than Alexa could ever dream of being. Yet from the way Bethany held her hand under the table, Alexa knew dealing with domestic tensions was something Bethany had just learned to do to – the same way she had learned to navigate boarding school. When the crowd inevitably became too much for Alexa to handle, she escaped to Marcus's room. That room had become Alexa's sanctuary. Bethany often stayed with her. Marcus came in and out, sometimes staying and keeping himself busy at his desk. More than once, he had offered to relinquish the room, but Bethany had thankfully been forward enough to tell him that his possession of it was half the appeal.

Bethany arrived moments later, wrapping her arms around Alexa. It was then Alexa realised Bethany was holding an envelope.

"It's for you. From me," said Bethany softly, her voice breaking slightly. "You want me to leave you while you read it?"

Alexa nodded. Bethany squeezed her tight and walked out of the room. The envelope was not sealed. Alexa pulled out the piece of paper. It reminded her of the letters they used to share when Bethany was imprisoned.

My beautiful Lex. I wish there was more I could do for you. You're hurt and I can't fix you. And I miss you. I'm selfish. My heart hurts every day I don't hear your voice. I know you can't talk right now, but if we write then maybe I can hear your voice – like I did when I was in prison. Don't do nothing that will hurt you more.

Tears slipped down Alexa's face as her fingers traced Bethany's words. She knew that was probably the most difficult letter Bethany had ever written. Bethany avoided anything that reminded her of gaol. Alexa was not sure she could do what Bethany asked, but she would try.

"What do you need?" asked Marcus in a concerned voice as he walked into the room. Alexa turned, feeling the shame of her actions as she rummaged through his desk, but the need to comfort Bethany was much greater. Mimicking the action of writing, Alexa tried to convey her message. "No, for some reason I like to keep my writing paper on the bookshelf," said Marcus. "What kind do you want? I have normal lined paper or nice writing paper. What's it for?"

Alexa looked over at the daybed. Marcus's eyes followed. He took a step towards the daybed and Alexa immediately rushed over to the letter, keeping it from his gaze.

"Beth?" Marcus asked kindly. Alexa nodded, her eyes downcast. "Then you need the nice paper." Marcus brought over a beautiful writing set. It was far too nice for Alexa to consider using. She waved her hand and backed away from the offer, but Marcus just sat down on the daybed next to her. "You don't like it?" Marcus asked. Alexa shook her head furiously. "You do like it?" he questioned with the shadow of a smile. "I bought it for someone. They didn't like it. That hurt a lot. They said they did, but never used it – even when they wrote – said it wasn't appropriate. When they left, they left it behind. It's yours if you want to use it. I'll leave it on the desk and give you some privacy."

When Marcus left, Alexa walked over to his desk. There was normal paper and pens sitting right next to the writing set. The desire to use the nice paper was overwhelming, yet it felt like an inexcusable extravagance. Then Alexa thought of Bethany. If anyone deserved a letter on fancy paper, it was her. There was no way she would have had beautiful paper in prison.

My Angel. I don't know how to write you the words I cannot speak. I feel like my words have gone – even from my hand. I thought I left that life behind. In our house a cruel stranger found us. I'm scared this is all our life can be. I don't want next time to take you from me. I don't want a next time. Bethy, how can this happen? Even when it's not me, they find me.

Alexa stared at the paper for another hour, but more words would not come. It would have to do for now.

Bethany's response was slower than Alexa expected. However, when it came it was in an envelope even nicer than the one she had given her. Looking over at Marcus's desk, Alexa saw another writing set next to hers. There was also a note from Marcus informing her and Bethany that there was more writing paper on the top shelf of the bookcase and they were welcome to use any and everything. Alexa could not help but look. The array of paper and envelopes was amazing. It still felt like a ridiculous indulgence to use it, but she wanted to – so much – and knew that Marcus was not being insincere in his offer.

This letter was not as difficult to write. Bethany's letter had not attended to what Alexa had written. Alexa knew Bethany did not have those answers either. Instead they spoke of better things – Bethany's carpentry; Marcus's brilliance; Charlotte's tender heart. They were good letters and helped Alexa feel connected to the world again. It just did not help her find her voice.

When Christmas Eve came, Alexa was tempted to curl up in Marcus's room and not emerge again until it was all over. Everyone was at the house. It made Alexa wonder if they had decided to start the celebrations early, although the house did not feel the slightest bit festive.

"Lex," said Bethany, creeping into the room. "Lex, will you come out with me?" Bethany's hand grasped Alexa's. There was pleading in her eyes and Alexa knew she had reached some unspoken deadline. They would probably talk at her now until she spoke. It made her wonder if she would be able to find the words to satisfy them.

Alexa let Bethany lead her into the lounge room where everyone was sitting. They sat down on the lounge together. Ben sighed heavily and moved in front of them, kneeling on the floor and taking Alexa's hands in his. "I've been waiting – Bethany told me why this is hurting you so badly. I've been debating with myself since it happened – I wanted to tell you – part of me thought you might work it out – understand – then come to me and ask questions," said Ben in a halting voice. "I made you a promise a long time ago to keep certain things secret. I can help you now, but only if I break that promise."

Ben was shaking. Her past. He was talking about her past. Something about her had drawn this attack. That changed everything, and Alexa was not sure she wanted to know anything – about her past or the attack.

"It will help you understand," urged Ben. "But only if you release me of your promise." Alexa eventually nodded. "I need to hear you say it. Please."

"Okay," squeaked Alexa, surprised that she managed to squeeze out the word.

"Okay," sighed Ben heavily. He took several more deep breaths before grasping Alexa and Bethany's hands tight and looking into their eyes. "This is not a simple story and it starts before I ever met the two of you."

Ben paused and Alexa knew he was waiting for some signal that she did not want him to continue, but perhaps her ignorance had stretched on for as long as possible. She had never wanted to know more, fearing it would only make her feel worse, but she was not sure she could feel much worse than she did right now. "Just tell me."

Ben nodded and gently stroked Alexa's hair, indicating this would be as bad as she imagined. "I always wanted to be a cop," he said, starting the story in a sedate manner. "I was young when I first started, already a Senior Constable when we got the call – getting ready to sit for my sergeant exams. I'd seen a lot and I thought I was a good cop – never got too attached, too rattled – learned to let things go.

"There was an emergency call – came through in the area next to mine – near the border of the two regions. We were close so we assisted. There was a man who had been badly injured – lucky to be alive, really. He had knife wounds to his pelvic region and a partially severed penis. Was in a very bad way. I still remember how much blood there was. The bed was soaked. The bedroom floor … it was among the worst I'd seen.

"The guy was Sean King. He told the officers and ambos that he'd been attacked by his wife. She'd caught him with another woman and taken her revenge, then fled with their kids. He said that his wife was a violent women and he feared for his children's safety. We searched everywhere for this woman for two days straight. When we found her things fell apart. Everything we thought we knew about the case just dissolved. While Sean's wife admitted she had considered harming her husband, she had an alibi. It wasn't great. She was a drug user and we couldn't rule out the possibility that she was lying, but there was also no evidence. Nothing except Sean's accusation. But worse than that, we had no kids. Sean's wife had left the children with him. The children – Caitlin, who was five, and Rebecca, who was three – had been missing for over two days.

"Every priority was on finding those two girls. There were sightings and leads, but they all came to nothing. It didn't matter. Every call we got, we chased. I was following one of those leads. Someone had seen a couple of young girls playing near an industrial area, but when they'd gone to check it out they couldn't find anyone. It was a large area. We walked it twice. There was this section with a whole lot of large concrete pipes. An adult would struggle to get into them, but they were perfect for kids.

"We heard them before we saw them. They kept hiding, but we finally cornered them. Two terrified little girls, covered in dirt, but alive. The older one had a knife. I sat down at the end of the pipe and introduced myself. I started talking. It was going okay until I called them Caitlin and Rebecca. Suddenly the older one was yelling at me, telling me that was not their names. Their names were Alexa and Bethany. It was the two of you."

"I don't understand," said Alexa. "You found us instead of his daughters and he thinks we're someone else? Didn't you tell him you found the wrong people? And why would he want to – if he thought I was his daughter, why'd he try to …"

Ben was shaking his head. There were tears in his eyes and when he spoke his voice crackled with emotion. "Alexa, you are Caitlin King. You were the girls we were looking for."

Alexa turned to Bethany, who nodded slowly. "I don't really remember it, but I remember – my first memory is you and me," said Bethany in a shaky voice. "We're not anywhere – just together – and you keep saying, 'We need new names. Two new names. Then they can't find us. If they find us they'll send me to gaol. I'll pick yours and you pick mine. Then we'll always be together.' It never made sense to me before. I thought it was a game we played. Wasn't til Ben told me what your dream meant – I'm sorry, Lex. I should've told him after the interview. Should've told Ben his name after he freaked you out. Then he could've never touched you."

Alexa turned and glared at Ben, now understanding why Bethany had not been by her bedside in hospital.

"I failed you – then and now – and I made the horrific mistake of blaming Bethany for something she could never have known," said Ben, keeping Alexa's gaze. "I didn't tell her your father's name. I never told you. I never warned either of you of the danger I knew still existed. What happened here was my fault."

"But you die in my dream," said Alexa, choosing not to have that argument.

Ben sighed heavily as he slowly shook his head. "We didn't know what was happening when you continued to claim to be someone else," he continued in a heavy voice. "Everything else fit, and either way we couldn't leave two young girls alone in an industrial estate. But you were armed and didn't trust us. We decided we'd wait as long as necessary for you to come out of your own free will. You seemed to like me better than my partner. You spoke to me and not to him. We figured you had to be hungry so organised food and drink. You both wanted pizza. It must have been something you had as a treat, because you asked for it like you were being demanding – testing to see if we'd comply. Even though we bought you a pizza each, Alexa, you made sure Bethany ate first. You were such an amazing child. My heart was breaking sitting with the two of you, fearing what you'd been through.

"It took such a long time for you to believe I wouldn't put you in gaol. I eventually managed to convince you that I'd believe your version of events. You and Bethany moved closer. You were both so scared. You kept asking if I promised – promised to believe you – and I promised over and over. Eventually you told me you'd been cutting up food for dinner as your father asked. He wasn't nearby. You heard sounds coming from his bedroom and went to look. You found – Sean was in there with Bethany," said Ben, his voice quivering. "He was naked. Beth was – he was making her – she told us he was giving her a lollipop."

"He hurt her!" gasped Alexa, grabbing Bethany tight, as if she could somehow now still shield her from that fate.

"Yes," nodded Ben. "And you protected her. You attacked Sean with the knife, grabbed Bethany and ran. You were both so brave talking about what happened. I promised we'd make sure you were safe and wouldn't be in any trouble. When you finally believed me, I got the two of you out of the pipe and into the police car."

"You don't get shot?" asked Alexa. Although the details were slightly different, so far Ben had explained her dream perfectly.

"Yes," answered Ben in a tight voice. "Sean turned up looking for you. He had a gun. I got in the way."

"I don't understand," said Alexa. "Why? How?"

"The why is easy," replied Ben, his voice stronger and more police-like. "Sean tried to blame your mother for the attack so he could have complete access to you and Bethany. He didn't want to share you any more. The how, that was never precisely determined. He accessed the gun illegally. How he found out where you were – how he got past the police guard – the police force back then – the only way would have been from one of us."

Ben's hands shook as he spoke.

"Never you, right?" asked Alexa in a timid voice.

"No, I promise, Alexa, never me. I wish I could tell you the world was a better place and bad cops didn't exist, but we know the truth."

"Is that what happened this time?" asked Bethany, speaking for the first time.

"We're investigating that," said Ben solemnly. "I don't have answers yet – and the answers we do get probably won't be the ones we want. The only difference this time is that Sean's dead. He can't hurt you again – either of you."

"But why'd he come back this time? Why'd he try and do that to me?" cried Alexa, her chest tearing with pain. "Why'd he keep talking about loving me and me loving him? That's not love."

"No, it's not," sighed Ben heavily. "When I was shot, you and Bethany disappeared again. In the commotion, no one saw you leave," Ben said, moving back to the original story. "I was hit, but only in the arm – flesh wound – I was back out the next day looking for you. I remember sitting at the end of the pipe thinking about how adorable you both were and how I'd take care of you if you'd been my children. I'd never had that connection before.

"We didn't find you. About thirty-six hours after you went missing, you both walked into a police station asking for me. You told them I was your uncle and that I was supposed to pick you up after school but forgot. It was a sweet lie. They played along, and I was rushed over to you. You both raced into my arms," said Ben, his voice breaking as a single tear fell down his cheek. "You hugged me so tight, but when the charade stopped – when we talked to you about what happened with Sean – we had to force you to stay. You wouldn't talk to us. Even then you were so stubborn and Bethany didn't do anything without your say so. I eventually managed to convince you it was safe to take you to the hospital. It was fine until the physical examinations. You refused to be separated from Bethany. When they asked her to take off her clothes, you started screaming. You were yelling at us not to hurt her – not to touch her down there."

Ben took a deep shuddering breath. His lips quivered slightly as he tried to talk, halting his words. No one spoke in the interim. The room was deathly silent. "They had to sedate you," continued Ben in a stronger voice. "They sedated you and Bethany and conducted full examinations. Bethany was okay. We were surprised. Besides the impact of the days living rough, she was physically fine. It was you, Alexa. You were the one hurt. There was evidence of sustained, ongoing sexual abuse. You'd never mentioned it once. In all those hours, your only concern was Bethany.

"After that, you didn't talk to any of us for a while. We interviewed your mother and Sean. Both denied any knowledge of the abuse. We didn't believe Sean. We charged him on the firearms offences and for shooting me. It kept him in gaol while we investigated. You were both put in care, but you didn't like it – kept running away. You eventually started to trust me again. Promised to tell me what happened if I let you and Bethany live with me. You didn't trust our promises," said Ben with a half-smile, reaching out and stroking Alexa's cheek. "You made us take you both back to my place. We settled you in. Two days later you agreed to talk."

"What did I tell you?" asked Alexa after Ben's pause continued into silence.

"Everything," Ben replied, his voice quivering once more. "Sean had been hurting you for as long as you could remember. It had escalated to penetrative sex in the year leading up to the incident. Your fath – Sean told you he loved you and that this was what people who loved each other did together."

"So I attacked him because I didn't think he loved me any more?" gasped Alexa, horrified that everyone's negative view of her was correct. "I was jealous? I wanted to be with him?"

"No, Alexa, no," cried Ben, holding her face in his hands so their eyes met. "No. He hurt you and you hated it. You told him to stop, that it was yucky and that it hurt. We think that was the trigger for him going after Bethany – except that instead of offering yourself to spare Bethany, you stabbed him. Personally, I think you made the right decision. He would never have stopped and I think he would've gone after Bethany in the end anyway."

"But why come back now after all this time?" asked Alexa softly.

"Because Sean believed he owned you. You, as a person, never meant anything to him. All he cared about was getting back his possession – maybe even getting back at me. He always blamed me. It may have even been how he found you. Through me. Because of me."

Alexa looked around the stunned room. Sam was next to Bethany, one of her hands in his, tears streaking his face. They had spoken many times over the years about her family, but neither of them ever suspected that this was her history. Marcus did not look shocked like Alexa expected. He looked pained. Gran, Pop and Maria all appeared quite stoic, though not unaffected by the revelations. Ben was the most broken – and most human – Alexa had ever seen him. He felt more real to her than he ever had before, and she did not doubt a word he said, she just did not understand.

"Why don't I remember any of this?" Alexa asked desperately.

"You do – bits of it, you do remember," replied Ben softly. "Your dream – for the most part, that was quite accurate. Just this year you spoke about you and Bethany naming each other. More was coming back. The more triggers from your past, the more memories came back. You never dreamt about the name Caitlin until after we met again."

"But the rest of it!" cried Alexa. "You said I told you about it. How could I have done that? How could I grow up and not remember something like that?"

"Probably because what happened to you was so traumatic," said Ben passionately, stroking Alexa's hair. "And you were so young. Most of us don't remember things that happened to us at that age."

"Most people would remember something like that!"

"But you didn't want to," said Ben over the top of her, continuing to stroke her hair to calm her. "You didn't want to remember. You never spoke about what happened after that day. If you were ever asked about it, you either ignored the question or just shrugged and said you didn't remember. When it came to court, neither you nor Bethany testified. We had to rely solely on the medical evidence and the statements made at the time. I won't deny that Sean's defence used that against us. The psychologists could not agree as to whether you had truly forgotten or not, but you were living back with your mother by then – I saw you once – afterwards – you didn't recognise me. You looked straight through me like I was just another person in the street. I'm not sure when your nightmares started, but that may have been your mind's outlet. That was where your memory went."

While everyone sat in silence, Alexa waited for her brain to remember. After all the information she had been given, she expected it to slot into place, piecing with the memories she had retrieved to give her a full version of her childhood. Nothing happened. Nothing clicked. It was then Alexa realised that though she now understood who Sean was – who she was – and why this attack had happened – nothing had changed. She did not feel better. Perhaps that would come, but right now she did not want to face this world.

"I need you not to be here," said Alexa, pulling Bethany into her arms.

Sam nodded, rising instantly from the lounge. His departure took

Gran, Pop and Maria with him. Marcus slipped out behind them.

"If it's okay, I'm going to stay the night – upstairs in the guest room – out of the way," said Ben. "I want to be close – just in case you need anything."

Alexa nodded. Ben smiled softly before kissing her and Bethany each on the top of the head. Charlotte rose awkwardly from the lounge, waving and pointing upstairs, but Bethany grabbed her hand and pulled her into their embrace. They stayed there for only a moment before heading to Bethany's bedroom and collapsing on her bed, their bodies entwined in a multi-limbed embrace.

Christmas arrived like a bad joke. The events of the night before did not enamour Alexa to the holiday, but before she could put a stop to it, the day had already begun. Charlotte was up when Alexa woke. There was food for lunch prepared in the kitchen, and when Alexa walked into the lounge room she found Charlotte decorating a Christmas tree she did not even know they possessed.

"Beth," said Charlotte, answering Alexa's unasked question.

Charlotte's tone made it clear she was not doing this out of her own desire to celebrate. Alexa grabbed some tinsel and ornaments from the box of decorations that had also found their way into the house. There was something soothing about the mechanical nature of the task. It required enough thought to distract her mind, but not enough to tax it.

"You're missing the star on top," said Marcus in a soft voice, walking into the lounge room.

"Short," replied Charlotte flatly, pointing between herself and Alexa.

Marcus held out his hand, and Alexa passed him the star. Bending the tree down, Marcus placed the star, but it shifted when he released the tree, leaving it tilted awkwardly.

"It's crooked," said Bethany, sweeping into the room. Alexa could see immediately that Bethany was forcing herself to make this a good day. Marcus stepped forward and righted the star. "Perfect," nodded Bethany, prancing forward and hugging Marcus. "Perfect."

Marcus held Bethany tight, cupping the back of her head, until she shivered. Pushing out of his arms, Bethany did a good impression of a smile before she danced out of the room. Marcus's eyes followed her, saddening at the sight. "I'd better shower," he said sombrely.

Alexa realised that was a sensible idea. The shower was more revitalising than Alexa thought possible. Weeks of baths while her wounds healed had allowed her to forget the pleasure of warm water cascading over her body.

Walking down the stairs, Alexa tried to find the courage to face the rest of the day. Marcus was waiting near the bottom of the stairs and Alexa could not help but muse that it had been a while since she had seen him dressed up.

"I have to head to my parents," he said when she reached him, looking as though he had waited to see her before leaving. "It's just one day and it's already more than a third over." Alexa nodded, thinking Marcus could not have said anything better. "And if you go to bed at eight, then there's only twelve hours left, so really it's half over," he added with a slight smile. Alexa smiled and shook her head. "Too far?" Alexa nodded. "Yeah, should've stopped at a third. I'll see you later."

Marcus's hand reached out to rub Alexa's shoulder before he changed his mind and stepped forward to hug her. It was a tender embrace, and Alexa loved that she felt no added intention in it.

Once Marcus was gone, Alexa headed to the kitchen. She and Charlotte cooked while Bethany prepared the house with Ben. Sam returned with Gran, Pop and Maria just before lunch. It was a somewhat sombre atmosphere. Charlotte tried hard to lighten the mood. Bethany looked like she wanted to join in, but her eyes continued to flick between Ben and Sam, who were keeping a strict eye on Alexa.

It annoyed Alexa that everyone was forgetting that this was Bethany's first Christmas outside of prison and Charlotte's first without her family. To ignore their need for a pleasant day was just rude. Maria seemed to understand and soon joined the efforts to make the day merry, pulling Gran and Pop into the fold. It worked for a while – until they moved from the dining room to the lounge room. Charlotte flitted around, doing everything. It was very thoughtful, but generally unrewarded, and without Charlotte's constant presence, Bethany lost her strength and buckled glumly under the weight of unhappy faces around her. Alexa wished she could have done what was required of her. She wanted to make this the day Charlotte and Bethany deserved, but it was simply not within her capacity.

Marcus returned late in the afternoon while the small number of presents under the tree were being distributed. He looked concerned by the mood of the room and Bethany's curled-up state on the lounge.

"Oh, Marcus, you're back!" cried Charlotte, when she walked into the room. She rushed forward and hugged him as though it was the first time she had seen him all day. "Merry Christmas. Did you have a nice lunch with your family? Did Rhianna come down?"

"Wasn't the best family Christmas I've ever had," replied Marcus grimly. "Don't know if Rhianna being there would've made it better, but she would've made it more interesting."

Alexa almost managed to smile, thinking about Rhianna jibing her parents.

"Charlotte, I think it's time you gave up the happy act," said Ben. "It's really not helping anyone."

Charlotte's eyes flicked between Bethany and Alexa before she dashed out of the room. Alexa saw Bethany's lips quiver as she curled her body into a tighter ball on the lounge. Alexa knew she should go after Charlotte, but was scared she did not have the words to make things better.

Marcus sighed heavily and walked up the stairs. He had not been beyond the first floor since Sean's attack. The room Sean had held Alexa in was shut up. The door was just closed, but the whole room could have been boarded up with how determinedly sealed it was. It made Marcus wonder how Charlotte was coping sleeping up here.

"Can I come in?" Marcus knocked, slowly opening the door.

"Sure," replied Charlotte with a shrug. She was sitting on her bed looking out the open balcony doors and down to the sun-drenched backyard. "When you just sit and stare, you can almost imagine you're somewhere else – exotic – when you look out there," she said softly, not turning her gaze.

"Where do you imagine you are?" asked Marcus, sitting himself on the bed a decent distance from Charlotte and following her gaze.

"Depends on the day. Usually just somewhere else."

"Must be hard, particularly on days like today – first Christmas away from your family."

"They're not my family," said Charlotte harshly, before her voice softened. "Besides, it's nothing. Alexa's the one having the bad day."

"We weren't talking about Alexa," said Marcus. Despite knowing Charlotte's disposition, he could not help but be infuriated by.

"Perhaps you should be. She needs support more than me," replied Charlotte in a dismissive voice, continuing to look out the window.

"You going for martyrdom?" asked Marcus. "Listen, Alexa needs time and I can't give it to her quicker than it'll come, but she also needs to know that you're all right. Seeing you hurt, it hurts her too."

"So you're really just here because of her."

"No. I'm here because I give a shit," replied Marcus with a frustrated sigh. "I just know there's no way Alexa's going to be upset that I'm up here talking to you – making sure you're all right – and not spending the rest of my Christmas staring at her."

"There's nothing to say," said Charlotte, with a disaffected shrug.

"I think I'd have a lot to say if I was in your position," said Marcus. "I'll trust you not to go around telling everyone, but my parents have all but disowned me – just because of the way I feel about Alexa – because I live here – choose to live here – and enjoy living here. I can't imagine the pain of your situation, but I know how much it hurts when the people you think will always be there for you suddenly turn against you."

"But they're your parents. They're not my family – never were. I don't have a family. My mother left because she hated me. My real father because he never wanted me. No one wants me."

"I thought your father – Dave – said he'd see you for Christmas," said Marcus, pierced by the hurt in Charlotte's voice.

"He changed his mind," replied Charlotte in a would-be calm voice, but it was full of bitterness and despair. Then the tears started slipping down her cheeks. "He rang – Carla was in the background – said he was sorry but there was just no point continuing a relationship with me when he wasn't my father," she sobbed. "Then – yesterday – that package – it was from him. They sent back the presents I sent the twins. He put a note in it. Just said sorry and had the name of another man he said I should try and contact." Marcus was hugging Charlotte before he knew what he was doing. He waited for her to push away, but she curled into him and continued to cry. "It's not fair, you know," said Charlotte, slowly moving out of Marcus's arms once she was composed. She shifted her position so that she was facing him. "I know I caused trouble, but why doesn't anyone want me? Why would everyone walk away from me like I mean nothing to them?"

"I don't think anyone has good answers to those questions," said

Marcus honestly. "Just like no one will ever be able to give Alexa and Bethany satisfactory answers as to why they suffered so much. There aren't always answers. Sometimes people just aren't as good as they should be." Charlotte shrugged, and Marcus thought she looked simultaneously comforted and disturbed to have her life compared to theirs. "I don't want to minimise anything you've suffered, but it's not true that you don't have a family. This here, this is your family. I think you know that. Beth and Alexa, they love you. You are they're sister. And they need you. They're so much better when you're around."

"You think it's bad if I forget them – make this my family?" asked Charlotte, looking up. "Part of me – sometimes I think I made this happen. I wanted to be – I missed being around them so much."

"Charlotte, you had no control over this," said Marcus intently, hoping she would believe him. "You don't need me to tell you how horribly you've been treated. It's wonderful that you can make this your family. I don't think you should feel bad at all. I think you're right to let that go and embrace this family. This family – Alexa and Bethany – they'll love and support you through everything. It's not what you should've had, but you deserve to be happy."

Charlotte's nod did much to assure Marcus that she would take on some of what he said. It made him think of Alexa and her refusal to believe that anything bad had not been caused – at least in part – by her. There was comfort in believing Charlotte was not so entirely like Alexa, yet the similarities between them – physical and emotional – were still striking. Sitting with Charlotte as the chatted more generically, Marcus tried to tease out what it was about Alexa that made her so attractive to him when he had never felt anything for Charlotte. That his feelings for Alexa had only increased with time – and her age – and that he had never found himself looking at his students in that way, never ceased to reassure him that it was not under-aged beauty that tempted him. All that left Marcus with was Alexa's vulnerability, which was something that could not be completely denied by his friendship with Charlotte. But while Charlotte was vulnerable, particularly now, she had never been broken. Alexa's vulnerability was so deep nothing could eliminate it, and Marcus wondered if the attraction was the knowledge that he might always be called on to be her protector, like some kind of reflected glory.

However, Marcus often felt that the last thing in the world Alexa needed was someone to protect her. Despite her fragility, she was the strongest person he had ever met. What Marcus believed Alexa needed was someone to journey with her, encourage her, assist when she felt weak, and celebrate and affirm her achievements. Visualising that future, Marcus realised all his previous desires for his own future had fallen away, replaced by the single desire of being with Alexa as she traversed her life. On one level that still sounded paternalistic, but Marcus also knew that in almost every couple, one partner had to sacrifice much of themselves if the other was to chase their dreams. It was just that he was the one prepared to give up everything to ensure Alexa did not have did give up anything.

Chapter Nine

THE MOOD IN the house lightened once Christmas was over. The lure of the new year was hard to resist, even for Alexa. She was not sure how one nominal date could make a difference, but she was determined, once more, that better things would emerge from the incoming year. The mysteries of her past had now been answered. There were no more secrets lurking in the dark corners of her mind. Her biological family now consisted solely of Bethany. The rest was annexed from her heart and mind. The challenge for the future would be to build a new family. Alexa only wished it did not have to be quite so treacherous.

With the Whites back in her life, and what appeared to be the permanent gulf between her and Ben, there were more questions over who her parental figures would be than Alexa previously considered. Even the issue of siblings was not straightforward. Any sibling had to be equally bound to her and Bethany. Alexa was not sure that would be possible with Hayley and Brett. When Alexa ventured to talk to Bethany about it, Bethany all but shut down the conversation.

"You – you should – they're your family and I want them to be," said Bethany, holding Alexa's hands and nodding. "But you can't force me on them. I ruined everything. I know what I did, Lex. You've been so kind and never blamed me or made me talk about it, but I know. I want you to be close to them, but it's something you have to do on your own, okay."

Alexa hated that idea. She did not want a sectioned up life, with those most important to her not able to be in the same room.

"It might only have to be a compromise for a short period of time," said Marcus, walking into the room after Bethany rushed out. "If the Whites want you in their family, they would know that'd involve contact with Bethany." Alexa nodded, feeling tears sting her eyes at the memory of Pam and Karl discussing how they would support her once she left school – when she would have gone for Bethany – before their family had been torn apart. "If the situation was reversed, you'd be as apprehensive as Bethany – more so," continued Marcus. "I don't think you can do anything but see them so often that interaction between them's inevitable. Then, once they get to know Beth, they'll love her the way we do. And Beth, she'll learn to believe that in time."

"You love her?" asked Alexa.

Marcus smiled, though it appeared to be more of an embarrassed grimace. "I'm not going to say that we always see eye-to-eye," he grinned. "But you know – she has a beautiful heart – the three of you, you're like family to me. I care about you all. It doesn't seem like it's just a year since I first moved in with you. I've never known a year like this."

"Not exactly the quiet life you crave," said Alexa softly, hating that her life would never be good enough for Marcus.

"This life – living here with you – there's nothing I crave more," replied Marcus in a husky voice, before grinning. "You should go visit the Whites. They said you were welcome any time. I'm heading out later. Beth's going out with Sam. Charlotte's working."

It was a suggestion Alexa was inclined to follow, but her nerves kept getting the better of her – until Marcus offered to catch the bus with her. He would stay on past her stop and then travel back. If she freaked out, he would meet her on the returning bus.

Marcus did not talk much as they travelled. Alexa was thankful. Her nerves were in overdrive. Even as the Whites' stop approached, her finger could only hover over the button to stop the bus. Then she felt Marcus's hand wrapping over hers, pushing her finger down. "You can do this," he said encouragingly. "Just try. I'll be on the bus back if you need me."

Alexa's heart was thumping anxiously. She felt like an idiot looking at the instructions for how to get into the house. It was very quiet and she wondered what she would do if the house was empty. However, as soon as Alexa opened the front door she saw Karl standing there with a broad smile on his face. "I saw you on the security screen," he said. "Was going to run out and let you in, but thought – didn't want you to feel like a guest. Want to join me in the kitchen? I'm making a cake."

"You're prepared to be in the kitchen with me?" asked Alexa sceptically.

"I'm game if you are," replied Karl. "The others are out. They'll be back in a couple of hours."

Karl immediately moved over to the radio when he walked into the kitchen, reaching to switch it off, but Alexa was glad this was one thing she had mastered.

***

When New Year's Eve arrived, Alexa tried to keep things as casual as possible, refusing every invitation to leave the house.

"One more day," said Marcus, joining her on the daybed. "And you get to leave this all behind. Start fresh."

"You really believe anyone gets to start fresh?" asked Alexa cynically, wondering why she continued to.

"No. Not in that way. But I guess there's the chance to reset psychologically."

"It's hard," admitted Alexa reluctantly. "Always trying to find something – some reason – I —"

"Of course it is," said Marcus, using his finger to turn her face to his. "Every year – to go through what you have – no one could ever blame you if you decided to curl up and never face anything again. You've been through – you know there are things worth you living for. You, Beth and Charlotte all have a future ahead of you. It won't feel okay straight away. It's not possible. But it will come. Things'll be okay in time. Just let it happen."

"You think I'm not letting it happen?"

"No. I guess I meant don't search for a way to make it okay. It'll come, and you're not doing anything wrong if it doesn't come as quickly as you need it to," replied Marcus tenderly, his finger gently stroking her cheek as he continued to hold her face.

Alexa allowed their eyes to meet. The rush of warmth to her stomach was intoxicating. Marcus smiled softly. When his hand fell from her face, it landed near her hands. Her fingers instantly slipped between his. It was not quite holding hands, but it was both more and less than she could hope for right now.

When Marcus left, Alexa stayed in his room. Even in his absence, he was the most peaceful person to be with. However, the sight of Bethany and Sam excitedly organising themselves for their night out dissolved the calm Marcus had created. Alexa only smiled at Bethany, but at the first opportunity, she grabbed Sam and pulled him to a secluded corner. "I know you guys are young, but no nightclubs, please," she begged him. "Too much temptation for her."

Sam took Alexa's face in his hands with a look of controlled patience. "Beth asked Charlotte to come out with us," he said slowly, as though she was a bit thick. "We're just having a picnic with whoever decides to turn up. Beth's idea. She doesn't want to take drugs any more."

"It's in her blood, Sam. More natural than breathing," replied Alexa, desperate for him to understand.

Although Sam nodded and said all the right things, Alexa was sure he thought she was being paranoid. It was frustrating. Alexa had spent her life trying to protect Bethany and was still paralysed by the fear of losing her, but she tried not to give into those gloomy visions. She needed to start this new year positively, but it was not working and she had to settle for watching the minutes tick by with glum impatience.

"I thought I'd find you doing something like this," said Ben, strolling into the room. He looked at ease, but there was something hesitant in his movements that made Alexa wonder if he was as scared of being alone with him as she was. "You don't really want to watch a clock all night, do you?" he asked. His voice was not accusatory, allowing Alexa to shake her head. "Want to do something fun?" Alexa sighed, dropping her eyes to the floor as she shook her head again. "It involves the pool."

That had Alexa's attention. She had not been able to swim after the attack, and even now she was allowed she had resisted. It was something she had wanted to start back with in the new year, but with Ben's encouragement, Alexa changed into her swimmers.

"Want to race?" Ben asked. Alexa nodded. "Laps or time?"

"First to stop," suggested Alexa in a soft voice.

"I had a feeling you'd say that," sighed Ben, making Alexa smile. "I'm on call, so can we agree that I don't lose if I have to stop to answer my phone?"

It was a fair concession, and Alexa really did not think Ben would last long anyway. When they pushed off the wall, they matched their strokes, keeping a steady pace. The movement was nice, and Alexa enjoyed the stretch of her muscles as she pulled her body through the water. She wondered how she could have kept herself from the pool over the last week.

Ben surprised Alexa by continuing well after her body began to tire. They both slowed, but this was one race Alexa did not want to lose. She needed some achievement to hold on to. However, as their laps continued, she began to wonder if Ben needed to win as much as she did, because he was not stopping. They were both slowing, but no one was stopping.

Then it happened. Ben's hand slapped clumsily against the wall. Alexa turned and pushed off for another lap. When she returned, Ben was leaning against the side of the pool, breathing deeply.

"You win," he smiled breathlessly. It was then that Alexa realised Ben had not been trying to win, just battling to keep up. It made her smile happily. "You're not even puffing," said Ben, dragging himself from the pool.

It was true, though Alexa's body felt like her bones had been replaced by jelly.

When they walked inside, Alexa glanced at the clock long enough to ascertain that the previous year had been truly buried behind her. With Ben continuing to praise her, she found herself smiling more broadly. After a quick shower, they made their way to the kitchen and conjured up a very large and very early breakfast.

They had finished eating by the time Alexa realised that she and Ben had been talking for over an hour with no discomfort or awkwardness. Perhaps it was what they talked about. For once it was not about her. For the most part Ben spoke about his life, and Alexa realised she had never known him at all. It was interesting to hear about his past, his work, plans for his career, even a bit about his stilted love life. He never seemed to mind when she asked him questions and always answered, no matter how personal or intrusive.

In those hours they spent chatting, Alexa felt like she and Ben finally managed to bridge the gulf that had separated them since Marcus's arrival. More than that, she felt like she knew something about Ben as a person and not just the man she had seen die in her dreams most nights of her life.

Those amazing gains allowed Alexa to laugh off Bethany's horror at how they had spent their evening. It also helped Alexa be much more hopeful about the incorporation of the Whites into her life. One thing they had touched on was Ben's feelings towards the Whites. Unconditionally supportive was his response. No matter how or what Alexa asked, he somehow managed to make that his answer to every question.

Bethany was also unconditionally supportive, but only as far as Alexa was concerned. As soon as she found out Alexa had invited the Whites to the house, she was making plans to be far away.

"Angel, I want you to meet them – just once. Please," said Alexa, as Bethany paced agitatedly up and down the lounge room.

"Lex, they hate me."

"No, they don't," replied Alexa truthfully. "They forgive you. You were just a child. What happened wasn't your fault."

Bethany glared at Alexa and stormed out of the room. It made Alexa wonder why no one ever pounded on Bethany for taking the blame for things. It was true there were aspects of Bethany's behaviour surrounding that event Alexa struggled to forgive, but it was not the real Bethany she blamed for those things. It was the horrible heroin-addicted imposter that invaded her body. But it did not matter which Bethany was to blame, the real Bethany refused to differentiate the two and Alexa had to accept that an introduction to the Whites would not occur this time.

However, with her focus solely on Bethany, Alexa was caught completely off-guard by Marcus's uncomfortable reaction to the news of the Whites' impending visit. His concern was not without grounds. Alexa could not imagine Karl reacting well to the sight of Marcus living in her house, though she refused to believe he would punch Marcus, as Ben had. It left her feeling terribly guilty when she suggested to Marcus that he make himself scarce. He seemed genuinely relieved by the proposal, making Alexa believe he would have stayed and risked another black eye if she had asked him to.

That left only Charlotte to meet the Whites, and Alexa found herself terribly conscious of the extraordinary size of the house – and the wanton excess it must present. Although no one said anything as Alexa showed them around, there was constant astonishment that there could be more to see.

"Okay, I'm going to ask the important question," said Brett. "Have you been baking in your extraordinarily gigantic kitchen?" His nose was in the air, taking in the smells drifting up the stairs.

"Charlotte, actually," Alexa smiled, walking them towards the dining room. "And I promise you'll be impressed. She's a much better cook than me."

"You ain't lying," hooted Brett, catching sight of the table laid out with afternoon tea. "You should start expecting me for meals."

Everyone took their seats, but when Charlotte did not materialise, Alexa dragged her into the room. Alexa tried to introduce her to everyone, but Brett was much more interested in interrogating Charlotte about what else she cooked.

"Oh man, if you need a taste tester, I'm yours," said Brett eagerly when Charlotte gave a very abbreviated overview of her cooking repertoire.

"What he means to say is that you bake very well," said Karl with a soft smile, his plate completely clean of crumbs.

Charlotte blushed and bowed her head. Alexa had yet to explain to the Whites much about her current living arrangements. So far their reactions had been quite muted, but their acceptance of Charlotte was a crucial test and one she could not delay. It meant there was a slightly hard edge to her voice as she explained the importance of Charlotte to her and Bethany and her permanence in their family.

"Sounds like you've been doing a lot of good things in the last couple of years," said Pam, giving her quiet acceptance, while Karl nodded. "So it's just the three of you living here then?"

"Err, not quite," replied Alexa hesitantly, deciding against lying.

"What?" asked Karl warily.

"We have someone else living in the front room," Alexa replied, trying to sound nonchalant, but not quite achieving it.

"Who?" responded Karl, sounding as though he was preparing himself for bad news.

"Marcus."

"Marcus? Who's Marcus?" asked Karl, genuinely perplexed. For a second, Alexa thought she might get away with it, but then a look of realisation flickered across Karl's face. "Marcus Knight? Your teacher? What the hell is he doing here?"

"I don't go to school any more. He's not my teacher," said Alexa immediately, though that response did not calm Karl. "He was in a car accident a few months ago. Really banged up, in a wheelchair, and he couldn't go back to his apartment. This place is pretty wheelchair-friendly, so he came to live here so he didn't have to stay in hospital."

"But he's still here?"

"Well, his girlfriend had to move cos they couldn't afford the rent and til they work that situation out, I said he could stay," answered Alexa quickly, making things up as she went along.

"How did you even know about the accident? Were you seeing him beforehand?" asked Karl sceptically, though the tone of his voice had softened slightly after hearing the word girlfriend.

"If you mean by 'seeing' that we saw each other now and then, then yes. We've never dated. He was involved in the court case Sam and the others had against Redgrove."

"I forgot about that," said Karl stiffly. "Yours was a separate case, wasn't it?" Alexa nodded. "He testify at that too?"

"They settled out of court, but as far as I know, he gave a statement, along with some of the other teachers."

"You in contact with any of them?"

"Darling, relax. He has a girlfriend," said Pam, placing a gentle hand on Karl's arm. "He had a lot to do with Alexa, remember. It's not a huge surprise they stayed in contact."

Alexa sighed softly, relieved by Pam's intervention. Marcus's presence was going to be a harder sell than she imagined, and she realised that her story would not hold up against any conversation Karl might have with Ben. However, Alexa hoped Ben might have adopted a more moderate opinion of Marcus over the last year – or at least realised how much damage opposition would cause.

Charlotte jumped in and saved the conversation from any more discussions about Marcus by asking Hayley about school. Pam and Brett joined in with surprising enthusiasm. Only Karl remained silent. He did not seem angry so much as contemplative. All the same, Alexa was not disappointed that Marcus did not arrive home before the Whites left, despite Karl extending their visit well beyond dinner.

"They're not here," said Alexa when she saw Marcus creeping into his room just before midnight. "They left half an hour ago."

"They know I'm here?" asked Marcus hesitantly.

"Yep. I get the feeling Karl may kill you if he sees you, so you may want to be prepared if you ever bump into him. Apparently breaking three-quarters of your limbs isn't really going to cut it."

"As an excuse or a punishment?" queried Marcus seriously. Alexa laughed. "How'd it go otherwise?"

"Pretty good, I think. Charlotte and Hayley seemed to hit it off. They ended up in Charlotte's room for over an hour. Never really thought of them being the same age. Always thought of Hayley as being so young."

"And Beth?" Marcus asked, looking around.

"Still hiding."

Always hiding became a more accurate description as the new year gathered momentum. With Charlotte and Hayley firm friends by the end of that first visit, there were numerous interactions between the two households. Barely a day went by that Hayley and Charlotte did not see each other at one house or another. If Hayley was visiting late, it was always Karl who came to collect her, his eyes scanning Marcus's room intently every time. Alexa quickly realised that it would be safer dropping Hayley home herself, but Marcus had an uncanny knack of just missing the Whites, causing Alexa to suspect he had inside information.

Bethany's lack of interaction with the Whites was not so much stealth as luck. Charlotte made no secret of the fact that she was trying to manoeuvre things to ensure an introduction. Alexa just never realised how serious Charlotte was – until the Whites turned up unexpectedly at their picnic lunch in the park that Bethany and Charlotte had been organising for a fortnight. Bethany did not see them at first. There was no reason for her to recognise them from so far away, and she was focused on making sure Gran, Pop and Maria were comfortable. However, life on the streets had made Bethany very perceptive of her surroundings, so when the Whites were just fifteen metres away, her head snapped around like a hunted deer.

"Sam, we've gotta go," Bethany said anxiously, pulling him away from the barbeque. "Quick."

"Beth, don't. Don't go," said Charlotte, blocking her path. Bethany hissed incoherent words in return, but Charlotte would not move and Sam was not dragging her away.

"Bethy, please don't leave," said Alexa, joining the mess of people around her. Bethany was shaking so violently Alexa feared she would break down completely. Ben quickly had Bethany in his arms, as the whole party congregated in a loose circle.

"Bethany, I know this has caught you off-guard. I wish we didn't have to scare you this way," said Pam tenderly, reaching out to take Bethany's hand even though she stood almost five metres away. "All we ask is that you please give us a chance."

"Give you a chance? Are you kidding? There're no chances, not ever," gasped Bethany, shaking her head jerkily.

"Angel, they're not taking me away. This isn't a choice, okay. I promise," said Alexa urgently, taking Bethany's face in her hands and staring into her eyes.

"What are you talking about? You deserve to be with them. You need parents – someone to take the pressure off you. They do that. I see it," cried Bethany. "You deserve all that, but I don't. Lex, this isn't right. I shouldn't be forced on them. Please don't make them know me."

"They want to meet you," said Charlotte, her hand on Bethany's shoulder.

"No, they don't. They can't. And I don't want to meet them. I can't. I can't," gasped Bethany frantically.

"Bethany, don't you think we've had all the time in the world to contemplate this meeting?" asked Karl, his forceful voice keeping Bethany from fleeing. "You were fifteen. I know you must've felt old. We know what Alexa was like and the life she'd lived by that age. I also know what Leo was like, how vicious he was, what kind of predator he was. We don't blame you for that."

"I was the one that told him about you," said Bethany in a small voice.

"What exactly did you tell him? Did you tell him that Hayley was worth coming after?" asked Karl seriously. Bethany shook her head as tears started to slip down her cheeks. "Tell him we were a soft target for money?" Bethany shook her head again. "Tell him you wanted Hayley raped, killed?"

"I told him I was jealous," breathed Bethany, choking on a sob.

"Of Hayley?" questioned Karl.

"Of Hayley, of the house, of you. Everything."

"And you think that's why Leo attacked us? Because you were jealous? Even you cannot be that naïve."

Bethany did not answer. No one did. Of course no one was that naïve, but it was a topic that was still too painful for most of them to confront. Their actions. Their guilt. Nearly all of them harboured some scar from that night.

"I'm sorry, Bethany," said Karl. "But we're not leaving – not this picnic – not your life. We knew the moment we decided to make Alexa a part of our family that one day you would join it too. That day is today. Every person in our family has been a part of making that decision. You're going to have to walk out of this family to not be a part of it."

Bethany still did not answer, but everyone else considered the matter settled. Brett and Sam got the barbeque going as Maria started the introductions. Hayley and Charlotte were already off together, happily congratulating each other.

"You okay?" Alexa asked Bethany, who was still huddled in Ben's arms.

"Can I use the bathroom," asked Bethany meekly.

Alexa nodded, feeling tears sting her own eyes as she wiped the tears from Bethany's. Bethany took a deep breath and walked away. Ben watched her for a few seconds before volunteering to shadow her. Alexa nodded, her breath shuddering as she released it. When she walked to the table, Karl and Pam immediately threw an arm around her shoulders and squeezed her tight. It was so comfortable with them, but it caused a guilty knot to tie in her stomach when she saw the pained expression in Ben's eyes when he returned with Bethany.

This was the relationship Alexa and Ben could never quite achieve. Their moment over New Year's Eve had faded to nothingness in the weeks that followed. It was such a contrast to Pam and Karl's ever-present ways. However, Ben did not hold a grudge, and whatever hurt she caused him by her closeness to the Whites he forgave as he came over and squeezed her shoulder and kissed her hair. Ben was even pleasant to Pam and Karl, chatting happily with them through lunch as he held Bethany close.

"You don't have to forgive me."

The words rang out across the table, stopping all conversation. Bethany had finally pushed out of Ben's arms, her eyes flicking between each member of the White family.

"I just had to say that," continued Bethany meekly. "I'm thankful you're being kind. That's enough. You don't have to forgive me." Bethany was looking at Hayley now.

"That's what Alexa said," replied Hayley, her voice wavering just slightly. "It's easy to be mad at the wrong person. I even got mad at Alexa for a while. But you never hurt us. And I think if you'd known what he was going to do – if you came there instead of the school with the gun – you would've shot him to protect us."

Alexa imagined that scenario. They would have used the gun. If Bethany hadn't, Alexa would have. She would not have thought twice about shooting Leo in the head. The problem would have been what came next. All Alexa could see was her nightmare – her and Bethany running from her crime.

"But I wasn't there and he was my boyfriend," countered Bethany. "I let him get you."

"He was a paedophile and a drug dealer who used you to get what he wanted," said Brett. "You can blame yourself forever if you like, but you'll only be holding yourself back."

Alexa had the feeling that Bethany spent the rest of the picnic trying to catch the Whites in their lie, with the number of times she apologised to them. She only ever managed to elicit to same response. The message was so consistent, Bethany appeared to start believing it. The result was that the invitation for the Whites to come back to the house was out of Bethany's mouth before she knew what she was saying. The twin terror that flickered in Bethany's eyes was something Alexa could relate to. Thankfully, the Whites ignored Bethany's fear of them and dispelled her fear of rejection, accepting the invitation with thanks.

"She's taken, you know," Alexa smiled at Brett as they packed up. His eyes had been drifting Bethany's way all day.

"She's pretty," replied Brett with a cheeky smile that would make him a knockout with almost every girl.

"I know," replied Alexa truthfully. Bethany really was beautiful.

"When you look at her, it's hard to think she's been through so much," said Brett softly, his look suddenly more thoughtful. "I never really thought about it with you. I saw you at home – saw your temper and the trouble you got into. It wasn't so well hidden."

"She has her moments as well, I assure you."

"So did we," smiled Brett, the cheekiness returning.

"Yeah, I guess we did," replied Alexa laughingly, although it felt strange knowing she had been Brett's first kiss.

"Do you remember that day?" he asked. Alexa nodded, looking around to make sure Pam and Karl were not close by. "Karen – she asked me out last week."

"What'd you say?"

"I told her to go jump," replied Brett with a hard edge to his voice. "Apparently I'm good enough for her now – after she found out we moved to a nicer house – or at least more expensive one – oh, and because I became so much more interesting after that night."

"She thought that was interesting?" gasped Alexa.

"She wasn't the only one. Changed schools to get away from it, but saw her out. Told me I became a celebrity at the school after that stuff – as if that was something that would actually impress me. Makes me wonder how I ever liked her."

"Everyone has their faults," said Alexa, worried he was becoming blinded to theirs.

"I learned to tell the difference between faults in actions and faults in basic moral character. You can help a good person make the right decisions. Not sure how you fix someone who's told they always make the right decisions, but they're not a nice person."

Alexa did not answer. She was intrigued by Brett's take on the world – and them. He saw her and Bethany as good people who made bad decisions. Redeemable. It was a nice thought, but the one thing Alexa struggled most to believe was that she was a good person. She always hoped she was – could be – but doubted it.

"Oh no, he's home," gasped Charlotte as they pulled into the driveway. "Why hasn't he been answering his phone, the idiot?"

Alexa did not have the chance to even throw Charlotte a confused look before she was out of the car and rushing into the house. The source of her anxiety was clear, but Alexa was not sure Marcus meeting the Whites would be so disastrous they had to prevent it. She changed her mind when they all gathered in the lounge room.

"So Marcus is out then?" asked Karl in a somewhat unfriendly manner. "Doesn't seem to be here much."

Alexa and Bethany both flicked their eyes to Ben and Sam, but neither of them countered Karl's observation.

"He does have his own life," answered Alexa.

"He's still with his girlfriend then?" queried Karl, his questions a little too informed to be coincidental.

"He hasn't told me any different," Alexa replied casually, though Lucy's absence over the last month made her suspect otherwise.

"So why's he still living here?"

Alexa could not help but laugh out loud, though it took effort to keep the smile on her face as she explained that Marcus was free to leave, but as they had become friends she had no intention of asking him to.

"I'm just curious. If there's nothing to hide I assume we would've seen him by now," muttered Karl.

"I would've thought you'd run into each other by now too," replied Alexa seriously, glancing between Charlotte and Hayley. "If you like, I can make sure he's around next time."

Pam quickly dismissed that as unnecessary. They would meet when the time was right.

Marcus listened from his bedroom as everyone said their goodbyes. Moving so that he could see them, he watched as Bethany stepped tentatively towards Pam. When Pam's hand reached out and brushed Bethany's shoulder, Bethany lunged forward and hugged Pam forcefully. Bethany's body was shuddering. Karl put a gentle hand on Bethany's back, resulting in an instant transfer of the hug. It was too heartbreaking to watch, so Marcus returned to his bed and picked up the book he had been reading.

Once the house returned to its quiet state, Marcus dared to venture to the kitchen to grab some food. He was hoping Alexa was still up so he could see how the day had gone, but there was no one around – until he returned to his room.

"Now we just have to introduce you," smiled Bethany from the daybed. There were no signs of the tears that had recently stained her face, and Marcus believed that Bethany's masks might be better than Alexa's.

"I think that can wait," replied Marcus. "Let everything settle down before we go and throw it into turmoil again. I almost tore Alexa's family apart once. I'm not keen on doing it again."

"But you have to meet them," cried Bethany. "How can you ask Lex out if you've never met them?"

"Who says I want to ask Alexa out?" asked Marcus, not keen on discussing this with Bethany.

"I'm going to pretend you didn't even say that. Why else would you've broken up with Lucy?" said Bethany with an air of supreme confidence. Marcus refused to reply. It annoyed him when Bethany was right. "Look, I'm all behind the two of you, but they love Lex and they're really protective of her, so you'd better start winning them over."

"You're all talk, you know that, Beth. Twenty-four hours ago, you never wanted to meet them either," Marcus retaliated.

"That's different," waved Bethany unaffectedly.

"Really? Listen, Beth, you have this beautifully romantic view of the world – and that's great. I don't know how you do it. But I don't think that way and, most importantly, either does Alexa. Don't force this. Alexa has to move at her own pace. She gets up and gets on with things, but that doesn't mean she recovers from them."

"I know her better than you," replied Bethany through gritted teeth.

"In some ways, but not all," replied Marcus earnestly. "If you want things between me and Alexa to ever happen, then let us find our own way. At our own pace."

The way Bethany slammed the door on her exit made Marcus realise they were not getting any better at communicating. It was frustrating, because Marcus did not want to fight with Bethany. Part of him even wanted to get to know the girl everyone else saw. And Bethany did have a point. He would need to win over the Whites, but in his mind that only mattered if he managed to win over Alexa. The real question was how. If there was one thing Alexa did not have a lot of, it was spare time. She was making sure she saw everyone at least once a week, often dedicating time to each of them. Marcus had once even seen a colour-coded schedule with arrows and squiggles everywhere. He had not been allocated a time. Rather his name was alone in a cloud bubble at the bottom of the page.

There could have been any number of reasons for his segregation, but Marcus eventually chose not to try and guess what it was. He let himself be guided by the mischievous grin and lively sparkle in Alexa's eyes the morning of Sean's attack, which told him her heart held the same desires as his. When he returned to work, he knew he would have to get more creative about finding time for him and Alexa to be alone, though all it really required was a disregard for cold water.

The smile that graced Alexa's face when she saw Marcus slipping into the pool on Tuesday morning was worth sacrifices a thousand times more torturous.

"Are you going to swim?" asked Alexa gleefully, her goggled eyes unable to hide their sparkle.

"Only if you promise not to make fun of how terrible I am," Marcus replied.

Alexa did not answer, only smiled more broadly as she dived back under the water and pushed off the wall. When she reached the other end she looked back at Marcus, nodding for him to start. Marcus complied and they swam in opposite directions until Alexa swam him down.

"You giving up?" asked Alexa, as Marcus pulled himself out of the water.

"You're still going?" he questioned, feeling like his body would dissolve if he tried to swim another lap. Her answer was diving back under the water.

Marcus wished that sight was enough to wake him up in time for every one of Alexa's morning swims, but if Alexa did not sneak into his room and on to the daybed, where he would always read her to sleep, he would miss her in the pool. Alexa noticed the pattern before he did, and she was soon spending every night in his room.

Most mornings Marcus felt strong and enjoyed the feeling of pulling himself through the water, but on others his body was so heavy he was sure he would sink. That was when he discovered the effect of wading in the water while Alexa swum. The distraction was always too much, dragging her towards him. They talked, floated, often bumping into each other. Every day their bodies moved closer. If it had been anyone else, Marcus would not have hesitated, but he would wait a lifetime to make the next move if it ensured he never pressured Alexa into a moment she did not want.

Alexa felt incredibly self-conscious. It was one of the first times she had ever worried about what she looked like in her swimmers. Every other day she just threw on her one-piece and jumped in the pool, but ever since Marcus had joined her, Jessica's voice had been swirling in her head. The result was her standing in front of the mirror in her bikini wondering if it was too obvious she was trying to tempt Marcus. Closing her eyes, Alexa ran from the room and down the stairs. Marcus was already in the pool, looking a little concerned by his solitary state – until he saw her. Alexa's heart stuttered erratically as she took in his wide eyes. He was looking at her like she was the most beautiful girl in the world.

Marcus moved to the side of the pool and waited as she sat on the edge, too scared to dive in. The fear of her top flying off did not explain why she did not slide her body into the water. Perhaps it was the fact that she and Marcus were now at eye level, and when he stood in front of her the last thing on her mind was swimming.

"You going to join me?" asked Marcus, his hand tucking a loose strand of hair behind her ear. His fingers held their position on her jawbone as she nodded.

When she did not move, his hands gripped her waist and gently lifted her into the water. For the first time, Alexa shivered as the water washed over her. They did not swim. Marcus dropped his body under the water, pulling her with him as they waded. Alexa finally felt her limbs come to life, but as they propelled her through the water, she found herself floating too close to Marcus. Their bodies collided. Marcus's hands were immediately on her waist, steadying her. Her hands came to rest on his chest. There was something surreal about being able to touch Marcus so freely. His hands slid down over her hips. Although they were only inches apart, he did not pull her into him. It left her free to explore. Her hands moved over his chest and shoulders, down his sides and back up again. Marcus did not move more than his head, which slid down to meet hers, their foreheads touching. When her arms eventually ended up around his neck, his hands moved over her back, encasing her tenderly.

Even after half a day of university, the feel of Marcus's hands on her had not left Alexa's body. She was still not sure what it was that had pulled them apart. Even more perplexing was what had kept them from kissing. The desire to be back in Marcus's arms was so strong that her body ached. It made concentrating in class very difficult, and Alexa needed to. These summer classes were run intensively, meaning few chances to catch up if she fell behind.

The moment class finished, Alexa practically skipped out of the room, rushing to make her way home. She was not sure what came next. All she knew was that they had both given up on resisting temptation. Dancing into Marcus's room, Alexa was caught short by his absence. He was usually home by now. The house was very big, and it took Alexa a while to ensure that he was not in another room.

Marcus's absence threw Alexa. All she had been able to think about was coming home to him. Clearly the same thoughts had not been circling his brain. When he did turn up after dinner, Alexa did not know how to face her confusion and escaped to her room. She considered going down to Marcus's room. Even if she had mistaken the meaning of the morning's events, they could go back to what they shared in the evenings. However, the thought of giving up what she had experienced was so painful she knew she had to rid herself of this foolishness immediately. Going further only risked more pain.

It was a sleepless night without Marcus's voice to ease Alexa into her dreams. The emptiness of the pool the next morning matched her mood. It meant she swam much longer and harder than she had in weeks.

"You swim?" asked Marcus, joining her at the dining table with his breakfast. Alexa did not look up, her heart stammering as she nodded. "Realised, oh, fifteen minutes ago that I haven't actually set an alarm for a some time now."

"You must've needed the sleep-in then if you didn't wake at the normal time," said Alexa, trying to convey more than that.

"Perhaps," Marcus replied sombrely. "Didn't sleep well last night, so probably did." Alexa nodded, unsure what to say. Just sitting so close, knowing she had read the signals all wrong was excruciating. "So what's the plan for Saturday night?" asked Marcus, pushing his empty plate away from him. "More study?" he queried, looking at the book next to Alexa's plate.

"No, I'm actually hanging with Charlotte, Hayley and Brett. Char has a party on Friday night so we moved our thing to Saturday," Alexa replied, her eyes down.

"So's that mean you're not doing anything Friday night?" asked Marcus in an overly casual way. Alexa's stomach suddenly felt as though she had eaten worms for breakfast. She looked up. Marcus was not smiling. He looked terrified. "I was hoping I might be able to take you out to dinner."

Alexa felt her eyes widen. She was trying to take everything in – figure out what Marcus really meant. They had been out for meals together before.

"There's a big part of me that just wants to – I thought it'd be best if we started slow," said Marcus, his voice stuttering as he spoke. "We can date for a while. See if it works."

"Really?" gasped Alexa.

"You don't want to?"

"No. Yes. No, I mean, I want to," Alexa said, unsure if yes or no was the correct response. "I just didn't think you did – thought I misinterpreted everything."

"You misinterpreted me getting up at five-thirty every morning just to be alone with you?" asked Marcus with a soft smile. "You misinterpreted yesterday morning?"

"Last night," Alexa clarified, shaking her head.

"Sorry about that," sighed Marcus. "I let Ryan convince me that being at the door for you when you came home last night would put too much pressure on you. It was torture being away from you."

Alexa was sure she would burst with relief. Then more recent memories returned and the smile slid from her face. "You sure?" she asked seriously. "You know – last time – you don't —"

"Alexa, you weren't being punished. It was just horrible, horrible timing. I've never been more sure about anything in my life."

Alexa would have responded if Charlotte did not walk in at that moment. It was so awkward Alexa had to flee the room. Just being around Marcus while others could witness their interactions was so difficult Alexa avoided him in a way she never had before. She hoped he understood, but there was never a chance to ask; he did not return to the pool in the mornings and she did not return to his room in the evenings.

"What's going on?" asked Bethany at dinner on Thursday night, looking between Alexa and Marcus.

Alexa glanced towards Marcus to see if he would answer, but looked away as soon as their eyes met. Just that momentary meeting of eyes was enough to set her body on fire and she did not want to start grinning like some drunk clown.

"Nothing," Alexa responded casually, though she did not look up as she spoke.

"Are you guys fighting?" asked Bethany, true concern in her voice this time.

"No, we're not fighting, Bethy. Everything's fine, I promise," Alexa replied, grasping Bethany's hand and smiling reassuringly.

Bethany nodded, but did not seem convinced. When Alexa carried the plates to the kitchen, Bethany was right behind her, asking the same questions over again. Alexa continued to reassure her, but that only set Bethany's mind on another, more accurate path.

"Then did something else happen? Did you and him – you know?" asked Bethany, her voice a swirl of emotions, as though she was waiting on the details to determine her reaction.

"No," replied Alexa, perhaps a little too quickly. "Nothing like that. Nothing's happened between us."

Marcus walked into the kitchen not appearing to have heard the conversation. Bethany looked at him with questioning eyes, but he just held her gaze with a stern stare, making it clear he was not interested in conversation. It seemed overly harsh to Alexa. Keeping things from Bethany did not have to include being mean to her, and she could see that Bethany was upset as she rushed from the room.

"That wasn't —" Alexa could not continue. Marcus was standing right next to her, smiling broadly.

"So nothing's going on between us?" he questioned playfully.

"No, I wouldn't say so," breathed Alexa, daring to look into his eyes.

"I hope you realise I plan to change that very soon," Marcus whispered in her ear.

Alexa's legs weakened. It felt like she was falling. Her body was on fire, her heart beating rapidly, stoking the flames. Marcus's eyes sparkled as his hand reached out and tucked her hair behind her ear. His thumb stroked her cheek. Her body was aching for her to reach out and pull his lips to hers, but this was not where she wanted them to have their first kiss.

The thought of how their first kiss could play out gave Alexa just enough strength to pull away from Marcus with a promise of seeing him at dinner tomorrow night. She hoped the smile that crossed his face meant he understood what she envisaged for their very near future. It was all she thought about as she lay sleepless in her bed, and as she pulled her tired body through the water. Marcus had left the house by the time she made it to the kitchen for breakfast, making her desire for the day to pass that much more urgent.

When Alexa did arrive home – after a hopelessly distracted day at university – she rushed straight up to her room and under the shower, paying more attention than ever to her personal grooming habits. She shaved her legs and washed her hair three times, scrubbed her face twice and smoothed her entire body with sweet smelling body lotion. Then came the hard part. Finding something to wear.

It was something Alexa was determined would not upset her. Marcus would not care if she turned up for their date in jeans and t-shirt, but she wanted to look nice. There had been so few happy moments in her life, and this was one event she wanted to approach feeling good about herself.

"Hey, Alexa, can I raid your closet?" asked Charlotte, walking into the room holding a selection of clothes. "Ooh, can I wear that?" she asked, pointing to the clothes Alexa had strewn across her bed. "I was trying to do something with these, but couldn't pull it off."

Alexa gave Charlotte free reign over her wardrobe while she examined the clothes Charlotte had brought up. Holding them up in front of the mirror, Alexa could still not decide what look she was going for. When Charlotte looked up, a smile of inspiration came across her face. Selecting clothes for Alexa in a way she never could for herself, Charlotte quickly coordinated the perfect outfit, insisting Alexa try it on to be sure.

"You look great. You should dress up more often," said Charlotte kindly, examining Alexa in the mirror. "Promise you'll wear it tonight.

Doesn't matter if you don't have anywhere to go – you look too good."

"Yeah, I'll wear this tonight," smiled Alexa, thinking Charlotte had to be one of the more perfect people in the world and was so glad fate had thrown them together.

"So is it okay if you give me a lift to the party," asked Charlotte as they walked downstairs.

"You going fishing tonight?" asked Sam, before Alexa could answer.

Alexa and Charlotte exchanged confused looks before they saw Bethany trying hard not to laugh behind Sam's back. "He means you make very good bait dressed like that and you may just hook yourself a catch tonight," smiled Bethany broadly.

"Oh, I'm sorry, I didn't realise you had plans. It's okay. I'll get there myself," said Charlotte guiltily.

"Get where?" asked Sam.

"Char has a party tonight. I told her ages ago that I'd drop her, but forgot when I said I'd go out for dinner."

"I can't imagine why," smiled Bethany.

Alexa glared at her, but Bethany simply shrugged before adding a wink and a smile. For some reason, that gesture made Alexa uneasy. It was clear Bethany had worked out what was going on since dinner last night. It should not have made any difference, but Alexa suddenly had the very unpleasant feeling she was not going anywhere tonight.

"It's okay, we'll take you," said Sam, nodding at Charlotte. "We were going to just hang here tonight, so you can give us a call when you need to be picked up as well – just not too late, hey."

"Thanks," Charlotte replied happily. "So what time you going out?" Charlotte asked Alexa, when Sam and Bethany left to get ready.

"I don't actually know," replied Alexa, feeling her stomach roll with dread.

"Where're you going?"

"Don't really know that either."

"Know who you're going with?" smiled Charlotte.

"Just a friend. He's supposed to pick me up."

Charlotte's squeal and excited hug were no doubt triggered by Alexa's blush and she was glad Charlotte said nothing more. It was nice to pretend she had some privacy. "Enjoy your dinner," smiled Charlotte, dancing to the front door.

"Yeah, I guess we'll see you tomorrow," smiled Bethany, joining

Charlotte at the door.

Alexa smiled back, but as soon as everyone had left she sunk into the lounge, curling her legs into her body. Marcus was still not home and he had not called. She wondered if she had misunderstood everything or if Marcus had changed his mind. Either way, he was not coming home to her. Dashing upstairs, Alexa changed into house clothes and tied her hair into a messy bun. It no longer mattered what she wore. There was no one to impress and that thought filled her stomach with lead.

Chapter Ten

MARCUS TRIED TO steady his hand. They were shaking so much he could not even get the key in the lock. It took everything he had not to break down right there on the doorstep. Maybe Alexa was right. Perhaps they were never supposed to be together. He kept trying to reason that this would have torn them apart anyway, but if he had known, he would never have let things go so far. He would have left weeks ago and spared them this heartbreak. Of all the ways he imagined this night playing out, this was beyond the realm of even his most pessimistic thoughts.

The house was quiet when Marcus finally let himself in, soft murmuring floating from the dining room. Alexa's voice sounded so sad. Marcus could only imagine how hurt she already was. He had planned to be home before her, waiting with flowers.

Bethany's head snapped up as soon as Marcus entered the room. Her eyes were like lasers, and he realised he had never put her off-side before.

"You're a real arse, you – what's wrong?"

It was Bethany's change in tone that drew Alexa's eyes up, her hurt turning to guilt in an instant.

"I need to talk to you," said Marcus, the words just squeezing out of his chest.

Alexa nodded, but stayed silent as she followed him out of the room. She sat down on the daybed and waited for him to speak, but all he could do was pace, trying to work out how he could possibly tell her what was going on. His hands ran agitatedly over his head. The absence of hair only increased his frustrations.

"What happened?" asked Alexa in an understanding voice, and Marcus could tell by the look on her face she knew whatever he had to say would tear them about.

"She's pregnant," gasped Marcus, his chest constricting, trying to keep those words inside, where he could tell himself they were simply not true. "Lucy, she's pregnant. She just told me today."

Alexa nodded, her eyes dropping to the floor. There was more to say, but he could not force the words from his mouth.

"When are you leaving?" asked Alexa, eventually looking up.

She was more intuitive than he gave her credit for. "Tomorrow – first thing," Marcus replied, his voice barely above a whisper.

"Okay," replied Alexa just as softly. She did not look up as she slipped from the daybed and out of the room.

Marcus turned away, not strong enough to watch her leave. He was going to be a father, yet all he cared about was losing the love of his life.

"No, no, it's not true," cried Bethany hysterically, bursting into the room. "It can't be."

Marcus could hear the tears in Bethany's voice, but kept his back to her. "Don't make this any harder than it already is, Beth. Please."

"No. Don't leave Lex for her. You can't."

"She's pregnant," cried Marcus, finally turning around. "I'm not going to abandon my child."

"You can be a father to that child here with Lex."

"No, I can't!" Marcus replied angrily. This was why he had been so late – arguing this point. "Lucy's already said that if I stay here I'll never see my child."

"She can't —"

"Don't be so naïve," spat Marcus. "She can and she will. You know. I know. Alexa knows. We all know what Lucy's like. I will not abandon my child."

"So you're going to go back to a person who'll put those sorts of demands on you?" asked Bethany incredulously.

"I'm going to my parents' place for now," sighed Marcus. After this stunt, he was struggling to ever want to speak to Lucy again. Being with her was out of the question, but he knew he would have little choice for now but to play along with her games.

"You don't even know if the baby's yours," said Bethany acidly.

"Don't," snapped Marcus. "That child is mine."

"Don't leave Lex for her. I'm telling you, you can't trust Lucy," replied Bethany, her voice more restrained and sincere, but Marcus could not trust her either.

"I'm leaving tomorrow, Beth. It's over, okay. Please, just accept it. It's over."

"No! You and Lex belong together! Why won't you see that?"

"Because this is not some damned fairy tale!" Marcus snapped, furious that he and Alexa could never have what Bethany dreamed.

"This is real life. You really think I should walk away from my own child? Is that romantic to you? Stop looking at me through rose-coloured fucking glasses. Of course this is the last thing I want."

"Then don't go. We'll get you a good lawyer. You can have them both," said Bethany, taking his hands in hers.

"The world doesn't work that way, Beth," replied Marcus with a heavy sigh, pulling his hands from her grasp as gently as possible. "Lucy doesn't work that way. Just let it go. Let me go. Alexa's young and beautiful. She'll move on. I'm not the only man in the world that will love her, but I might be the one who does it the worst."

Alexa did not sleep. She was out on the balcony before the sun came up, watching Marcus pack his car. He looked up continuously. The lights were off so she doubted he could see her, but she could see the heartbreak in his eyes. Perhaps now he understood they were never supposed to be together.

It was still dark when Marcus drove away. Alexa waited for the rush of tears, but nothing came. She had given Marcus her heart long ago and he had not given it back, leaving her feeling so empty that not even tears remained. Bethany's panicked frame appeared in the front yard minutes later. When the realisation of Marcus's departure hit, her eyes turned immediately up to the third floor. Moments later Alexa was being crushed in her heartbroken embrace, Bethany crying her tears for her.

"We have to fight, Lex," urged Bethany. Alexa shook her head. If there was one thing she had run out of, it was fight. "But you know – Lex, the baby might not be his. Did you tell him? Did you tell him Lucy's cheating on him? He'll believe you."

"He'll believe that I believe you," replied Alexa flatly. She had learned the hard way what Marcus would believe. "He's sure the baby's his. Maybe they already did tests."

"But you love him – you love each other. It's not fair."

Tears slipped down Bethany's cheeks as she finished those broken words, finally brewing the sadness in Alexa's heart. Tears burned the corners of Alexa's eyes at the truth of that statement and why the loss hurt Bethany so much. It was not fair. After all they had suffered, fair seemed like a reasonable expectation.

A sombre mood fell over the house. Alexa found solace in study.

Moving back down into Marcus's room, she devoted herself to her books. She tried to moderate her study habits so no one could accuse her of hiding from the world, but commenting on the way she lived had practically become part of everyone's routine that it seemed a little too hopeful for it to stop now. However, Ben and Sam kept very quiet on the issue. Alexa had the feeling they were so relieved Marcus had left they did not want to risk any actions that might invite him back.

As they all sat quietly eating dinner, it gave Alexa hope she would be left to mourn in peace. The sound of the front door slamming shattered that. Heavy footsteps proceeded towards them as Ben jumped from his seat, reaching for the gun he was not wearing. He and Sam moved to the doorway, but Marcus was there before them and pushed them aside as he charged towards Alexa.

"Did you know?" Marcus spat, tossing a large envelope at her. Alexa was not sure she had ever seen him so angry. "Did you know?" he cried again, though this time with desperation.

Confused by what was happening, Alexa picked up the envelope. It contained photos – of Lucy lip-locked with a man – a man who was clearly not Marcus.

"You knew!" cried Marcus, correctly interpreting the lack of surprise on her face.

"Bethy told me – a long time ago – that night – when you left," confessed Alexa, remembering her torment over that decision. "I've never seen these."

"Why didn't you tell me?" gasped Marcus.

"You loved her," replied Alexa softly.

"And you might not have believed her," said Bethany, drawing Marcus's hateful glare. "I saw her. I was the one who knew Lucy was cheating on you. I tried to tell you – more than once – but you chose not to believe me."

"She's pregnant with my child! How is this the right time to tell me?" cried Marcus. "What right do you have to tear my life apart?"

"You don't know that it's yours!" replied Bethany passionately. "I couldn't let you walk out of here – your home – for a lie."

"It's mine," said Marcus, his voice resigned and barely above a whisper. "That child is mine. You had no right."

Bethany opened her mouth to retaliate, but Marcus was already gone. It made Alexa wonder what would happen if the child was not his, but that speculation was useless.

Three weeks later a note from Marcus arrived with a copy of a medical report. The baby was his.

For Alexa that had to be the end of it. She wanted Marcus to be a good father. She could not interfere. Bethany was not convinced, positive Lucy could not legally keep Marcus from his child. She had even consulted Peter for his professional opinion. From Peter's lack of reassurance when she returned to work, Alexa could not have the optimistic outlook Bethany did.

But in the end, the most telling factor was Marcus's silence.

The emptiness that accompanied Marcus's absence was hard for Alexa to shake. As soon as semester started, her friends picked up on the difference in her demeanour. Alexa had not spoken to Amy or Jessica all break, only communicating via text, and when she had last seen them her life had been moving in the right – if hectic – direction.

When it became clear Alexa would not open up at uni, Jessica arranged for a girls' night in. Alexa was tempted to bail, but decided it would be better to get out of the house, though she was determined to stay silent on recent events. When Amy started to tearfully recall her break up with Jake over the summer, Alexa suddenly found herself overcome by emotion. Amy and Jessica were immediately on either side of her.

"What's going on?" asked Amy.

Alexa could not answer, horrified they were ignoring Amy's heartbreak, but neither Amy nor Jessica let it slide. Even when Alexa composed herself and claimed to have just been upset for Amy, they kept pressing. Alexa finally caved and told them about Marcus.

"But I don't get it. What stopped you getting together before Christmas?" asked Amy. "Things happened so you didn't go to the beach that day, but – I don't get it. What was wrong with the next day?"

Alexa did not have the words. She had never thought about how unreasonable her story would sound when everything else was left out. Raising her shaking hands to her neck, Alexa undid the silk scarf she wore whenever she left the house. The scar across her throat was still red and stood out dramatically. The doctors promised it would fade with time, but it showed no signs of doing so yet.

"He did that?" gasped Jessica, her hand over her mouth. "Why would you —" Alexa shook her head. "Not Damien?"

"No. My father," replied Alexa softly, retying her scarf.

"That Ben guy?" asked Amy, her voice quivering.

"My biological father."

"Shit, Alexa," gasped Jessica, her eyes wide. Until now the quirks in Alexa's life had been more amusing than frightening, and it was clear Jessica now understood how much Alexa had been hiding. "You know we'd never force you to tell us stuff. We just want to know you're okay."

Alexa nodded. She did not talk straight away, but when Amy asked the first question, Alexa answered. More questions inevitably followed, and over the next few hours Alexa divulged much of her life, opening up about things she had never told anyone outside her family group.

"I still can't believe you almost died," choked Jessica. "Your family knows we care, right? That we'd want to know – visit you."

"You won't tell anyone, right?" asked Alexa frantically, ignoring Jessica's comment. "You won't tell people what I told you."

"Of course not," said Amy, Jessica immediately agreeing. "But you don't have to be ashamed. All that shit – that's not your fault."

"Some of it is," muttered Alexa.

"You mean working as a pro, right?" asked Jessica, reading Alexa's mind. "You realise you're not the first girl to do that, right? I mean it's not called the oldest profession in the world for nothing."

"Men just have these fucked up double standards about women and their sexuality," added Amy. "Men are the reason that profession exists and they call women whores for providing them with what they want. They should be calling them goddesses."

"I thought about it once," said Jessica, smiling more broadly as Alexa stared. "I was too chicken. I don't have money. My parents don't have money to support me and it seemed like an easy option."

"So what happened?" asked Alexa, suddenly wishing she had had this conversation years ago.

"Well, I got my crappy job at the supermarket. It gave me enough to pay my bills. And then I started seeing my ex. I think I could've done it, but not if I had a boyfriend. That would've felt too much like cheating."

Alexa started to realise other people's lives were more complicated than she ever gave them credit for, and that it was possible for her to relate to them. Yet confiding in people was still terrifying and Alexa feared returning to university and a world that suddenly knew her secrets.

"Wow, you're really not the trusting type, are you?" said Jessica with a laugh. "I could be insulted."

"Can you really blame me?" Alexa asked seriously. Damien was three tables away, stubbornly refusing to look their way.

"Yeah, that was bad, but at least he seemed to learn his lesson – even if he has been a complete dick to you ever since. You would've thought you'd made the fake profile of him with the way he acts towards you. But if it makes you feel better, you're definitely not the first girl to have an arsehole for an ex-boyfriend."

Alexa could only nod. Talk of Damien only served to prove how amazing Marcus was. Just the thought of Marcus, the knowledge of his permanent estrangement from her life, brought tears to her eyes. Jessica's hand reached out to hers and squeezed it tenderly.

"Don't get mad, but me and Amy were talking about this last night," said Jessica.

"About what?" asked Alexa, pulling her hand back.

"You – well, you and Marcus," smiled Jessica, reclaiming Alexa's hand. "What would be the best thing to say. I mean, it's kinda the best and worst situation, isn't it. You've met someone you love so much and they love you just as much. Me and Amy, we've never known that. But the rest of it – we've known the crap side of love pretty intimately. So we won't tell you what to think or feel, but we are going to make some suggestions about how you act."

"Like what?"

"Well, mainly just doing stuff that keeps your mind off Marcus."

"Fake it til you make it?"

"Exactly," smiled Jessica. "Except we kinda hope you don't have to fake having fun with us."

Alexa didn't. As far as distraction went, Jessica and Amy were amazing. It did not remove the ache in Alexa's heart or the emptiness she felt in her huge mansion, but it did make the days more bearable. And since home was where her heartache was, Alexa found herself spending less and less time there. When she was not out with her university friends, she was over at the Whites or visiting Maria. Ben had still not invited her over to his place, so Alexa never went – despite him giving Bethany a key to pass on to her. Although Alexa and Ben got along better in company than they had for a long time, it was still not the relationship Alexa craved, and she had not worked out how to be the daughter Bethany was.

The constant socialisation would have provided a useful mode of distraction if it were not for the way people were watching Alexa. Those who knew the truth about Marcus were waiting for her to fall apart, while Pam and Karl seemed to be watching for signs that Alexa had been lying about the nature of their relationship. The one person watching the closest was Ben. He was always at the house and always appeared on the brink of talking to Alexa about something. Alexa was not in the mood for a lecture, but if Ben had something to say she knew she would hear it eventually.

"Can I come in?" knocked Ben on Alexa's bedroom door.

"Sure," replied Alexa, taking a deep breath, recalling what she had been preparing in response to the inevitable conversation.

"There's something I need to talk to you about. I wanted to give you time to digest everything about your father first – I was going to tell you a couple of weeks ago, but with everything – there's no real good time, I suppose," said Ben in an uncharacteristically hesitant voice.

"What are you talking about?" asked Alexa, thrown by Ben's comment.

"It's about your father – about what he did to you."

"I know all that now. I'm over it. I don't need more explanations," sighed Alexa agitatedly. Despite the revelations, she still had no memories of those childhood years and was determined to never think about that time.

"I left something out," said Ben, sitting down on the bed. "Something I thought you had the right to know without everyone else hearing. It has to do with the damage he did to you – physically."

"What do you mean?" asked Alexa hesitantly. This was not right. She had had many tests after Leo's attack. She had been thankful not to have contracted any diseases – one of the only blessings she felt she had ever received. If they had told her nothing then, she could not work out what else could be wrong with her.

"You were young when Sean started molesting you," explained Ben gravely. "At the hospital – when they examined you – back then – the doctors said the damage was so great that …" Ben hesitated, true heartbreak in his eyes. "I'm sorry, Alexa, you're infertile. You can't have children."

"No – but I fell pregnant – to Clinton – I was pregnant," Alexa stammered, sure Ben was wrong.

"You said yourself you never took a pregnancy test," said Ben gently, not rebuffing her completely. "Maybe you were never pregnant. I'm sorry. I wish I was – that the doctors were wrong, but they told me. I remember going in and sitting with you – playing with you – barely able to speak with all you'd suffered. It's not fair and I'm sorry I can't change it."

There was no reason for Alexa to doubt Ben's word. There were tears in his eyes and despite all the difficulties they had in their relationship, he was not cruel. He would never joke about these things. It had to be true. She could never have children. All those desires to right the wrongs of her childhood now taunted her. She would be childless. Alone. Alexa was glad now that Lucy had fallen pregnant. If Marcus had stayed for her she would have stripped him of the possibility of every worthwhile future. For the first time, Alexa hoped that Marcus and Lucy were able to make their relationship work. A happy family was the least Marcus deserved.

Ben stayed with Alexa and comforted her as she cried, but as much as she appreciated his support, his arms were not the ones she needed.

"Can you tell Bethy?" Alexa asked meekly.

"Of course," said Ben. "I'll do that right now."

It felt like only seconds later that the sound of feet came thundering towards her. Bethany did not knock. She just closed the door behind her and entwined her body with Alexa's. They both cried. All night. When morning came, Sam crept into the room, taking Bethany's place after she finally managed to fall asleep. Sam cradled Alexa tenderly. The way he held her told her that he was not just there as her friend. In their recklessly romantic moments, they had always spoken of the family they would have together. Even if they had ventured to imagine a future in which they were not together, their futures had always involved their two families growing up together. Now that dream was gone – half of it erased permanently – and Alexa wondered if Sam spent as many hours as she did praying the same fate did not lay install for Bethany.

When Alexa finally pulled herself from her room, the world seemed that much darker. Even the bluest sky seemed grey, and though she lost weight, she had never felt heavier. Motivation was much harder to find. It no longer seemed to matter how many gains she made, because she knew, in the end, everything would be stripped from her. The only thing that kept her going was routine. It was harder to come up with excuses than to trudge on. Stumbling blindly from one day to the next was what she had always done. She could just no longer do it with a smile.

Thankfully, there was one part of her life that did not require Alexa to be cheery. In fact, studying was sometimes easier when her mood was lowest. That her assessment marks had so far benefited from her gloomy lifestyle provided some comfort. So did the fact that Charlotte liked to focus her energies into study as well. Alexa and Charlotte spent most evenings studying together. They never spoke about their troubles, but Alexa could tell Charlotte was not coping well. There was something particular about the pain of abandonment. It did not always peak at the start, and Alexa knew Charlotte would not be able to weave a shimmering story to explain her living arrangement to her peers. Their lives were not normal, and that alone eradicated all hope of them ever feeling like they could truly fit in.

With the days passing so bleakly, Alexa was surprised by the sudden arrival of Easter. Time without Marcus seemed to stretch on indefinitely, and yet somehow it still passed. Life was moving on. And, because it was what they normally did, Alexa and Charlotte hosted the Easter gathering. In many ways, it was the best day they had had in a long time. Dancing and singing to the radio while they cooked was a carefree way to pass the morning. If everyone who arrived could have seen that as a good sign, the whole day may have passed that way.

Alexa could not blame the Whites for their concerns. They were still in the dark about her near-relationship with Marcus. As soon as Karl heard that Marcus had moved out because his girlfriend was pregnant, he became much more generous towards Marcus, his suspicions seemingly erased. It left them with the news of Alexa's infertility as the cause of her melancholy, and regarding that, they had been nothing but supportive. Karl, in particular, had taken it upon himself to research different fertility options.

It was really Ben and Sam who had once more decided Alexa was not living her life the right way. Even the fact that she was going out more concerned them. Six months ago they had complained she was shutting herself off from the world and not meeting new people. Now she was escaping her problems by fleeing the house and indulging in reckless behaviour. They had even gone as far as asking if she drank or took drugs when she went out with Amy and Jessica. Alexa never answered those questions. That took things one step too far and erased the ground she and Ben had been making up until that point.

The fear of what would be said today kept Alexa on edge. What was worse was that Ben and Sam recruited Bethany into their crusade. It was a low tactic, because Alexa would never dismiss Bethany's concerns. So when Bethany snuggled in close on the lounge, as they gathered for afternoon tea, and asked how she was doing, Alexa had to temper her annoyance.

"Bethany's right," said Ben, talking before Alexa could. "You've been very down this last month. We want to make sure you're okay."

"Can I ask when exactly I was supposed to be happy again?" asked Alexa, her voice calm but unimpressed. "I don't know which of the things that've occurred recently I'm supposed to be all that happy about."

"Don't get defensive," said Ben.

"No, you keep telling me I'm depressed, hinting that I'm not supposed to be. I don't recall you giving me a deadline for getting over it when you told me I'd never have kids because my own father fucked me so hard he tore my insides to shreds."

Bethany grabbed Alexa's arm and buried her head in Alexa's shoulder blade. Alexa immediately took Bethany's hand, but Bethany's fingers pushed against her palm. It took a second for Alexa to realise that Bethany was not mad at her. Her fingers were tracing the word sorry on to her palm. It was the way they had silently communicated as children – writing words and tapping code.

"That wasn't necessary," snarled Sam, looking over at Bethany.

"And this is?" snapped Alexa. Sam's eyebrows rose expressively. "Can you just tell me what you want from me and I can give it to you. I'm sick of always getting it wrong."

The petulance in Alexa's voice left the room silent for many minutes. Ben and Sam exchanged looks, possibly coordinating their response, but thankfully Brett spoke first. "I think you're doing fine," he said with a casual shrug of his shoulders. "Everyone reacts different to things. You're still living your life – getting up, going to uni. Things'll fall back into place in time."

There was something more to Brett's response than just support. There was lived experience; which made Alexa wonder how difficult it was for him to get up in the morning and make it through each day.

"I think you're doing fine too," said Karl supportively. "All three of you. There's been nothing easy about your lives – ever, probably. That gets on top of you. But life doesn't get better while you're focusing on what you don't have. You need to focus on the good – the things you're thankful for. Start small. Be thankful for just the briefest moment that makes you smile, for the people in your life and then slowly you'll find you've got more to be thankful for than not."

"I get it," muttered Alexa. "I'm being selfish."

"No," replied Karl forcefully. "There's very little that's selfish about you, Charlotte and Beth. Now perhaps Bethany's benefited from more structured assistance over the last couple of years." Alexa knew Karl was referring to the counselling Bethany had been forced to receive in detention and remained a condition of her parole. It was something Alexa had refused to undertake, despite the suggestion from many sources. "You and Charlotte – just understand that you don't have to cope alone. We're in this together."

Although all Alexa wanted was for everyone to leave so she, Bethany and Charlotte could be alone, she smiled and said everything that was expected of her. It seemed to appease Ben and Sam to a degree, though she was sure they realised she was putting it on for their benefit. The only consolation was Hayley and Brett both urging them to ignore the pressure. They had copped the same kind of stuff from people over the last couple of years.

When it became clear Sam was going to stay wherever Bethany was, Alexa was selfishly glad they decided to go back to Sam's. From the way Bethany hugged her and Charlotte on her departure, Alexa was sure she was doing it for her. "Sorry, Lex," whispered Bethany. "Never wanted them to say all that. I just want to see you smile again. I want you to have what I've got. I hate that I stole it from you."

Alexa was about to refute that, hating that Bethany still held on to guilt about their pasts. Then Bethany's eyes flicked to Sam, and Alexa could not help but smile. "You didn't steal him from me, Angel," said Alexa, stroking Bethany's face. "I think sometimes I found him for you. You guys are so good together. Trust me, you've never stolen anything from me."

Bethany smiled broadly, engulfing Alexa in a crushing hug before dancing to the door where Sam was waiting for her. The tenderness with which Sam took Bethany's hand and kissed her as he walked her to the car was so sweet that it helped to erase some of the annoyance Alexa still felt towards him.

"She's happy, isn't she?" asked Alexa, sitting down on the lounge with Charlotte.

"Yeah, I think so," nodded Charlotte. "I try and catch her out sometimes, see if it's fake, but I don't think it is."

"You think she's doing something we're not?"

"Complying with people," smirked Charlotte. "We know it doesn't always help her, but she seems to know how to work them – make them think she's doing what they want. We're not good at that."

"No, we're definitely crap at that," smiled Alexa. Then she realised she was smiling – genuinely – and there was no one around to see it. No one would even believe her if she told them.

"Did you think you were doing that bad?" asked Charlotte, her voice losing its playful edge.

"I knew I wasn't super happy. I just wanted to focus on the things that could go well – you know, uni, friends, us."

"Me too. But somehow when we say it, it's different to what they want – even though it sounds exactly the same to me," said Charlotte, astounding Alexa with the accuracy of her assessment. "I know you don't want to talk about it, but I miss Marc. He seemed to understand – like cos he knew you so well that he got me too. Used to make me feel like I was making progress, even if I wasn't doing that well. You think it was just cos he's a teacher?"

"I don't know." Alexa's voice was barely above a whisper. It was hard to listen to Marcus being spoken about in such an affectionate way. Charlotte had just encapsulated one of his very best traits and it made Alexa miss him so much more than any of Bethany's comments about him being her soulmate ever had.

"I know everyone else thinks I'm doing bad, but I don't," said Charlotte firmly, as though she had finally found the courage to disagree with them. "It's just not that easy to feel grateful for shit when things always turn out bad and you're waiting for everything else to turn to crap. Hasn't so far. That's cos of you, but sometimes I feel so ungrateful. I wish I could repay you somehow. You never even had to talk to me and if I'd never met you I'd be on the streets all alone."

"You are repaying me," said Alexa earnestly, grabbing Charlotte's hands. "You just being around – no, I mean, doing well at school, working and making lots of friends. I'm sorry I haven't shown you how happy it makes me having you around. You being here – for me and Bethy. We love having you as our sister."

"So you really do consider me to be like your sister?" asked Charlotte tentatively.

"No. Not like. Are," replied Alexa forcefully. "You are our sister. That's a done deal. So's Hayley and Brett. So you'd better not have any issues being one of five. The five of us – it's unbreakable. You're a part of that, okay."

"Yeah, okay," smiled Charlotte. "And let's give this whole grateful shit a go. How hard can it be?"

Harder than it appeared was the answer. To Charlotte and Alexa, it felt as if Ben and Sam had an intricate web of double standards that was almost impossible to navigate. If they studied too hard, they were not being social enough. If they were out of the house too much, they were avoiding the family. If they were too depressed then they were giving into their melancholy, yet if they appeared too happy then they were denying their true emotions.

Although Charlotte was not really the focus of the surveillance, she often copped the worst of the comments, as though Ben and Sam were blaming her for Alexa's moods and behaviour. That frustrated Alexa more, though it was nothing to the hurt she felt when Bethany took sides with Sam and Ben.

"I can't do it any more, Charlotte, I can't," cried Alexa, slamming the door behind her as she rushed into Charlotte's room and away from yet another conversation about her mood. "What the hell do they want from us?"

"Why do you think I've been in here all night?" muttered Charlotte, true despair in her voice.

"I just need – I don't even know any more – l almost don't feel like I can stay here. I know they love us and we're probably being so ungrateful and selfish, but – why can't they just let us live our lives?"

"Makes you want to run away, doesn't it?"

"Char, that's perfect. Let's do that!" cried Alexa.

"Seriously?" questioned Charlotte. Alexa nodded feverishly. "Bit drastic. And where'd we go? You don't want to leave them forever. I know you."

"Not forever, but why do we all have to live together like this? I want a life – my life. I don't know what that life is yet, but it doesn't feel like it's here any more."

"What about uni? School?" asked Charlotte hesitantly.

"There are universities all over the world – and schools. I can get a job. The only barriers are the ones we put in front of us," said Alexa.

"But where?" asked Charlotte, and this time Alexa got the feeling that the plan to leave was no longer the stumbling block.

"Wherever we want. We can start researching it – maybe take a taster trip to check things out," Alexa replied, feeling freer every minute they spoke of their escape.

"Do we have to decide now?" queried Charlotte tentatively.

"How about we think about it for a bit," Alexa suggested. "If we find we're spending heaps of time thinking about it – planning for it – then we seriously do it. But just keep it secret. If you thought the hovering was bad now, just wait til they find out about this."

Alexa and Charlotte did not talk about their plan again for two weeks, when they finally had the house to themselves. That was when they each discovered just how much they were relying on this new future to get them through each day.

"Language is the main barrier," said Charlotte, laying out her research on her bed. "But I'd love to live somewhere like Rome."

"We can learn a new language," smiled Alexa, picking up the world map. "New York has a much bigger circle than the other cities."

"Beth thinks she's found my dad. He's a lawyer. I mean, he probably doesn't want me either."

"I can talk to Peter," said Alexa softly. This was something Alexa knew nothing about, but there were strangely few pangs of jealousy. Bethany was a wonderful confidant and she was glad Charlotte had her too. "Maybe we can get him to make an appointment – make it seem more official. Then you can decide what you want to do after you've met him."

"Probably no point. He won't want me," mumbled Charlotte.

"Maybe," shrugged Alexa. "But New York would still be worth checking out, right? I mean, it's supposed to be one of the best cities in the world. If I confess that I'd like to go there, will you come with me?"

"Yeah, definitely," smiled Charlotte broadly.

Alexa hugged Charlotte briefly before grabbing the map again. Their plan started to come together immediately, becoming more definite by the day. They would leave for their scouting trip as soon as Alexa finished her end of semester exams. When they would leave for good was less clear, but neither of them felt as though it would not happen eventually.

Though they never spoke of their plan to, or even in front of, anyone else, their newfound focus and determination soon became apparent. Ben and Sam were impressed by their behaviour and attitude. It was ironic.

There was only one person who did not see the situation through their own biased filter. The concern and fear that filled Bethany's eyes at times told Alexa that Bethany knew something was going on, but that she had no idea what the plan was. It made Alexa wonder if she would take Bethany with her when they did leave for good.

"What's going on?" Bethany eventually asked. Unfortunately, Ben and Sam were also sitting down to dinner with them – as they always were these days.

"Nothing," replied Alexa firmly.

"I guess we're just curious how this change of heart came about," said Ben, though Alexa had the strange feeling he was saying that to support Bethany more than to interrogate her.

"Me and Charlotte just started taking on everyone's advice," Alexa replied, trying to stay calm. "We started thinking further ahead, not just on what's happening now. Making plans for the future."

"What kind of plans?" asked Bethany, her voice wavering.

"Finish uni. Get a job," answered Alexa casually, wishing she could speak to Bethany more honestly about this.

Bethany was placated – until she found Charlotte's map. Charlotte managed to calm the situation with a story about plans for a gap year overseas when she finished school, but even that was too much for Bethany. Bethany was suddenly telling Alexa – multiple times a day – how much she still needed her and how she could not survive without her. It had the opposite effect. Alexa's life had become too hard. She could no longer live her life and Bethany's, and if Bethany insisted on that, the only outcome would be a premature end to both their lives.

"Lex!"

Alexa and Charlotte turned to each other as they sat on Alexa's bed. Hurriedly packing away their stuff, they were at the top of the stairs when Sam reached them, panic in his eyes.

"Lex, you have to help me," gasped Sam. "I thought it was just a craving – a bad one – but I can't calm her. I thought I was getting to be okay at it, but she's losing it. I don't understand."

Alexa bolted down the stairs and into Bethany's room. Bethany was pacing agitatedly. When their eyes met, Alexa's heart sunk. She rushed at Bethany. The imposter was not inside her, it was outside, tugging her away from them. Despite Bethany's best efforts to resist, Alexa grabbed her and wrestled her to the ground.

"Where is it, Bethy? Where is it?" asked Alexa forcefully, pinning Bethany's hands to the bed as she tried to break free. Bethany did not answer, so Alexa began to frisk her. "Please, Angel. Don't let it take you from me again."

Something flickered in Bethany's eyes. Her body loosened. When Bethany's eyes met Alexa's, Alexa sighed. She released Bethany's hands. Bethany did not resist when Alexa shoved her hand straight down the front of her pants and pulled out a small foil package.

"It's okay," said Alexa gently. Heart beating so hard it hurt, Alexa placed the foil back in Bethany's hands. "It's up to you. You want to take it?" Bethany's eyes widened. Alexa felt sick. They would have to begin their battle all over again if Bethany said yes. Thankfully, there was only a moment of hesitation before Bethany shook her head.

Without looking at anyone, Bethany pushed off the bed and out to the bathroom. She opened the foil and flicked the powder into the sink. Turning on the tap, she washed the heroin away.

"What happened, Angel?" asked Alexa.

Bethany collapsed on the floor and hugged her knees to her chest. Alexa dropped next to her and held her tight as she rocked back and forth. She had never wanted to push Bethany to this.

"I never wanted to take it," gasped Bethany, tears spilling down her cheeks. "Never bought it to take it. Just wanted – in case – I don't know. I'm sorry, Lex. All I could think about was that I had it. All day. Every minute."

"I know. But the important thing is you fought it. You fought so hard. You didn't give in."

"You don't hate me?" asked Bethany, looking into Alexa's eyes.

"Never, Angel," answered Alexa sincerely. "Never, ever."

"Promise."

"On my life."

Bethany nodded, burying her head in Alexa's shoulder. They stayed there for a long time. Even when they did move, it was only as far as Bethany's bedroom, where they curled up together on the bed. No one disturbed them until the next morning when Sam arrived. Alexa could not blame him when she saw how terrible he looked. He sat down on the bed, stroking Bethany's hair as she slept. Bethany woke almost immediately, scuttling away from him.

"All I want to know is if this is the life you want to live – here, clean, with me," asked Sam in a broken voice. "Just tell me that and I'll be here to get you through – as long as it's what you want."

"You don't want to be with a heroin addict," replied Bethany, tearing Alexa's heart. She was giving Sam an out and Alexa hoped he did not take it.

"I don't want to be with a heroin user," said Sam firmly. "Through no fault of your own, you were born a heroin addict. Up til yesterday you'd chosen not to be a heroin user. If you still don't want to use, I'll help you fight this. Just tell me what you want."

"I want to be a good person," answered Bethany, her voice breaking as tears tumbled from her eyes. "I don't want to use drugs. I don't want to hurt people I love. I don't want you to hate me."

Sam scrambled across the bed and took Bethany's face in his hands. Alexa rolled out of the bed. It was strange watching him profess his love to someone other than herself, especially when he was demonstrating all the traits that had made her love him in the first place.

Trudging back up to her own bed, it took Alexa a while to realise that Charlotte was waiting for her. "How's Beth?"

"Not good. Okay, but – I don't know, Char. I've never seen her like that. She's never brought drugs into the house before."

"We still going? We can't leave her like this."

"I know," replied Alexa softly.

There was still time to make that decision, and for the next couple of weeks Alexa wavered wildly over what the best course of action was. If she thought only of herself, the answer was easy. But ignoring Bethany's needs was not something she knew how to do. Then came the news Alexa had been dreading.

Amy was out on a nursing placement for her course. It seemed fated that she would somehow be placed in the hospital – the very maternity ward – where Lucy gave birth prematurely to a daughter. Amy was even involved in the care of Marcus's daughter. Although Amy said little about the situation – just telling Alexa of the birth was saying too much – she did let Alexa know that it did not appear as if Lucy and Marcus were romantically involved.

Bethany knew nothing about this so continued to quietly assure

Alexa that Marcus would be back as soon as the baby was born and he had visitation sorted out. Alexa was not sure how long that would take, but if Marcus had any intention of returning, he was giving no sign of it. With each day that passed and Marcus stayed silent, Alexa's will to stay and live this life of pain diminished. The result was that her plans for her departure became more concrete by the day.

"I'm sorry I keep asking you for all these favours," said Alexa, as she sat across the desk from Peter. It had taken her entire shift to muster the courage to ask for his assistance. It had resulted in questions – and confessions – but Peter said nothing of her planned trip.

"You have given me the number of an American lawyer and want me to call and make an appointment for you to see him when you're in the States. Alexa, if all my clients wanted favours like that I would be a very happy man."

"So I'm not being a pain?"

"Far from it," smiled Peter. "Though you did steal my thunder slightly. I'd been waiting for the chance to speak to you."

"About what?"

"Well, you know that we've been going through our archives," said Peter.

"You wouldn't let me help," muttered Alexa, still feeling the sting of that rejection. It was one of the few times she had put herself forward to work with other staff, but when Peter had found her sorting through the archive boxes he all but dragged her away.

"Unlike my other staff, you are one of my clients. It wasn't appropriate," said Peter, repeating what he had said before. "Some of those files relate to your family."

"So what did you need to talk to me about?" asked Alexa, pulling her arms around her chest. She hated the idea that her own demons were lurking in this building.

"A couple of things, actually. The first one is about Beth," said Peter somewhat tentatively, making Alexa's heart stammer. "Now that the Whites are back in your life – well I guess I've been waiting for you to storm into my office to confront me. The fact that you haven't means that no one has told you."

"Told me what?" growled Alexa, barely keeping her composure. She was sick of being left in the dark.

Peter sighed heavily and sat forward. "When you came back from the city – after trying to set up a place for you and Beth – I became worried about the two of you – about your survival. I didn't want to see Beth die on the streets and I knew if anything happened to her you would follow soon after." Peter stopped talking and Alexa had to urge him to continue. "I wracked my brain for days trying to think of what I could do. I still couldn't offer you a home or a family. I just – I bought Bethany the heroin – well, paid for it, anyway. I paid for the needles. I financed everything she needed to stay high. I paid the rent at the boarding house. I paid for it all. I visited her every week, though she was not always there, and I made her write to you and tell you not to come back, because I knew you would. Maybe not immediately, but I knew you would eventually."

"Every week?" whispered Alexa.

"Yes. I didn't always enjoy it. Bethany on drugs is not – you know the difference – but she was alive. I will never know if I did the right thing – giving a fourteen-year-old heroin – but she was going to take it whether I was around or not. I thought it better she had clean needles and didn't have to work the way you did. And that you would never have to work that way again either."

"Then how did she get into so much debt?"

"I'm not sure she ever did," said Peter, clearly uncertain about this point. "Money did go missing. I think Leo was stealing from her. Perhaps creating a debt at the same time."

"I don't understand. Then why'd she give him Hayley – tell him where they lived," cried Alexa, more confused than ever.

"I don't believe she did," replied Peter with firm sincerity, and Alexa knew he was telling the truth – or what he believed to be the truth. "There's little doubt Leo found out the Whites' address from Beth, but I still don't believe she ever intentionally gave it to him. She refused to talk much on that point. I think he either tricked or tortured it out of her."

"But why?"

"Leo told Beth that he was going after you. That's why she had the gun. Everything she had went to buying that – almost everything. She never sold the locket. I think that was the one thing that retained the bond between you, but Leo used it against her. It was her weakness and he exploited it. You know as well as I do that Bethany was just a toy to him. Maybe she knew that too. She went to your school prepared to kill him to protect you. When she found out you weren't there, she tried to get money from your roommates to pay Leo off – to save you."

Alexa closed her eyes as memories of that night flicked by, but this time she did not feel sorry for herself. She hated herself. She hated that she ever believed Bethany would put them in danger and the anger she felt towards Bethany – the anger she had never been able to fully release – began to slide away.

"When Beth found out what happened she was angry and confused. Leo didn't tell her the truth. He told her he found you and that you willingly paid off the debt by sleeping with him. When she asked where you were, he told her that the last time he saw you, you were alive. I don't know if that was why he didn't kill you. He had lied to Bethany enough that he surely could have lied about that. I'm sure he never expected you to survive the fall or the cold."

"Then why was she given such a harsh sentence?" cried Alexa. "If you knew all this why didn't we fight? I would've fought for her. You knew that! Ben knew that and you kept me from her!"

"The sentence was mainly for shooting the girl," replied Peter calmly. "She was made an example of, there's no doubt about that, but Beth decided not to fight. It took a while to convince her that Leo had lied to her. I don't think she wanted to believe it. She didn't want to be responsible for what happened to you. Beth felt very guilty. And she was scared. She was scared that if you got her off, she would have nowhere to go. She was scared she would put you back in the same situation that almost killed you. None of us expected the sentence she received. A different judge – I'm sorry."

"I hated her. All this time. I hated her and she never did anything wrong," Alexa gasped as tears rolled down her cheeks.

"You never truly hated her," replied Peter soothingly. "We both know you're not capable of that, but perhaps now there doesn't have to be this unspoken gulf between the two of you."

"But how can I forgive myself? The Whites – they all understood. Everyone understood, but me."

"They understood, because I told them what I just told you."

"When?"

"When I gave them the money from you."

"But I told you that I wanted that to be anonymous," said Alexa, though she knew that hardly mattered now.

"I had some dealings with them while working as Bethany's

lawyer. I needed information only they could give me," replied Peter in his impeccably calm manner. "They knew who I was. Now, you told me that I was to give the money to the Whites. You refused to let anyone else handle it or even know about the money. I never told them who the was money from, but they were capable of making an intelligent guess."

"Did you stay in contact with them?" asked Alexa coyly, wondering how his answer would differ to Pam and Karl's.

"No. They stayed in contact with me."

"Did you tell them about me being in the hospital last year?"

"Yes. No. No, but for all intents and purposes, yes. It was my information that allowed them to know where you were. The media never referred to you by your current name. Sean King, he was well known. What happened to you as a child. It was a very big story. I know you don't want to know this, but you look a lot like your father. They saw his photo and asked me what hospital you were in."

"I need to get out of here for a bit," said Alexa, pushing out of her seat.

"That's okay. Just let me give you the other stuff," said Peter, rising from his chair.

"What stuff?"

"Some of your mother's belongings that were in our archives."

"Things I gave to you?" asked Alexa, struggling to think of what Peter would have of their mother's.

"Do you remember giving me anything?" asked Peter. Alexa shook her head. "Beth was in hospital. You were in foster care. There was no one else to manage her possessions."

"So what is there?"

"Just some personal effects. It's wasn't my place to decide what was kept and what was discarded," said Peter almost apologetically. Perhaps he understood just how much she did not want these things. "The box is in Marian's office. You can collect it on your way out."

Alexa nodded and headed to the door. "I can't come back here for a while," she said, not turning to look at Peter.

"I understand."

All Alexa could do was nod. There was no one in Marian's office and she was glad. There was a box on the desk with her mother's name on it. She grabbed it and walked towards the door, but as she turned she noticed another box sitting on the floor. It looked the same except that the labelling was slightly different. It was also sealed – heavily. New tape had been plastered over the old, which looked intact, if a little fragile.

With a heavy sigh, Alexa collected the other box. She did not want these things, but Bethany had been through enough. It would make her happy to have some of their mother's belongings. More than once Bethany had lamented the fact that they had nothing to remember their mother by – not even a photo.

Arriving home while the house was empty, Alexa tipped the contents of the first box on to her bed and began sorting. There really was not much. Some cheap jewellery and a few trinkets. It amazed Alexa that this was all her mother's life amounted to. Then she remembered the other box. It struck her as odd that it was sealed so solidly, but it had been much heavier.

Using scissors to cut the tape, Alexa was surprised by how quickly she recognised the contents. Diaries. Hers. Her mother's. Her father's. Grabbing hers first, she felt sick with the contents. They were filled with professions of love – from her to Sean – written in her own hand. All of them. Every single one. Grabbing her father's, they were similarly annotated. This time there were pictures too. They started innocently enough, but as the years went on they became more graphic, more intimate. Then it struck Alexa. Sean was not taking these photos. Someone was watching them. Someone else was there while he groped her and raped her. Unable to stop herself, Alexa grabbed her mother's diaries. Her mother had known the entire time. Alexa had been all but bred for Sean's pleasure. Bethany was her mother's consolation.

Shaking, Alexa could not decide what to do. She could not keep these things in her house. But she could never let Bethany find them either. Bethany had lost too much already. It was not fair to strip her of the little that remained. Throwing everything back into the boxes, Alexa stumbled with them out to the backyard. Bethany had bought a clay urn for the winter so they could enjoy the backyard on even the coldest of days. Filling it with kindling and paper, Alexa lit it and waited for the fire to take hold.

That was when she noticed the photos. The lid of the small box had dislodged. Alexa gasped as she flicked through them. Most of them were normal family photos, but intersperse between them – as if they were nothing unusual – were ones of her and her father.

"Stop! Stop, stop!"

Hands suddenly grabbed Alexa's as she tossed a stack of photos into the fire. Alexa felt herself being restrained and hugged at the same time. Peter was holding her tight, his heart beating so hard she could feel it thumping against her chest. But with Peter restraining her, there was no one to stop Bethany pulling out the contents of the boxes.

"What's this!" cried Bethany. "You gave her mum's stuff to burn! How could you? I've asked a thousand times about her stuff and you've lied to me!"

"Beth, I am not lying to you now. That box of books – you and Alexa were never supposed to see that," said Peter in a strained voice. "Your mother never wanted you to see it. It was supposed to stay sealed until after all your deaths. I have a very big problem right now and I'm begging you not to make it worse. Let me take that box. Alexa was only ever supposed to take the other one."

Perhaps Peter knew Bethany was never going to obey such a request, because he did not let go of Alexa as Bethany reached out for the diaries. Bethany did the opposite to Alexa. She went for her mother's first.

"Just because our mother loved me better doesn't mean you get to keep her stuff from me," spat Bethany viciously.

Peter held Alexa tighter, as if he feared what she might do, but Alexa had no idea what she would do if he let go of her – until she saw the expression on Bethany's face change. Bethany scrambled through the diaries, flicking through each of them. Alexa felt herself reaching out for Bethany, knowing she had to shield her from this.

"No, she needs to see this," said Peter, but when Bethany started moving towards the fire he finally loosened his grip. "Run. To your room. Go. Now."

Peter pushed Alexa towards the house. Her brain was not working well enough to do anything but comply. When she reached the top floor, she rushed to a window overlooking the backyard. There were diaries and photos sprawled everywhere and Bethany was shaking and crying in Peter's arms. They were there for a long time. When they did finally move, Peter collected all the photos and diaries, placing them back into their box, while Bethany walked over to the other box of her mother's belongings. It made Alexa sick to think that Bethany still wanted that stuff after all she had seen, but just as she was about to turn away she noticed Bethany trying to break and smash all the cheap jewellery before flinging it into the fire. When that was done, Bethany grabbed one of the pool chairs and smashed it to the ground. Over and over. Again and again. Until there was nothing left.

It took another ten minutes, but Bethany eventually arrived at Alexa's bedroom door, tears still streaming down her face. Alexa wished she could believe Bethany's love for their mother had finally died, but was not sure even this was enough to break that bond.

"I'm sorry," said Alexa when the silence stretched on. "I wanted to keep the little stuff for you, but after I saw the diaries I needed to burn it all. I felt so guilty over hating you for Leo that I was going to let you keep her stuff, but I couldn't. I'm sorry."

"What do you mean hating me?" gasped Bethany. Alexa choked up a sob and confessed all she had felt and all that Peter had set right. "So you picked me – looked after me – all this time, even though you really thought I set Leo on Hayley?" asked Bethany with wide eyes. Alexa nodded shamefully. "And today you were going to burn our mother's diaries to keep the truth from me and let me live on in happy ignorance – just to spare me pain?"

"You don't ever deserve to be in pain. I'm so sorry, Bethy."

Bethany lunged at Alexa, hugging her tight and pulling her to the bed. They cried as they apologised over and over, but it would never be enough, because it was not their sins that needed to be forgiven.

"We don't need them," said Bethany firmly, her tears finally running dry. "We have each other and we have Ben. They can rot in hell. As long as I have you and Ben, I don't need anyone else."

"Yeah," replied Alexa, squeezing Bethany's arms to her as her heart ached. She did not feel as though she had Ben. She had Bethany and that would have to suffice, though she was not sure it would.

Heavy clouds let Alexa sleep in well beyond her normal time. Bethany must have already woken as the bed beside her was empty. It took a second for the memories of the day before to seep back through Alexa's brain, but when they did she found the desire to get out of bed desert her. Her last exam was tomorrow and she and Charlotte were booked on a plane the day after. They would only be away a little over a month, but so far they had told no one. She and Charlotte would have to make some tough decisions very quickly, but Alexa was not sure if she could sacrifice both her own and Charlotte's future happiness for Bethany – a previously unimaginable concept.

Walking down the stairs, Alexa heard Bethany and Ben speaking. It was clear Ben knew what happened yesterday and Alexa wondered if Peter had told him. It did not sound like Bethany had just explained the situation. Sitting on the steps out of sight, Alexa listened to what they were saying. She wanted to know how Bethany was really coping and if Ben would be enough of a support base for her when she left.

"How are you feeling?" asked Ben.

"Empty, betrayed … did you know?" asked Bethany in the most accusing voice she had ever heard her use with Ben.

"Not for sure. I suspected," answered Ben gravely.

"You didn't like my mother, did you?"

"No."

Ben did not elaborate despite Bethany staying silent. Perhaps he, like Alexa, suspected Bethany had not yet dissolved all her tender feelings for her mother and was desperately clinging to the hope some miracle would absolve her.

"I did," said Bethany eventually. "I loved her so much and always hated Lex for hating her. But Lex never tried to take her away from me. I remember Mum being mean to her, but Lex never tried to turn me against her. Never made me feel as though I had to choose and all that time she knew. She knew and never even tried to stop it. Lex was right all along."

Alexa could hear Bethany crying and was sure Ben was holding her to his chest, tenderly embracing her the way he always did with Bethany – and never with her.

"How's Alexa?" asked Ben, his voice so controlled.

"She's okay. She just takes it all on as usual."

Alexa could not help but smirk at the dual visions her family had of her. On one hand they thought of her as controlled and measured, always taking everything in her stride. Yet on the other side, she was emotionally unstable, never dealing with anything and refusing to move on.

"I don't think it'll be that easy for her," said Ben in a thick voice.

"At least she always hated the bitch. I loved her – more than Lex sometimes. Why didn't you tell me, Dad? We talked about her so much. Why didn't you just tell me?"

Alexa could see that Ben could not answer – not when she was standing at the top of the steps staring at him with wide, hurt eyes. "Alexa, wait," he cried, but the sound of Ben's voice tore through her chest like a knife as she dashed back up the stairs.

Pacing back and forth, Alexa tried to control her gasping breaths and the overwhelming desire to leave and never, ever come back. Ben entered her bedroom ahead of Bethany, who he kept behind him, as if protecting her. That only infuriated Alexa more. Bethany looked confused and Alexa could not honestly believe Bethany would think she would be okay with this.

"Alexa, please, let me explain," said Ben, putting his arm out as if to place it calmingly on her shoulder.

Alexa pulled away from him. "When did she start calling you Dad?" Alexa demanded. Ben stammered, but could not articulate an answer. "When!"

"While she was still in gaol."

Anger and fury tore through Alexa's heart. They had never told her. They had this connection and they never told her, or even thought to invite her in.

"He's always wanted to be our father, Lex. Don't shut him out," said Bethany, moving out from behind Ben.

"Shut him out? You're the ones that have shut me out! Why didn't you tell me? If it was no big deal, if you wanted me to be included, why didn't you tell me? Why keep it a secret?"

"Calm down. We've never shut you out. You won't let yourself in. When are you going to start trusting people?" countered Bethany.

Bethany's arguments were so flawed that Alexa wanted to scream. "Trust? Honestly? What reason do I have to trust anyone? Tell me who should I trust?"

"Us … Ben. God, he's my father. He's our father."

Alexa turned and looked at Ben. He looked scared, yet hopeful. Then the images of her and Sean together swirled in her mind. The touch of Sean's hands on her body shivered through her and she could not help but scream out in response, "You are not my father!"

"No, I am not your father," said Ben in a low, hurt voice. He turned and left the room without another glace.

Bethany stared angrily at Alexa. "That wasn't fair. He's done more for us than anyone."

"He left us!" replied Alexa, trying to cover her pain with anger. "He left us and sent us back to our mother – the one who hated me and poisoned you."

"He wants to be our father now – make up for that," replied

Bethany, trying to speak calmly as tears slipped down her cheeks.

"If he'd truly wanted to be our father he'd have nothing to make up for."

Alexa turned away to stop Bethany from trying to change her mind. Right then, her mind had never been more set. Bethany had found her place in the world. She had managed to put their past behind her. Now Alexa had to do the same.

Chapter Eleven

BEN TRUDGED THROUGH the front door of his apartment and headed straight to the fridge. He did not turn on any lights. From the lounge, Alexa watched as he pulled out the single bottle of beer sitting centre stage of his fridge and placed it on the counter. It made her heart stammer. Perhaps this was a very bad idea. She had finished her exams that afternoon. By morning she would be on a plane out of the country. She knew she could not leave like this, but the fear that pulsed through her body as she watched Ben stare at the beer made her wonder if this would be yet another thing she had to escape.

Ben stared at the bottle for almost five minutes, before finally putting it back in the fridge, swigging instead from a half-empty bottle of Coke. Walking out to the lounge room, he jumped back in fright when he turned on the light to see Alexa sitting bolt upright on his lounge. "What are you doing here?" he asked in a kind and gentle voice.

"I needed to see you. Can you sit down and talk to me for a bit?"

Ben nodded and moved next to Alexa. Tears began tumbling down Alexa's cheeks as soon as he looked into her eyes. She had put him through so much and in reality he had done nothing but be there for her – always.

"I don't know what's wrong with me," Alexa sobbed. "I want you to be my father more than you can ever know. I just can't let you in. I don't even know why." Ben squeezed her hand, but stayed silent. "I want it so much it hurts, yet the thought of you being my father scares me even more. Why am I like this? Why can't I be like Bethy? Why can't I trust you?"

"This isn't all your fault. I'm as much to blame," replied Ben in a heavy voice.

"No —"

"Let me finish," he interrupted. "You don't trust me, because I betrayed you. I never betrayed Beth, and you gave her the capacity to love and trust; something that's been severely damaged in you. I'm going to tell you something I haven't even told Beth – about how you came to be in my life."

Alexa could not help but pull away from Ben. Her eyes dried up and she wiped away the remaining tears. She knew this was not going to be a happy story and wondered how it would affect her plans to never return home.

"When you walked into that police station looking for me, I was rapt. Penny and I could never have children. I can never have children. We were young. We'd spoken about adopting, and in those hours talking you out of the pipe I fell in love with you and Beth. I wanted to take you in, but they put you into foster care. It was just standard procedure. By the next morning you were both missing again. I walked out the front to drive to the station and I see the two of you playing in the gutter across the road.

"You just smiled awkwardly, knowing you'd done the wrong thing. Bethany waved frantically. I took you both inside and Penny cooked a huge breakfast. The pair of you ate about three helpings. I'd never seen so much food disappear into such little stomachs."

"How did we find you?" asked Alexa curiously.

"I have no idea," smiled Ben. "I eventually worked out that you asked if I lived near you – asked me my favourite number and if that was the number of my house. And all these other little, indirect questions. Still don't know how you managed to put it all together to find my house and travel there. You were only five.

"But I was so glad you came. I thought you must've loved me the way I did the two of you. You asked if you could stay, but again you were taken into care. You ran away every time. Back to me. By the third day they were considering letting you stay, but you wouldn't talk to the police so I made you a deal. You could stay with me if you told us what had really happened at home.

"You agreed. I sat there as we questioned you for over eight hours. You told us everything. I'd never been so shocked, or proud, in my life. The things you'd endured and your bravery at recounting it. I never wanted to see you go through anything like that again. I spoke to Penny and convinced her to foster the two of you, with the hope of one day adopting you both. It took a while, but it wasn't long before she fell in love with Beth." Alexa smirked sadly. "She liked you as well," Ben added quickly. "We started you in school when you trusted Penny enough with Beth and you were happy. We even took you to the zoo. I've still never seen your face light up so much. It was one of the best days of my life as well. I felt as though I had everything I could ever hope for. We bought you a book and Bethany a toy. I remember the look of pure surprise and this most amazing joy on your face. I think they were the first presents you'd ever been given."

"What happened? Where'd it all go so wrong?"

"Your mother wanted Beth back, but that meant both of you – you couldn't have one without the other. She'd been through rehab and was clean. I didn't want to give you back, but there was pressure from everyone to give you up. You begged me to let you stay. 'I'll be good. I promise. And I'll take care of Bethy. You won't have to do anything. Please, let us stay,' you said. I cried all night thinking about it. In the end the courts said your mother had the right to take the two of you. When it came time for you to leave, your eyes turned to stone. Beth was excited about going home. She'd missed her mother and so for her sake you said nothing. All you let pass was a single tear. After you'd gone I found the book we'd bought you and the toy we'd given Beth. She never noticed, but I knew you left them behind on purpose.

"I tried to keep track of you, but Penny got upset and everyone at work said I should leave it be. Sean was gone and your mother was clean. You'll be fine, they said. The next time I saw you was in court. You looked straight at me without a flicker of recognition. You'd forgotten everything and everyone, including me. My heart broke, but as far as I knew you were happy at home.

"Now you see. You do know how to be happy. It was a long time ago, but you know and there's a reason you've never fully trusted me. I've kept my distance too. I never quite forgave myself for everything that happened to you. Beth can love and trust. It was easy with her and I never felt as guilty. She never pleaded with me to keep her safe. You did and I let you down."

"Could you have kept me?" asked Alexa.

"No," replied Ben sadly, shaking his head. "The removal order was only temporary and there was no case to make it permanent. The fact that there was some suggestion of police involvement in Sean's escape from the hospital didn't help. I know I had no choice but to let you go, but that never stopped me feeling guilty. I knew if anything ever happened to you it'd be my fault." Tears were sliding down Alexa's face. She could recall none of what Ben told her, but the emotion of it rang true. "Wait here a minute," said Ben, walking to his bedroom. When he returned, he was clutching a hardcover children's book. "I used to read it when I thought about you, wonder where you were and how you were doing." Alexa took the book. It was in perfect condition. Inside were drawings and pictures of animals with a description of their diets and habitats. "You had it virtually memorised in two days. I didn't know five-year-olds could really read let alone memorise books."

Alexa traced her fingers over the cover. "Who taught me to read?"

"Your father," answered Ben softly.

"Between raping me?"

"Something like that. It's the strange thing about human behaviour. If Sean hadn't been an incestuous paedophile, then you would've called him a good father," said Ben, looking disgusted. "You were a very intelligent little girl. You could read and write. You were amazingly dextrous. Sean was a very intelligent man. Perhaps too intelligent – or just too aware of it. He was too good for other people, even though he couldn't keep a job. But he was charming and had a way with people. Very manipulative. Very arrogant."

"What was my mother like?"

"Stupid. Senseless was perhaps a better descriptor," added Ben, softening his tone. "The kind of person you just wanted to shake some sense into. I think under the right circumstances – the right guidance – she could've been a very good person, but she was easily corrupted. Sean was much older than her. He was twenty-eight when he met her. She was just sixteen. By the time she was eighteen they were married and she was pregnant with you."

"Do we have grandparents?" asked Alexa, deciding it was probably better to know it all now. There seemed no reason for secrets any longer.

"Yes. Somewhere. Sean's parents – it was never considered suitable to send you to them. Sean was bright, but he didn't come from a good family. I'm sure he always intended on making it out, but he somehow managed to sabotage his situations to bring him straight back down. Your mother's parents, they were prepared to take you, but not Bethany."

"What do you mean? Why?"

"I'm only speculating – putting together bits of information – but I think Sean taking you from your mother – I think that was the trigger for her drug abuse. There's no doubt Sean lured her in with a combination of sex and drugs, but it appeared to be recreational until after your birth. Over time, it appears as though he managed to normalise his behaviour towards you. Or perhaps that's why she hated you – to give her some way of making what he did to you acceptable.

"Bethany was the child your mother was supposed to have had with you, but Bethany was born addicted to heroin. Sean never really took drugs. He was the reason your mother never lost the two of you. He presented as the good parent who was taking care of the two of you and looking after your mother. It was a cover that was never exposed until your attack on him."

"But why did they want me and not Bethy? Everyone loves Bethy."

"Your mother came from a – what you might call a nicer family. They disapproved of Sean. Cut your mother off – or a combination of that and Sean dragging her away. They never wanted Bethany because she was born addicted to heroin. We did consider splitting you up. You refused. That was the end of it. Your grandparents were fickle. They did not take your rejection of them well. They never wanted anything to do with you after that."

"I don't want to know who they are," said Alexa firmly.

"That's what Bethany said," smiled Ben.

Alexa nodded and looked back down at the book. She flicked through the pages, hoping for some memory – a happy memory – to hold on to, but it triggered nothing. Between the back pages was a photograph. Alexa pulled it out and looked at the smiling faces. She had never seen a genuine smile on her face before. Her arms were around Ben's neck, his arm around her waist as she stood next to him. He was seated on a bench next to Penny, Bethany sitting happily on Penny's lap. Even then Bethany looked almost as big as Alexa. It was so hard to reconcile that photo with reality. It encapsulated the life Alexa had only been able to dream of, and though she recognised their faces, it did not seem real.

"Do you still want to be my father?" asked Alexa tentatively.

"More than anything," replied Ben, one of his hands cupping her cheek.

"Even after what I said to you?"

"I understand why you said those things."

"I wish you were my dad," gasped Alexa, tears once again slipping down her face. Ben pulled her into his arms with a sigh of relief. "Can I keep these?" she asked when Ben released her, holding the book and photo to her chest.

"They're all yours."

Alexa smiled slightly and nodded, hugging them tighter. Ben suddenly looked at her intensely, his hand grasping hers. "When do you leave?"

"Tomorrow," Alexa replied, not quite meeting his eyes. "Can I stay tonight, though?"

***

Marcus collapsed on the lounge, his hands covering his face. He could not remember being this exhausted in his life. Tracey's early birth had left him completely unprepared for her arrival. In truth, he was not sure the extra seven weeks would have made much difference. He had been unprepared because Lucy had been so difficult. As soon as Lucy had realised he was not taking her back, the trouble began. If she could have, Marcus was sure Lucy would have terminated, but that part of her plan backfired. She had waited until after she could easily terminate to tell him about the pregnancy, to ensure he could not force her to. In the end, she did her best to poison the pregnancy by drinking and smoking. Lucy's behaviour remained erratic right up to Tracey's premature birth, when she made the decision to give her up.

It turned out Lucy tried alternately to get pregnant to Marcus and her pilot ex-boyfriend, who had been on the periphery since she and Marcus got together. For some reason, Lucy had considered it fate that she fell pregnant to Marcus, as though it was a sign they should be together, when it was clear all she had ever wanted was to get back with her ex.

Marcus might have felt sorry for Lucy if not for the way she continued to manipulate him. Despite not wanting Tracey, Lucy made Marcus fight for her. The legal wrangling and compensation Lucy insisted on for giving up her parental rights broke Marcus financially. Although he had taken twelve months paternity leave, it was all unpaid. It left him no choice but to continue living with his parents. He had thought about going back to Alexa more than once. He knew if he turned up on her doorstep that she would take them in. He also knew she would automatically start mothering Tracey. It was not as though Marcus believed that would be a bad thing for Tracey, but Alexa was not even twenty-one. He could not make her a mother like this.

Everyday Marcus wondered whether he should call Alexa. He did not have to live with her to be in her life, but he knew he could not call her while he was in turmoil – not again. He did not know how long it would take to get settled with Tracey, but once he was, he would call. He wanted to see Alexa, hear her voice and have his friend back. Tracey made a relationship unrealistic, but they could be friends.

Truthfully, Marcus imaged two very different futures. The first was the one he knew was best for Alexa, where they would just be friends and she would go on to meet a great guy who she would marry and have her own children with. The second, selfish, future was the one where Alexa never found anyone else. In that future, when she had had her chance to be a carefree adult and was ready to settle down, Marcus would be there waiting for her.

Loud insistent banging on the front door saved Marcus from dwelling on the pain of the first future or the guilt of the second. Opening the door, Marcus was shocked, and yet somehow not surprised, by the sight of Bethany before him. He did not greet her, just turned and walked inside. Whatever conversation she wanted to have with him was not being had in the street.

"Who is it?" called Marcus's mother from the kitchen.

Marcus had to stop himself from rolling his eyes. "It's okay, Mum. It's for me," he replied, leading Bethany in the other direction towards the lounge room. "What can I do for you, Beth?"

"Come home – where you belong."

This was not the time for this conversation. Not when he had just been thinking about Alexa, missing her so much that even an argument with Bethany would make him feel happier than he was living with his parents. "I'm where I belong," Marcus muttered unconvincingly.

"Are you happy?" asked Bethany pointedly.

"Not as happy as I could be," Marcus confessed. "But I've made up my mind."

"She's leaving, you know," said Bethany, a slight wavering in her voice. "I don't think she has any intention of coming back."

"Where's she going?" asked Marcus, trying to keep his voice indifferent, but his plans for his future, even the terrible plan A, were being thrown into disarray and his heart was pounding erratically at the thought of Alexa leaving him alone.

"I don't know. She hasn't told me anything. She doesn't even think

I know, or that I know she's taking Charlotte."

"Then how do you know?"

"Because I know her better than myself," spat Bethany angrily. "And if you were there you'd know as well. Lucy can't keep the baby from you. I sent you the lawyer. Why won't you come back and make the both of you happy for once?"

"It's not that simple."

"I know you probably want to wait until the baby's born, but it can't be that far away. Just call her. Talk to her. Make her stay."

"Beth, I —"

A piercing cry suddenly filled the house. Marcus jumped from the lounge to Bethany's look of astonishment. Walking back into the room, Marcus held a tiny child in his arms, settling her with a bottle and gentle bouncing.

"This is my daughter," said Marcus, showing the baby to Bethany before sitting back down on the lounge.

"She's so small."

"She was premature."

"What's her name?"

"Tracey," answered Marcus, his heart skipping a beat.

Bethany smiled. "That's Lex's middle name."

"I know."

"You still love her, don't you?" asked Bethany tenderly.

"More than you could ever imagine."

"Then why are you here and not with us?"

"Because I can't do it to her."

"What?"

"Lump this burden on her. We've never kissed, never even held hands and you want me to walk into her life, when she's just twenty, and make her a mother."

"Alexa would never consider Tracey a burden."

"I know!" hissed Marcus. "She'd give up her entire life for Tracey. I don't want that. Maybe in a few years it'll be different."

"So you thought that one day you'd meet again and she'd accept Tracey as her own and maybe you'd even settle down and have your own children?" Marcus hated the way Bethany broke down his selfish future as though it was an itinerary. He had it mapped out much more romantically, though had to admit it would probably never play out that way. Nothing ever did with Alexa. "I can understand why you feel that way," said Bethany, her voice full of sympathy. "But it's never going to happen. Once she leaves, Lex's first priority will be ridding you from her heart and … Lex can never have children. You'll never have children with her, no one will. Her only chance is Tracey."

Marcus remained glued to the lounge as Bethany rose and left. If her only argument was that Alexa was determined to move on from him, Marcus could not have objected, but the idea of Alexa being robbed of motherhood – after everything else she had been forced to endure – was heartbreaking. Marcus knew in his heart the only mother he foresaw Tracey having was Alexa. What use was it keeping them apart for a few years so Alexa could grow up? Alexa was more mature than most of the women his age.

"What are we going to do?" Marcus asked Tracey as she slowly closed her eyes.

"Do about what?" asked his mother as she walked into the room. "What did that girl want? Cause trouble, no doubt." Marcus could not answer. "You want to stay away from them. I don't want Tracey influenced by people like them."

"Yes, because Lucy was mother of the year material," spat Marcus, rising from the lounge with Tracey still asleep in his arms. He hated that his mother had pushed him to say such a thing. He had determined that when it came time to tell Tracey about Lucy he would only ever do it in the most sympathetic terms.

"If it wasn't for your unhealthy obsession with your students, then perhaps she would have coped better."

Marcus opened his mouth, but nothing came out. The frequency with which his own mother all but accused him of being a paedophile was much higher than he wanted to admit. Pacing his room in an agitated manner, Marcus tried to determine what the right thing to do was. For a moment his heart truly softened for Lucy. If he chose Alexa, then Lucy would be the one to give them the gift of a child. However, Marcus could not think of Alexa without considering his mother's comments. He could never allow himself back into Alexa's life if he was going to hurt her the way so many others had.

It took Marcus half the day to convince himself he was not a predator. He thought of all the students before and after Alexa and the lack of sexual interest he had in any of them. He found many of the girls he taught interesting, engaging, personable and pretty, but not one of them had he found attractive. The deciding factor was

Charlotte. Charlotte was Alexa remade, yet if he was not attracted to her, then it could not have been Alexa's youth that had made her so appealing. Truthfully, he had never loved Alexa more than in the last two years. The less child-like she became, the more he loved her. However, looking down at Tracey as she lay peacefully on his chest, Marcus knew that he could not just move back in with Alexa. There had to be something more than all or nothing.

Marcus started devising a new plan. He would ask Alexa out. If he lived with his parents, there was no reason for Alexa to feel like a mother straight away. They could find their feet as a couple first and then they could become a family. It would not be perfect and Marcus could only imagine what disasters they would face as they tried to forge their relationship, but it no longer mattered. He would not give Alexa up – not as long as she would still have him.

It took another two days before Marcus could con his parents into taking care of Tracey so he could go out without them questioning his motives, though they remained suspicious. Driving towards his old home, Marcus had never felt so nervous. Scenarios, good and bad, raged through his head, to the extent that he bordered on tears when he thought of Alexa rejecting him and smiled stupidly when he imagined her kissing him.

Pulling up to the gate, Marcus wondered if his access code would still work. Bethany had put extensive security around the property after Sean's attack. Alexa had never even thought about locking the gates. Marcus could not help but smile when the gates swung open. He wondered if it was Alexa or Bethany who had allowed his code to remain in the system. He suspected Bethany.

It felt like a lifetime before someone answered the door. When Bethany's face greeted him, it was not the expression he had hoped to inspire.

"She's gone," said Bethany, not waiting for him to speak.

"Where?" Marcus managed to ask, though it did not matter.

"I don't know. She wouldn't tell me where or for how long." Bethany's voice broke as she spoke. "It was like it wasn't her any more. It was just like she needed to escape. I don't even know if she's coming back."

Marcus found himself leaning against the wall, unable to withstand the weight of his own body. He knew that look in Alexa. What shocked him was that she had left Bethany behind. He could only imagine the pain Alexa was in if she had needed to escape so desperately she had left her main reason for living behind.

Bethany watched Marcus leave. He looked like a broken man. She was surprised then that he called her the next day, asking if she had heard from Alexa, but she had no news to give him. Marcus continued to call every day, but there was nothing Bethany could say. Alexa wrote, but never gave any indication of where she was or when she was coming home. Sometimes she would let slip where she and Charlotte had been, but for the most part the emails were reminders of what needed to be done in her absence. It was the first time Bethany truly understood what Alexa and Charlotte did for her.

Never before had Bethany been required to cook and clean for herself. Her meals were always ready and she never shopped, except for personal pleasure. Her laundry basket periodically emptied itself and clean clothes returned, folded neatly on her bed. The communal rooms in the house were always clean. She had never even cleaned her own bathroom. Then there were the bills. They were more expensive than Bethany had ever given any thought to. When the first one came in, Bethany put it to the side, assuming Alexa would never leave her to deal with it. It was not the case. In response to her query, Alexa emailed a reply to let Bethany know she would have to take care of the house completely until their return. Bethany felt a sense of pride on paying that bill, but when others arrived she started to feel sick.

"I guess we know why Alexa used to complain about having no money," said Sam, sifting through the bills with her.

"I don't even know how I'm going to afford them all," moaned Bethany.

"It has to be possible. Alexa gets the same amount from the trust as you and she doesn't have a job. I know your apprenticeship doesn't pay much, but it's more than nothing."

"She gets Charlotte's rent," argued Bethany, sure that Alexa had more money somewhere. All this expense did not add up.

"Face it, Beth. Until Alexa returns, you're not going to be able to afford anything either," said Sam.

Suddenly Marcus's scathing assessment of her carefree lifestyle seemed somewhat generous. Ben tried to reassure Bethany it was not true and offered to assist in every way he could. He practically moved in at the end of Alexa's first week away, but Bethany found it did little to improve the state of the house. Ben had always been a kept man and he too began to realise just how much he relied on Alexa's hospitality to keep him going.

With these revelations, Bethany was determined that Alexa would understand how much she missed her. She wrote emails every day. In each one she made it clear she understood the amazing input Alexa had in her life and how grateful she was. Alexa responded to most, but never commented on anything she said. It was as though Alexa was not even reading them. Angry, Bethany made her recognition of Alexa and Charlotte more pointed and explicit. It had no effect. After a week of rejection, Bethany read through all her emails to see how Alexa could have possibly ignored her. Then she understood. She sounded like a petulant child. She missed having someone around to take care of her.

"You do like being taken care of," smiled Sam, sitting on the lounge facing Bethany.

"So you think I'm a selfish prat too?"

"No. I never said that, but you get used to having people do stuff for you. I'm guilty of it too. I've taken Gran and Pop for granted far too many times. I know that now and I'm old enough to try and change it. It's hard work and not very satisfying. I still haven't learned to enjoy washing, but it's just a responsibility I can't shirk any more."

"I haven't been shirking my responsibilities," sulked Bethany. Sam's situation was different. Gran and Pop were old.

"Really? Have you even tried cooking a meal? Alexa has like twenty tonnes of cook books. Have you opened any? You're not as useless as you make out."

"Help me?" Bethany asked hopefully.

"That's not taking responsibility," smiled Sam, shaking his head.

"Last time I tried to cook I set the kitchen on fire. I think I am being responsible," retorted Bethany.

Sam gave into that logic and Bethany was glad. She really did not know her way around the kitchen. That was where Maria and Gran stepped in. They had more skills and patience than Sam. Maria, in particular, was thrilled to have the opportunity to teach Bethany to cook. She regaled stories of teaching Alexa new dishes when they first met. They did not inspire Bethany. She was still struggling to master the basics.

"Relax, Beth," said Maria soothingly when Bethany collapsed on the floor in tears. "It's food. It doesn't have to be perfect. It just has to be edible. If you undercook the meat, you put it back. If you overcook it, you squirt more sauce on the plate."

"Lex and Char don't mess up like this," cried Bethany.

"They did when they were learning. It just happened that they started cooking very young. I grant you, Charlotte has some real flare in the kitchen. But you know what, Alexa's not an amazing cook." Bethany glared up at Maria, disgusted by the insult. "What she does do – better than anyone I've ever met – is make something edible from very little."

"There was this one place – I swear, Maria, the only thing they bought was baked beans. There were a couple of other foster kids there too. The kind of place you only stay for a few days. By the end of the day, one of us would've pissed them off so they'd send us all to bed without dinner. Lex made sure we ate whenever we could so we wouldn't go hungry. Don't know how many meals we had there, but I remember thinking that baked beans were awesome. They had so many different flavours and ways to use them. Every cupboard in every house, there was always baked beans. I tried to cook them when I was at the Christies'. They were crap."

"Do you know the big difference between you and Alexa?" asked Maria. "She wouldn't dare ask for help. If she can't do something, she'll avoid it or pretend she can. By the time you work out there's a problem she's become proficient enough to counter your concerns. But what you do share is a shocking lack of faith in yourselves. You can do this, Beth. I know you can and I'll keep telling you so until you can say it yourself."

Bethany nodded, wiped her eyes and rose to her feet. It might not be an achievement in the eyes of the rest of the world, and there was much more she needed to achieve before she could count herself as Alexa's equal, but she was determined to be able to cook by the time Alexa arrived home. Maria was pleased by the change of heart, and progress was swift enough that Bethany felt like she had something to tell Alexa in her next email. Instead of whinging about everything being too hard, she detailed the small achievements she was making. Bethany did not want to feel as though she was boasting, but she was proud of herself and after a few emails in the same vein it appeared Alexa was too. Alexa's replies started to sound like the sister Bethany had always known, but still Alexa gave no hint as to where she was or when she was coming home. Bethany resisted the urge to ask. It did not matter. Alexa would come home when she could face her life again.

By the end of four weeks, Bethany felt like she was learning to stand on her own two feet, but her heart was breaking with every day Alexa's absence extended on. Bethany could not believe it had been such a short period of time and was learning to accept the role she had played in Alexa's depression. Alexa had always supported her, but Bethany realised she had never reciprocated that care. It was a situation Bethany was determined to remedy – if she was only given the chance.

"I still don't think she'd leave forever and not say goodbye," said Sam, as he, Bethany, Ben and Maria sat glumly in the lounge room. "It's not like her. She does the right thing no matter what it costs her. Even if she's planning to move away, she'll come back first."

"Maybe," said Maria, clearly unconvinced. "But we all miss her so much that we wouldn't let her go without a fight. Maybe this is her way of avoiding the fight."

"I just want more time to make things up to her," said Ben. "I owe her so much."

"I want her to know how much I love her and miss her and how sorry I am for taking her for granted," sighed Bethany, trying to keep from sobbing.

"I already knew."

"Lex!" screamed Bethany, jumping over the lounge.

Alexa and Charlotte were standing at the entrance to the room, having crept quietly into the house. They never thought they would make it this far without being noticed.

"I'm sorry I thought I needed to run away from everything – from you," said Alexa, embracing Bethany. "I missed you so much."

"I've missed you more. I can't believe how much you two did for me. I can't believe how lazy I was," said Bethany, tears slipping down her cheeks as she pulled Charlotte into their embrace. "I'll show you how much better I've gotten. I'll even cook dinner tonight."

"Should we alert the fire brigade?" laughed Alexa, but quickly decided not to joke. It would have taken a lot for Bethany to return to the kitchen after that debacle.

"It's good to have you home," said Ben in a gravelly voice as he pulled Alexa into a hug as soon as Bethany released her.

In turn, Alexa and Charlotte greeted Maria and Sam, insisting on coffee before any conversations about their trip.

"It was so good," exclaimed Charlotte, smiling more broadly than any of them had ever seen. "First we went to Europe. Lex took me to London and Rome and this country town in Germany she stayed in when she went over last time."

"You let her call you Lex?" questioned Sam.

"Okay, so I was a little attached to that name, but Bethy's never leaving me and I'm never leaving her, so it's okay. You can all call me Lex if you want to."

"Anyway," sighed Charlotte, desperate to tell the rest of her story. "After that we went to the US to see if we could track down my father. Beth helped me find out where he was ages ago and Lex organised a meeting with him. He never even knew that my mother was pregnant. She broke up with him without telling him and he didn't leave me. He even liked me."

Everyone smiled happily in response to Charlotte's story and after answering a few brief questions, she bounded up to her room to unpack like a new person. But things had not gone as smoothly as Charlotte implied. Peter had set up the appointment, but Wes Cassidy's secretary postponed it before they even arrived in New York. That made Charlotte nervous – as though, without even knowing her, her father was trying to ignore her. It had taken a lot of convincing before Alexa managed to get Charlotte to accompany her to the rescheduled meeting. Wes Cassidy's reaction did not inspire much confidence.

"What can I do you for?" Wes asked in a friendly-enough manner, but his eyes kept flicking uneasily back to Charlotte.

Charlotte was unable to speak, so Alexa made up a story. She told Wes that she was looking for her biological father and that she thought he lived in New York, but that she could not be sure if he would end up being her biological father. "Is there some way of contacting him discretely? Or even if we work out he's the person I'm looking for, can I force him to take a paternity test?" asked Alexa.

"What are you expecting from this man?" asked Wes warily.

"Answers. It'd be nice to know him. I don't need money. I just want to get to know him," replied Alexa, hoping they were Charlotte's answers.

The phone rang and Wes grabbed for it immediately. He spoke rapidly for over five minutes and when he finally got off the phone he abruptly ended their meeting. "I'm sorry to do this, but it's an emergency," he said hastily. "Get my secretary to reschedule and I will look into what rights you have."

Charlotte had been prepared to walk away then and never come back, convinced that Wes somehow knew who she was and wanted her to realise how unwelcome her intrusion into his life was. Alexa persisted, though was disappointed that it would be two days before Wes Cassidy could fit them in. When Charlotte insisted they just leave, Alexa knew the rest of the negotiations with Wes would have to happen in secret.

"You don't seriously think that the only reason I came to New York was to hang out in an office for five minutes with a guy that may have once shagged your mother, right?" asked Alexa when Charlotte started packing her bags. "We're in New York. I'm not leaving early for you."

It took a trip to Coney Island for Charlotte to loosen up to the idea of having fun in spite of the reception she received from the last person she held out any hope of loving her. When Alexa told her that she had another meeting with Wes Cassidy, Charlotte refused point blank to accompany her and even threatened at one point to not be there when Alexa returned. Confiscating Charlotte's passport, Alexa made her way to the meeting.

"You're alone today," said Wes as soon as Alexa walked into his office. "Where's Charlotte?"

Alexa was impressed Wes remembered Charlotte's name. He had forgotten hers. "At the hostel," Alexa answered. Wes looked thoroughly thrown. Alexa took her seat and waited for him to speak, but he just stared at her. "You were the one who was going to give me the legal advice, remember."

"Yes, right … sorry, I just assumed …" Wes looked as though he was about to stand up, before sitting back down and looking at Alexa. "Why are you here?"

"For advice."

"On finding your biological father?"

"No. I know who my biological father was," replied Alexa darkly. "Advice on how to approach the man we believe is Charlotte's biological father."

Alexa noticed that her answer did not seem to surprise Wes. "Where did you get the name of this man?" he asked.

"From the man who raised her," replied Alexa. Wes nodded before asking Alexa for the name of that man and if he ever did a paternity test. "I don't think there have ever been any paternity tests, but he seemed to know he wasn't her father."

"I think that if we are going to continue this conversation, then Charlotte should really be here."

"She won't come here. I had to take her passport to stop her from leaving."

"Then I'll come with you."

Wes got up and walked out of the office. By the time Alexa managed to find her feet to follow him, he was already asking his secretary to cancel all his meetings for the rest of the day and call his wife. Alexa thought that Wes would not be a very good man to be a secretary for.

They travelled to the hostel in silence. Wes did not seem to want to speak and Alexa did not try and make him. It was obvious he had some idea that Charlotte thought he might be her father, but could not be sure if he wanted to tell her to her face if that was true or not.

"I want to talk to her alone," said Wes.

"I'll let you talk to her in private, but I won't leave her alone with you," replied Alexa forcefully. Wes nodded, eyeing her carefully.

Whatever Charlotte and Wes said to each other over the next hour remained their secret. Alexa was surprised when she saw each of them swabbing their cheeks and placing them into plastic bags and an envelope. Wes did not stay long after that.

"Said it was the right thing to do – have the test," said Charlotte once he was gone.

Although Charlotte did not complain about staying until the tests were processed, she also seemed to have little interest in the results – until Wes turned up two days later.

"It's not one hundred percent definitive," Wes said, handing over the test results. "It would have been more accurate with your mother's DNA, but I could be your father – I am your father."

"Biologically," clarified Charlotte, handing back the envelope after glancing at the results. "Doesn't make any sense to me."

"I did know you existed," said Wes, nodding. Charlotte instantly stepped back. "You were two when I first found out about you – I was

213

about to marry Lindsay. I confronted your mother. She told me David Jammel was your father – that she'd cheated on me with him and that's why she broke it off. They'd been on-again–off-again for ages. He was her first boyfriend. I wasn't always sure the maths added up, but I saw David with you once – when I was visiting my family. He looked like he truly loved you." Charlotte nodded, but did not look as though she really understood where the story was going and appeared too scared to ask. "You would've had a better life than what I could've offered you back then," said Wes. "David was so successful. They could afford a house – everything. I was struggling to get work. I didn't want to tear all that apart for a miscalculation, but I did think about you."

"We weren't rich," said Charlotte darkly. "We never had any money. That's why they fought – why she left. He got a bit better after she left, but then Carla came along."

"There's a lot I still need to find out about your life, but I want to find those things out – the good and the bad. I know I've missed out on many years, but I'd like to be there for the rest of them."

Alexa had expected Charlotte to rush to Wes then, but she never did. Even after leaving them alone for over an hour, Charlotte seemed to distrust Wes and his intentions. The next day they met his wife. Lindsay's warm embrace and self-confessed joy at finally meeting Charlotte went a long way to easing relations. Lindsay was a natural conversationalist and talked openly about the discussions they'd had over the years concerning Charlotte's existence and whether they should ever become involved.

"So you really didn't know? You didn't walk out on her when you found out she was pregnant?" asked Charlotte timidly.

"No. Part of me always hoped you were mine. Never understood why."

"So? Was your holiday as productive?" probed Bethany, bringing Alexa's attention back to the present.

The question made Alexa's stomach turn. She wanted to come home and was even excited about returning to university, but she did not want to be grilled on her feelings about life right then. "I know this is where I want to be. I know I love all of you and missed you," she smiled, sidestepping the question.

"But you're not as happy as Charlotte?"

"Charlotte just found out she wasn't abandoned by everyone who should've loved her. I don't think much could happen to me to make me that happy."

"So what are you going to do now?" asked Ben.

"Study. I had a great time, but now I have to get my butt back into gear."

"And beyond that?"

"I'm not thinking beyond that," answered Alexa truthfully. "One day at a time. That's all I can do and right now that's working. Please, let me handle this on my own."

Ben and Bethany tried to question Alexa more, but she sidetracked them again, this time with gifts. Alexa knew the balance and calm she had created overseas would not last. Just walking past Marcus's old room had told her that. However, she was getting better at shutting out those feelings. She would shut Marcus out of her heart forever, or shut off the part of her heart that contained her love for him. The problem was that she felt sometimes as if her heart belonged almost wholly to Marcus.

It would have been easier if Alexa could blame Marcus for leaving, but the arguments never stuck for long. All that mattered was that he was not coming back. He had moved on with his life – a life she could never have given him – and she had to as well.

Unpacking by throwing all her clothes in her dirty clothes basket, Alexa sat on her bed and looked out the window. It pleased her to realise she was happy to be home. Her heartbreak over Marcus was no worse than anyone else's after a break-up, and Jessica and Amy would help her through it. There was only one person who would dominate the direction of her life and it was not Marcus.

"Alexa," whispered a voice behind her.

Alexa did not register the word properly until she turned to see Marcus standing, breathless, in her doorway. She was surprised by the immediate stonewalling of her heart. She was used to a very different reaction on seeing him, but knew, despite Bethany's obvious match-making attempts, that this was going to end very badly, and she needed to be prepared.

"Oh, Alexa. I thought I'd lost you," gasped Marcus, though he did not move any closer.

"You never had me to lose," replied Alexa tonelessly.

"I'm sorry. I should have, but … I've only ever wanted what was best for you. I always thought that was what I was doing, but …"

"Why are you here?" asked Alexa when Marcus failed to finish his sentence, wondering if it was some sort of test of her new resolve.

"I don't want to lose you."

"You don't have me, so that can never happen. Nothing's changed – how – what … nothing's changed," cried Alexa softly.

"I've changed. I want to be with you," said Marcus, stepping tentatively forward. "Damn the consequences. I want you. Please, don't let it be too late."

Alexa did not know what to do. Marcus had left her. He had chosen another life and she had let him go. Why was he back now, acting as though they could be together? Standing in defiant silence, Alexa stared at Marcus, waiting for him to understand.

When Marcus turned away, Alexa slunk slowly back on to her bed. Marcus had come back. For her. And she had sent him away.

Before Alexa could think herself out of it, she bounded out of the room. Marcus was stopped two steps down, one hand grasping the banister, the other covering his face. With a thumping breath, Alexa reached out for him, his head immediately snapping up.

"It's not too late," she whispered, her voice failing her. "It's not too late."

Marcus rushed up the steps and around to Alexa, stopping just inches from her. The air between them became electrified, tingling every inch of Alexa's body and she wondered if Marcus felt it too. Managing a smile, she took Marcus by the hand. Whatever was going to happen next was not going to happen in public.

Locking the door behind them, Alexa turned to see Marcus standing awkwardly in front of her. Making sure she did not allow herself to think her way out of this situation, she stepped forward and ran her hands up the side of his face. Cupping his cheeks gently, she rose up on her tippy-toes and pressed her lips gently against his. She was surprised by how soft his lips were and how much she liked the taste of him.

Marcus's arms remained by his side as Alexa slipped back down flat on her feet. He looked in a state of shock and it made her smile. She was obviously not the only one trying not to overthink the situation. Taking Marcus by the hand again, Alexa led him to the bed, sitting him up against the padded headboard. She straddled his lap and felt his hands move over her hips. Leaning forward, Alexa began to kiss Marcus and was glad that this time he was kissing her back.

Unbuttoning his shirt, she moved her kisses down his chest. She felt his hands tighten around her hips as she continued to move lower and she knew he was enjoying what she was doing. But when her hands reached for his belt, Marcus suddenly pushed her off him.

"No, this isn't right."

Chapter Twelve

ALEXA STARED DEEP into Marcus's eyes, her heart breaking in an instant. She rushed across the room, but did not know where to go. She could not go downstairs – not where people were – but she did not want to stay near Marcus either.

"Wait, I didn't mean it like that," said Marcus urgently, jumping off the bed. He grabbed Alexa's hand tight as she tried to pull away. "I'm sorry. This was what was supposed to – it was meant to be like this."

Alexa resisted, but only for a second. The way Marcus's hand stroked her cheek, the movement of his body into hers and the feel of his lips was enough to smother any desire to flee. Marcus's kiss was so intense Alexa felt as though he was breathing fire into her body. Every cell was alight with passion. Her feet rose up on to their toes to pull her body closer to his. Marcus's hands moved over her back, holding her to him. Though her feet started to ache, she could not pull away. Moving her hands down his chest, she pushed aside his unbuttoned shirt.

Marcus pulled back. When Alexa looked up she could see him trying to assess the situation. When she immediately stepped back in towards him, he guided them to the bed. Marcus instantly drew their bodies close as their lips met. Alexa stroked his face, shoulders, arms – any part of his body she could reach. She could not let go. She could not stop. Every part of her body yearned for more, but she noticed Marcus would not move forward without her prompting. Sitting up slightly, she stripped off her top and slid Marcus's off his shoulders. The feel of his skin against hers made her gasp, fuelling the passion she was starting to believe had no end.

The need to experience the feel of just skin on skin saw Alexa strip them both naked. She could feel Marcus's breath shuddering as they pulled in close. He slowed his movements, taking her face in his hands. She was glad he did not speak. When she nodded once, he pulled her lips back to his and kissed her passionately before gently lifting his body on top of hers.

If Alexa could have thought rationally, she would have known this was the point where things would go wrong, but she could not think about anything but the fire that was burning through her body. Entwining her legs in his, Alexa felt her heart thumping against her ribcage. Marcus's hands moved to her cheeks. He pushed gently against her as he kissed her lovingly.

Everything slowed. Marcus's movements became soft – a tender flame emerging from the passion. His arms slid under Alexa's torso and held her tight as their bodies moved together. When his lips found hers once more, the burning passion returned, engulfing them entirely, Marcus holding her close right to the end.

"Are you okay?" asked Marcus, brushing the hair from Alexa's face. "How do you feel?"

"Scared," replied Alexa immediately, as she tried to prevent that fear taking hold of her body. Panic streaked across Marcus's face. "I never had you before," she explained in a shaky voice. "I hated it, but I could live without you. Now I know how perfect being with you feels, I'm so scared I'm going to lose you."

"You're not going to lose me," Marcus replied immediately, looking straight in her eyes with firm conviction. "I couldn't imagine my life without you. Every day away from you's been torture."

"Does that mean you're going to move back in?"

"I don't know," Marcus murmured, rolling off Alexa to lie next to her. "It's not just us we have to worry about now. Perhaps we shouldn't get in too deep until we know it's going to work."

Alexa rolled over, turning her back on Marcus, trying to supress the fear that was threatening to consume her. "Maybe we need to get in too deep," she said in a timid voice. "Then we have to make it work." Marcus urged her to roll over and face him. "I mean, otherwise we just end up talking ourselves out of what we want – the way we always have."

"You prepared to do that? Damn the world and bear the brunt of its anger to be with me?" asked Marcus seriously. Alexa's eyes widened. "Because I am. Say yes and I'll take you now and never let you go. You'll be stuck with me forever – through everything life throws at us."

"Yes," replied Alexa immediately.

Marcus lunged forward and kissed her passionately, enveloping her in his arms.

There was nothing more perfect Alexa had experienced than

having Marcus's arms around her, and while they lay together his hands never stopped stroking her, as his lips caressed her skin, hair and mouth.

"Oh my God, what time is it?" asked Marcus suddenly, practically jumping out of the bed.

"Five. Why?"

"Mum's looking after the baby. I've got to get home. This was all a last minute thing. She wasn't happy about me going. I think she suspected I was coming here."

Alexa was confused, though the last part she understood. His parents still hated her and it made her feel strangely vulnerable as she sat naked in bed, her legs curled into her chest and her arms wrapped around them. Marcus was half dressed before he looked over at her. He pulled on his shirt as he sat slowly sat back down on the bed, curling her into his arms. "I'm sorry. That was so rude," he said softly. "I just never expected this. It's not what I'd planned."

"Not quite the welcome home I expected either," replied Alexa softly. "You're coming back though, right?"

"Absolutely," replied Marcus firmly, pulling her closer. "I'll pack a few of our things and come right back over. I'll move the rest of our stuff later. I don't want to be apart from you for a second longer than I have to."

Alexa smiled and stroked Marcus's face. "I love you," she said softly, before sliding her arms around his neck. Marcus froze. Alexa pulled back to see his stunned expression. It took her a moment to realise why he was so surprised. She had said those words so many times in her head over the past few years that it felt natural to finally say it out loud.

"Are you trying to make leaving you impossible," gasped Marcus, his hands stroking her hair and face. "I love you so much. You're my world. I'm sorry I have to leave, but I'll be back as quickly as possible. Wait up for me?"

Alexa nodded, but when Marcus stood to leave she found it hard to let go of his hand as he moved towards the door.

A strange feeling swamped Alexa as the door closed behind Marcus. Jumping out of bed, she dressed quickly to lessen the feeling of vulnerability, but then found herself turning in circles, pondering where she should go. Creeping down the stairs, she wondered who was still in the house and who knew of Marcus's visit. So scared of the reception she might receive, her whole body was shaking as she moved slowly towards the voices in the lounge room.

"It's just us," said Bethany, standing up from the lounge and hugging Alexa tight. "Thought we needed the night alone together."

Perhaps Bethany truly understood how terrifying these events were for Alexa, because she said nothing about Marcus, even though she had clearly orchestrated the reunion. She and Charlotte acted as though they knew nothing of the situation. Their focus was on dinner and Bethany showing off her newfound cooking skills. Alexa joined them in the kitchen, but did little more than stand absently out of the way while Charlotte enthusiastically encouraged and praised Bethany.

Every minute saw Alexa expecting Marcus's return. She tried not to look at the clock, reasoning that it would take time for him to return home, pack his and his child's belongings, and then drive back to her. It was clear that neither Charlotte nor Bethany was expecting him for dinner, because they did not make provisions for a fourth serving. That helped reassure Alexa that Marcus had not abandoned her, but it was harder to maintain that faith once dinner was finished. Every second that passed was a reminder that Marcus was not back. It left Alexa sitting nervously on the lounge, her leg shaking continuously, as she tried to pay attention to the television flickering in front of her.

"What time did he say he was coming back?" asked Bethany warily.

"He didn't," replied Alexa absently, though she was comforted slightly by the fact that Bethany believed he was coming back. However, Bethany's faith could not change the fact that Marcus had now been gone over three hours. Alexa knew something had gone wrong. She was almost in tears with the thought that he had been hurt – possibly even killed – because of her weakness.

"He'll be here," said Charlotte confidently. "When has he ever not kept his word? Something's just held him up. He has a baby. Everyone knows they mess up schedules. They need to eat, then poo, then sleep. And they scream all the time in between."

"Yeah, I know," murmured Alexa. "I just hope I wasn't so stupid as to give him what he wanted, so that now he doesn't need to come back."

"That's a hell of a long time to wait for a lay," said Bethany frankly. "I think he would've left long ago if that's all he was after."

Two hours later, they were still waiting. Alexa had stopped fidgeting. Her body was like a statute carved into the lounge, her legs curled up into her body. No one spoke, but from the looks that crossed the room, Alexa knew Bethany and Charlotte were beginning to wonder if they had misjudged Marcus. Then came the short wrap at the front door that caused their heads to jerk up.

"I'll get it," said Bethany, holding her hand out to Alexa to keep her seat.

It was a sweet gesture, but Alexa could not be kept from her mistake. She needed to know what her decision had cost them. The sight of Marcus looking dishevelled on the doorstep was almost a relief. He was in one piece. Bethany quickly grabbed the bags from his shoulders, though it was difficult with the little baby in his arms. Marcus may be alive, but from the look in his eyes she knew all was not well.

"What's wrong?" Alexa asked tentatively, walking slowly towards him.

A flustered and angry look came over Marcus's face, stopping Alexa in her tracks. Marcus looked around and smiled slightly. "Nothing's wrong," he said confidently. "I'm here. We're here," he added, looking down at the baby.

Almost on cue, the baby started to whimper. Marcus was not confident about being able to settle her, given the upheaval of the evening, again hinting at more than simple logistics having held him up. When he started directing Bethany to his bags to find what he needed to fix a bottle, Alexa tentatively asked if she could hold the baby. "Of course," said Marcus, directing Alexa to a seat on the lounge before gently placing the baby in her arms.

A strange bond began to weave between this child and Alexa's heart. This was Marcus's baby – a little piece of him. It did not even matter that Lucy was its mother. Alexa suddenly realised that she possibly thought it was better that way. Examining the tiny creature in her arms as she stroked its head, she noticed that it had pale features that did not seem to come from either Lucy or Marcus, though she did recognise Marcus's mouth.

"Do you want me to take her?" asked Marcus, holding out the bottle to Alexa.

Alexa liked that he was not questioning her competence, and slowly shook her head. When Marcus smiled, she took the bottle from him. He sat next to her and silently directed her until Tracey was feeding happily. Alexa loved the way he smiled as he watched them.

"What's her name?" asked Alexa.

"Tracey," replied Marcus with a slight blush.

"That's my middle name," replied Alexa with a surprised smile.

"He knows," said Bethany happily as she peered down at them from behind the lounge.

"Tracey Alexandra," said Marcus proudly, though he was still blushing.

"My name's not short for Alexandra, though," said Alexa, before looking down, realising how conceited she sounded.

"That was my cunning plan to stop people realising I named her after you," grinned Marcus, making Charlotte and Bethany laugh.

"Lucy was okay with you naming Tracey after me?" asked Alexa, suddenly realising that fathers did not usually have sole naming rights over a child.

"In the end," answered Marcus. "She did like the name Tracey."

"Did she know it was my name?" asked Alexa curiously.

"No," laughed Marcus. "You were always going to be a part of my child's life – one way or another," he added more seriously. "Even if only by name."

Alexa thought her heart might burst with that confession. She looked into Marcus's eyes and realised she did not have to hide how much she loved him. Shuffling her body towards him, she leaned back against him and allowed her head to rest in the crook of his neck. She felt him sigh heavily as his arm slipped around her shoulders.

"I don't know where we're going to put Tracey," said Marcus, when Tracey finally closed her eyes. "I didn't get much in the end, just the essentials. I don't even have her cot."

"Don't worry. I've got that covered," said Bethany, directing Marcus's attention to the base of the stairs, where a beautiful wooden cot sat.

"Did you buy that?" asked Marcus, his voice full of surprise. "When?"

"No, I made it," replied Bethany in a small voice. "I was sure you'd come back eventually. Just thought it'd be sooner than this."

"Thank you, Beth. That's really beautiful," said Marcus, taking her hand and squeezing it. "I'm sorry I thought you bought it. I'm still not used to knowing anyone who can make furniture better than what you can buy in the shops."

Alexa knew Marcus was sincere in his praise. Perhaps Bethany did too, because she was suddenly flitting around the room to cover the tears that were building in her eyes. When Alexa and Marcus moved towards the stairs, they saw Bethany rush over to Charlotte and hug her tight.

"Start of the good times now, Bethy," whispered Charlotte, but they could hear her in the quietness of the house.

Bethany nodded and pulled away, but Charlotte took her hand and shook her head. Bethany smiled, before dancing over to the stairs and grabbing the cot. Charlotte raced up the stairs with her and they were waiting in Alexa's bedroom when she and Marcus arrived with Tracey.

"Since she's so new, she'll probably have to stay with you, but when she gets bigger you can put her next door," said Bethany.

Alexa was thrown by that suggestion. Next door was her study. She and Marcus walked out of the bedroom and to the next room. It was a nursery. And every piece of furniture had clearly been made by Bethany.

"My contribution looks pretty lame now," said Charlotte in mock annoyance as she held up a hamper of items. "I bought a present for the baby in every place we went."

"I didn't know that," said Alexa, shocked by this development. Then she saw Bethany's smirk and realised there may have been some double-crossing going on while they were away.

"Thank you," said Marcus in a thick voice, hugging Charlotte and Bethany in turn. "They're the best welcome home presents ever."

"We'll see you guys in the morning," smiled Bethany, her arms around Charlotte's shoulders. They were hugging as they walked down the stairs.

Alexa smiled as Marcus guided her back to the bedroom. There was a strange unreality to his presence, yet he would be there in the morning. He had come home.

Marcus put Tracey down in her cot and placed the blanket from Charlotte's hamper over her. Tracey looked so peaceful as they stood watching her sleep. Alexa reached down and stroked Tracey's cheek, startling her, though she did not wake.

"Is she okay? What happened to her?" asked Alexa urgently.

"Nothing, she's fine, I promise," replied Marcus, turning Alexa to face him. He stroked her cheek tenderly, holding her gaze as he nodded. "I promise. No one's harmed her. Come on, let's get to bed and catch some sleep before she wakes up. She doesn't sleep through the night yet."

Alexa nodded, but she felt strangely self-conscious getting changed in front of Marcus. When she turned away, she was glad that Marcus also turned his gaze. What pleased her more was that he wore pyjamas to bed too. It made it that much easier for her to snuggle into him.

"Why were you so late?" asked Alexa tentatively.

"My parents objected to me leaving – ferociously," said Marcus, pulling her tight into his chest. "They don't agree with us being together. As soon as they found out – it just took a while to sort out."

"They're okay with us now?" asked Alexa.

"No. By sort out, I meant leave," Marcus replied, stroking her hair. "When they tried to stop me taking Tracey, they left me with no choice but to call the police." Alexa felt her body go stiff. "It's all fine now, I promise. I just had to sort a few things out. It took time and I needed to calm Tracey down. I'm sorry I didn't call. In the end I just grabbed a couple of bags and left."

"What did your parents say?" asked Alexa. They had agreed to be together in the face of all disasters, but she was sure Marcus had not realised they would strike so soon.

"They told me that I was no longer their son."

"Marc, you can't —"

"No, don't. Whatever you're going to say, please don't. I love you," said Marcus, looking deep into Alexa's eyes. It was hard to argue when he was looking at her like that. "We've tried to deny our feelings for each other and I know there's an age gap, but you're not my student any more. I'm not your teacher and the older we get the less the age gap is going to matter. Don't let it trouble you. It's their loss, not ours."

"What about Lucy?" Alexa asked cautiously, shaken by Marcus's revelation.

"What about Lucy?" asked Marcus back.

"She's Tracey's mother," replied Alexa, wondering why he was being so coy. "Does she know about us yet? Will it cause problems? When do you have to give Tracey back?"

"I don't. Tracey has no mother," answered Marcus, a hard edge to his voice. "It's just me and her."

"What do you mean? Lucy doesn't see – I don't get it – what do you – where's Lucy?"

"Lucy chose to no longer be Tracey's mother," said Marcus, his head turning towards his sleeping daughter. "It's complex and I don't want you to think badly of Lucy. She's back with her ex. It worked out for the best."

Alexa stayed silent for a while, curling into Marcus's chest. She was sure she would find out the full story eventually, but was shocked it had come to that. She always assumed Lucy had become pregnant on purpose.

"Then why weren't you coming back?" asked Alexa. She sounded petulant, but it hurt to think Marcus had deliberately stayed away. "If Lucy wasn't a problem, why weren't you coming back?"

Marcus pulled Alexa closer to him and kissed the top of her head before he answered. "I didn't want to burden you," he said finally, his voice gravelly. "I didn't think it was fair to turn up on your doorstep with a child and expect you to take us both in. We'd never even kissed, held hands or gone on a date."

"And now?"

"And now I'd rather take that risk than lose you forever. I guess I assumed we'd have years of chances to get it right. Maybe there is no right time and we just have to make the most of it."

"So it's just us and Tracey?"

"Yeah, just the three of us. I hope that's all right with you," said Marcus, stroking Alexa's face.

"That's great with me," smiled Alexa, lifting her lips to his.

When Marcus kissed her back, the passions that had engulfed her body that afternoon returned full force. She could not pull herself away and was glad that Marcus held her close. Yearning to feel his skin on hers once more, she slipped off her top. It was beautiful, but she still felt so exposed. Something of her hesitation must have shown, because Marcus pulled back, his eyes searching hers.

"Can I ask you something?" he queried cautiously. Alexa looked at him warily. "This afternoon – did you enjoy it?"

"Of course I did. Didn't you notice?" asked Alexa defensively, crossing her arms over her chest.

"Not quite what I meant," said Marcus, continuing to hold her gaze, though he did not reach out for her. "Did you find it …

pleasurable?" he asked. Alexa looked at him quizzically. "Personally satisfying? I got the feeling you didn't … you know."

"Climax?" offered Alexa helpfully, finally understanding what he was getting at. Marcus nodded. "Nope," replied Alexa simply, but was concerned by the contorted expression on Marcus's face.

"You don't seem concerned," he said. Alexa shrugged, wondering if she was supposed to be. "Have you ever?"

"Not like that," answered Alexa, her cheeks on fire with what that was inferring.

"Ever? Not with Sam? Or Damien?" asked Marcus in a shocked voice. Alexa shook her head, wondering if Marcus thought she was deficient. "Ever at all?"

Alexa's fierce blush was the only answer she could give. Marcus shook his head, a smile creeping across his face. When he moved forward to kiss her, it did not last as long as she expected. Instead his lips moved further down her body as his hands discovered her in a way no others had before. Alexa had never been very comfortable with guys, but if they had touched her the way Marcus was now, she was not so sure she would have pushed them away. When he eventually rolled on top of her, Alexa felt sure she might explode. She bit her lip and held Marcus tight to contain herself, but could not help but be slightly embarrassed by her reaction.

"I hope that was a little more satisfying for you," smiled Marcus.

"I'm sorry," Alexa replied automatically.

"For what?" asked Marcus in a controlled voice. Alexa could only blush. "You can apologise for holding yourself back," he whispered in her ear. "But not for enjoying yourself. Get used to it. I plan to make you a very happy women."

Alexa was glad Marcus said nothing more and just held her close as they finally fell asleep. However, Tracey did not let them sleep long. Marcus tried to insist on Alexa staying in bed, but she was already awake. As Marcus had the most experience with Tracey, he fed and changed her before putting her back to bed, but she did not want to sleep straight away. When they finally got Tracey back to sleep, Alexa was sure she was asleep before her eyes were even closed.

***

Marcus watched Alexa from the kitchen window as he prepared their breakfasts. She was holding Tracey tenderly, Bethany sitting behind them. It was so beautiful it made him wonder why he had been so concerned about bringing Tracey into Alexa's life. Bethany turned and caught his eye, somehow managing to wipe the grin off his face. She rose and strode into the kitchen. Marcus closed his eyes, praying for patience. If he wanted Alexa, he was going to have to find a way to get along with Bethany.

"You haven't cured her, you know," said Bethany, not even bothering with a greeting. "You've made her truly happy, perhaps for the first time in her life, but that doesn't change much."

"I never thought she needed to be cured," retorted Marcus.

"Don't take it the wrong way," said Bethany, placing a gentle hand on Marcus's arm that he struggled not to throw off. "I just don't want you to be disappointed in Lex, cos you had false hope about her. Her past hasn't changed and there might be some time when she's terrified of you. You just have to realise that this hasn't erased all that."

"I know," conceded Marcus, the anger dropping from his voice. "I know. But we can't predict what'll set her off. We don't know what'll cause her next panic attack, but I'll be there for her when it happens. I'm never going to walk away from her, but I'm also not going to sit around and wait for it. She deserves more than that. We're going to enjoy every moment and when we have to face hard times, we'll do it together."

Bethany smiled, before wrapping Marcus in a warm embrace. This time, he hugged her back. Bethany was annoying and infuriating, but she had a good heart and had all but brought him and Alexa together. He would love her for that. "Now, are you going to join us outside, because we could really use someone that isn't half asleep, Aunty Beth?"

Bethany smiled brightly, tears forming in her eyes as she lunged forward and hugged Marcus again. It reminded him that Alexa was not the only one who needed their importance reaffirmed.

Alexa closed her eyes, hoping she could snatch a few moments of rest. Tracey snuggled against her shoulder, finally settling into sleep.

"You look comfortable," said Sam softly, appearing at her side, nudging her awake.

"I'm not," laughed Alexa. "She's heavier than she looks, but she's restless, won't let me put her down."

"Maybe she's worried you'll leave her," suggested Sam. Alexa did not answer, only stroking Tracey's tiny head. "I always said you'd make a good mother."

"I'm not sure that's what I am right now," murmured Alexa. She wanted to be, but would never force the issue.

"What do you mean?" asked Sam. "I thought Lucy was out of the picture."

"She is, but Tracey's Marcus's daughter. He's never actually said he wants me to be her mother."

"Of course he does. He just assumes you'd know that. He thinks you're perfect," said Sam almost mockingly. Alexa rolled her eyes, but managed a smile. "Where is he, anyway?"

"Picking up the rest of his things," answered Alexa softly. "His parents aren't happy about us."

"I heard, but that's only because they don't know you. Are you happy about Tracey?"

"Yeah, but I always expected that she'd be living with Lucy. This full-time thing is a bit of a surprise, but I wouldn't swap it for the world. I love them both so much."

"Well, I know you'll do fine. Look at the job you did with Beth," smiled Sam, stroking Alexa's hair. "It makes me so happy to see you like this."

Alexa smiled down at Sam's glowing face. She could not believe he was finally supporting her. She had expected opposition to her and Marcus being together and had not wanted to consider how he would react to Tracey, but his acceptance of her new relationships was very welcome.

"Oh, hey, Sam. How you doing?" asked Marcus, stumbling into the room, laden down with bags and boxes.

"Do you need any help?" asked Sam, rising to his feet, his hand still on Alexa's.

"Yeah, we have a truck load of stuff to bring in. Alexa, do you mind if I just store it in my old room for now?"

"Go ahead," smiled Alexa.

She could still not get over the fact that she and Marcus were finally together. Marcus, about to rush back downstairs, turned and hugged her, kissing her forehead and cupping Tracey's tiny head. Tracey woke at Marcus's touch, becoming restless once again.

"You want me to take her?" asked Marcus.

"No, you unpack, get the truck back. You can have her if she's not asleep by the time you're finished."

Marcus smiled and dragged Sam downstairs. Tracey settled, but every time Alexa tried to put her in her cot she woke up and cried, sending Alexa back to her chair to calm her once more.

"You don't think I want you to be her mother?" asked Marcus, bursting into the room an hour later as Alexa finally managed to put Tracey down to sleep.

"Sam spoke to you?"

"Oh, Alexa, he shouldn't have to. Don't ever be scared to talk to me about things." Marcus pulled her into his chest and kissed the top of her head. "I don't want you feeling inadequate or unequal in this relationship. We're partners, okay?" Alexa nodded. "And I want you to be Tracey's mother. I want you to raise her with me. I want her to call you Mum."

"I want that too," replied Alexa softly.

Marcus smiled, before releasing Alexa and closing the bedroom door. "No holding back this time," he said, pulling Alexa to the bed.

Alexa giggled before Marcus cut it off with a kiss. She tried to please him, but he refused to let her. He was determined to focus all his attentions on her, muttering in her ear that she needed to learn the right way to make love. "I don't know what I'm doing?" she asked tentatively.

"Well, no, you do, but it's hard to learn the rest when your partners don't know what they're doing," Marcus replied with a slightly smug smile.

Perhaps he had every right to be smug. Alexa had to admit he did know what he was doing and he did it well.

The news of Marcus and Alexa's union spread quickly through the family, though Alexa made sure word did not reach the Whites. She was not yet sure how she would handle them. They were already upset about her sudden departure overseas and she had not even had time to deal with that problem. However, Alexa was not looking forward to the confrontation with Ben either, and made Bethany promise she would be with her at the first meeting with him and that it would not occur in the house.

"So, you and Marcus," said Ben, as he, Bethany and Alexa sat in a beachside café. Alexa could see he was trying very hard to appear calm and cool.

"You're not happy about us, are you?" asked Alexa.

"I didn't say that. I just worry about you," said Ben.

There was something in his voice that made Alexa recall their conversation before she went overseas. "Marcus is nothing like Sean," she said firmly. "He's not like that and I'm not my mother."

"I know," nodded Ben. "But I'm your father. It's my job to worry, but that doesn't mean I disapprove. I've seen you together. He loves you, I know that."

"Yeah, he does."

"Dad's not attacking you, Lex," said Bethany. She had not backed away from calling Ben dad and, now Alexa knew, insisted on always calling him dad. It still made Alexa uneasy, but she did not need any more battles – and truly wanted Ben to be their father as well – so said nothing.

"No, I don't want you to feel as though I'm not on your side," smiled Ben. "I am. I want to be more on your side – permanently."

"What do you mean?" asked Bethany in an excited voice, while Alexa stared back sceptically.

"It means I want to adopt the two of you. I know I should've done it ages ago, but there's nothing stopping me from doing it now. Better late than never, they always say."

Alexa wondered how long Ben had been planning this – and how long he had been waiting to ask them.

"So you'll be our Dad for real?" cried Bethany, throwing her arms around Ben's neck.

Alexa suspected this was not a complete surprise to Bethany, and it was not as though it was unexpected, but Alexa did not know why her reaction was so different to Bethany's. She was struggling against the desire to vomit as her heart pounded out of time in her throat, chest and stomach.

"Yes, for real," smiled Ben, hugging Bethany warmly.

"Isn't this great, Lex?"

"Yeah, um …"

"What's wrong? Why aren't you happy about this?" asked Bethany, truly heartbroken by Alexa's muted reaction. "Ben's wanted to adopt us from the beginning. Now he can."

"I'm glad he wants to adopt us, but there's more to consider than whether or not he wants to."

"He wants to adopt us. I want him to adopt us, so unless you don't, there is nothing else to consider."

Alexa could not look at Bethany. It was more complex than she wanted to admit. In the Whites she had a family she loved and in Pam and Karl, foster parents who thought of her as their daughter. She did not want to risk losing that, or make Charlotte feel as though she was being abandoned.

Ben was clearly disappointed and Alexa hated that. Things like this wreaked havoc with the delicate mental and emotional balance she had, and the desire to avoid potential pain was always so much greater than the desire for potential happiness, even when she knew her fear of pain was somewhat irrational.

"You don't have to do this," said Ben, when Bethany went to the bathroom.

"I never said I don't want it," murmured Alexa. "I just need time."

"Take as much as you need."

Yet time was a precious commodity that Alexa found she rarely had enough of. Behind at university, she was struggling to catch up. Marcus did all he could to accommodate her, but Alexa's problem was that he was so much more appealing than her textbooks. However, Marcus was insistent and forced Alexa to write up a schedule she promised to keep that included swimming, studying and spending time with Charlotte, Bethany, Maria and the Whites.

Alexa managed to smooth things over with Pam and Karl concerning her unannounced trip – and won Hayley and Brett over with gifts – but she chickened out on telling them about Marcus or Ben. Charlotte must have been worried about their reaction too, because Alexa had the feeling Hayley had no idea about Marcus's reappearance in her life. That was a very good thing. Hayley could not keep secrets. Strangely, that meant that it was with the Whites that Alexa found the most peace. At home, Bethany never stopped questioning her about Ben's offer to adopt them.

"What's the problem?" asked Marcus as he sat on the lounge feeding Tracey. "You don't want him to adopt you?"

"It's not that," replied Alexa uneasily, not looking up from the pile of clothes she was folding.

"You do know that he'd never hurt you, right? And that he really doesn't want to sleep with you," said Marcus seriously. Alexa could not articulate an answer. "And that just because he becomes your 'father' those things aren't going to change."

Tears begin to slip down Alexa's cheeks. Marcus jumped up and nudged her towards the lounge where he juggled Tracey until he had a free arm to wrap around Alexa's shoulders.

"Shh, it's okay. You're scared and that's fine, but don't lose Ben to that fear. If you can't do it, he'll understand, he will, but if you want this, don't let this chance pass you by."

"It's all I've ever wanted," whispered Alexa, burying her head in Marcus's shoulder. "Even in my dreams – I just wanted him to take me and Bethy and keep us safe. But every time he came close …"

"He died," said Marcus, speaking the words she couldn't. "You're not a bad omen. All those things that happened to us – they were just coincidence. We're not being punished for being together."

"Your parents don't talk to you because of me. What do you call that?"

"Stupidity," answered Marcus immediately. "If anything, they're punishing themselves. Nothing'll happen to Ben if you say you want him to adopt you."

"What if it does? What if he gets shot because of me? How will I live with myself?" Alexa asked. Marcus stayed silent, eventually shrugging, but she could see in his eyes that he was just holding back from speaking all the arguments she would immediately reject. "What about Charlotte?" she asked, throwing up another obstacle.

"If you're so worried about how she feels, then why not just ask her what she wants. Find out if it's a problem, then go from there."

When Charlotte walked innocently into the lounge room, Marcus immediately left, with a significant stare at Alexa.

"What's that about?" asked Charlotte.

"I need to talk to you about something," replied Alexa glumly.

"The adoption?" suggested Charlotte with a smile. "Beth's already spoken to me – and I know she's already told you I'm okay with it."

"You sure though? Bethy can be a little forceful when she wants something," said Alexa, fearing even that was an understatement. Charlotte smiled broadly. "I mean, I feel wrong. It's been the three of us for so long, I feel like I'm disowning you – disowning part of me – if I agree to this."

"Did you know Ben spoke to me about it before he spoke to you?" asked Charlotte, sitting down on the lounge with Alexa. Alexa shook her head. "Yeah, I didn't tell Beth. She gets jealous. Ben's been really good to me – almost like a father, too, since I came here. Before we went away, he spoke to me about wanting to one day adopt you and

Beth – like he'd always wanted to. He asked me what I thought about him and how I'd feel about it – if I wanted to be a part of it."

"What'd you say?" asked Alexa, dumbfounded by this news.

"I said maybe. Then after meeting Wes – that changed things – not the way I see Ben, just that it would seem strange trying to get to know your biological father while being adopted by another man. But I know how you feel. It does feel like I'm losing you, but because of Wes not Ben."

"You being close to Wes would never make me stop thinking of you as my sister," cried Alexa.

"Just like Ben adopting you can't change how freakishly similar we are," smiled Charlotte. "So maybe you have your answer."

"Maybe. There's still one more sister, a brother and foster parents to go yet." Alexa hesitated for a moment. "It matters to me, so don't tip Hayley off, okay."

"I think it's good I have so much school to catch up on, cos there's a lot I'm not tipping Hayley off about at the moment."

Besides the awkwardness surrounding Ben and the Whites, Alexa had never been happier. With Marcus still on paternity leave, he did all he could around the house to take the pressure off her and allow her to focus on university. He also made sure she never had to worry about Tracey, although Alexa would have preferred to be more involved.

"Don't you trust us with Tracey?" asked Bethany, when Marcus again insisted that Alexa continue her study and he feed Tracey.

"No, of course I trust you," replied Marcus, looking between Bethany, Charlotte and Alexa.

"Then how come we're never allowed to do anything?" asked Bethany somewhat aggressively. "Every time we offer, you say no. I get that you don't want to pressure Lex, but uni, work, she's always going to have something on. You can't protect her forever – and me and Char don't want to be shut out either. We love Tracey too."

Alexa was surprised Marcus did not did not immediately respond and that his eyes were downcast. "It's not that I don't trust you," he said in a quiet voice that was unlike his own. "I just – I don't want to be that bad father that neglects his child and casts her off to other people. Tracey's already been abandoned by her mother. I just – I want to be a good father."

Bethany jumped from her seat and rushed over to Marcus. Sliding down behind him on the lounge and wrapping herself around his body, she hugged him intensely. When she buried her head in Marcus's shoulder, Alexa realised Bethany was actually crying. "You couldn't be a bad father," she said, her voice unsteady despite her best efforts to control it. "It's not possible."

Marcus gestured to Alexa, who put her books down and went to try and extricate Bethany from him. She knew how little Marcus liked Bethany's physicality, but Marcus held Tracey out to her and as soon as his arms were free, he pulled Bethany around and into his lap, hugging her tight.

"You won't be a bad father, you won't be," repeated Bethany as if it were some kind of mantra, and Alexa knew that Bethany was trying to convince herself more than anyone. It made Alexa ill. She had suffered at the hands of Sean and had an irrational fear of Ben, but never had she worried that Marcus would be anything like Sean. It was then Alexa realise that Bethany just pointed her fears in different directions.

"You know I don't really think of you like that," said Bethany half an hour later, still curled up in Marcus's lap. "I don't think you'd ever hurt Tracey. I don't."

"I know," replied Marcus, gently tucking Bethany's hair behind her ear. "Just like Alexa doesn't really think of Ben that way."

Bethany looked up at him, holding his gaze thoughtfully. "Can I hold Tracey?" she asked hopefully.

Marcus nodded and Bethany slipped out of his arms. Alexa held Tracey out to Bethany, who took her immediately and held her close. Marcus walked quickly towards the kitchen and Alexa followed.

"I'm sorry about Bethy. She's —"

"I love you," said Marcus, pulling Alexa into a tight embrace. They stood together for many minutes, until Marcus pulled away with a wild glint in his eyes. "Swim?"

Chapter Thirteen

"ABOUT THIS WEEKEND," said Marcus, prodding Alexa on Wednesday morning. "You got plans?" Alexa groaned. Saturday would be her twenty-first birthday. Bethany wanted a party. Alexa wanted to hide. "I was thinking of an early morning escape – breakfast by the beach. You up for it?"

"You're the most perfect guy in the world," smiled Alexa, and Marcus smiled back broadly.

When Saturday morning came, Alexa was up early, forgoing her morning swim in the pool with the anticipation of once more swimming in the ocean. Marcus had not planned for their morning to be quite so early, but with Tracey already awake there seemed little point in delaying their departure.

Slipping out unseen by anyone, Alexa put her hand out the car window, allowing the breeze of freedom to wash over her. Marcus stayed with Tracey on the beach while Alexa swam, before offering her warm, dry clothes she had never thought to pack herself. Alexa could not help but smile happily as they sat down to breakfast. Marcus held her hand across the table, but she pulled back when he tried to stroke her face. She was not very comfortable with public displays of affection. She was still coming to terms with their private ones.

"Can we talk about a few things?" asked Marcus, squeezing Alexa's hand. She had been expecting this since Bethany's episode and was only surprised it had taken so long. "You really okay with this – us?"

"What?" gasped Alexa.

"Don't panic. I just have to be sure. I couldn't live with myself if I felt like you ever believed you'd been pressured into this – or that you didn't feel equal in our relationship. I just want to know how you feel about this – all of it. Are you really okay with the fact that we met while you were in high school – while I was you're teacher?"

"I understand how I feel about you. I'm not completely blind to my own emotions and what I want," replied Alexa angrily, pulling her hand out of Marcus's and crossing her arms over her chest.

Marcus grinned. "I never said you were. I am," he confessed. "I need you to convince me I'm not a predator." Alexa instantly reached forward with both her hands and grabbed his, but she did not speak. He smiled ruefully. "You can't do it, can you?"

"It's not that. I don't – my feelings for you changed – I don't want you to think the wrong thing," Alexa said hesitantly. "I don't want to hurt you."

"I need to know."

"I don't think I really loved you in high school," Alexa confessed, looking up timidly. "I loved the concept of you. I loved that you liked me – that no matter how many more bad things you knew about me that you kept liking me. I never really thought you loved me – not truly. I just needed to survive – and you were what I needed."

"That was all I wanted for you, too," said Marcus softly. "I still remember that last Friday – when you left for the Whites – I'd never seen you so alive. I saw your future more clearly then than ever before and I knew it should never include me. You were a kid and I just wanted to get you through Redgrove and hand you over to that future. I thought maybe we could be friends. I just never planned on it ending the way it did."

"It probably saved us from a bad decision," shrugged Alexa, refusing to think about those events. "As soon as I left for overseas I knew I needed to move on from you. I was really grateful for everything you'd done for me, but I wanted a new life." Marcus nodded. "When I came back, everyone thought I was still pining for you, but I wasn't. I was struggling and I missed you – that person who didn't judge, who knew when to talk and when to stay silent."

"I didn't always know those things," smiled Marcus.

"No – and Sam used to. More than anything, I'd made you my yard stick. You and Sam. If I couldn't like someone even close to what I'd felt for either of you, then I didn't want to be involved with them. That's why Damien was such a mistake. There was just never a connection that way. When I met you again – it brought back a lot of feelings, but I was content being your friend. We were good friends. You let me feel like I could trust myself. Everyone else made me second-guess everything. Sometimes it slipped over to something more, but mostly, you were just my friend."

"Do you regret us now – want to be just friends?" asked Marcus seriously.

"No," smiled Alexa. "I fell in love with you the more I got to know you. There was always chemistry, but I missed you so much when you left this last time. I felt like I'd fallen in love with you as an adult, not a child, and I thought you'd fallen for who I really was."

"You still think I'm the only person who'll love you once they know about you?"

Alexa smiled again. It always seemed to come back to this question eventually. "I don't know. No, probably not. I don't think everyone will be able to overlook my past. But I found one person who can – who I love – and I don't know why I'm always being asked to throw that away just to prove that there's someone else out there who'll love me as much as you."

"You never ask me about school though," said Marcus, seemingly continuing down a list of concerns.

"Don't take this the wrong way, but I don't want to talk about school."

"Not your school, my school."

"I don't really care much for what you did at high school either," smiled Alexa, before realising how unsupportive that sounded. "I mean, if you want to talk about it, I will. I just don't think we'll have much in common with our high school experiences."

This time Marcus laughed, then ruffled his hair before trying again. "No, I mean me at school now. You never ask me about it."

"What would I ask? I know I'll have to get over my aversion to school when we send Tracey, but til then, I still don't really want to talk about it. It's all the same stuff, right?" Marcus gave Alexa a crooked smile and raised his eyebrows. "I'm being unfair, aren't I? Whatever you want to talk about, we can talk. I'll get over it."

"You really don't know what I'm getting at, do you?"

"Apparently not," replied Alexa, feeling her stomach turn over.

"I mean that you never ask me about any of my female students."

"What do you want me to ask?"

"You're really not concerned I might find one of them attractive?" asked Marcus with a hint of incredulity. "You're not worried I might leave you for one of them?"

"No," laughed Alexa, this time with genuine mirth. "You're not like that."

"I was like that with you. I left my fiancée for you."

"You left your fiancée for more reasons than that. You told me what you really wanted was to just see me through high school, so you really didn't leave her for me."

"I left her for the possibility of you."

"And you never touched me. I think I could've been seduced by you – I would've been seduced by you if you'd tried," said Alexa, speaking the truth she had never wanted to admit. "If you'd have done that, then you would've been taking advantage of me. You didn't. You're not that kind of man. You know that, right?"

Marcus squeezed Alexa's hand tight, but he did not respond. He did not ask her any more questions either. They ate their breakfast in near silence, but Alexa did not want to go home that way. Taking Marcus by the hand, as he held Tracey in his other arm, she walked with him along the beach until they reached the rock cliff at the south end. There they all sat together, in silence, but in peace.

"I love you," Marcus whispered in Alexa's ear.

"I love you right back," Alexa smiled, turning and allowing him to steal a public kiss.

The drive home was spent talking about more menial matters. Alexa carried Tracey from the car, but Marcus held her back from the door, turning her gently to face him. He leaned down and kissed her passionately, stroking her face and holding her close.

"Happy Birthday, Alexa. I love you so much. I never really thought I'd be with you, but I'm so happy it worked out this way."

"Nothing ever works out the way you plan, but at least this time it worked out better. It's a nice change."

Marcus smiled and took Alexa's hand as they walked inside.

"HAPPY BIRTHDAY!"

The chorus cry was so loud it startled Tracey, sending her into a fit of tears. Alexa quickly tried to calm her as she got her own heartbeat under control. Alexa could not believe she had been fooled into thinking they were not celebrating her birthday.

"Sorry," smirked Bethany, moving forward, looking somewhere between apologetic and triumphant. "Happy Birthday, though. I know you don't celebrate, but I thought maybe it was time to change that and well, even if you don't, I'm not letting you forget your twenty-first."

"Thank you," smiled Alexa, knowing it was too late to be mad. "I think maybe we have something to celebrate now and I'm so glad you're here to celebrate it with me."

Hugging Bethany tight, Alexa suddenly noticed Pam and Karl and the strained looks on their faces. Karl looked murderous, though was doing his best to keep it in check, if somewhat unsuccessfully. Walking in with Marcus, his hand around her waist and his child in her arms, Alexa knew there was no way she could avoid explanations now. Urging everyone to move the party outside, Bethany managed to clear the room to leave Alexa and her foster family in the lounge room. Marcus kept his place by Alexa's side, his hand firmly on her waist, but Alexa could see that this conversation was not going to be made easier by his presence. Handing him Tracey, she indicated that she could handle it. It took a moment for Marcus to be convinced, and Alexa was not sure the tender, defiant kiss he placed on her forehead really helped the situation.

"I can explain," said Alexa, managing to be the first person to speak.

"You'd better," said Karl, barely containing his anger. "He's your teacher."

"He was my teacher."

Karl's eyes flashed at her clarification. "Just how long has this been going on?"

"A little over a month. Yes, we were attracted to each other back in high school," Alexa added quickly, knowing there would be questions on that point. "And we even made plans to get together when I finished, but nothing ever happened between us until a month ago. We fought against this for a long time, but I love him and he loves me."

"So you're really together?" exclaimed Hayley happily, rushing forward to hug Alexa, though the embrace was short-lived when Hayley saw the look on her father's face.

"So who else knew?" stammered Karl.

"I guessed," said Brett, sitting down on the lounge with a shrug of his shoulders.

"I had my suspicions," said Pam, placing a calming arm around Karl's shoulders.

"And the baby?"

"The baby is his, but he wants us to raise her together," answered Alexa.

"What about the mother?" asked Pam, her eyes full of concern.

"She doesn't want Tracey," said Alexa softly, hating telling people that.

Karl sat down on the edge of the lounge. He was clearly still angry, though he seemed deflated by the calmness that surrounded him. "Are you sure you're ready for a child?" he asked eventually.

"No. Is anyone ever ready for a child?" asked Alexa with a slight smile. "I love Marcus and I love Tracey. I don't feel like I'm being burdened here. I know I'm only twenty-one and that's young, but I'm not like other people my age. I can't go and be young and carefree. This is what I want – for better or worse – this is what I want."

"He never pressured you. I mean ever – at school or even now? He's much older than you and I just don't want to see you used by another man," said Karl passionately. Alexa moved forward and hugged Karl. His hesitant arms made her realise he was as surprised as she was by her actions, but when she went to quickly move away, he pulled her back and hugged her properly. "Promise me," he urged.

"No, I swear, he never pressured me," replied Alexa earnestly, stepping back so she could look into Karl's eyes. "He always tried to do the right thing by me. We were both determined to just be friends for a long time, but after a while it stopped making sense to deny how much we loved each other – and how good we were together. I've given up a lot, I don't want to give up this. Please, tell me you support me."

It took me a while, but Karl finally nodded. Alexa was glad, but this was not the only thing that needed to be dealt with and it seemed better to face it all at once. "There's something else we should cover while we're here," said Alexa. "You have to know that I really do consider you my family and I love you all. I just …."

"You what, Alexa?" asked Karl kindly, taking her hand.

"Ben wants to adopt us," Alexa finally blurted out.

"I assume this is what you want as well?" asked Pam in a gentle voice.

"Yes," nodded Alexa, keeping her eyes to the ground.

"Alexa, there's no need to be ashamed," said Karl, standing in front of her and forcing her eyes to meet his. "Ben's a very important person in your life – and Bethany's. He's always seen the two of you as his daughters. We know that. He's told us so himself. If him adopting you is what you want, you shouldn't let us hold you back. You'll never be any less a part of this family."

"Really?" asked Alexa, looking directly at Hayley.

"We never had the same parents before and I called you my

sister."

"You sure?" asked Alexa again, looking around the room.

"Yeah, we're sure," said Brett. "You can't get rid of us that easy."

Alexa looked at Pam, who nodded warmly. Then she turned to Karl. He was really the one she was worried about – not because he was the one with the temper, but because she owed Karl more than she could ever express and, in reality, she was much closer to him than Ben.

"You'll always be our daughter," said Karl earnestly. "You, Bethany and Charlotte, you're all part of our family now. But, Alexa, you're so special to us, please don't be scared of coming to us about things. We'll support you through everything. Good and bad."

Alexa nodded and let Karl's arms envelope her once more. Keeping his arm around her shoulders, Karl placed a kiss on the top of her head before insisting they join her party. However, as soon as they got outside, Karl and Brett detoured away from Alexa and headed straight over to Marcus.

"I hope you realise," said Karl, cornering Marcus, Brett standing on the other side as Alexa tried to get past them. "That if you hurt her in any way you'll have me to deal with."

"If I hurt her," replied Marcus with a wry smile, waving his hand to Alexa to reassure her. "I'll be nothing but a broken corpse by the time you get to me. You're joining the end of a long queue here."

"Does that worry you?" asked Brett.

"No, I have no intention of ever hurting Alexa. I'm glad there're so many people who think so much of her."

"Happy Birthday," said Ben from behind Alexa, steering her away from the scene and towards all the food Bethany, Charlotte and Maria had organised. "Listen, I didn't mean to put any pressure on you about the adoption. I realise you're very close to Pam and Karl and they've probably been better parents to you than I have."

"Ben – I mean, Dad … I want you to adopt us." Alexa swallowed hard on those words, but she owed Ben this much. "I love the Whites, I always will, and I know you would've taken care of us if you could've. I want you to adopt us. Charlotte doesn't mind and – I want you to be our … I want you to adopt us."

Ben hugged Alexa warmly and Alexa had to fight against the irrational fear that was building in her body. Then she was suddenly smothered from her other side.

"What are we hugging about?" asked Bethany.

Alexa loved Bethany's physicality.

"Alexa said yes," said Ben.

Bethany screamed in Alexa's ear as she ripped her out of Ben's arms and hugged her properly, jumping up and down with her.

"Oh, Lex, thank you. You won't regret this, I promise. We're finally a family, Lex. We finally have our family."

Alexa could not answer. She hoped one day she would find herself in the same place Bethany was, but right now, the idea of having parents, even Pam and Karl, was still so foreign and frightening.

Bethany's excitement quickly drew everyone's attention and Ben made the smiling announcement. No one was surprised. Ben and Bethany had been vocal about their wishes. Alexa was just glad when the congratulations were over and was even more relaxed when the birthday formalities had finished. Sitting through the Bethany-led Happy Birthday song was almost as much as Alexa could handle and she was thankful when Tracey's tired crying gave her an excuse to go inside.

"Want to go out for dinner?" asked Marcus, walking into their bedroom behind Alexa.

"I'm so full. I don't think I want to eat for another year."

"Want to pretend we're going out for dinner? Charlotte and Bethany offered to look after Tracey."

"You're letting them?" asked Alexa sceptically.

"Ben and Maria are staying as well," smiled Marcus guiltily. "And Beth's going to think I don't trust her if I don't let her look after Tracey soon."

"But you don't," replied Alexa.

"Shhh," Marcus smiled, and Alexa fell into his arms, kissing him tenderly. "Dinner?"

"Swim."

Marcus led Alexa back downstairs to the pool, letting Bethany know that her little charge was upstairs asleep and was hers for the night. Charlotte turned to Bethany, a smile on her face as they raced into the house.

"Hey, good morning, sleepyhead," smiled Marcus, watching Alexa's eyes slowly blink open. "Did you have a good birthday?"

"Yeah. I didn't think I would ever be able to say that, but I might even celebrate it next year if things keep going this well."

"Well, maybe I can give you something to celebrate a little sooner than that."

"What do you mean?" asked Alexa.

"Sit up, Tracey and I have something to discuss with you," said Marcus. Alexa shuffled herself up and sat nervously watching as Marcus picked Tracey up out of her cot and sat back down on the bed with her. "Now, I know it's only been a few weeks since we arrived and you've been doing a really wonderful job. I've never been happier and you're wonderful with Tracey, but right now I just don't feel like it's enough."

Alexa's heart raced. Marcus was not happy. She had not answered his questions properly yesterday. He was leaving her. She was not doing enough for him and he was leaving her.

"So I was thinking that perhaps there was a way we could remedy that," continued Marcus, smiling inexplicably. "What I want to know is if – maybe – you would consider being my wife."

The cogs stopped turning in Alexa's mind. She could only look at Marcus with wide, confused eyes. He smiled and stroked her cheek. Her eyes followed his hand down to his lap and his other hand that was holding a small box. Ever so slowly, as if it was all happening at half-speed, Marcus opened the box to reveal a glimmering ring. It was a white gold band with diamonds studded all the way around it.

"But … are you – but we've only been together – what – six weeks – less," stammered Alexa.

"I know. I know, but I've loved you for years," said Marcus tenderly, grasping her hand. "There's no one else in the world I want to be with and whether you marry me today or in ten years I don't care. I just want to know that one day you'll be my wife, because there's simply no one else for me. Why should I wait to ask? We're together, raising a child. Get in too deep, and then we have to make it work, right?"

"Right," nodded Alexa, her voice thick with the tears that were slipping down her face. Marcus placed the engagement ring on her finger. She had honestly never thought anyone would ever want to marry her – not even Marcus.

Putting Tracey back in her cot, Marcus slipped back into the bed and pulled Alexa into his arms, kissing her passionately.

Tingling and in a state of shock, Alexa lay in Marcus's arms, stroking his chest, her eyes constantly drawn to her bejewelled finger. Engaged. They were engaged.

"Listen, there was something else I was supposed to ask before I got carried away," said Marcus, lifting himself up to look down into Alexa's eyes. "I was wondering if perhaps you'd consider doing a little adopting yourself once we were married."

"You mean adopt Tracey?"

"Yes. You're her mother in every way that counts. Why not make it official? I want us to be a proper family and I never want you to doubt your place in our family for a second."

"Are you sure?" asked Alexa tentatively.

"Is that a yes?" asked Marcus, refusing to answer her question.

"Yes," smiled Alexa, nodding just to be sure. "That's a yes."

Marcus's arms enveloped her again, but just as his lips met hers Tracey started crying.

Alexa could not help but feel like the day had a strange unreality to it. Having taken her engagement ring off for her morning swim, she dressed nervously, wondering how she would break the news to her family. The Whites had only just found out about her going out with Marcus. Even Ben's reaction was hard to predict.

"What is that?" cried Bethany, as Alexa walked down the stairs.

"What?" asked Alexa, looking around her.

"On your finger!" Alexa could not quite answer, but Bethany's loud cries had drawn Charlotte and Marcus to the hallway. "You're engaged?" Alexa could still not answer. It seemed impossible that she could answer yes to that question. "Since when?"

"This morning," replied Marcus.

"But – but … you guys only just got together," stammered Bethany. "I don't understand. Are you serious? Don't you think this is a little extreme?"

"I thought you'd be happy," said Alexa meekly.

"Are you?" retorted Bethany. "You don't have to prove anything here. I'm all for you two being together, but marriage? Really?"

"I understand," said Charlotte simply, before congratulating Marcus then Alexa and walking up the stairs. "But I'm guessing I'm keeping this quiet for a while."

"Yes," sighed Alexa. "I think that's best."

It took much longer than Alexa expected to get Bethany on board and Alexa was not prepared to face the rest of the family without

Bethany onside. To avoid unintended announcements, Alexa put the ring on her necklace and wore it under her clothes. However, she could not keep her engagement a secret from everyone; she was too happy for that.

"We get to come to the wedding, right?" asked Amy. "I know you're going to have some small thing, but after two years, we have to count as close friends, right?"

Alexa smiled and nodded.

"This is a great excuse for dress shopping," said Jessica happily. "When's the wedding?"

"Haven't gotten that far. I'm still worrying about what everyone's going to say," answered Alexa. "It could be never."

"Don't take this the wrong way, but you freak out a lot about these kinds of things," smiled Amy. "We don't lose our minds when you tell us your crazy shit – and nothing we say ever seems to shock you – with the possible exception of me getting along with my parents. So please, don't ruin this for yourself. This is such a happy time and your family – the whole, crazy, haphazard lot of them – will be stoked. Once they get over the shock."

It took almost two weeks for Marcus, Charlotte, Jessica and Amy to convince Alexa that she was ready to announce her engagement. The process was helped by Ryan and Rhianna's enthusiastic reactions. However, Bethany's continuing concern, that had spread to Sam, was what really worried Alexa. She never thought they would disagree on something like this. The tension was also piquing Ben's interest, so when everyone was gathered in the lounge room, Alexa just spat it out.

"You don't seem very happy about it," said Pam.

"I am," replied Alexa, trying to keep her voice from being an agitated growl. "I'm stoked. I just want you guys to be as well."

Alexa waited, but the room remained in silence. Karl looked mutinous, while Ben was stony-faced. Even Sam was unhappy and he already knew. At least Charlotte and Hayley were smiling. Maria looked as though she wanted to be, while Pam, Gran and Pop seemed more ambivalent.

"I know this seems a little rushed and that we're getting carried away," said Marcus finally, when it became obvious no one was going to talk. "I'm not sure I can explain the way we feel for each other, but I love Alexa. I don't want any other woman – ever. I want Alexa. I want her to be my wife. I want her to be Tracey's mother. I want us to be a family. I'll wait forever until she's ready to marry me. I just wanted to know that she would."

"So you're not getting married right away, then?" asked Karl.

"We haven't decided on a date," answered Marcus.

"I don't plan on having a long engagement," said Alexa. "I want to marry Marc. I don't care to wait."

Tracey's grumbling interrupted the conversations. Marcus gave her to Alexa and went out to the kitchen to fix her bottle. Alexa was not surprised to see Ben and Karl walking out of the room, Sam trailing behind them. Alexa followed, trying not to be seen.

"If you're going to object, will you just get it off your chest. Tracey's hungry," said Marcus.

"She's too young," said Karl. "She's not ready for all this."

"She thinks she is."

"You selfish bastard," hissed Ben, moving forward.

Alexa was behind them now, but they did not notice her.

"You should've been sent to gaol for what you did. I should've reported you years ago – got you kicked out of your profession," spat Karl.

"You don't think that I feel sick about that?" cried Marcus. "You think I'm ignorant of everything I did? I could never protest my innocence and if you ever reported me, I'd cop it. I wouldn't even fight it. I'd be a cleaner if that's the only job I could get, but I didn't molest her. I didn't take advantage of her. I never kissed her. I never touched her."

"You still wanted to," snarled Ben.

"Well, this whole thing wouldn't have been an issue if I hadn't. I'm not saying our relationship has perfect origins. But our physical relationship didn't start until she was twenty. She's not a child any more."

"Thanks to men like you, she's never been a child," spat Ben.

"You're comparing me to Sean? To Clinton?" asked Marcus incredulously. Ben did not answer. Apparently he was not prepared to go quite that far. "What exactly do you want me to do? Leave her? You think that'll make things better? I've left her before."

"She'd get over you. You're not irreplaceable," said Sam.

"I'm sure she would. She's had to come to terms with a lot of loss in her life. Would you expect her to smile through it? Would you expect her to just pick up and move on? That's what you've all expected before and you nearly drove her away with the pressure of not living up to your standards of how she was supposed to live her life."

"You've got no right —"

"Damn it, Ben, I've got every right. I don't care how much you disapprove. I'm not leaving her. I'm never leaving her."

Alexa pushed through with Tracey and hugged Marcus warmly. He held her tighter as her body shook. "I'm not leaving him either," she said in a quivering voice as she turned to face Ben, Karl and Sam.

"Alexa, you're too young. You're not ready for this," said Ben sincerely.

"Don't tell me what I am and am not," replied Alexa forcefully. "I know, better than any of you, what I am. And Marc's the only one who lets me feel safe in that. You used to," she added looking at Sam. "Then you stopped believing in me. You stopped trusting my judgement."

"Well you kept making bad decisions," said Sam gravely.

"My decisions don't affect you. I'm the one who paid for the bad ones. And not every decision I've made has been wrong."

"Most of the recent ones have been," Sam muttered.

"I'm not going to let you force me to choose between you guys and Marc. I'm staying with Marc. I want you all to be a part of my life – our life. You choose if you can deal with it."

The shivering in Alexa's body became worse as they all stood there looking at each other. Knowing she needed to get away from the conflict, Marcus led her out into the backyard. He took Tracey from her arms and nudged her towards the pool. He would never fully understand the calming powers water had on Alexa, but was glad they had the pool. Even after swimming just a couple of laps the tension dropped from her face. It was just difficult for Marcus to acknowledge that he was part of the reason she felt so stressed. However, this time, he had no thought of walking away. That was no longer an option.

Charlotte, Hayley, Brett and Maria joined them half an hour later. Everyone else was still debating. Marcus was disheartened by Bethany's absence and could tell Alexa was too, though she tried to hide it as she mucked about in the pool with the others, but Bethany was not absent for long.

"Hey, brother," she said, hugging Marcus from behind and kissing him on the cheek. Marcus thought he would shrug Bethany off, but surprised himself by hugging her arms warmly. "Can I hold her?" asked Bethany softly. Marcus handed Tracey over. Tracey snuggled happily in Bethany's arms. "I never disapproved. I just worry that Lex takes on too much – too much responsibility. She won't let you help her – won't even let you know she needs help."

"You think I'm pressuring her?" asked Marcus seriously, wondering why he never considered confiding in Bethany.

"Maybe. I don't know," shrugged Bethany, not looking up from Tracey. "What I do know is that Lex craves security. You give her that. I think that outweighs everything else. She makes stupid decisions when she feels insecure. You marry her and she gets to relax and live a bit. I just have to remember sometimes that me and her are very different."

"I like the security too," confessed Marcus. "Things've been ripped away from us so often. It makes me nervous. I know it's just paper, but to us, it makes a difference."

"Yeah, I know. But the pressure thing – you need to help out."

"What do you mean? Tracey? Uni? I've tried hard not to put too much on her. I don't want that."

"Money," said Bethany, looking into Marcus's eyes. "You know she's broke? Well, not completely, obviously, but in terms of her allowance. I offered to take over some of the bills when she returned – after I realised how much they all were – even to just go through the household budget with her, but she wouldn't. Charlotte wants to contribute more, but Lex won't have it. Do you pay anything?" Marcus felt ill. He had not paid a single bill or any rent since moving back in. All he could do was shake his head guiltily. "Help me fix this?"

"This doesn't really sound like you," smiled Marcus.

"I grew up a lot when Lex and Charlotte took off. I'm going to disappoint you, but I am trying. I'm not proud of what I've put her through, but all that stuff, I just never had to deal with it – and I don't think I could've. Surviving was about all I could do and I didn't even do that very well."

"You did okay, Beth. You did as well as you could. Remember, Alexa wasn't perfect either. You guys are doing great. Don't expect too much. You'll get better at this whole living thing. And I'm here for you too, little sis."

Pam, Karl, Gran and Pop were the next to arrive in the backyard. When Karl walked over to Marcus and shook his hand, welcoming him to their family, Alexa jumped out of the pool and hugged him, drenching him in the process.

"All I want is for you to be safe and happy," said Karl, holding her tight. "He's a good man, I know that. I could do much worse for a son-in-law."

"So you don't mind that I'm making you a granddad?" asked Alexa with a watery smile.

Karl did not answer. Ben and Sam had just walked out into the backyard and the hurt in Ben's eyes was obvious to everyone. Karl released Alexa, but she did not move forward, too scared to take that first step.

"I'm not asking you to choose," said Ben finally. "I choose you." Alexa did not move and Ben strode over to her and hugged her gently. "I'm sorry."

Sam did not say anything, but walked over and sat with Bethany and gently stroked Tracey's head.

"So we're all excited about the engagement, then?" asked Maria in a chirpy voice, eliciting only concerned looks. "Wonderful. Then I insist on hosting the engagement party. It'll be my present to you. Give me a list of who you want to invite and we can get it started."

From the look on Alexa's face, Marcus knew that, halfway through a semester she was already behind on, an engagement party was the last thing on her mind. However, the concept was so appealing to Bethany, Charlotte and Hayley that in the end they really had no choice. Nothing could have stopped them once they started feverishly planning. Even postponing until a later date was incomprehensible. They wanted to celebrate, and Marcus knew he could not take that from them. When they promised all they needed from him and Alexa was their invitation list, there was nothing left to argue.

Sitting down together, Marcus was strangely pleased that Alexa found the task as difficult as he did. Beyond their closest friends and family, no one knew they were even together. That conversation had been too fraught to consider engaging in until they were more settled, but it would be considerably harder now that it had gone a long way beyond dating.

"I need you to do this," said Bethany anxiously a week later. "Just write the names down. If they don't approve, they won't come and we don't want them there anyway."

The very slight quiver in Bethany's voice as she spoke allowed Marcus to understand that Bethany was not being unreasonably demanding. She understood as well as they did the potential backlash this event could cause, but appeared determined to ignore it. Alexa was right, Bethany was not as ignorant as she often appeared to be, and Marcus wondered just how taxing it was for her to maintain her positive outlook.

As they drove towards Maria's apartment on the day of the engagement party, Alexa was struck by a terrifying realisation. Marcus had never been there before and he had no idea how she and Maria became friends. Marcus said nothing as he parked the car or as he carried Tracey to Maria's apartment. It was not until he walked out on to Maria's balcony and looked out on the park below that his expression changed.

"You okay?" asked Alexa, following him out on to the balcony while Maria played with Tracey inside.

"Yeah, sorry," said Marcus shaking his head. "Just thinking about something for a minute."

"What?" asked Alexa, wondering what he would say about that day. Marcus turned to her, and she could see him looking back at a dark past, before he smiled and kissed her forehead.

"Nothing," he answered casually.

"I knew I could never completely give up on a man who'd spend an entire day sitting on a park bench just hoping for the chance to say he was sorry," said Alexa softly.

Marcus's eyes widened as he looked between her and the park bench below. "You … you were – here – you were here?"

"That's how I got to know Maria in the first place. I was worried about seeing you, but I had to know if you'd turn up. I came here – to the park – a lot to try and find a place to watch to see if you'd turn up."

"Why … but if – if you were here …"

"I couldn't. I couldn't face you," answered Alexa truthfully. Marcus's head dropped as he nodded sadly. "We both knew we had to walk away, but I don't think I could've. You didn't realise it, but you gave me your apology just by showing up. I needed to grow up. I loved you, but if anything was ever going to happen I wanted it to be with us as equals and not me as the damsel in distress."

"I wish I'd known," moaned Marcus, sounding pained. "I would've waited til the end of time for you. And maybe then I wouldn't have hurt you the way I have."

"Maybe, but what we have now is pretty awesome," smiled Alexa. She had spent too much of her life wondering what if. "Because of Lucy we have Tracey. She gave us a gift I can't give you. Maybe all the pain was worth it in the end. I don't wish it any other way. I don't want you to either."

Marcus hugged her warmly, whispering in her ear how amazing she was. Alexa was going to reply when Maria interrupted them, holding Tracey out to Marcus.

"I signed up for grandmother duties, which is all the fun stuff," Maria smiled. "And right now, she doesn't smell fun." Marcus quickly took Tracey and held her close, kissing her over and over until she giggled. "I never thought I'd hear you be thankful for any part of your past," said Maria when Marcus had left.

"Me either," laughed Alexa, unaware of what she had professed. "But I finally feel like I'm getting a handle on who I am."

"Because you're going to be a wife and mother?" asked Maria seriously.

"No, I thought a lot while I was away. When I decided I'd come back, I made a lot of pacts with myself – about what I would and wouldn't do, what I would and wouldn't let other people talk me into doing. Marc actually made a big mess of my plans, but he lets me feel like I can be with him without compromising on who I want to be."

"You've grown up a lot," smiled Maria, taking Alexa's hand. "You should be proud of yourself."

It was something Alexa never had been before, but with a deep breath, she felt like she might be partway there.

The family arrived over the next fifteen minutes and helped set up. Marcus had invited his parents, but they had so far not even responded. It was something Marcus refused to talk about. However, Rhianna did not disappoint, coming straight from the airport.

"I'm glad you made it," said Marcus, hugging Rhianna warmly. "I wasn't sure you would with such short notice. I wasn't even sure the invite would find you up there in the Territory."

"Smug city boy," replied Rhianna, playfully punching Marcus in the ribs. "Civilisation – and mail – has made it all the way up there too. Besides, Bethany emailed me mine. We even have internet."

Marcus smiled as Rhianna continued to mock him. "You staying there for good?" he asked. "It's been a while. Almost like you're settling down."

"Don't start on that. I'm happy for you and your boring, old-fashioned ways. Be happy for me in my hectic, hippy ways. Besides, you never know, I might even come back here for a while. I've missed my little niece." Almost as if commanded, Charlotte appeared with Tracey and smilingly handed her over to Rhianna. "Don't worry about Mum and Dad," said Rhianna, noticing Marcus's strained look. "They'll come around. They miss this little tyke too and are starting to think Alexa can't be all bad if you guys are marrying and you want Alexa to adopt Tracey. I don't understand their problem. There's eight years between them. Me, I think it's great."

Alexa could not help but smile as she watched Rhianna hold Tracey above her head, wiggling her until she smiled. No one had ever accepted Alexa without question the way Rhianna had and now they were going to be sisters.

Once the guests started to arrive, Alexa could feel the tension in the room rising. It had been a task getting their families onside and no one was quite sure how their friends would react. Alexa was glad Jessica and Amy were the first of her friends to arrive. At least she did not have to explain anything to them. It was just a matter of introducing them to everyone they had heard so much about.

"Nice," smiled Jessica, when Alexa introduced her to Marcus. "I would've been mucking up in class too, if I was scoring detention with him." Marcus looked scandalised by the comment, but the laughter of Jessica, Amy and Alexa did a lot to diffuse the tension. "Sorry, congratulations."

"Yeah, congratulations," said Amy.

"Sorry," smiled Alexa when they walked off. "Jess makes jokes out of everything."

"It's not funny," said Marcus in a low voice.

"Sometimes it is," countered Alexa. "They're the only people who ever make jokes about us – me, my life. Everything everyone else takes so seriously, they laugh at – and let me laugh too. They're serious when I want them to be, but they're incredibly unserious when I really need to them to be. They help me let go."

"They were helping you let go of me?" asked Marcus seriously.

Alexa nodded. "Succeeding?"

"Well, obviously not too well," smiled Alexa, kissing Marcus swiftly on the lips and flitting away.

Nick and Alan had arrived, and were soon followed by the rest of the Redgrove group. Within minutes they had collected Alexa out on the balcony with a stockpile of drinks and food.

"So, engaged," said Lizzie, as Alexa sat down.

"Yeah," replied Alexa sheepishly.

"But I thought you just had a crush on him?" blurted Lizzie, as though she had been holding in the comment since she received her invitation.

"It was a bit more than a crush," confessed Alexa with an embarrassed smile.

"Obviously!" Lizzie's face was red and her voice bordering on hysterical. Alexa was bemused by Lizzie's reaction and relieved there was more surprise than disapproval in her voice. "When did this all happen? I mean you have a baby, you're getting married. How did all this happen without us knowing?"

"Me and Marc being together's only fairly recent."

"Yeah, exactly how recent?" asked Chad with a smile and glinting eyes. "Tracey does look a lot like you."

"Ha ha, I didn't quite manage to sneak a pregnancy past you," said Alexa, sticking her tongue out at Chad. "A couple of months."

"And now you're engaged. Sure don't waste no time tying a man down," laughed Chad.

"Well, I think it's really good," said Ezra, smiling. "A little strange, perhaps. I never intended on going to any of my teachers' weddings, but you were never going to do life normally."

"I don't know if it's that strange," said Chad in a more serious voice. "Look at everything that happened in high school. It'd be hard for them not to at least like each other. I think you make a really great couple – and a great mother."

"Well, like you really need us to say anything, but we think it's great as well," smiled Nick, nudging Alan, who then smiled as well.

"Hey, Alexa, can talk to you for a minute?" asked Bianca, speaking for the first time that evening.

"No, come on, Bianca," moaned Chad. "This is her engagement party. Don't make a scene."

Alexa stared at Chad, wondering what he knew. She might have asked, but Bianca was already walking inside and towards the front door. It was odd, but Alexa followed her out into the corridor.

"What's going on?" asked Alexa.

"Are you sure about this? I mean marriage, a baby. He was our teacher," said Bianca in the same condescending tone she had often used when they were in high school.

"Bianca, please don't. I'm happy. For the first time in my life, I'm happy," sighed Alexa, trying to contain her annoyance. "I'm sorry we're not really friends any more and I know that's my fault, but please don't come into my life and try and take this away from me."

"I don't want to take anything from you. But this is wrong. You don't want to do this. It won't make you happy."

"But I am happy!" cried Alexa, before realising Bianca must want some credit for that. "I've been able to do everything I need because of the money we won and I really should thank you for that."

"I'm sorry we ever won that money," muttered Bianca.

"Why?" asked Alexa automatically, shocked anyone could say such a thing.

"I'd give it all up to be happy again. That money destroyed my life. It's the only reason people talk to me. Everyone asks for money. You offer people money and they don't even take it! I wish I'd never been so jealous of you."

"It's fine," said Alexa cautiously, worried about the way Bianca was linking her in with her troubles.

"That money was the worst thing that ever happened to us," said Bianca more forcefully.

"It was the best thing that ever happened to me," replied Alexa, refusing to agree with Bianca.

"You would've had all this anyway," waved Bianca agitatedly. Alexa wondered if that was the problem. "All these people would've been here by your side whether you had money or not. I would've been happy without it. We would've been friends without it. I just want to get rid of it and never think about it again. I have to go."

Alexa was left dumbstruck. It was a lie that she and Bianca had ever been great friends, even in high school, but not once had Alexa seriously considered that Bianca would regret winning the money or care that they were not close friends now. Still confused by what had just transpired, Alexa walked back into the apartment, only to be cornered by Alan. "Can I talk to you for a minute?"

"Only if it's good news," smiled Alexa, unsure she could take more confusion tonight.

"I'm not sure I can guarantee that, but it's not bad news," replied Alan, not quite managing a smile. There was something in his face that made Alexa curious. It was the same thing she had seen at Sam's place the night she broke up with Damien. "I wanted to give you this," he said, taking a small pouch from his pocket and laying it her hand. She opened it and a silver charm bracelet fell into her hands. "I know it's a little childish. I actually bought it for you when we were in year nine."

"What?"

"I had a massive crush on you in high school," confessed Alan with a blushing grin. "Even past high school, really. I knew I never had a chance, but I bought it thinking one day I'd have the courage to give it to you."

"I'm sorry, Al," gasped Alexa, feeling tears sting her eyes.

"For what?"

"For not knowing."

"That's okay," smiled Alan. "I didn't really want you to. Hell, everyone knew nobody stood a chance against Sam, and we had a feeling about you and Marc. I just wanted you to have it and thought maybe I could steal a kiss – just on the cheek." Alexa smiled and nodded. Alan moved and gave her a long and tender kiss on the cheek. "And Chad's right. You make a great mum."

"Thanks," gasped Alexa, hardly able to breathe as Alan brushed her cheek.

Alan took her by the hand and delivered her to Marcus, shaking his hand. "We doing speeches soon, mate?" asked Alan. "Let's get the formalities over so we can crank this party up."

Marcus looked down at Alexa as she grimaced. "We can just thank everyone for coming – get it over and done with," said Marcus, squeezing her hand.

"No, you can't be serious," said Brandon, suddenly grabbing Marcus's arm. Alexa had not even noticed him standing behind Marcus. "Have you honestly become so delusional as to think this will actually work?"

Alexa felt herself immediately flanked by Charlotte and Bethany – Sam, Hayley, Brett and her high school friends around them.

"No one here's delusional," said Ryan in a calm voice, appearing on Marcus's other side. "We all know Alexa and how much she and Marc love each other."

"Love? This isn't love, it's sick," spat Brandon. "She's twenty-one. She's a kid and he's her teacher."

If Alexa had not been able to hear the disgust in Brandon's voice, she would definitely have seen it on his face. She looked up at Marcus to see what he would say in response, but he appeared too stunned to speak.

"Listen, you don't have to understand it," said Ryan. "You just have to accept it and if you spent any time with them, then you'd know how good they are together and how great Alexa is."

"You," said Brandon scathingly, turning on Ryan. "You're the reason Marc thinks this whole thing's okay. We've spent years trying to get his head right and suddenly you come along and tell him it's all okay. Do you even know her history? Do you know what that thing has done? Who knows what sorts of things she's infected with. Have you even had her test—"

Alexa was quicker than them all, standing in front of Marcus with his balled fist in her hand. "Please, don't," she pleaded. "Please don't hit anyone."

Marcus looked down and Alexa felt his body instantly relax. Pulling her into his chest, he kissed the top of her head as he apologised quietly in her ear.

"I love Alexa," said Marcus firmly, looking at Brandon. "I don't think there's anything wrong with us. I was her teacher and I am ten years older than her. I can't change any of that, but she's the love of my life and I'm not going to miss out on happiness because of how and where we met. If you – any of you – can't accept us, it's time for you to go. I'm not leaving her."

Brandon looked around the room as the room watched him, waiting for his decision. He gave Marcus one last disbelieving look before walking out the door, followed by many others. Marcus moved forward and hugged his mates who remained, before introducing them to Alexa. It was awkward and left the room in a strange state of tension.

"So maybe we should leave that as the speeches for tonight," smiled Alexa nervously, looking around at her friends, hoping for some assistance.

"Sweet," smiled Alan. "Party time! I get first dance."

Alan grabbed Alexa and pulled her to the centre of the room. Bethany instantly cried out that she would handle the music. Alan did not wait for it to start playing before breaking out the moves. Nick, Chad, Hayley and Charlotte quickly joined them on their newly designated dance floor. Their enthusiasm caught on and Chad even managed to get Sam to join in the festivities.

"Forgiven me yet?" Alexa asked, when Sam took her by the waist and started dancing close. It did not matter that Bethany was playing a dance song, Sam swayed Alexa slowly to their own rhythm.

"You ever get jealous looking at me and Beth?" responded Sam, speaking in her ear so no one else could hear.

"I don't know what to call it," replied Alexa honestly, her heart thrumming.

"There was a part of me that always assumed we'd end up together – like it'd be forced on us. I started to think you felt that way about Marcus – like there was just no point moving on because you'd just end up together whether you wanted to or not. I didn't want that for you. I wanted you to have more. I wanted you to have what I found with Beth – what I thought I'd never find."

"I know you care. I just think you care too much," said Alexa.

"No, you were right. I stopped seeing you as you," said Sam intently. "I'm going to make it up to you. I'm going to give you your best friend back."

Alexa smiled and hugged Sam tight, forgetting all about dancing. It was the best engagement present Sam could have given her.

"Do I get a get a look in?" asked Marcus, tapping Sam on the shoulder. "Beth sent me. I warn you, she wants to dance."

Chapter Fourteen

ALEXA FOUND HER life falling into a hectic new routine. University and study took up most of her time, but she was determined she would not let herself lose touch with friends and family. Friday nights were spent with Charlotte, Bethany and Hayley. Monday nights were dinner with Maria. The Whites were visited on the weekend and Marcus was everywhere in between. What surprised Alexa was Ben's early arrival on Monday to join her for her morning swim. It was pleasant, particularly breakfast afterwards. It was the first time they had really spent any time together since New Year's Eve. Ben came back the next day and the day after. By Thursday morning, Alexa was sure he would be sick of her, but, weary-eyed, he walked out to the pool and slipped in. Alexa smiled and pushed off. Ben finished well before her this time, but waited for her to finish before leaving.

"You're not staying for breakfast?" she asked, trying to keep the disappointment from her voice.

"Not this morning. I have to get to work," smiled Ben, gently stroking her wet hair.

"Something big?" asked Alexa, her fear piqued by something in his voice.

"Just preparing for a raid."

"Dangerous?"

Ben smiled and chuckled slightly. "Not today."

Alexa was going to ask him more, but decided it could wait until tomorrow morning. However, Ben did not show up the next morning. Alexa waited in the pool for him, turning at every noise, but the only person to arrive was Marcus.

"No Ben?" asked Marcus. Alexa just shook her head. "Why don't you just have your swim and I'll make breakfast. Tracey didn't feel like sleeping in."

Marcus tried to make conversation at breakfast, but Alexa found it hard to join in. She wondered if something had happened to Ben or if he was just sick of seeing her.

"Something's probably come up at work. He'll call and explain when he can," said Marcus reassuringly, as Alexa swung her bag over her shoulder.

"You think they know about us?" asked Alexa, biting her lip. "I mean, legally, we're nothing to him."

"I'm positive he would have you down as next of kin," replied Marcus soothingly. "You'd know if something happened to him. He's just been caught up with work, I'm sure of it. He'll call."

But Ben never called and when Alexa returned home Marcus could not get her to talk about it. Marcus offered to call Ben and make sure he was okay, but Alexa just shook her head.

"You sure you don't want me to take her tonight?" asked Marcus, watching Alexa pack Tracey's bag as she prepared to go to dinner with Charlotte, Bethany and Hayley.

"It's girls' night out and she's a girl," replied Alexa softly, trying to rouse her mood.

"I know, but it's your night off and I want you to relax."

"You do realise that I hardly spend a minute with Tracey when I take her to dinner, right," laughed Alexa. "Hayley has her out of my arms as soon as she sees me and Charlotte and Bethy can't get enough of her. Besides, I love being able to spend time with Tracey. I feel like I'm not doing enough for the two of you at the moment."

"Don't think that," said Marcus, though it was almost a command. "You have to study. It's your second last semester and you want to get into honours next year, don't you?"

"Yeah, of course I do. I just wish I had more time for everyone, but especially you two."

"When your exams are over, you can spend every spare minute with us. We'll have two whole months off together," smiled Marcus.

"I know," nodded Alexa. Marcus pulled her into a gentle hug, before picking up Tracey and carrying her downstairs. At the front door, Charlotte eagerly took Tracey from his arms before he could say a thing. Alexa smiled as he shook his head. "I did tell you," she said, kissing him goodnight.

"Do you want me to take her?" Bethany asked Charlotte eagerly when she arrived at the door.

"No, I'm good," said Charlotte.

"Let's go. Hayley'll want a chance at Tracey as well," smiled Alexa.

At dinner, Tracey's every whimper was attended to by her three doting aunts. Alexa was sure Tracey was very aware she only had to make a noise to get attention and was consequently a loud and bubbly child. The attention doubled when she smiled and positively exploded when she giggled, though the men of the family were no more immune to her charms. That made Alexa think of Ben. She had still not heard from him and wondered if she should ask Bethany if he was okay, but did not want to worry her. Trying to distract herself from thoughts of Ben, Alexa concentrated her mind on her sisters' lives.

"Mum's already said that," sighed Hayley, as they discussed school. "You don't have to make everything so serious. Can't you go back to being my cool big sister? I don't need another mother."

Alexa apologised quickly, but was not sure what else to say. Bethany smiled and took her by the hand. "Lex, you have to stop thinking you have to take care of us," she said. "I know you're getting married and have a baby and that you even pretty much raised me, but you're still only twenty-one. Don't try and be older than you have to be. With us, you need to relax and be our big sister and not our mother."

"Yeah," agreed Charlotte softly. "We all have Pam and Maria. Pam's actually been really good to me and Beth and gives us the support and advice of a mother – like she does for you. We don't need you to be a mum to us any more. You can relax. Just be our sister."

Alexa nodded. It was not as though she was she was upset by the request, more that she had not been aware of her actions. "I'll try, okay," she said finally.

"Well, perhaps I can be your first test," said Charlotte nervously. "I'm not going back to my school next year."

"What!" cried Alexa, Bethany and Hayley in unison.

"It's not that bad," laughed Charlotte, who had clearly said it that way for effect. "I'm just changing schools."

"Why? I thought you were going well?" asked Bethany. "You being bullied or something?" she added with a tone very intent on taking care of it.

"No, it's not quite that dramatic," replied Charlotte, squeezing Bethany's hand. "I didn't want to discuss it before I had it all sorted. My new school's pretty expensive and I didn't want Lex to feel pressured into paying for it."

"Who is paying for it?" asked Alexa.

"My dad. We've kept in contact since I came home. He wants me to go to university over there. It's harder to do that if I don't do the IB and my school doesn't offer it."

"What's the IB?" asked Bethany, turning to Alexa, who just shrugged.

"The International Baccalaureate," answered Charlotte. "I can use it to get into any university around the world easier than I can with our normal exams."

Alexa took a deep breath and swallowed. Charlotte still had two more years of school ahead of her, but the idea of her leaving was horrible and Alexa did not know what to say. However, the need for her to not appear too motherly was removed by the tears slipping down Bethany's cheeks.

"Beth, it's okay," said Charlotte tenderly.

"I'm going to miss you so much," Bethany sobbed, wiping away her tears, though they kept falling.

"Maybe going away to uni and definitely not for two years," smiled Charlotte reassuringly. "It's just an opportunity. I haven't promised them I'm going over there."

"Is Wes really okay with paying for it?" asked Alexa tentatively.

"I think so. I'm still a bit nervous about that, but I have money saved and I think I can cover next year's fees if I need to – with a bit of help."

"Anything you need, Char," said Alexa firmly. "I'm your big sister, but in terms of money, anything you need, okay?"

Charlotte's news had the house abuzz. Alexa found her happiness mixed with pangs of jealousy and regret. She knew everything she had ever done for Charlotte was to help her avoid her own fate and so far it looked like it was working as well as she could have hoped. However, the slight smile that often sat on Charlotte's lips made Alexa wish there had been someone who had been able to spare herself more. It made her think of the Whites and all they had tried – and all she had rejected – and it made her think of Ben, who she did not hear from again until he turned up for breakfast on Sunday morning.

"Dad!" smiled Bethany, rushing into his arms. Ben hugged her warmly in response before looking over at Alexa, clearly hoping she would demonstrate the same enthusiasm, but Alexa could not move towards him. She felt Marcus's eyes on her as she walked back to the kitchen to collect more food.

"You okay, Alexa?" asked Ben, his arms still around Bethany as they followed her.

"Yeah, just tired," murmured Alexa.

"You swim this morning?" asked Ben. Alexa nodded. "Maybe you swim too much. You're taking on a lot at the moment."

Alexa nodded again, excusing herself to go to the bathroom. She stopped just outside the room, leaning against the wall as she mastered the urge to cry.

"You sure she's okay?" asked Ben. Alexa was sure he was talking to Bethany, but it was Marcus who replied.

"You're kidding, right?" said Marcus, his voice almost a snarl. "You have no idea why she's upset?" There was only silence. "You come by every morning for four days, tell her you're preparing for a raid and then just don't show up the next day. You don't call or let her know you're all right. You don't tell her you won't be coming by. I thought you'd made some epic breakthrough, realising that you really don't know Lex because you've never spent any real time with her and then you do this."

"Why didn't she just call me if she was so worried?" asked Ben.

"Because she didn't want to find out that something had happened to you. She doesn't even know if she'd be told if something did happen to you because, after all, she's nothing to you. Her words!" cried Marcus, and Alexa guessed Ben had been about to argue. "Her words. But you know, I don't think that would've stopped her. If she really thought something had happened to you, she would've been doing everything to find out. She didn't call because she didn't want to find out that you don't care whether or not you see her."

Ben stormed out of the room, but pulled up when he saw Alexa against the wall. She did not move, but she did not have to. Ben pulled her into his arms, hugging her tight as his breath hitched. He apologised softly, but she did not reply. She was still too hurt to throw her arms around him the way she wanted to. When he promised he would not make the same mistake again, she felt so sick she ran to her room.

Things were never the same after that. Ben stopped just showing up at the house. He would call and ask to come by. He would make arrangements to see Alexa, then turn up fifteen minutes early. It annoyed her at first, but after a while she noticed her distrust waning. He had been making promises, just so he could keep them. Even when her classes finished and exams loomed, Ben did not disappear. Although he pulled back from engagements with her – as everyone else did – he was often at the house with Bethany. That was when he started doing all the things she wished he had been around to do before. He brought her cups of tea and bowls of chopped up fruit, talking to her for a minute before leaving her to study. He even cooked meals with Bethany. When they ate together he talked as much to Marcus he did to Bethany and Charlotte, and even took an interest in Tracey.

All this attention made Alexa feel like she was outright neglecting her family. She tried to take on more, insisting she could handle it, but Marcus was amazingly stubborn on these points. He refused to let her do anything but focus on her studies. However, the way he spoke of the coming months when they would both be at home together was so enticing it made it hard to concentrate.

Thankfully, the hard work paid off. The exams generally went well, and Alexa did not return home after any of them on the verge of tears. She hoped that would translate into better marks, noting how beneficial it was not to have everything fall apart just before her exams. When pens down was called on the last exam, Alexa was practically bouncing in her seat, waiting to be dismissed. Jessica feigned shock at Alexa's apologies for not being able to stay for their traditional post-exam celebrations.

"Yeah, yeah, I know," laughed Jessica. "I can't compete with the love of your life and your new daughter."

"Sorry," grimaced Alexa again, though her smile quickly overrode it.

"You can make it up to me by making sure I'm on the wedding planning committee."

"Yeah, definitely," smiled Alexa, thinking it would be great to have a normal person around to help explain how weddings worked.

Racing home, Alexa flew into the house, almost colliding with Marcus who was waiting near the front door for her.

"Ace it?" asked Marcus, pulling her into his arms and hugging her tight.

"Maybe, we'll see," replied Alexa smilingly. "Where's Tracey? I want to hang with the two of you."

"Sleeping," said Marcus apologetically. "She has no sense of occasion."

Alexa was disappointed until she realised that left her alone with Marcus, something she had not been for quite a while. "I guess I'll just have to hang with you," she said, as she slowly unbuttoned his shirt.

Marcus kissed her passionately, before breaking away to lead her up to their room. Once there, Alexa stripped off his shirt. She had planned to tease the moment out longer, but it had been a long time since Marcus's hands had played on her skin. There were too many reasons to follow the pace their bodies dictated, and this time Alexa tried not to hold back.

"Do ever think we rushed into this?" asked Marcus, suddenly thoughtful and pensive.

"Yeah, sometimes, of course," replied Alexa, confused by the question. She was not sure there was anyone who would say they had taken things slowly. "I mean, that week before you left – I thought so much about what would happen. I thought about our dates and where you might take me – where I might take you. I thought about what our first kiss would be like and how long I'd make you wait. I wanted to know that you'd wait until I was ready before things got more serious." Marcus's face contorted and Alexa hugged him tight. "Doesn't mean it would've happened that way," she smiled. "Neither of us were really interested in slowing things down once they got started. It may've happened this way anyway. I sometimes think that's why nothing ever happened before. Maybe we always knew it would be all over with that one kiss."

"And you're happy?" asked Marcus seriously.

"Of course I'm happy. What's wrong? What's going on?" asked Alexa, realising there was something larger at play.

"What scares you most?"

That question confirmed Alexa's suspicion, though it gave little indication of what was wrong. However, she barely hesitated with her answer. "I'm scared I haven't created a safe enough world for my family and that I'll be forced to defend them and forced to endure all that pain again," she answered seriously, before pausing for a moment. "But that's not my greatest fear. Mostly I'm scared that I am my past, that I'll never be separated from it, and that people will believe I wanted my father – that I've never been raped – that I wanted it – all because – that you might look at me the way others do."

Marcus's head dropped. He did not try to deny it and Alexa was glad. She had known exactly what he had been thinking when he had pushed her away that day.

"It wasn't just that and I wasn't thinking badly about you," said Marcus with soft sincerity. "I was so used to denying myself, denying you. That, and it suddenly occurred to me that you, this angel-like creature, was the very same person who'd been with men like that. I couldn't help but wonder why none of them realised just how amazing you were. Part of me feels like I should've been the man who found you there and noticed you and taken you away. You did what you had to do. I wish you never had to, but I don't think any less of you because of it."

Alexa squeezed Marcus's hand and accepted his explanation, but she knew this conversation had never been truly about her. "So what's your greatest fear?"

"That you will bore of me," Marcus sighed, looking up at the ceiling.

"How? What do you mean?"

"I never told you why Lucy started cheating on me, did I?" said Marcus in a shaky voice. Alexa shook her head and squeezed his hand. "It was before we met again. We'd been going out for a while and she wanted to get more adventurous in the bedroom. I'm – I wasn't really into that. I think sex is for love. It's old fashioned for a guy and I don't admit it to anyone, but I've only really done it one way."

Alexa smiled.

"I guess you noticed," Marcus muttered in a defeated tone. "The only times I didn't was here, when I was in the wheelchair. She made all sorts of noises to get at you ... and I used her. I didn't want to be with her, but I used her for my own satisfaction. I guess I'm just worried that you'll want more from me than I can give you."

Feeling his body sag around her, Alexa could not imagine the amount of courage it must have taken Marcus to say those words out loud. "We could use the same position for the rest of our lives and I would never bore of you," said Alexa truthfully. "Did you know I never let Damien on top of me?" Marcus's eyes widened slowly as he shook his head. "It's harder for someone to rape you from underneath you. The one time I did was that night – the night we broke up. I felt like I was being raped – even though I knew what was happening, it still felt like he was violating me. You've never – well you have made my heart race and given me tingles down my spine, but for very different reasons."

"I'm so sorry," cried Marcus earnestly.

"For what?"

"For not giving you the choice."

"You've never made me feel unsafe. You notice everything and I don't have to tell you to stop or that I feel uncomfortable. You seem to know before I even get a chance to panic. Damien never noticed anything. I was just a body to him, I think. But with you – I like what you do. I love what we do."

Marcus's arms enveloped Alexa in a crushing embrace just as Tracey's cries drifted into the room. After another fierce hug, they jumped out of bed and raced to Tracey's bedside.

The end of Alexa's exams meant that she had much more time to spend with everyone and to tend to matters she had been neglecting. Foremost on her mind was Charlotte's schooling and how they were going to pay for it if, for some reason, her father withdrew his financial support. Calling a family meeting with Charlotte and Bethany, Alexa walked in with a plan, but they had come prepared.

"We're not letting you give up more money and continue to pay all the bills with your share. You deserve to have a life too," said Bethany forcefully.

"You two are too young to be taking on all this responsibility," said Alexa, smilingly squeezing Bethany's hand, then trying to move on with her plan.

"I'm nineteen, Lex. When you were my age, you were dealing with all of this. I'm doing well and I want to start taking a bit more responsibility for my life. I can't live with you and Marc forever. I want to feel like I can stand on my own two feet. Don't make me feel useless and inadequate."

"And I don't want to feel like a burden," said Charlotte.

Alexa got the feeling that they had pre-planned their remarks. Every one of her arguments was countered by a remark about how her actions were impinging on them. They were fighting her at her weakest point and they were winning. Marcus just sat at the table smiling smugly.

"So are you ready for our plan now?" asked Bethany. Alexa nodded and let out a defeated sigh. "You take sixty percent of the interest payments. Ah, don't speak," added Bethany as soon as Alexa opened her mouth. "Charlotte and I split the other forty. We both work and we don't really need that much. We've worked out our personal budgets and I want you to look at mine. It doesn't balance yet." Alexa smiled. "Charlotte and I are going to contribute a hundred dollars a week to housekeeping – and so are you and Marc. This pays for bills, food, whatever we need."

"Nope," said Marcus quickly. "Charlotte pays fifty until she gets a proper job – or leaves school. Lex and I will pay one-twenty-five each. That's fair."

"And we each pay for our own expenses," added Bethany, nodding in agreement with Marcus's proposal.

"That all sounds pretty good," admitted Alexa. "But I don't think I should get more than half of the money. If we're all contributing to the bills and food, then it should be a three-way split."

"We actually did a five-way split," smiled Charlotte, as though she had pre-empted this very proposal. "You, Marc and Tracey, and me and Beth. Twenty percent each. The rest of us have jobs and you guys have a baby. She's not cheap. We know how much she craps."

"So we agree then?" asked Marcus.

"Yeah, okay, I agree," sighed Alexa.

"Roughly translated: she's run out of arguments," laughed Bethany.

Everyone except Alexa laughed merrily, until Ben turned up looking curious. Bethany could not hide her joy as she explained how they had finally snookered Alexa into relinquishing some form of financial control.

"You think you could relinquish a bit more?" Ben asked. "I was hoping I could take you out for dinner?"

"What, just me?" asked Alexa, before realising how horrible she sounded.

"No, I assumed Marcus and Tracey would come along," replied Ben calmly.

"But what about Bethy and Charlotte?"

"We're planning pizza and popcorn," smiled Bethany. "And we actually see quite a bit of Dad."

Alexa looked at Charlotte who nodded in confirmation, which surprised Alexa. She had never really seen them together. It made her feel terribly out of touch.

"Only if you want to, of course," said Ben.

"I'm keen," smiled Marcus, taking Alexa's hand, which allowed her to nod slowly.

Alexa found dinner more awkward than she knew she should. Marcus tried hard to keep the conversation going, but the real icebreaker was Tracey. Ben held her through most of dinner and tended to her every need, even trying her on small amounts of their food. Watching Ben with Tracey allowed Alexa to see him in a different light. For the first time she saw the man who had been desperate to be a father – had longed to be her father – and she found herself yearning for the childhood they could have had if he had been the one to hold her so innocently.

"I know I haven't been very supportive, but I'd like the chance to change that," said Ben as they sat talking at the end of the meal. "I want to be a part of your family's life, be a part of Tracey's life."

"You were always going to be her grandad," said Alexa, the words spilling out of her mouth so quickly they surprised her as much as Ben. "I have some intimacy issues, but you were always going to play that role in my life – I mean Tracey's life."

Ben smiled and looked down at Tracey, his eyes watering slightly as he introduced himself as grandad.

That was the beginning of Ben's frequent visits. Although the number of morning swims decreased to just two a week, he was always around and often when Bethany was not home. Alexa paid more attention and realised that Ben and Charlotte did spend a lot of time together, often discussing the law. Charlotte had done her year ten work experience with Peter and Alexa thought she had her sights set on a law degree, though she would never discuss it with any of them. Whenever they asked Charlotte what she wanted to do when she left school, she would simply shrug and say she had not decided yet.

Alexa was glad that Ben played such a paternal role in Charlotte's life, but was even happier that he was playing that role in her life. At least once a week he would make sure they had some time together and he was spending an increasing amount of time with Marcus as well.

"I have to admit, I was wrong about the two of you," said Ben as they sat down at the beach with their coffees. Marcus had insisted they have the afternoon alone together.

"I thought you'd already done that," replied Alexa.

"No, I'd accepted that I'd do more damage trying to break you up. I assumed it'd fall apart. I really thought you were being manipulated by him. I thought he had you under some kind of spell or something and that if we just kept you apart you'd snap out of it."

"And what do you think now?"

"That you were right. He's not Sean. Nothing like him. That you're actually really good together," answered Ben sincerely. "I think if anyone's spellbound, it's actually Marcus. He adores you. I see it every time he's near you. I was worried he saw you as something to take care of and control, but he just loves you."

"I could've told you that if you'd asked," replied Alexa, perhaps more harshly than was necessary.

"Alexa, you have to see things from my point of view. I'd already seen what Sean had done to your mother – then to you. I'd seen what Clinton had done to you. What Leo put you through. To think you were being lured into the same trap. That day – when I saw the way you were looking at each other – it'd been hard enough to leave you in that place after organising that damned plea bargain, but to see that – I almost never took you back to school that day."

"What do you mean organise the plea bargain?" cried Alexa. "Peter did that – he organised it – because I was too tainted to make a case against Clinton."

"They were never going to plead that case out," replied Ben with an agitated sigh, making Alexa realise how long he had held on to this secret. "They would've put you through trial. Your mental health really didn't matter to them. When Peter couldn't argue his point he tracked me down. Gave me the background. I was so mad at him for not telling me about your mother – about the foster homes. He didn't trust me, I don't think. He was always so protective of you. Anyway, I pulled every string I could and called in every favour. I was coming for you then, was going to get Beth, but Peter talked me out of it. After all, you had no idea who I was and you were supposed to be safe at school, and the Whites were good people, he assured me. If I took Beth, you'd freak out. He was right, but I still wish I'd ignored him. Maybe then I could've stopped what happened next."

"You might've stopped Leo getting me, but he was always going for Hayley. If Bethy left him, he would've just gone for Hayley sooner. I don't regret sparing her. She never would've survived that. But I don't know if you could've ever stopped Marcus and me."

"Destined to be together?"

"No," replied Alexa tersely. "If you guys had trusted us and let us be, then I don't know that anything would have happened – not then. Even if things hadn't ended so badly at school and we'd met up like we planned, I still think we would've gone our separate ways. Marc never would've started anything with me unless I was completely sure and I wasn't back then. I knew it was wrong. I knew I was too young, and so did he. We would've stayed friends and I think I would've survived better."

"So nothing would've happened between you?" asked Ben, and Alexa could hear the regret in his voice.

"I don't know. Marc would've helped me move on, but that doesn't guarantee that I would've met someone else and fallen in love. And I think, eventually, if we were both single at the same time and I didn't feel immature any more, I think we would've tested us out. But it happened the way it did and I don't regret it."

"Well, everything happens for a reason. Perhaps yours was Tracey," offered Ben with a smile.

"Maybe, but I don't like to think things happen for a reason," said Alexa, trying to repress a shiver. "Give me a good reason for what happened to me and Bethy?" Ben did not answer. "Things happen the way they do and you just deal with the consequences and take heart from the unexpected good."

"I wish I'd trusted you," said Ben sombrely.

"So Marc wouldn't be your future son-in-law?"

"No," smiled Ben, and Alexa thought he liked the way she phrased that. "No, because I've spent all these years never really knowing you. I got to know Beth. She's forceful and physical and you get to know her whether you intend to or not. You're closed off and I made the mistake of thinking that's all there was. And you suffered so much more than Beth and all I wanted in the world was to protect you – and I failed in that too, because the person I thought you were wasn't even real. I was so scared of letting you fall that I was holding you down when you were really preparing to fly. I'm sorry."

Alexa found herself suddenly crawling into Ben's lap. His arms instantly wrapped around her and she allowed herself to be pulled into his chest.

"You weren't real to me either," said Alexa, tears in her eyes. Ben stroked her hair as she wondered what else would be okay to say. "That day in court, do you think I'd really forgotten you?"

"I don't know. You were almost seven by then. I thought I saw a flicker of recognition, then your eyes went blank. Peter told me you coped by shutting down. You just blocked things out."

"Except in my dreams," she said softly. Ben nodded. "I'm sorry."

"For what?"

"Hurting you. I see the way you are with Tracey and how much you must have wanted that with us."

"You didn't take you and Beth away from me," said Ben, holding her tighter as he stroked her hair. "You should've never been sent back to your mother. I'd petitioned to adopt the two of you, but when your mother died the system's solution was to send you into temporary foster care. They should've called me. I just wish they called me."

Alexa was sure that was the last good talk she and Ben would have for a while. Their breakthrough conversations always seemed to be followed by weeks or months of silence, but this time was different. Ben continued to come by the house and after noticing that she almost never visited him, Alexa made more of an effort herself. They also talked more about their past. Despite all the revelations after Sean's attack, Alexa had no sudden flashes of memory. That past remained hidden in the darkness of her mind, but sometimes she wanted to know more.

"What was I like?" Alexa asked Ben one morning when they had finished their swim.

"Rough," smiled Ben. "You used a lot of words I didn't expect young children to know."

"But I didn't think I swore much."

"We were teaching you words more suited to everyday conversation. Maybe something stuck."

"So I was an adorable little potty-mouth, then?"

Ben laughed. "You were more than that. You were very much like what you were when I met you again. But I remember thinking how bright you were. We had you in school for a while and you were – still are, even – this amazing mix of experience and naivety. You were very dexterous, but toys and children's thing were like a mystery to you. You could read. Then once you started school, you just took off academically. You picked things up so quickly. The school wanted you to have an IQ test."

"But you didn't agree?" asked Alexa curiously.

"We ran out of time."

Alexa jumped out of the pool and grabbed her towel, but before she could make it inside Ben enveloped her in a wet embrace. "It's hard not to wonder, isn't it?" he said in a thick voice. Alexa nodded.

"I know, but don't dwell on it. I find it hard too, but we have a great life now – and I want you to have a great night too."

"Huh?" asked Alexa, pushing out of his arms.

"Maria and I want some grandparent time with Tracey," smiled Ben. "We're stealing your child and sending you and Marcus out to dinner. No arguments."

Alexa did not argue and neither did Marcus. Time alone together was too precious to be denied.

"You almost ready?" asked Marcus, walking into the bedroom. "Beth is feeding Tracey. You almost have to fight to hold her at times in this house. I think Charlotte was upset she didn't get to feed her."

"Did you tell them they're welcome to change her nappies," called Alexa from the bathroom, letting out a small chuckle.

"That, they don't seem interested in."

Alexa walked out from the bathroom half dressed, her pants unbuttoned around her waist as she searched for the top she wanted to wear.

"What?" asked Alexa with a smile when she noticed Marcus sitting on the bed watching her.

"Nothing, you're just beautiful," he said, walking over and placing his hands on her waist. "It's hard to believe that we're really together and I get to hold you like this."

Alexa immediately stopped worrying about finding more clothes to wear and with a devilish smile set about them wearing less. Leading Marcus to the bed, she saw a look of concern cross his face as she straddled his waist. "Roll me over as soon as you stop enjoying it," she said, placing a finger on his lips before quickly replacing it with her mouth.

Alexa loved the way Marcus's hands held her. They were strong, yet tender, and never forceful. They enveloped her and made her feel safe.

"You better be close," gasped Marcus as he kissed her lips, but she just smiled and shook her head. It had not been her concern. Marcus groaned, his lips moving to her chest and his hands below her waist. This time it was Alexa's turn to gasp.

"Wow," breathed Marcus, Alexa lying on his chest, his arms wrapped tightly around her.

"Yeah, that," said Alexa, her heart still thumping erratically.

***

The smell of Christmas began to slowly invade the house as shops became a swirl of fairy lights and tinsel. Bethany and Charlotte made furtive efforts to bring many of those decorations into the house, but Alexa was resisting all efforts to involve her.

"Lex," said Bethany, as Alexa started lunch.

Alexa knew what was coming. It would be the fifth time they had had this conversation this week. "You want to talk to me about Christmas?"

"Don't be like that," said Bethany playfully, hugging Alexa from behind. "I want to celebrate this year. I want to experience a happy Christmas like everyone else talks about. There's no reason why we can't have that too."

"Everyone I know talks about excessive alcohol consumption and family feuds," smiled Alexa. Bethany did not return the smile. "I'm sorry. What do you want to do?"

"I want a Christmas tree. I want decorations. I want presents and a feast. I want it all, every last bit of it," said Bethany, desperate desire in her voice. Alexa stood mute. She wanted all that too, but was just too scared to hope it was possible. "Tracey deserves it too – and Marc. You know he'd never force you to celebrate, but do you really think he wants to just skip over his daughter's first Christmas? Do you want to skip over your daughter's first Christmas? Do you want Tracey to grow up scared of Christmas like we are?"

"You're still scared?" asked Alexa, turning out of Bethany's arms to look in her eyes.

"Yeah, Lex. I know how you feel," nodded Bethany, tears filling her eyes. "But I don't want to feel this way no more."

"Okay, let's do Christmas. Let's have the whole catastrophe," said Alexa, forcing a smile on her face.

"Oh, Lex, you're the best!" cried Bethany, hugging her tight. "It's going to be great, you'll see. Nothing can go wrong, Lex, nothing."

"What's not going to go wrong?" asked Ben, walking into the kitchen, a large grin across his face.

"Christmas. Lex is letting us celebrate," explained Bethany.

"We'll give it a go," smiled Alexa nervously. "What brings you here, Ben – I mean, Dad?" She had been trying hard to call him Dad in front of Bethany, but it still made her stomach turn.

"I thought maybe the three of us could go out to dinner tonight – to celebrate," said Ben hopefully.

"Celebrate what?" asked Bethany, positively beaming.

Alexa knew it did not matter what Ben's good news was. Bethany just loved reasons to celebrate. Ben handed Alexa the envelope he was holding. It had already been opened. Alexa pulled out the documents. They were birth certificates. One for her and one for Bethany. They were now officially Alexa and Bethany Shepard.

A high-pitched, excited scream filled the air as Bethany dashed over to Ben and hugged him tightly.

"You're our Dad! You're our Dad now!"

Ben hugged Bethany, but Alexa could feel his eyes on her. Her hands were shaking and she had to counter the urge to vomit.

"Just give us a minute," said Ben quietly, when Bethany noticed Alexa's lack of enthusiasm. Bethany left hesitantly. "You okay?"

"Yeah," replied Alexa absently. "I'm sorry, I'm not being fair," she said before looking up at Ben. It was too much. Tears slipped down her cheeks as fear engulfed her. "I don't want you to be my dad."

Ben rushed forward and hugged her. Alexa hated herself. She tried to push out of Ben's arms, but he would not let her. "I will never be Sean. Never. I promise," he whispered.

Alexa's whole body began to shake as her sobbing increased, drawing Bethany back into the kitchen.

"I – I don't want you – I don't want you to be my dad."

"Lex! You said – he is – why are you –"

Ben held up his hand and shook his head, immediately silencing Bethany.

"I'm never going to be like Sean. Look at me, Alexa," commanded Ben. Alexa would not look up and he had to force her chin up. "I'm not Sean." Bethany gasped, tears slipping down her own cheeks. "Listen, if it makes you feel more comfortable you can just keep calling me Ben. I'm never leaving the two of you. I know you love me. I know how you feel. You don't have to call me Dad. I'll be whatever you need me to be."

Alexa managed to push out of Ben's embrace. Bethany tried to hug her, but she stepped away. She knew it was irrational, but she could not yet face the idea of having a father again, especially not when she knew what some people thought of her and Ben's relationship.

When Ben returned for his next morning swim, Alexa was glad he said nothing about the adoption. Alexa liked the idea that on paper Ben was her father and that no one could take that away from them, but somehow could not bear to think of it more intimately than that.

This complication did not add to Alexa's enthusiasm for Christmas. Although she had agreed to celebrate, she could no longer bring herself to take an active part in its organisation. Bethany did not seem to mind. She was so excited she did not care that Alexa was leaving it all to her. What that meant was that as December neared an end, the house looked as though Father Christmas had vomited all over it. It turned out to be an omen. Tracey came down with a stomach bug that quickly travelled through half the family. Only Bethany and Marcus were spared.

"This is the real omen," smiled Bethany, as Alexa laid curled up on the lounge clutching her stomach. "Me not getting sick. It's a sign Christmas should go ahead. You getting sick, that's just being a mother. Nothing to do with Christmas."

Alexa would have countered that argument if she did not need to rush to the closest bathroom. Marcus did as much as he could to make her feel better, but with everyone else so sick he was tasked with taking care of Tracey. Being so premature, the doctors wanted to keep a close eye on her to ensure she stayed hydrated. Even the mildest infections were much more dangerous to Tracey than the rest of the family. Despite that, Tracey was the first to recover, followed swiftly by Charlotte.

Only Alexa continued to suffer the ill effects of the infection. Long after everyone else was better, Alexa was sent scurrying to the bathroom by the nausea that could hit at any time. She tried to keep eating and drinking, but the idea of putting anything into her mouth was very hard to contemplate when it kept coming back up. As Christmas approached, Alexa woke every morning expecting to feel better. All she got was another dose of nausea and vomiting that saw her weight plummet. Everyone was worried about her, but she just brushed off their concerns. It was too difficult to deal with them while she was being paralysed with her own fears.

"Amy, please give me another reason for this," said Alexa anxiously, making the call from the corner of a spare room on the third floor. "This really can't be happening."

"You've been sick, right?" asked Amy. Alexa murmured an agreement. "And you've lost weight?" Alexa nodded before agreeing verbally. "Alexa, you never had much weight to lose. Once you fall below a certain threshold your periods can become really irregular."

"Yeah, they're not that regular normally."

"I didn't think so. Get over the stomach bug – that's probably what's still making you sick – put some weight on and things should go back to working the way it should. Don't stress. You're infertile, you shouldn't be worrying about being pregnant."

Amy was right, but as the days continued on – with the nausea – and her period refused to materialise, it was hard to dismiss the possibility of the impossible. Even on Christmas Day, as a hot wind blew through the bedroom, another wave of nausea forced Alexa back to the bathroom to expel the little contents of her stomach.

"Merry Christmas!" cried Marcus, waltzing into the bedroom, Tracey sitting happily in his arms, dressed in an elf outfit.

Alexa quickly washed her mouth and walked out into the bedroom, forcing a smile on to her face. "You're really going to do it to her, aren't you?" she asked on seeing Tracey. "She'll hate you forever."

"Think of the gorgeous photos we'll have of her."

"Think of the therapy sessions." Alexa quickly held a hand over her mouth as her stomach rumbled uneasily.

"You still feeling sick? I thought you were almost better," said Marcus, his voice clouded with concern.

"I am better," smiled Alexa. "Just still not quite right."

"Now, Tracey," said Marcus sternly, holding his daughter up above his face. "That really wasn't a nice thing to do to your mother. After all she's done for you, you go and give her your stomach bug for Christmas. You had better make it up to her."

"It's okay," laughed Alexa, thinking grimly that it was actually him who had done this to her before catching that thought. There was no way she was pregnant. It was impossible and she had to stop thinking about it.

"My poor baby, sick for Christmas."

Marcus wrapped his arm around Alexa's waist and rubbed her stomach gently, but Alexa could not help but push it away.

Walking down the stairs, Alexa could smell that Charlotte had already been busy in the kitchen. Ben was talking to Marcus at the bottom of the stairs and admiring Tracey. He smiled warmly when he saw Alexa.

"Merry Christmas, Dad," Alexa said, trying to keep it from a sigh, as she hugged Ben. Ben pushed her away and looked at her quizzically. It took her a moment to realise why. Since the adoption, she had called him by no name. "Just don't expect miracles. The problem was never you adopting us. I always wanted that."

"Merry Christmas to you too," smiled Ben. Alexa was glad he did not try to carry on the latter half of the conversation. "You feeling okay? Marc said you're still a bit queasy." Ben placed the back of his hand on her cheek before moving to her pale forehead.

"I'm okay, Dad. Don't fuss."

Ben smiled broadly as he nodded and walked towards the lounge room. Alexa followed and was almost overwhelmed by the staggering number of presents. They did not all fit under the tree and quite literally took up an entire corner of the room.

"See, would you have denied her this?" asked Bethany, taking a momentary break from official photographer duties. Alexa smiled and shook her head. "We get to create the kind of Christmas we want for her. We don't have to be scared of this day any more."

Alexa hugged Bethany, then found Marcus and Tracey and pulled them before Bethany's camera.

With her nausea all but gone, Alexa found herself eating heartily at lunch and joining in the festivities. It was only when Karl donned his Santa hat and started to distribute the presents that Alexa began to feel uneasy. That last Christmas with the Whites was the last one she had tried to celebrate and she had to swallow hard on the fear that rose up in her at the memory.

"You okay?" asked Marcus when she held on to her unopened present for a little too long. Alexa nodded and started to tear the paper. "You're doing great," he whispered in her ear. "Don't expect miracles. I think you're doing great." Marcus trailed a finger down her cheek. When she looked up into his eyes, she was met by a lustful smile and she could not help but smile broadly in response.

It took almost an hour to distribute the presents and another hour to extricate them and the happily crawling Tracey from the floating sea of wrapping paper. Tracey was old enough to enjoy the ripping and tearing around her, but her mini mountain of presents remained largely untouched. She was far too concerned with getting her share of attention and everyone happily obliged.

Dinner became a desperate attempt to finish off the mass of food left over from lunch, but most people's stomachs could not handle much more. The result was a jam-packed fridge and a bag of leftovers for everyone when they left. Ben stayed around to help Alexa clean up. Bethany had gone home with Sam. Charlotte was on the phone to her father and Marcus was trying to put an overtired Tracey to bed.

"You have a good day?" asked Ben as he passed Alexa plates to put in the dishwasher.

"Yeah, it's been really good. Nice to have an uneventful Christmas for once," said Alexa, trying not to sigh. "It's just a shame Marc couldn't convince his parents to come. No one should miss their granddaughter's first Christmas."

"They'll come round in time."

"Ben, can I ask you something?" asked Alexa, not really paying attention to what he was saying. Ben nodded, though she could see the concern in his face. "You know what you said about me – about having kids – there wasn't any chance you were wrong, was there?"

Alexa felt herself suddenly enveloped in Ben's arms as he held her tight and kissed the top of her head. "I'm so sorry. I realise that with the wedding and Tracey that you were going to always think about not being able to have your own children," he said in a gravelly voice. "I know that adoption isn't the same, but it comes really close."

"It's not that. I love Tracey and it doesn't matter to me that she's not mine biologically. It's just – it's only – I mean, I swear I fell pregnant to Clinton."

"I know. I know. Maybe you did, but the doctors told us that they just didn't think it would be possible for your body to be able to carry a child to term. They considered it impossible that you would ever fall pregnant. I'm sorry, but I think something else must have been going on. Stress, it can make things fall out of whack. Penny, she had a couple of times where she skipped her period and we thought we'd fallen pregnant – it just wasn't to be."

Alexa took a deep breath. Amy was right. She was just nauseous from her stomach bug and had an irregular period – and even if she did fall pregnant, she would lose it anyway. It made her think of trying to blackmail Clinton and how futile the whole plan had ultimately been. She had never even been pregnant. She probably had this stupid stomach bug then too.

"You okay?" asked Ben, pushing Alexa out of his arms so he could look at her.

"Yeah, I'm fine," smiled Alexa, wiping the tears from her eyes.

"You have a right to be upset about all that's been taken away from you."

"No, I've been given too much that's wonderful. No one can have it all and I have everything I need and nearly everything I could possibly want. I'm not going to regret the rest. I refuse."

***

The sky crackled with light as fireworks erupted overhead. Alexa and Bethany leaned forward on Maria's balcony, necks craned, perpetually enchanted by the sight. Their wide eyes and bright smiles followed every burst of light, until the sky was filled with smoky silence.

"Happy New Year, baby," said Marcus from behind, his hands wrapped around Alexa's waist.

Alexa released Bethany's hand and turned in Marcus's arms to face him. She could not remember a time in her life when she was happier. "Happy New Year," she smilingly replied.

"Just think, next New Year's Eve, you'll be my wife." Marcus's eyes sparkled as he spoke those words and Alexa could not imagine what he saw. She loved that he loved her so much, but was still perplexed that it was even possible. It made her stomach twist, wondering if he would love her as much if he knew she was pregnant. But as soon as she had that thought she tore it away from herself. Whatever was going on with her body, it was not a baby.

What it was that was afflicting her was something Alexa tried to sporadically figure out as the new year rolled on. She looked up false pregnancies on the internet, but the results were often more disturbing than the alternative. Amy kept insisting that she just go to the doctor, which Alexa knew was the most sensible approach, but she was too scared about what she would hear. If she was pregnant, she would miscarry soon enough anyway. If it was something more sinister, she was not sure she was strong enough to handle that either.

Walking into the bathroom, Alexa continued to expect the event that never came. Standing in front of the mirror, she lifted up her top and examined her stomach. She wondered if the slight bulge she could see was a baby or just lunch. The thought of it being a child sat heavily on her heart, knowing her body would betray it.

"You still feeling sick?" asked Marcus as Alexa walked out of the bathroom.

Alexa looked down and realised she still had her hand on her stomach. "A little, I guess," she replied, quickly moving her hand and stretching a smile across her face.

"Why don't you have a lie down and I'll wake you up in a few hours. You hardly slept this morning looking after Tracey."

Alexa was going to argue, but with the mention of sleep her body suddenly felt tired and heavy. When a yawn escaped her, Marcus smiled and led her to the bed.

"You don't want to get undressed?" asked Marcus.

It was a strange question, since he knew she always slept in pyjamas, though she guessed he was talking about sleeping in actual clothes. Alexa shook her head, slipping off her shoes and sliding under the covers. Marcus smiled again and sat on his side of the bed, stroking her hair.

"Don't let me sleep too long," Alexa mumbled, sleep already coming over her. "I still want to take you out to dinner tonight."

"I'm not about to miss out on that."

As Alexa's eyes closed, Marcus reluctantly moved his hand away. He would have sat and watched her sleep for hours, but he found it too difficult to resist touching her. Even now, she flinched if he accidently touched her during the night, though she nearly always snuggled back against him afterwards. Leaving her to sleep, Marcus walked downstairs. Tracey was playing with Charlotte, both of them giggling happily.

"She been okay?" asked Marcus.

"Yep, but she needs changing," smiled Charlotte, holding Tracey up. Marcus rolled his eyes, but before he could take her, Bethany swooped in and bundled Tracey into her arms.

"I can do it," Bethany called, already out of the room.

Marcus followed Bethany and stood in the doorway as she tried to change Tracey's nappy, but Tracey could see him and was struggling to get to him. Marcus moved by her side to calm Tracey, but he noticed Bethany looked unhappily defeated when she pulled Tracey's pants back up and Tracey lunged into his arms.

"She usually doesn't do that. Usually she just lies there and smiles or giggles," shrugged Bethany.

"She usually screams at me," laughed Marcus.

"I can take care of her, you know. I'm learning. I'd be able to take care of her if anything ever happened."

Marcus looked at Bethany cautiously. He found her much harder to read than Alexa. "What's going on, Beth?"

"I know what you think of me. I know I deserve it – I just want … I'm not that girl you hate."

"Oh, Beth, I know we clash sometimes, but I know who and what you are and you're as amazing as Alexa in many ways – more amazing in others, I think."

"Then you would leave Tracey with me if anything ever happened to you and Lex?"

Marcus could not answer for so many reasons, but Bethany assumed the worst, and with tears in her eyes turned away.

"Beth, wait."

Marcus was glad Bethany retreated outside and not to her room. As soon as Tracey saw Bethany, she became restless and Marcus was thankful Bethany looked up right when Tracey practically leapt out of his arms. Bethany hugged her warmly and Tracey nestled contentedly into her.

"You're worse than Lex, you know," sighed Marcus. "I didn't answer because I just don't know what we'd do. Not because I don't trust you. You and Sam, you're young. You're happy now, but you guys might not be together forever. Ben is relatively young now, but might not be by the time – then there's my sister, Pam and Karl, my parents – if we were all dead." Bethany smiled slightly at that comment. "I don't know. I don't like to even think about it. Why are you so worried about that? You really started to change her nappies because you're worried me and Lex might die?"

"It's a good reason. I'm no use if I can't," replied Bethany defensively.

"But why, Beth?"

"Bad things happen to us. Haven't you noticed? Even you. You start living with us and look at the things that've happened to you. You almost die in a car accident. You almost die protecting Lex. Lex almost dies. Charlotte gets hijacked in a stolen car. You really need me to go on?"

Marcus shook his head. He moved and sat next to Bethany on the deck chair and pulled her and Tracey into a warm embrace.

"I'll talk to Lex about a making a will. We'll make sure Tracey's looked after. We're family – a big, crazy family – and we'll make it through every disaster together. You'll take care of us and we'll take care of you. We're not cursed. Don't waste your time trying to see the bad things coming. You'll always be looking in the wrong direction. May as well focus on the good, okay, and we have plenty of good."

Marcus could feel Bethany heaving tearlessly against his chest, so held her tight until she was completely calm.

"So you really trust me with her?" Bethany asked looking down at Tracey.

"Want me to prove it?" asked Marcus. Bethany nodded, her eyes still wide and sad. "Want to look after her tonight while Lex and me go to dinner?"

"I was going to see Sam tonight. Will you let me take her with me to visit him? I won't stay, but she's never been to Sam's place, and Gran and Pop would love to see her."

"Sure," smiled Marcus.

Bethany smiled as she jumped up, speaking quickly, though to who Marcus was not really sure. "Maybe Charlotte will come too. She'll love that. It'll be a great night. This is awesome."

Marcus looked at his watch. Without Tracey they did not need to eat so early, but he had plans for other ways they could pass the time until dinner. He was disappointed to find Alexa still asleep. He hated waking her up, so settled for sitting in the armchair by the side of the bed and reading, but after an hour he could wait no longer.

"Lex," Marcus whispered, holding her hand gently. "Lex, you want to wake up?"

Alexa did not wake. Marcus brushed his hand gently over her forehead, tucking her hair away from her face. Alexa's fingers began to wiggle slightly in his hand and he smiled down at her, but as her eyes slowly opened, they widened in fear. Her breathing hitched fearfully as she stared at him in horror.

"Lex? Hey, look at me. I'm here. It's okay," Marcus said softly, stroking her face and holding her hand. Her breaths became faster and more frantic as tears slipped down cheeks. Her whole body was shaking. When he tried to stroke her face again, her arms lifted up protectively across her face. "Alexa, wake up. It's okay. Lex, please," cried Marcus, trying to pull her arms away from her face. That was when she started screaming.

Alexa's body shook and jerked as Marcus tried to calm her and pull her arms down. Their eyes finally met. Alexa looked stunned. Her head flicked around the room as if she was disorientated. When she finally looked back at him, the terror was gone. Her face was full of shame and another type of fear. Marcus climbed on the bed and pulled her into his arms, holding her shaking body tight. He looked over and saw Charlotte and Bethany's worried faces at the door. Alexa's head popped up for a second, but as soon as she saw them, she buried her face in shame. They quickly left.

"Please, Lex. Please tell me what's wrong. You're safe now, I promise. Please tell me what scared you."

"Stop!" Alexa cried in agony. "Don't call me that."

"What? Call you what?" Marcus asked confusedly. Alexa's body shook along with her head. He repeated his question, holding her tenderly. "Lex, ple—"

"That!"

Marcus was stunned. They all called her Lex now. He had called her Lex to her face many times before. Then it struck him. Alexa had not been awake. He had been sitting by her bedside, stroking her face and holding her hand.

"Is that what I called you back then?" asked Marcus, his voice shaking.

Alexa nodded into his chest as her arms clung to him tighter, as if she expected him to push her away. He wondered if he should ask her to confirm what he suspected, but thought better of it. He did not want her to feel ashamed, but he never wanted her to relive that horror again either. He still remembered how sick he had felt when she told him that it was his image that came to her every time another man raped her in Leo's filthy apartment. He could see it – how Alexa's mind had misconstrued the present setting – and it made him sick to think that he was a link that could transport her back to that horror.

"I won't ever call you that again, okay," Marcus said in a soft but determined voice. Alexa nodded. Her arms loosened their grip on him, so he pulled her tighter to his chest.

"Do you hate me?" asked Alexa timidly, after a long silence.

"I will never, ever hate you," Marcus answered, his voice almost a growl.

"I'm sorry," replied Alexa, making his heart twist. He had not meant to sound angry.

"I don't want you to ever say that. You have nothing to be sorry about. I'm not angry with you. I just want you to know that you don't ever have to worry again. I'm here with you. I'll never leave your side and no one's ever going to hurt you again."

Marcus was still simmering when they made their way to the car for dinner. Alexa was almost sorry Tracey was not with them. It might have helped calm him down and break the tension.

"I'm sorry," Marcus said, after they had ordered. "The thought of what happened to you and what you went through just makes me so angry. I think rape's the worst thing a man can do to a woman. It's a control and violation that should never be forced on anyone."

"I didn't want to make you feel bad, or make you angry," replied Alexa softly, not quite meeting his eyes. "I'm not scared of you and I don't want you to think of me as some kind of freak."

"I don't think you're a freak," smiled Marcus. "It's just a sensitive issue. I don't think I'm a violent person, but I think I could've killed Leo or Clinton or Sean for what they did to you. It's not right you've suffered so much. It doesn't even seem possible that so much could happen to just one person."

"So you really think rape's the worst way a man can hurt a woman?" asked Alexa.

"Yes, I do. I don't think there's a greater betrayal of trust between a man and a woman. A guy has the position of power in sex and I don't think any man has the right to abuse that."

"Then what do you think is the worst thing a woman can do to a man?"

"Lie about a pregnancy."

"Really?" gasped Alexa. She could feel Marcus's anger rise again, causing a trickle of fear to run through her heart.

"Yes, that's the power you hold over men. Tracey may never have been mine. If Beth had never sent me those photos and forced me to believe Lucy cheated on me, then I'd never've known there was a chance Tracey was another man's child – all because Lucy chose not to tell me. Only a woman knows who the true father of her child is and the worst thing they can ever do is lie about it."

Alexa felt her chest constrict. Her body was still not doing what she expected or needed it to do and she was lying to Marcus about it. It was not quite what he was saying, but it was close enough to know how angry he would be if he ever found out that she had let herself fall pregnant.

Marcus's eyes were wide and sorrowful when Alexa looked up,

and she tried to smile as she once again told herself that it was not possible for her to be pregnant.

"New topic?" Marcus asked, squeezing her hand. Alexa nodded, smiling with relief. "How to wake you up without scaring the crap out of you and me? Bucket of water?" he suggested, trying to sound jovial.

Alexa liked that Marcus was attempting to make a joke out of the situation – like Jessica would have. "Fog horn?" she offered and they laughed together, their ideas becoming more ridiculous until their food arrived.

Chapter Fifteen

MARCUS DROVE HOME wondering how a year that had started so well could turn disastrous so quickly. The worst part was that he had no idea what had gone wrong. There had been changes in his relationship with Alexa, but he had put them down to the effects of him going back to work, then her returning to university, and all the challenges that encompassed.

One obvious sticking point had been Tracey's care, but Marcus thought they struck on the perfect compromise. Their neglect at even thinking about childcare for Tracey had been a near-disaster, but after getting lucky and finding childcare for two days a week, Maria stepped in and offered her services on the other three. Despite them both agreeing with the plan, Alexa continued to suggest that she defer for a semester, but Marcus considered it completely unnecessary. When he pointed out to Alexa that she had spent the last couple of years trying to catch up on the semester she felt she had missed, she just shrugged.

It was a level of self-sacrifice Marcus refused to let Alexa engage in. It was not necessary and his stubbornness on that point had not always been well received. Yet at other times, he was not convinced that was the real issue. When Alexa returned to university, it was impossible for her to hide how much she enjoyed it. Jessica and Amy were great friends and she was always in contact with them. She liked her classes and brought textbooks to bed with her; although Marcus often felt that had a secondary motive.

As the weeks went on, Marcus and Alexa slowly become much less intimate. It had been easy to dismiss at the start; they were both so tired and their schedules often mismatched. However, when Alexa started to distance herself from hugging and kissing, Marcus knew something was not right. She became very self-conscious, particularly of her body. Her clothes became less fitted. She started locking the bathroom door when she showered and would wrap the towel around herself as soon as she got out of the pool, never walking around in her swimmers the way she once had.

There was no doubt Alexa had put on weight. She was eating

much more heartily and consistently. The results were predictable, but far from undesirable. If anything, Marcus thought she looked better – healthier – than she had in a long time. He made the mistake of saying that to her, but he was not the only one who thought so. Sam had immediately concurred, though in a much blunter manner, which sent Alexa rushing from the room in tears. Marcus had gone straight after her, apologising for his comments, but things were never quite the same after that. They drifted apart, slowly but surely. Alexa shied away from his touch. Sadness crept back into her eyes. Even the cold defiance returned to her voice and she became defensive whenever they spoke. It was not like her, and when everyone else drew blanks on what the issue could be, Marcus had to assume the worst.

"I think she's seeing someone else," he said, sitting with Ryan at the pub.

"No," replied Ryan instantly. "She's just not that kind of girl. Nope, I refuse to believe that. I don't think you even believe that."

"No, maybe not," sighed Marcus. "But something's not right. I don't know – I mean, maybe – maybe it could be something else."

"What?"

"Maybe she's finally lost the love goggles," offered Marcus. It had been at the back of his mind from the very beginning. "I think she finally sees me the way everyone else always has. She thinks I took advantage of her."

Ryan could not immediately counteract that argument. They had spoken many times about the fact that Alexa had never believed he acted inappropriately or seduced her into this relationship. It was not until after Ryan convinced Marcus to arrange a dinner with all of them so he could see their interactions with his own eyes that he gave Marcus his full assessment of the situation.

"She still loves you to bits," said Ryan. "Though something's definitely going on," he added quickly. "But she loves you. When you're not looking, she's just sitting there adoring you. But she seems really scared – or guilty, maybe – about something. I don't know what, because, you're right, she looks great."

Sometimes it was easy for Marcus to believe things were okay. As long as they weren't being physical, or talking about her staying at university – or a raft of other things – they were great. In their quiet moments together, it was difficult to believe there was anything wrong. Alexa would still smile at him and stroke his face tenderly. She was still loving and tender to Tracey, but there was a definite sadness about her now. It was as if she expected everything to be suddenly torn away from her.

Then Marcus finally understood. If Alexa believed he had taken advantage of her, pressured her into this situation, their only option would be to separate. But if they separated, they would not only lose their relationship, Alexa might believe she would lose Tracey and her one chance at motherhood.

It was selfish, but Marcus refused to confront Alexa. Being with her, even as their relationship was falling apart, was better than being away from her. At least he knew she did not hate him, she just could not love him – because he was someone who had taken advantage of a vulnerable child, then made her believe it was okay. Their physical relationship would eventually deteriorate to nothing and perhaps all that would be left would be their friendship. It was fantasy, but even fantasy was better than thinking this would all be over soon.

"Good morning," said Marcus, walking into the full dining room.

Alexa was feeding Tracey. She greeted him with a broad and genuine smile, but he noticed it did not penetrate her eyes, which had the look of sadness he knew only too well. The sight made his heart twist. It was that smile that made him stay – and that sadness that made him realise how wrong it was to do so.

Watching Alexa through breakfast, Marcus became only more convinced that her animosity towards him was due to her growing conviction that they would have to break up. She held Tracey tight and when Maria turned up tears burned in the sides of her eyes.

"So I'll see you this afternoon," said Marcus at the front door.

"Yeah," replied Alexa.

There was coldness in Alexa's voice that Marcus had not heard for a long time, but the look in her eyes told him that part of her still loved him. He kissed her lightly on the cheek, but when he moved to hug her, she backed away, claiming to hear Tracey crying inside. Slumping against the wall by the front door, Marcus wondered where they went from here. Then he heard Alexa talking to Maria inside and stayed to listen.

"You okay?" Maria asked gently.

"Yeah," replied Alexa softly. "I'll see you this afternoon. Marc will be home first, if you need to go before I get home."

"You don't mind me looking after Tracey, do you?"

"No. I love that you're looking after her. I'm glad we have you. I hate the thought of her being in any danger because I hired some psycho to look after her."

"Then what's wrong?" asked Maria almost imploringly.

There was a long pause and for a minute Marcus thought Alexa might answer, but she just rushed out the door, right past him, out the gate and down the street without a single backward glance.

It was no surprise to find Alexa with Charlotte later that night. Charlotte was the only one of them not to question Alexa about what was wrong and would let her just curl up on her bed, as if everything would resolve itself if she closed her eyes for long enough.

"Alexa," said Marcus's gently from the door. "Can we talk for a minute? We need to sort things out. We can't go on like this." Alexa nodded slowly, tears welling in her eyes, as she approached. "What's going on?" asked Marcus, when they walked into their bedroom. "Why won't you let me near you?"

"Nothing's going on," replied Alexa defensively.

"Just tell me. It'll be all right. Whatever it is, we can face it together." It was a lie, but Marcus wanted it to be true.

"There's nothing to face. Nothing's wrong," gasped Alexa.

"Nothing's wrong?" cried Marcus incredulously. "You haven't let me touch you in weeks. You won't be near me unless you're fully dressed. It's been going on for months. I want to know what's wrong."

"Nothing's wrong," repeated Alexa, her voice breaking.

"Don't lie to me!" Marcus's frustration was getting the better of him, but the fear of what was about to transpire was overwhelming his better senses.

"Don't yell at me!"

"Then tell me the truth!"

Alexa jumped, looking up at Marcus fearfully. His heart twisted, knowing he had scared her. She pushed past him and rushed down the stairs. He let her go. He would have to let her go, he thought desperately, but he had promised never to leave her. He did not want to break that promise. He wanted to believe in her loving smile and the desperate hope that there was another explanation for what was happening to them.

Washing his face in the bathroom sink, Marcus looked around the room as though the answer would be written somewhere on the walls. Staring at the mirror, he tried to put the pieces together in different ways. None of the scenarios he conjured seemed very likely. Tears started slipping down his cheeks as he forced himself to face the inevitable truth. Standing tall, wiping his eyes, knowing what he had to do next, Marcus tossed the tissues into the bin. That was when the most unlikely scenario streaked through his head. It was impossible, but it fit – though not nearly as well as the truth. Marcus knew it could not be true, but he could not let go of the possibility.

Stumbling down the stairs, Marcus tried to hold on to the terrifying hope that was building within him. Alexa was alone in the kitchen. Her back was to the door, but she must have heard him, because she froze.

Marcus could not speak straight away. "Are you pregnant?" he finally murmured, his voice barely audible, but he knew Alexa heard him when her head dropped and gave a faint nod. He was not sure what to ask next. He ran his hands through his hair, his arms shaking. "How far along?"

"I don't know," breathed Alexa. "Four or five months, maybe."

"Four to five months!" Anger superseded every other emotion, as a sense of betrayal ripped through Marcus's heart. "When the hell were you planning on telling me? What, when the baby was born? We're supposed to be getting married in three weeks and you can't even tell me that you're fucking pregnant! Is the baby even mine?"

Alexa spun around in horror. Marcus felt a rush of shame, but it could not compare to the anger boiling within him. Not wanting to say anything else he might regret, he turned and left.

***

Alexa felt her head lift involuntarily. She gasped painfully and curled further into her body, rocking slowly back and forth. Marcus had been gone four hours and twenty-seven minutes. She could not help but think that when he did return to pick up his belongings, her body would have dispelled the baby. She wondered if he would take her back then – if she begged and swore it would never happen again. Just a few more days, she thought bitterly, and she would have miscarried. It would have been over and she could have gone back to loving Marcus the way he deserved and stopped pushing him away from her and her mistakes.

There was a click of the door. Alexa's head snapped up. Marcus was standing in the doorway. She wanted to fall at his feet and beg forgiveness, but the best she could do was roll on to her knees on the bed – staying out of his reach. "I'm sorry," she cried, fresh tears spilling down her face. "I didn't mean for it to happen. It should've been gone by now. I don't know what to do. I'm so scared. Please don't leave me. I promise the baby's yours."

Marcus rushed forward and Alexa could not help but back away. He grabbed her hand and pulled her into his arms. He did not release her hand until he had manoeuvred them so she was cradled in his lap. "I'm not leaving," he said sincerely.

Alexa thought she could smell alcohol on his breath. She wondered if he had been at the pub this whole time, but he did not appear drunk – something he certainly would be if he had been drinking for four hours.

"I didn't know what to do," Alexa whispered, hoping he would say he forgave her. "Ben told me I could never have children. He said I would've miscarried Clinton's baby if I hadn't lost it. I just – I just thought I'd miscarry this one. I didn't tell you – I wanted to, but I didn't want to think about it. It was going to die anyway. Then I just kept being pregnant. I wanted the baby, but we'd never spoken about it. I didn't want you to be mad that I was pregnant or upset that we were going to lose it, so I just kept waiting for it to go away."

Marcus took a deep breath before sighing heavily. "It's all right," he said, holding her closer. "Whatever happens, it's going to be all right. We'll face it together. You can tell me anything. You're going to be my wife, I need you to trust me. I could never hate you."

"I'm sorry I got pregnant. I didn't mean to hurt you."

"I'm not upset you're pregnant. I'm just sorry you didn't trust me enough to tell me. We'll go to the doctor tomorrow and find out what's going on, all right."

The next morning Alexa fidgeted anxiously as they waited to see her doctor. Dr Carter had not been shocked when Alexa had disclosed her apparent infertility. Although she had suggested Alexa undertake further investigations, it had seemed like a ridiculous proposition at the time – more tests and invasive procedures to confirm what she already knew. When Marcus told Dr Carter why they were there, the surprise on Dr Carter's face did much to alleviate Alexa's feelings of stupidity.

"When did you do the pregnancy test?" Dr Carter asked.

"I haven't done one," replied Alexa softly.

"What?" asked Marcus, turning and looking at Alexa as though this was all a rouse.

"Let's do one now," said Dr Carter quickly, handing Alexa a jar. "Just to be sure."

Alexa grudgingly did as she was asked, sitting silently as her fears were confirmed. She would have gone straight home after that, but as soon as the results were revealed Marcus started asking questions. Dr Carter refused to speculate how the pregnancy would progress, and Alexa was horrified when she started talking to her about emergency referrals. Thankfully, Dr Carter and Marcus took care of everything. Alexa just closed her eyes and pretended it was not real.

What followed was a week of tests and specialist appointments. Alexa felt like a lab rat, and far too many of the tests were of a gynaecological nature that left her feeling powerless and scared. Marcus went with her to every appointment and held her hand during every test. Alexa appreciated it, but could not show it. She and Marcus barely spoke and when they did it was never about the pregnancy. They did not tell anyone what was happening and when Alexa was at home, she was always holed up in her room. Amy called a number of times, reassuring Alexa that the tests were completely routine and that there was nothing to worry about. Alexa struggled to believe her. She struggled to even speak at most of the appointments. Marcus the one answering the doctors' questions.

"Well, it looks like the two of you should start preparing for a new arrival," said their specialist, after looking through all the test results.

"But —" stammered Alexa.

"I can understand the assessment that was made at the time. There's quite a lot of damage. The majority of it is to the birthing canal and the cervix. There's also damage to the lower part of the uterus. There is a section of your uterus at the top that appears relatively healthy. That is where the umbilical cord is attached. It will be a matter of whether the lower part of the uterus can sustain the pregnancy in the later stages. A natural birth would not be wise under the circumstances. There's a high risk of complications."

"What kind of complications?" asked Marcus, squeezing Alexa's hand.

"There is a lot of scar tissue and I'm not convinced that the birthing canal will be able to stretch the way it should. If Alexa went into labour the stress may tear the tissue."

"She could bleed to death?" asked Marcus, his voice shaking as his face went white.

"It would risk both her life and the baby's. There's no need for that. We'll deliver the baby via caesarean section when required. You both need to understand that this is a high-risk pregnancy. I will ask that you take it easy, Alexa, and don't exert yourself. We'll need to monitor you very carefully until the birth."

Alexa said nothing. They would have another appointment in two weeks – and within four months they would have a child. It seemed impossible. Alexa had accepted long ago that she was pregnant, but she never once believed she would ever actually be having a baby. It was too much to comprehend, and even though Marcus continued to look at her all through lunch with concerned eyes, she said nothing.

"Are you all right?" Marcus asked as he started the car.

"Can we just go home for a while before we pick up Tracey? I just need a bit more time," Alexa replied in a soft voice.

Walking behind him, Alexa followed Marcus up the stairs and into the bedroom. He sat down on the bed and she immediately crawled between his legs and leant against his chest. His arms held her tight to him, stroking her hair. "I'm scared," she whispered, pressing harder into his chest. He held her close and kissed the top of her head, but said nothing. "We never talked about having a baby. Tracey's not even a year old. Are you okay with this?"

"I never thought we'd ever have another child. Beth told me you couldn't have children," replied Marcus softly. "I believed her, just like you believed Ben. I suppose otherwise it wouldn't have taken me five months to figure it out. But I want this baby."

"Where'd you go? That night," Alexa asked tentatively.

"The pub. That's why it took me so long to come home. Ryan dragged me to his place to sober up," said Marcus with a heavy sigh. "He drove me home. Even brought my car home for me. I handled this whole thing so badly. If not for Ryan I would've handled it much worse. I'm so sorry I hurt you."

"So I still drive you to drink?"

"No," replied Marcus emphatically. "I was just so scared that I was losing you. It won't happen again."

Alexa nodded, but was silent for a long time. "So we're having a baby then," she said timidly.

"Looks like it."

"I've missed having your arms around me," said Alexa sadly.

"Oh I missed you too, baby."

"Make love to me?" she asked, hoping he would not say no.

Marcus nodded. He was very gentle, always holding her close. His tenderness when she had hurt him so badly made her eyes sting, but he did not let her go and kissed away the tears as they fell.

"Do you know what I keep wondering?" asked Marcus, stroking Alexa's back as she lay in his arms. "When we actually conceived the child. It would be nice to know when it was."

"I thought you would've worked that out."

"You know? But you didn't know how far along you were," said Marcus in a surprised voice.

"I didn't know how to calculate it – where you started counting from," Alexa admitted timidly. Marcus did not smile as he stroked her cheek. "It happened – it was that time you said 'Wow'. Remember?" Marcus smiled softly as he nodded. "Tracey got sick after and then me. We didn't have another chance until I was already pregnant."

"That was a good day," said Marcus, his manner still very subdued. Alexa just nodded. "I guess now all we have to do is tell everyone."

That part frightened Alexa almost as much as the pregnancy itself. If it was up to her, she probably would have continued to avoid it, but Marcus helped her through, announcing it to Bethany and Charlotte. Alexa had never actually seen Bethany speechless before.

"But you said – the doctors – I don't get it," Bethany eventually stammered.

"Me either," replied Alexa softly.

"Can you – will you be – can your body –" questioned Bethany, unable to finish her sentences.

"It's all fine, Bethy," smiled Alexa reassuringly, squeezing Bethany's hand. Bethany smiled back, her face full of relief.

"Is that true?" asked Charlotte, but she was not speaking to Alexa. She was asking Marcus.

"Not quite," he replied, and, despite Alexa's discomfort, he detailed the doctor's concerns.

"But the doctors are going to take care of her, right?" asked Bethany anxiously.

"Of course," answered Marcus soothingly.

Charlotte and Bethany had lots of questions. Marcus answered them all as best he could while Alexa sat silently next to him. Bethany only became more concerned the more questions she asked, but Alexa was surprised by how stoic it made her. She did not break down in tears the way she would have even a year ago.

"We're just going to have to take care of you," Bethany smiled, before laughing. "You think we'll be able to do it, Marc? We might have to sedate her or something for the rest of her pregnancy."

They teased Alexa for the next half an hour, but she did not mind. It was nice to be smiling again.

"Wait, so did you find out if you're having a boy or a girl?" asked Bethany.

"No," replied Marcus and Alexa together.

"That was about the only time Alexa really spoke up. We're not finding out until the day," smiled Marcus, squeezing Alexa's hand.

When Alexa faced her family the next day, flanked by Charlotte and Bethany, it was clear they were expecting a different announcement.

"So you and Marcus, you're breaking up?" asked Ben. Alexa shook her head. "Then where is he?"

"Upstairs with Tracey," replied Alexa coolly.

"We've seen how strained you've been. If there are problems, it's better to face them now. You don't have to marry him," said Ben.

"I know that."

"Alexa, we've seen the rift," said Ben. "You two are barely on speaking terms."

Alexa tried to believe that Ben was speaking purely out of concern for her and not because he was desperately hoping to break her and Marcus up.

"Why don't you tell us why you asked us to come here," said Karl, sparing Alexa the need to answer Ben.

Alexa opened her mouth, but the words would not come out. Bethany's hand slipped into hers while Charlotte's arm wrapped around her waist, as they gently urged her on.

"I'm pregnant," Alexa said finally, not meeting anyone's eyes.

"What!" cried the room in unison.

Marcus moved hesitantly towards Alexa. Tracey was sitting in his arms, fidgeting wildly at the sight of so many people. As he walked behind Alexa, Tracey leapt into Bethany's arms, making Bethany smile.

"This is why you've been fighting?" asked Ben confrontationally, looking at Marcus. "What? You don't want another child?"

Marcus did not answer. He looked down at Alexa, but she would not look at him. "We're a little bit nervous about this," Marcus said eventually, pulling Alexa into him and placing his hands lovingly on her enlarged stomach. "It's been a bit of a shock. And we don't have much time to get used to the idea, but we both want this child. I can't really speak for Alexa, but I don't think we're really excited about it yet. We're still in shock."

"How far along are you?" asked Pam, her eyes on Alexa's stomach.

"Five months."

It took a long time for everyone to come to terms with the news. There were lots of questions and not a lot of excitement. Alexa still had her doubts about Marcus. He had so far said and done everything right, but he was not the same man he had been a few months ago. When everyone left, she found him sitting by the pool with the ultrasound picture of their child.

"You okay?" asked Alexa.

Marcus shrugged, then looked up and shook his head. "Today was much harder than I expected. I didn't know what to say – how to explain."

"What do you mean?"

"Everyone wanting to know why we've been fighting. Me wondering if I should say anything," he murmured in broken voice. "They all still see me … they see me the way I see me sometimes – the way I thought you'd begun to see me. I thought it was over. The only reason I stayed was because you hadn't asked me to leave. Yet I was positive the blinders had finally come off and you realised that I'd seduced you – forced you – into this. You'd finally seen the age gap and what I did to you in that place. I knew I'd have to leave, but I couldn't. Now it's turned out to be something else – something wonderful, but terrifying – and I'm still scared that you'll open your eyes and tell me you don't love me any more."

"You're leaving?" stammered Alexa, her eyes full of tears. She knew Marcus had said more than just that, but that was all she could really comprehend. It was true, fathers never stuck around. The terror of having to raise their child on her own overwhelmed Alexa. She looked down at her ring and tore it off with fumbling fingers. Throwing it away, she dashed back into the house, her breaths coming in unsteady gasps as she held on to the kitchen bench.

"So the engagement's off then?" asked Marcus angrily, storming into the kitchen.

"Well you just said you're leaving. How can we get married when you're walking out on us?" cried Alexa, her voice almost failing her.

"I never said that!" cried Marcus. "I was trying to confide in you how hard these months had been. I wanted you to know how I felt – how you ripped my heart out. And, yes, if you could only see me as someone who'd taken advantage of you – abused your trust and forced you into this situation – then of course I would leave you! I could never make you – I could never stay feeling like I was forcing myself on you."

Alexa stayed silent, her hands across her chest. She knew Charlotte, Bethany and Sam were at the door to the kitchen, but did not acknowledge them.

"I am not leaving you – not unless you ask me to. I'm not walking out on you or our children. But I'm not giving you that ring back either," said Marcus firmly, pointing to the backyard. "You threw it back at me. You want out – then you walk out. You're not the only one terrified this is all going to be torn away. You're not the only one who gets scared."

Marcus stormed out. A door near the front of the house slammed shut. Charlotte reassured Alexa it wasn't the front door.

"Did he really say he was leaving?" asked Bethany.

"He said he would have to," replied Alexa.

"Why?"

"I don't know why! What's it matter? He just said he would."

"You're going to have to snap out of this, Lex, if you want that chance at being happy you go on about," said Sam angrily. "I know I've not been there for you – been the friend I once was – but I'm with Marcus on this one. You shut everyone out. None of us knew what was wrong. Marcus eventually guessed, but he had to guess. He loves you so much. Even if I still loved you, I couldn't compete with that. He adores you and I reckon sometimes he wishes he didn't, because he's not a paedophile. I know what I've said before about him, but he's torn himself apart over you.

"If Beth kept a pregnancy from me. I think I'd forgive her. If she had some crazy excuse like you, then I'd make myself get over it, but it'd hurt. I'd feel like I'd lost something.

"Marc would've helped you through this. He would've been everything you needed and you walked away from him. And now, when he's stuck by you – not once mentioned to anyone that you'd kept this from him – you've gone and torn him down because he dared to tell you how much you hurt him."

Alexa stormed out into the backyard. They didn't understand. None of them did. Marcus had told her he could leave her. She did not want to be with him if he was thinking about leaving every time she became a little dysfunctional. She was dysfunctional too often for that.

Marcus waited anxiously in their bedroom. He was determined Alexa would have to come to him, though was unsure it was the best strategy. Alexa was not herself. He wondered if the prolonged state of fear she had been in had damaged her psychologically and if she would cope with this pregnancy.

Ordinarily, Marcus would have tried to pull Alexa out of it, but he was still too wounded by the way things had played out. He did not resent Alexa, but could not deny how difficult it had been for him – and it was clear trying to express that to Alexa now would do more harm than good. The problem was that Marcus was pinning all his hopes on Alexa dragging herself out of this state and quickly. If she could not do it, he wondered who would assist him. Bethany and Charlotte, definitely. Maria and the Whites, probably. Sam and Ben, it was hard to tell. All their support to date appeared very shaky and conditional.

Noticing it was so quiet, Marcus realised Tracey was still downstairs. He assumed Bethany would look after her, but his and Alexa's decision to get in too deep felt a little foolhardy right now and he wondered how Tracey would be affected. However, no matter how Marcus looked at it, he knew there were few options other than make it work. Even if Alexa decided to call it quits, she was not vindictive. Marcus could not foresee any malice in their relationship, and knew Alexa would always put their children's needs first. It was that need for constant interaction that Marcus felt would ultimately secure their future. It did not matter how Alexa achieved it, but the truth was that once she was stable again, she would begin to resemble the girl he had fallen in love with. If he was there always supporting her – as he intended to be – no matter how difficult she made it – he was sure they would pull through eventually. The only question was how long that would take – and how long he should lock himself in their room, waiting for her to come back to him.

"Still want to be my husband?"

Marcus's head snapped up. It felt like he had been waiting a lifetime to hear that voice. Not just Alexa, but the real Alexa. She was back, standing in the doorway of their bedroom. It was almost as if it was a different person to the one he had been living with for the past few months. Just as he had learned to recognise the shadow of heroin on Bethany, he was starting to learn what the shadow of fear looked like when it descended on Alexa. This was what Bethany had been trying to warn him about when they first got together. Not Alexa fearing his touch while she slept. It was the deep fear and consequential dysfunction that Alexa would never outrun. She could recover, but she would never be able to completely prevent herself from reacting exactly as she had.

Not even bothering to answer, Marcus rushed to Alexa, pulling her into his arms and kissing her. She pushed away, holding up her left hand. There on her third finger sat her engagement ring, looking much more sparkly than when gave it to her.

"Sorry I took so long," Alexa said apologetically. "I threw it pretty well, apparently." She shrugged, as if unsure what to say or do next. "Sorry I made you doubt yourself," she added quietly. "I don't see you that way – not ever. I've tried – not recently – but I have. After school, while I was away, I was searching for a reason to distrust you and dismiss you. You're just not like that. Our minds might have wandered. We might have been attracted to each other when we shouldn't have, but you never took advantage of me. There were so many times – most of the time I was with you in high school – I was vulnerable. At the end, when we decided that we liked each other enough to give it a go, you could've taken it further. I don't think I would've stopped you. I think I would've known that you were taking advantage of me, but I would've felt like I owed you that much for what you'd done for me."

"Do you feel like you owe me now?" asked Marcus, terrified of the answer.

"No," smiled Alexa. "I liked being able to help you when you got yourself in trouble with the unit. I didn't feel like a little girl waiting to be rescued. And you never tried to take care of me. When we were friends, I felt like your equal and that never changed when we got together."

"What happened, then?" Marcus asked. "Why were you so scared of telling me?"

"Lots of little reasons," replied Alexa, her voice quivering. "It wasn't supposed to be possible, so I spent a lot of time denying it – especially at the start. Then even when I was pretty convinced I was pregnant, I was positive I'd lose it. I wanted to spare you. Part of me was scared of your reaction, then the other part didn't want to hurt you, cos I wanted to believe you'd have been excited. Then another part of me thought I needed to be able to deal with it myself, you know, cos it was my fault it was all happening.

"Amy kept telling me I just needed to face you and take the test, but I didn't want to be wrong. I wanted to have a baby with you – wanted it to be possible – and if I told you and took the test, I was so sure it would all disappear and you'd think I was crazy."

There was so much Marcus had planned to say, but the words disappeared. He could not fight that kind of fearful irrationality. Even knowing what had happened this time would not necessarily help him figure out what was going through Alexa's head next time. All he could do was accept that Alexa was as much a victim of this as he was and believe things would be all right if he just stuck around and supported her through it. It made him think of her devotion to Bethany and why she always persisted, even when it hurt her terribly to do so.

"You're not crazy. You're my beautiful fiancée, who's about to be my wife and give birth to our child. You're everything I ever wanted from life," Marcus said, moving towards Alexa. Her smile was full of relief, though she did not move into his arms until he pulled her into his.

"I'm sorry," Alexa said again, holding him tight.

"I know, but we have so much to look forward to. There's no point dwelling on the difficulties. I think I can foresee only one problem," said Marcus. Alexa's head snapped up, her eyes full of fear. "Your dress," he smiled, rubbing her swollen belly.

This time Alexa smiled. "Jess and Amy convinced me to hope for the best and prepare for a big belly."

Chapter Sixteen

PULLING UP IN front of Maria's apartment, Alexa closed her eyes and counted to five. Slowly opening them, she was somewhat surprised the same vista greeted her. It was not a dream. This life was real, and she was about to be married to one of the most amazing men in the world.

"You okay?" asked Bethany, as Alexa continued to sit.

"Just trying to see if I wake up."

"You thinking we should be back in the park, shacked up in the boarding house and living horrible lives?"

"You ever think that? Feel like it's a dream?" asked Alexa, strangely surprised by how accurately Bethany had encapsulated her feelings.

"Every day," replied Bethany seriously. "Keep waiting to wake up somewhere else. Sometimes I dream about being back home – with them. They're not dead and we never escaped. Sometimes takes me a while to convince myself it's not possible."

Alexa reached over and hugged Bethany tight. There was nothing she could say, but they held each other as they shook slightly, waiting for their fears to subside and reality to take back over.

"Come on," smiled Bethany, suddenly excited. "Let's see Maria try and stuff your huge baby boobs into your dress."

Alexa shook her head as Bethany cackled. It had turned out to be the one oversight in her planning. She had counted on her abdomen expanding with her pregnancy and secretly planned accordingly, but she had never realised her chest would expand just as rapidly. The last fitting – after her confession – had highlighted the deficiency. Maria had been working tirelessly since then to make the adjustments and today was the last fitting before the wedding on the weekend.

Dancing into Maria's apartment, Bethany immediately went over to her dress and put it on. The bridesmaid dresses were almost identical to the wedding dress, with the exception of their deep sea blue colour. The long, flowing material danced over Bethany's body, making her usual graceful movements look shockingly elegant.

"Don't you go near the kitchen in that dress," scolded Maria playfully.

Bethany wore the dress every time she visited Maria, and Maria had confessed that she was only planning on washing it the day before the wedding.

Just as Alexa had her dress on, Karl arrived with Hayley and Charlotte, who both tore off their uniforms and threw on their dresses. Karl said nothing as Alexa stood in the middle of the lounge room in her white dress.

"Aw, you think she looks beautiful too," gasped Bethany, on seeing the smile on Karl's face. She rushed at him, hugging him as tears slipped down her cheeks.

The tenderness with which Karl held Bethany was truly beautiful. Alexa could not comprehend how he of all people could be so kind when others had been so cruel.

"She looks amazing," smiled Karl, pushing Bethany slowly out of his arms. "But look at you! It's almost a shame it's your sister's wedding and you're not allowed to steal her limelight."

Bethany responded too quietly for Alexa to hear. She must have been seeking reassurance, because Karl had his finger under her chin, forcing their eyes to meet. When Karl nodded firmly, Bethany pulled her body straighter and nodded, before dancing over to Hayley and Charlotte. Alexa doubted either of them would ever realise tears had recently burned Bethany's eyes as she smiled and gushed over them.

The whirling movements of everyone made Alexa dizzy and she was thankful Maria did not need her for long. Some very minor adjustments were needed, but it would not require another fitting. Finally free, Alexa slumped on the balcony, thankful when Karl came out and sat with her, handing her a coffee. Her consumption of caffeine had decreased dramatically, but he assured her one coffee would not harm her.

"You didn't bring Tracey today?" asked Karl.

"Tracey in all this mayhem? No, I thought it'd be chaotic enough without adding her to the mix," laughed Alexa.

"I was kind of expecting to be the entertainer," smiled Karl.

It was funny how quickly Karl had overcome his initial objections to her relationship with Marcus. When she almost ruined everything by throwing Marcus's ring back at him, it was Karl who had come over and calmed her enough to see reason. He had a way of dealing with her that few others could accomplish. Perhaps it was because he was unequivocally supportive, even when he disagreed with her.

"You excited about this little tyke yet?" asked Karl, gently rubbing her stomach.

There was a nudge in Alexa's belly in response to his touch, and she found the strength to hold Karl's hand to her body so he could feel it. "Not yet," she admitted. "It doesn't quite feel real. And even after the wedding's over, I have to get back to my studies and finish my exams."

"You know you look beautiful in that dress, right?" said Karl. Alexa shrugged and nodded at the same time. She felt beautiful in. It made her almost not care if she looked it or not. "You having someone walk you down the aisle?"

"No," replied Alexa, shaking her head as her stomach twisted uncomfortably. She shifted in her chair causing Karl's hand to slip from her stomach.

"Independent woman, belong to no man and refuse to be given away type thing?" asked Karl, his tone even and non-judgemental.

"Yeah, sort of," conceded Alexa, but from the way Karl was looking at her, he knew that was not the full answer.

"I think you should consider asking Ben," said Karl seriously. "You don't need to explain your other reasons for avoiding this question and I think some of them you'd struggle to describe."

"You don't want to?" asked Alexa softly.

"If you asked, I'd be honoured, but Ben is your father now. You and I – I never thought we'd get to this point. Pam and I, we don't really feel like your mother and father. We feel like your parents and definitely feel like Tracey and this little tyke's grandparents." Karl placed his hand back on Alexa's expanded belly and rubbed it gently. Alexa grabbed it and held it there. "You're the only person who's never asked us what the difference is," he smiled. "We still remember that argument and we've seen how difficult it's been for you to accept Ben as your father. In a way I think it's easier for us. You had a mother and a father, but you never had parents.

"Ben will have this opportunity with Beth. Beth wants all those traditional moments she never thought she'd have. But I think you want them too in many ways. Ben would never pressure you – never even ask. But I know what it'd mean to him – to have a chance to be there for you. Just think about it. Hell, you don't even need to decide until the day."

Alexa did think about it. She wanted to discuss it with Marcus, but knew what he would say. He would support anything that helped heal the rift between her and Ben, but not at the expense of her own happiness.

"You're just going to have to talk to him," said Charlotte, the only person Alexa managed to confide in. "You real concern is that he's not supportive of the marriage, right?" Alexa nodded. "Then find out."

When Alexa hesitated, Charlotte grabbed her phone and texted Ben. He was at the house forty minutes later. Thankfully, Bethany arrived five minutes before him. "I need to talk to Ben about some stuff and I need you to be there," said Alexa urgently, grabbing Bethany as soon as she walked in the front door. "I need you on my side. Please."

"Sure, Lex," nodded Bethany, squeezing Alexa's hands.

Ben seemed surprised by the united front he was presented with. When Alexa started the conversation by calling him by his name, rather than Dad, both he and Bethany knew it was serious.

"I need to know if you support me and Marc," said Alexa firmly, looking straight at Ben.

"Of course I —"

"No, not just in words. In reality," said Alexa over the top of him. "You seem to be looking for the cracks, just waiting for us to fall apart. I love him. I don't see that changing – even when I'm busy messing things up between us. I don't like thinking you're lurking in the shadows waiting for the chance to say 'I told you so'."

"I've seen the two of you together. I've seen the way you look at each other. Before Christmas, I stopped doubting – I started to see what you saw," said Ben sincerely, holding Alexa's gaze. "That changed this year. When he stood there as though he'd known about the pregnancy the whole time and – I couldn't help but think he was the reason you had been so – I don't know, distant, I guess."

"But that was all my fault," cried Alexa.

"No, I don't think so. A lot of it was my fault," added Ben over the top of her. "I should've told you there were problems – that there was damage, but that we needed to get it checked. I just remember them telling me back then and looking at you, wondering how I'd ever explain. When. I'm not against you and Marc."

"But?" questioned Alexa, sure there was more.

"But I just think that when things are going wrong, I might get a bit protective. I don't want you to stay with someone because you're too scared to leave – or too loyal."

Alexa turned to Bethany. Bethany's fingers were tapping her palm, reassuring her. Just like her, Bethany indicated. Alexa thought about that; considered what she would be like if it was Bethany or Charlotte in her position – with a man she had struggled to approve of. It was possible she would have reacted much worse than Ben. Alexa nodded, holding Bethany's hands to stop her from leaving.

"There's something else – something else I need to ask," said Alexa, her heart pounding furiously. Ben nodded, waiting for her to speak, but it had suddenly become very difficult. "Will you walk me down the aisle?"

Bethany seemed to understand the question first. Her arms were shaking, trying to restrain her reaction. Ben looked taken aback, and it took a couple of attempts at speaking before the words came out. "You know the answer is I'd be absolutely honoured to," he said in a thick voice. "But I didn't think you'd have anyone give you away. You don't have to."

"I'm not," said Alexa in a short voice. "You're not giving me away. You're just walking me down the aisle."

Bethany laughed and hugged Alexa tight. It took a moment to realise how angry she had sounded.

"Karl's okay with this?" asked Ben.

"Yeah," smiled Alexa, deciding against divulging more. "Thank you for asking."

Ben moved off his lounge to sit next to Alexa. Bethany proceeded to gather them in her arms, while Ben did the same from the other side. Terror was building in Alexa's body, but she forced herself to suppress it. She would not let herself fear those who had done nothing but try and protect her. When Ben detangled himself from Bethany, laughing that they were crushing Alexa and the baby, Alexa could not stop herself from taking his hand and placing it on her bump so that he could feel the baby moving.

***

Marcus stood in front of the mirror, his fingers fumbling as he tried to tie his tie. He had worn a tie on most days of his adult life and yet today, on the most important day, he was struggling to get it right.

"I seriously don't know how you're even awake enough to be this amped," said Ryan, pulling the tie from Marcus's neck and throwing around his own.

Ryan had not been the only one to question the timing of the wedding. It was something Marcus had questioned himself, but he had known from the moment he decided to ask Alexa to marry him that he would trade every vision of his wedding for hers if he had to. Planning their wedding had been one of the few bright points in those dark months, made brighter by the fact that he had had to compromise very little. It was rare that they had not wanted similar things for this day. Timing, however, was Alexa's choice.

The symbolism associated with their marrying as the sun rose on a bright new day was too beautiful to argue against. Marcus's main concern was how Alexa would be affected by a gloomy morning. The forecast was for a cloudy day, but with the night sky still a dark, inky blue, there was no telling if it was correct or not.

Driving out to the clifftop near their bay, it was difficult to stifle the yawns that were circling the car. Ryan tried to curse Marcus, but was cut off by his own yawn. Alexa had been horrified when she learned they had to pay to hire the location from the local council. She suggested they just turn up, but Marcus was too conservative for that. He hated breaking the rules. And given the cost of their wedding compared to the average one, he felt they had some room to move with the budget. He was sure at one point Alexa was trying to have the cheapest wedding on record.

Although there were many traditional elements to their wedding, all the fancy ceremony had been stripped back. Their small gathering of guests would just huddle around them. Alexa had not even wanted to pay for a photographer. She researched it and found it impossible to justify the costs. Bethany would have her camera, which would be passed around, and that would make do. It had been strange for Marcus to feel like the demanding one, but thankfully word spread and Alan sent Alexa a message telling her that his sister was a budding photographer and that she would be his wedding present to them.

The next shock most people got was that they had no plans for a reception. Neither of them cared much for that part and had planned for a picnic breakfast on the clifftop, but Peter had stepped forward just a few weeks ago with another offer. This one Alexa struggled to accept. Peter knew the owner of a nearby café on the beach and arranged for a breakfast reception there. The look of consternation on Alexa's face made Peter smile as he reassured them it would be completely in keeping with their style. That was something they would have to wait and find out about, because beyond the location, they knew very little about what lay install for them.

There were people already at the clifftop when Marcus arrived. Karl was coordinating the guests who had come early to help set up. They had a cluster of lanterns which lit their area beautifully. They had managed to convince Alexa that she should be the last to arrive, knowing she would not have been able to relinquish responsibility if she had been here. This was everyone's gift to them – getting up in the middle of the night to spend the early hours of a chilly morning setting up a wedding in near complete darkness.

"She still asleep?" Marcus asked Karl in a soft voice, as he approached Tracey's stroller.

"Snug as a bug," smiled Karl.

Marcus did not dare check. Tracey was wrapped up in a thick sleeping bag with a heavy blanket over the stroller to keep out the cool breeze. Karl and Pam assured him they had checked on her several times and she was warm in her little cocoon.

"Marc!" squealed Rhianna, rushing over to him. "Crazy idea, this wedding. It's freezing!"

Marcus hugged Rhianna. She really was cold. She did not own a suitable coat for the event and had hoped it would not be as cold as predicted. Thankfully, Bethany stepped in, opening her wardrobe to Rhianna. It had been a beautiful bonding moment. Marcus had never seen Bethany so happy as when she thought she was truly able to assist someone. It was something that had helped ease away some of the lingering dislike he still harboured. In many ways, Marcus was disappointed in himself that he held any kind of resentment towards Bethany. He truly loved her as his sister, but was starting to realise that when he developed grudges, he held them very tight.

"You're looking good, Rhianna," smiled Ryan.

"Thanks. Beth dolled me up after you guys left," smiled Rhianna, posing for them. "She's great with make-up and hair. If she doesn't sleep for a week after today, I'll be surprised. She's been up for the last two days straight, I swear."

"You come with Sam and Brett?" asked Ryan, looking around with squinting eyes.

"Yeah, they're over with Sam's grandparents and Maria setting up the celebratory drinks. I'll go get them and send them over," smiled

Rhianna.

Marcus waited for Brett and Sam to join them, thinking of how this contrasted to every previous vision he had had for his wedding day. Most of the people he had envisaged being here were no longer part of his life. It was something that would have concerned him more if he were not so content.

Choosing Ryan to be his best man was so simple it bordered on automatic. The selection of Sam and Brett in the bridal party was not only the consequence of Marcus running out of good friends after Ryan, but also acceptance of the fact that Alexa's world was now his.

"Hey, brother!" called Brett, walking up behind Marcus and clapping a hand on his shoulder. "Too late to back out now."

Marcus smiled, thinking it had probably been too late five years ago when Alexa's deep sea blue eyes had pierced their way through to his heart. Although it was still difficult to acknowledge that Alexa had been his student then, with each year that passed, those origins became less painful; made easier by the attitudes of those around them.

"Ready to officially join this very impressive sibling group?" asked Brett jovially.

"You betcha, little brother," laughed Marcus. "Always wanted a brother."

"Hell yeah. That's the only good thing about so many sisters – most of them will marry men – finally balance things up. Very glad to have another guy in the family."

Karl walked over and joined them, placing a loving arm around Brett's shoulder. For a moment Marcus imagined what Alexa would have been like if she had been able to continue living with the Whites through and beyond high school. Today's eventuality would have been highly unlikely, but Marcus would have preferred that to what Alexa went through. Shaking his head, knowing the past could never be changed, Marcus just delighted in the news that Alexa was on her way.

"Just make sure no one steps past those lanterns until the sun comes up," said Karl, pointing towards the edge of the cliff.

The lanterns had been set out as a large open love heart. People were gathering inside it, all holding lights of various forms and colours. There were even a number of glow sticks. Rhianna was by far the most colourful, practically decorated in glow sticks. It was no wonder she and Bethany got along so well.

"Let's go do this, boys," said Ryan.

Sam put his hand on Marcus's shoulder to hold him back for a second. "You're the best person for her," he said feelingly. "I couldn't have asked for a better husband for her. I just wanted you to know that."

Alexa's heart was thrumming as Ben parked the car. She felt a little ridiculous in her dress, but also the prettiest she ever had. When she looked out at the colours dancing across the lightening sky, her heart flipped again, knowing Marcus was waiting for her.

"Let's go get you married," squealed Bethany.

Alexa turned to Ben. When she nodded and took a deep breath, he jumped out of the car and moved around to her door. He helped to gather her dress off the ground as she slid out of the car. She shivered slightly in the cool dawn air, causing her to rub her arms. It made her very glad Maria had the foresight to realise she would be cold in only her dress. The long white jacket suited the dress perfectly. It had been Maria's – something she had been holding on to for years without really knowing why. The gift was so sweet and generous that Alexa had to wonder if she could truly be this lucky.

"Ready?" asked Ben.

They all looked across to the eastern horizon. Light was breaking over the edge of the ocean, orange burning through the clouds strewn gently across the sky, splattering them with colour.

"Yeah, let's do this," replied Alexa.

Bethany and Hayley squealed excitedly as they linked arms with Charlotte. Alexa had never been to a wedding before and had no fixed concepts of what they were supposed to be like, so had had no qualms when they had come to her asking to walk arm-in-arm to their positions rather than one after the other. Ahead of them, Alexa could see their guests waving Bethany, Charlotte and Hayley into the correct position with their flotilla of lights. Bethany was practically skipping, and Alexa knew when she reached Marcus because she suddenly broke away and threw her arms around him.

"I think that's our cue," said Ben. "Better leave now or Beth will drown your husband in tears."

Alexa smiled broadly. Since she had asked Ben to be involved in the wedding, he had been doing everything he could to show how much she supported them.

"Dad," said Alexa, halting Ben's movement towards the wedding. "Thank you – for everything. Thanks for wanting us."

"Shhh," said Ben quickly, wrapping his arm around her shoulder, but not pulling her into a hug. "This is all I've ever wanted. Now let's get you to that clifftop before we miss the sunrise. I'll hug you when it's over. I can't bear the thought of scrunching you up before everyone sees you looking so beautiful."

Soft music drifted through the air. Alexa looked around, but could not see where it was coming from. She had never even considered having music. It seemed so impractical when they were outside, but it was a lovely addition as she and Ben walked towards Marcus. The illumination of the sky and their gathering was so pretty, Alexa almost wished she could have just sat and watched it, but when she reached Marcus all she could do was throw herself into his arms.

"Huh-hmm. I think we need to get you hitched first," called Alan, causing a chuckle to ripple through the air.

Alexa smiled and took a step back, but did not let go of Marcus's hands. The celebrant spoke, but Alexa barely listened. They had run through the proceedings before and she knew what she needed to say and when. What she had promised herself she would do was pay attention to the moment. Her eyes roved the whole scene, taking it in. From the changing colours of the sky to the smiles of her friends and family, and the look of absolute adoration from Marcus, they were images she promised herself she would never forget.

When it came to the exchanging of vows and rings, the ceremony had a much greater hold on Alexa's attention. This was the part that really mattered and she loved the feeling that accompanied Marcus slipping the wedding band on her ring finger, and the smile that adorned his face when she reciprocated. It felt like from this point forward their relationship – their marriage – was something no one could strip away from them. She could still ruin things with her dysfunctional lunacy, but they were now bound together by more than their will.

"I now pronounce you husband and wife," said the celebrant. "You may kiss the bride."

Marcus smilingly obliged to the cheers of not only their gathering, but also a few residents and passers-by who had stopped to watch.

"Okay, trust that I'm only making your day more memorable and follow my directions quickly," said Lily in an urgent voice.

Alexa was too stunned to do otherwise and posed as required by Alan's sister as she clicked away. The light was changing so rapidly that there were no second chances for the shots, but it quickly became very fun and wild on the increasingly bright clifftop.

When the sun had risen completely, everyone started to relax. Bottles of sparkling grape and apple juice were cracked open and congratulations passed around.

"That was a beautiful ceremony," said Peter, walking up to Alexa and Marcus. "Can I introduce you to my wife, Jian."

"Congratulations," smiled Jian, moving forward and kissing Alexa and Marcus in turn. "It really was a lovely ceremony."

"I'm so glad you could come," said Alexa. She had been so afraid that it would be inappropriate to ask Peter that she had even made a point of asking him to attend as her boss, not as her lawyer. Peter had responded that he would attend as her friend. "Would you like to meet Tracey? I can't believe she actually slept through the whole thing."

Peter opened his arms and Tracey had little hesitation reaching out for him. She was so used to being held by different sets of arms that she had no fear of meeting new people.

"She's very beautiful," smiled Peter, holding on to his glasses as Tracey reached for them. "Has anyone ever told you that she actually looks a lot like you?"

"I've told her, but she doesn't believe me," said Marcus. "Thank you again for organising our reception. It's a very generous gift."

"It's the least I could do," nodded Peter in a thick voice. "The very least," he added as he leaned in and placed a gentle kiss on Alexa's cheek and passed Tracey back to her. "We're going to go ahead and get your reception ready. We'll see you again soon."

Peter's departure started a trend. After so many hours up and about, stomachs were rumbling and everyone was keen to make their way towards a guaranteed food source. Lily insisted that the bridal party stick around for a few more photos. The beautiful coastal scene was so mesmerising, it was not hard to convince Alexa to stay. However, after half an hour of photos she was finding herself becoming more and more fatigued.

"You okay?" asked Bethany, sitting down next to Alexa while the boys took more photos.

"Yeah, but this thing is heavy," said Alexa, her hand on her bump.

"Ah, I saw that!" cried Sam. "Rubbing your stomach. You're hungry too! Let's go. I love you dearly, but if you don't feed me soon I don't want to be held responsible for my actions."

Ryan and Brett gave instant, loud backing to Sam's sentiment, herding everyone towards the cars.

"Happy?" asked Marcus softly as he and Alexa snuggled together on the back seat of Ryan's car.

"It feels impossible that I've been given so much," Alexa replied.

"Nothing more than you deserve," said Marcus earnestly, leaning in and kissing her passionately. Alexa kissed him back, wrapping her arm around his neck and holding him close.

"You guys want us to just leave you in the car?" asked Ryan, pulling up outside the café. "You can finish your tonsil hockey session in peace."

Marcus shoved Ryan playfully in the shoulder as they clambered out of the car and into the café. A section of the café had been cordoned off for them, with a large table laden down with breakfast foods.

"Ah, we're not speeching before eating, are we?" asked Alan, holding his fork halfway between his plate and mouth.

Chad's fork slipped into his mouth as he registered Alan's words. He chewed quickly before speaking. "Don't listen to Al," Chad laughed. "He's getting all sensitive because he loved you in his prepubescent years. We know you care so much about us that you'd never let us starve in our sleep-deprived state."

"Just remember I'm eating for two, so if you don't have a plate of food waiting for me by the time I squeeze my way between you, you're both barred from my life," called Alexa. "And no speeches!"

There was a loud cheer from the boys as Chad, Alan and Nick started piling a plate high for Alexa. Marcus kissed her tenderly before releasing her and sitting at the other end of the table with Ryan and Rhianna.

The next few hours were the best Alexa could remember ever experiencing. Everyone was in a good mood, and with no formalities to break the flow, all they were left with was enthusiastic celebrating. Alexa and Marcus did the rounds of all their guests. The boys from high school all teased Alexa about her pregnancy, joking that most people had the wedding before they started showing. It was nice they were all so chilled about it, but as the reception was wrapping up, she realised all was not quite as rosy as it seemed.

"Is she really okay?" Alan asked Marcus in a concerned voice, Chad, Nick and Sam all standing around them.

"No," replied Marcus seriously. "It gets more dangerous by the day. We're having pretty regular check-ups. Last one showed some strain that wasn't there a couple of weeks ago. Doctor warned that she'll probably be bed-bound before the end of the pregnancy."

"Does she know?" asked Chad.

"She knows, but I'm not sure she always understands," Marcus replied, annoying Alexa with his response. "Or just ignores the risk," he added with a smile, suddenly noticing her scowl.

"You could've asked me these questions," snapped Alexa, moving into the circle with crossed arms.

"Yeah, we could of," said Nick. "But you would've lied."

Alexa stuck her tongue, but it did not stop their questions – or Marcus's honest answers.

"Wedding dance time!"

Heads snapped up everywhere. Alexa looked over to see Bethany's beaming face next to Rhianna's mischievous one. Alexa started shaking her head, but Marcus was already leading her to a small section of cleared floor.

"You'll thank us later," whispered Marcus softly in her ear.

"After I fall on my arse? I can't dance," Alexa replied.

"I sincerely disagree, but just trust me, okay."

Alexa nodded and let Marcus take her in his arms. The music was soft and slow, and he moved her gently, twirling her every so often as Lily flitted around them taking photos from every angle. Just as Alexa started to feel herself smile, a frustrated cry filled the air and the sound of cutlery hitting the floor clanged around the room.

"And party's over, people," called Chad. "Baby has spoken. Time to leave the overtired toddler to the newly-wedded couple."

Everyone laughed, but Tracey was threatening a full-blown meltdown. When she refused every set of arms but Marcus's, they all started to pack up. It had been a long day already and there were very few people who were not talking about going back to bed. With one final group photo – Tracey whimpering in the centre – the reception finally came to an end.

When Marcus and Alexa slipped into the back of the car, Tracey in between them, they both released long, contented sighs of relief.

Chapter Seventeen

ALEXA GENTLY OPENED the front door, trying not to be too loud, but Tracey woke, her whimpering turning immediately to cries.

"Too good to be true," sighed Marcus, adjusting Tracey's position in his arms to try and soothe her. Tracey had cried much of the trip home, only knocking herself out in the last hour of the drive.

"Maybe it's a good thing the doctor refused to let me fly," said Alexa. "We would've been very unpopular if she'd screamed like that on a five-hour flight.

Marcus said nothing, just rubbed Alexa's shoulder, before placing Tracey on the lounge room floor with a toy and going to fix her bottle. It had been the one part of the wedding Marcus had wanted to do all himself and his plans had been amazing. The enticement of a five-day island holiday in the Pacific was overwhelming, but a fortnight before the wedding their specialist refused to give Alexa clearance to fly. There were too many risks of complications. The compromise was a beach holiday up the coast. It had been beautiful and relaxing, but Alexa had the feeling Marcus was still disappointed he had not been able to give them the honeymoon he planned.

Tracey cried and grumbled until Marcus returned with her bottle. Despite being hungry, she would not immediately feed, but she eventually settled and halfway through her bottle was sound asleep.

"She's going to wake hungry in an hour," said Marcus in a tired voice, holding up the half-full bottle. "Better than nothing, I guess."

"I know how she feels," yawned Alexa.

"Go have a nap," suggested Marcus, standing to put Tracey to bed, but Alexa just shook her head. However, by the time Marcus returned, Alexa was already half-asleep on the lounge. There was a gentle chuckling near her ear as she felt her body being shuffled. When her shoes were flicked off her feet, she felt warmth engulf her as Marcus laid her body down with his and wrapped her in his arms. Alexa felt her eyes close more solidly as Marcus's arms held her tighter.

The sound of heavy footsteps made Alexa turn. She saw the arm just in time. Grabbing it, she held it firm, twisting it away from her – away from Bethany.

"Ow, Lex, ow. Let go!"

"Wake up. Alexa, wake up."

The number of hands multiplied, spewing out from Sean's body and engulfing Alexa like a hideous octopus. A gunshot tore through the air. Sean's hands still clung to Alexa's body, but Ben pushed between them and held her protectively.

"He's dead. He's dead. Let go now. He's dead."

Alexa opened her hands at the same time as her eyes, confusing her brain with the scene in front of her. Ben was still holding her, but so was Marcus. Bethany was beside Ben rubbing her wrist. When Alexa realised she was laying down, she got Marcus to sit her up.

"You okay?" Alexa asked Bethany, reaching out and stroking her wrist.

"Yeah," nodded Bethany. "You? Must've been a bad one."

"He went after you again," said Alexa softly. "But you killed him this time," she added, looking at Ben.

"That's good," said Marcus. "It's good you dreamed that. Might not get rid of your nightmares completely, but you always said they were so scary partly because you knew what was coming. Maybe now that's changed. Maybe it'll be changed for good."

"I think that could work," said Bethany, squeezing Alexa's hand.

They all knew there was nothing they could do to actively alter Alexa's nightmare, but she did like the idea that it could change to reflect reality. Sean could never hurt them again. He was not even their father any more. In the eyes of every law, Ben was their dad. He had slayed their dragon, and for the first time Alexa felt something close to hope after a nightmare.

Almost on cue, as if hearing the extra voices in the house, Tracey started to cry.

"Can I go get her?" asked Bethany excitedly. "Please!"

"Oh, thank you, yes," cried Marcus. "You please make her happy and I'll start dinner. You guys," he added, pointing at Alexa and Ben. "Catch up. And don't let her strain herself."

"He getting all overprotective?" asked Ben, moving on to the lounge next to Alexa once they were alone.

"Something like that," replied Alexa in a tired voice. "We spent half our honeymoon organising how I'd finish the semester. We called and emailed my lecturers. Will have to submit a whole lot of paperwork, but they're going to give me special provisions as I require them. I was going to just apply to graduate after this semester, but one of my lecturers was really insistent – said I should just take a year off and then come back and do my honours. I'll get in," Alexa added with a slight smile.

"You qualified?" asked Ben happily.

"Yeah, got the required average. They said there was never any doubt, but everything seems to always get real complex in my life around exam time."

"True, but we'll manage. We'll even look at finding ways to drive you to class if you need it. You deserve to get your degree – with honours."

"You think I'll be able to get a real job at the end of it?" asked Alexa, hoping Ben understood what she meant.

"Might take time," nodded Ben. "Might not be your dream job, but yeah, I really do believe you will. And when you get that job, I'll think you'll do fine. It'll be scary, but we all believe in you."

Alexa nodded, trying to weave Ben's confidence into her soul. Living had always proved to be so much harder than surviving. She felt like she was starting to understand how to live her home life, particularly as her home encompassed those she loved most and who loved her enough to put up with everything she put them through. University and friends was something she had basic competence at, but that was after years of practice and moulding from school. Working for Peter was only possible because it was Peter. Moving beyond that realm was terrifying.

"Alexa, don't take this as a sign of a lack of faith, but you're in a very good position financially. You don't ever need to do anything you find uncomfortable – even work. You were right when you told me you don't ever get to be normal. Even after we've removed all those threats in your life, there was never normal in your life. There's nothing for you to go back to. What you get is to live the rest of your life in peace and security."

Alexa curled up into Ben's arms, trying desperately to hold her tears at bay. This was the man she had always wanted Ben to be.

"Thank you for killing him," whispered Alexa, grasping Ben's shirt.

Ben did not answer immediately. "I'll always try and protect you and Beth – this whole family."

"You think Marc's right? You think you can kill him in my dreams now?"

"Yeah, I do. Your dreams have always been pretty truthful. You dreamed those things because I wasn't there for you – there to help and protect you the way I should've – even when I was around – and with Sean still alive – still a threat. Now that's changed. Sean can't ever hurt you again and I'm going to be the person you always needed me to be. I'm going to trust you and support you – be there for you rather than tell you what you're supposed to do."

"So there's hope?" asked Alexa sitting up.

"There's definitely hope," smiled Ben.

Dinner was a rowdy affair. Bethany had somehow managed to get Tracey out of her dark mood, meaning she was happy and vocal at the dinner table. She was clearly excited to see Charlotte and Ben. Marcus even suggested that Tracey might have been unhappy with them for taking her away from the rest of the family for so long. Charlotte agreed and insisted they make up for that by letting her and Bethany take Tracey for the night. Bethany had even made a second cot for Tracey.

"I didn't plan it this way, but I think my initial distrust is working in our favour," smiled Marcus, when he and Alexa were alone in their room. "Everyone practically begging to look after Tracey when we're so tired. It's gold. I just hope they don't catch on too soon."

"They will," laughed Alexa. "But it won't change anything. You just have to say the word and they'll help us. You know that, right?"

"I've always known it in theory. I think with the way things turned out in my family that it's a bit hard to believe in practice. My parents always helped with Tracey, but not without letting me know that she was my responsibility – not something to be palmed off."

Alexa found it strange that she somehow managed to have the better family out of the two of them. She had always imagined her life being worse than everyone's, but the family that had built up around her was perfect. That realisation made her appreciate them even more – and gave her the patience to deal with their evermore overprotective ways.

All it took was one wince. Moving a little too rapidly, Alexa had not been able to hide the pain that had tickled her pelvis. When it became harder to hide just how frequent these painful niggles were as the pregnancy progressed, the more overbearing everyone became. Thankfully her doctor was still allowing her to keep swimming as long as it caused no issues, because most of her other movements were heavily restricted. Once she was down the stairs, Marcus refused to let her back up, fetching anything she needed.

"You don't need to do this," sighed Alexa.

"Yes he does," snapped Bethany. "You need to listen to the doctor – and us."

Marcus had been refusing to keep Bethany in the dark about the pregnancy, realising what an ally he had when it came to keeping Alexa well. While Alexa loved that they cared, she hated their concerns. She hated the fear this pregnancy was instilling in her. She hated the pain it was causing her body and the strain on her mind that was making the completion of the semester more tedious than she wanted it to be.

Alexa had already stopped attending lectures. The university had agreed to provide her all the material she needed so she could complete her subjects from home. They had even given her a parking space on campus so she could drive to her tutorials. It all helped, but none of it stopped the situation being painfully difficult.

Those struggles made Alexa glad she and Marcus had not delayed their wedding. It was technically only a piece of paper, but for Alexa the commitment behind that symbolism was more important than she could explain. It helped to stop her mind twisting situations into her believing that Marcus would just walk out on them. That she had something to reassure herself things were not about to fall apart helped her cope while the world felt like it was speeding along without her.

When Tracey progressed rapidly from tottering to running before her first birthday, it felt like the house descended into chaos, as a whole new world fell into her reach. It made them all realise how thoughtless they were with numerous, suddenly dangerous household items. There was nothing Tracey would not grab. Fear was something she had shockingly little concept of.

"I think we need to re-child-proof this house," sighed Alexa, after gently taking the fork from Tracey's hand that she had grabbed from the table. Tracey whinged and ran from the room, a giggle trailing in from the hallway.

"If she wasn't so tall we wouldn't have such a problem," said Charlotte, pushing the cutlery further towards the centre of the dining table.

"I don't think we'll have a problem with this one," smiled Alexa, rubbing her swollen stomach. "If it takes after me, it'll be five before it reaches anything dangerous."

"Dangerous? We wouldn't be talking about our little terror, would we?" asked Marcus, walking into the kitchen with Bethany, large wads of toilet paper in his hands. "She discovered toilet paper."

"And she was only a few metres in front of me," said Bethany, wrestling Tracey playfully. "She can move fast when she sees something she likes."

"Yep, that's our girl," smiled Marcus, tickling Tracey's exposed tummy, making her giggle.

When Marcus took Tracey into his arms and kissed her over and over, Alexa had the feeling Tracey already had him wrapped him around her little finger. Thankfully, Tracey generally needed little reprimanding. Despite her antics, she was rarely naughty and usually only grumpy when she was tired. Even now that Alexa could not play with Tracey as actively as before, she would often sit happily with her and listen as Alexa read to her. Truthfully, Marcus would not let them do much else. With Tracey's first birthday coinciding with Alexa's exams, Marcus was not only being very insistent about how little Alexa moved, but how much she studied. The only consolation was that this semester was a much lighter study load, after she had tried, unsuccessfully, to complete her degree in two and a half years.

However, it was difficult to study while everyone else organised Tracey's birthday; though once Bethany got involved, Alexa found the hardest thing was containing the celebrations.

"It's her first birthday!" cried Bethany. "You can't let that go. I don't want her growing up like you – thinking no one likes her – no one wants to celebrate her."

"Of course we're going to celebrate," said Marcus softly, squeezing Bethany's hand as she bit her quivering lip. "I think Alexa just wants to keep it to something we can fit in this house."

"I like that we can give her everything," said Alexa in a wavering voice. "But I don't want her growing up thinking that things come that easy to everyone."

Bethany rushed over and wrapped her shaking arms around Alexa. "She'll love us," she whispered, hugging Alexa tighter. "We're nice to her. She'll love us even though we're not like her."

Marcus's eyes clearly showed that he had heard what Bethany

said, but he stayed quiet. Alexa knew that part of him expected all their fears to slide away, but the reality was that every new thing only brought forth a new wave of terror.

"Morning," smiled Marcus, ignoring the way Alexa flinched away from him when he stroked her arm. "Big day."

"You let me sleep in?" asked Alexa, noticing the light in the room.

"Of course I did," chuckled Marcus. "I had orders from Bethany. She wanted no interference in the extravaganza that is your daughter's first birthday."

"What have they done?" asked Alexa curiously.

"It's pretty amazing, actually. The cake is a lady bug – well, the three cakes they baked have been turned into a lady bug. And they have outdone themselves in the kitchen as usual. And maybe gone a tad crazy with gifts. Oh yeah, and the house is full of balloons."

From the way Marcus was smiling at her, Alexa knew he had no fears that she would object. Bethany had not moved away from her over the top celebrations, they were just completely homemade.

"Want me to help you to the shower?" asked Marcus, trying to sound casual. He had recently changed that question from need to want after Alexa continued to rile against her need for assistance.

"I'm fine," Alexa sighed, but it was impossible for her to hide the pain moving caused her. Tears slipped down her cheek as Marcus helped her shift her body into a seated position then up on to her feet.

"I've gotcha," said Marcus softly, keeping his arm protectively around her waist.

Despite Marcus being nothing but wonderful, Alexa hated that her body was betraying her. Her frustration and self-loathing was only made worse by the fact that Marcus would not condemn her and leave her to manage on her own. In some ways she wished he would. It would have been incredibly painful and tiring, but she would have felt like she had achieved something.

"I love you," said Marcus softly, when Alexa continued to sit on the bed, despite the fact that she was dressed and ready to head downstairs. "I'll just go check on things and come back up in a minute to help you down the stairs if you need it."

Alexa nodded. The baby kicked, causing her to grimace. This was the part she hated the most. Every movement the baby made pained her more and more the longer the pregnancy went on.

"Now, I know you're not going to be keen on this idea, but Charlotte has just brutally savaged my concept of my own physical strength, so you're going to have to help me out." Alexa turned around to see Ben standing at the door with a strangely disgruntled look on his face. "I'm serious. Beth told Marc that he had to carry you down the stairs – that you weren't allowed to walk any more. Then I suggested I could go and get you and Charlotte cried that I'd have a heart attack. I was too old."

"That's a terrible cover story," said Alexa. "What if it's true? You'll feel awful if you drop me down the stairs."

"You do realise that you have to pass a pretty strict physical to become a police officer," replied Ben in an unimpressed voice.

"Yeah, to get in. You can get as weak as you want after that."

"And that if you wanted to walk down those stairs by yourself you're saying all the wrong things? You're leaving me no choice but to prove myself."

A slight smile came over Ben's face and Alexa realised she did not really care if it was all a rouse. Ben had given her a genuine excuse to avoid the pain of the stairs. "Yeah, okay, Dad, come prove how strong you are," she sighed. "Can we just test it first over the bed? I really don't want to fall down the stairs."

Ben did not appear impressed by her comments, but when his arms slid under her body he was very gentle. "Okay?" he asked, lifting her up against his chest.

It surprised Alexa just how benign Ben's touch felt despite the intimacy of his hold. However, even that realisation made her mind swirl. "I'm just going to close my eyes and pretend you're not my dad for a minute, okay," she whispered, burying her face in the crook of his neck.

"I won't let anything hurt you," Ben replied softly.

Alexa could feel the movement under her body. It was sickening with her eyes closed, but she knew it was better than the panic attack that might take hold if she dared to let herself think. It was not until she was placed gently on the lounge that she looked up to see Ben's smug smile.

"I think you might owe Ben an apology, Charlotte," said Marcus, sitting down on the lounge and handing Tracey gently to Alexa. "She wants you," he added with a smile. "Won't eat breakfast with us."

"Fine," sighed Charlotte. "You guys need to swap bodies then," she said, waving her hands between Ben and Marcus. "Then you'll look as strong as you are."

"When did this extend to insulting me?" cried Marcus. "That's a low blow."

Charlotte just smirked as Bethany giggled, before they both danced back to the kitchen. Alexa watched them with a strange sense of envy. She knew she could no longer be like them, but missed the carefree moments they had shared.

Despite people always being around, Alexa felt isolated. Eating and playing with Tracey helped improve Alexa's mood. It was hard not to have fun with a one-year-old in a room full of balloons. When people started to arrive, Alexa even began to feel like she was not confined to the lounge, as everyone moved around and took the time to sit with her.

"I can't believe how fast she's growing up," said Karl, holding Tracey tenderly.

"I might need to borrow your children occasionally, Alexa," smiled Pam. "The way Karl talks, he's so clucky he'll be wanting us to have another baby."

Karl dismissed Pam's jibe, but did not let go of Tracey until she decided she wanted more variety in the arms that held her. Tracey was delighted by the number of people at the house intent on giving her whatever she wanted. The steadily growing pile of presents in the lounge room also attracted Tracey's attention, eventually proving to be too much of a temptation.

"No, no, Tracey," said Alexa, pulling the present from her hands. "You have to wait."

"No," cried Tracey. "Me."

"Tracey," replied Alexa sternly.

"Mmeeeee," answered Tracey. "Mum," offered Tracey, grabbing another present and offering it to Alexa. When Alexa took the present, Tracey smiled and started distributing more presents.

"I think it's time to do presents," smiled Ben. "I'll go get everyone."

Charlotte, Hayley and Bethany came bounding in from the kitchen and dropped to the floor near the slightly smaller pile of presents. Tracey immediately joined them.

"Me," said Tracey, hugging her present.

"Yes, all for you," smiled Bethany, stroking Tracey's cheek. "All for you!"

Tracey squealed with delight. When Bethany indicated that she could open her present, Tracey tore it with vigour, but appeared much less sure of what she should do with the clothes that were inside. Throwing them to the side, she waved her hands for more presents. Marcus sat down next to Alexa and took her hand. They were both watching Bethany. Alexa had heard Marcus telling Bethany that young children often did not appreciate presents when they unwrapped them. Bethany's hands were shaking as she handed Tracey the present. She was smiling assuredly, but Alexa could see that she was steeling herself for rejection. However, this time, when Tracey opened the present to find a range of books – all with some form of interactivity – Tracey was won over. Tracey grabbed the middle book and handed it back to Bethany before moving into her lap.

Reading was something they did so often with Tracey that she often preferred books to toys. As soon as Bethany finished the first book, Tracey grabbed the next. There was no care for presents now. When all the books were read, Tracey picked up the first one and moved towards Alexa.

"We'll get lunch ready," smiled Marcus. "You read with Mummy?" he asked Tracey. Tracey's only response was to snuggle in closer to Alexa.

Everyone started to move towards the dining room. Bethany stayed back, curling up with them on the lounge. Even when lunch was served, Tracey brought her books with her. The rest of the presents were opened after lunch, but Tracey seemed more bemused than excited by the continued unwrapping of presents around her. Every so often she would find herself attracted to one of the gifts, but it was the coloured paper that now had her attention.

The need for Alexa to push herself off the lounge to use the bathroom had everyone else moving as well, with talk of birthday cake and coffee to come. Alexa took her time before emerging, slipping into the kitchen.

"No sneaking a piece," said Charlotte. "You know you get to eat cake for two. No need to try for a secret extra."

"It's a great cake," said Alexa, loving that Charlotte was not commenting on how much she was moving.

"Yeah, Beth's pretty proud of it. She designed it. You know that?

She tell you?" asked Charlotte. Alexa shook her head. She had assumed they had just followed a recipe. "She takes her aunt duties pretty seriously. I mean, I love Tracey – so much – but Beth – she's intent on her having everything. All the things we didn't."

"Has she been getting more serious the more pregnant I get? The more Marcus tells her about my specialist appointments?" questioned Alexa.

"Yeah," nodded Charlotte solemnly. "You can't think her being ignorant would be better. She's terrified of losing you, but she's not being irrational. This pregnancy – it's dangerous. We're all scared."

Arms gently snaked around Alexa's body. Bethany buried her head in Alexa's neck as she held her from behind. "It's scary, but we love you and this little one so much. We know it's going to be okay. Bad things aren't allowed to happen to us any more," said Bethany softly.

"That's right," replied Alexa. "It will hurt a bit as it grows, but then the doctor will just cut it out and I can go back to being unstretched."

"Let's go give Tracey the best lady bug cake ever," smiled Charlotte, rubbing Alexa and Bethany's arms.

"Can I take it out?" asked Alexa.

Charlotte lifted the large tray off the bench, handing in carefully to Alexa. Bethany kept hovering, but Alexa could tell Bethany was actually much more concerned that she would drop the cake than hurt herself. Walking slowly into the lounge room, they were met by Marcus's apologetic eyes. "I don't think we need that just yet."

Bethany quickly grabbed the cake and whisked it back to the kitchen. Marcus took Alexa's hand and walked her to the lounge room, and there was Tracey fast asleep in a bed of wrapping paper.

"One minute she was crawling and tossing things, the next she was fast asleep. At least she's having a good day. Kinda wish we could just sneak away and have a nap too," Marcus added in a whisper. "Better just make some coffee, huh?"

"Probably better," smiled Alexa.

Marcus pulled Alexa into a gentle hug before they headed back to the kitchen. It was nice that everyone was letting her move and do things without comment, though she could not deny that she was very happy to be sitting down at the dining table with her juice. They all chatted as they waited for Tracey to wake up. As soon as they heard the whimpering, Bethany was up and heading towards the kitchen.

"Mummy," called Tracey from the lounge room.

Alexa liked that Marcus did not push out from his seat. They had learned the hard way that when Tracey called for someone that was who she wanted and no one else would suffice. Thankfully, Tracey had started to understand that Alexa could not bend down and pick her up, so when Alexa sat on the lounge Tracey pulled herself up and into her arms. Closing her eyes, Alexa pushed off the lounge. Pain speared through the left side of her pelvis. Taking a deep breath, Alexa held Tracey close and carried her to the dining room.

Still tired, Tracey kept her face hidden from the family as they sat around the dining table. As soon as she turned around, Bethany, Charlotte and Hayley were pulling faces at her from the other side of the table. It did not take long before Tracey was giggling softly, and once Bethany had her attention, she pushed the cake into her line of sight. Tracey started bouncing, waving her hands and squealing loudly.

"I believe she likes the cake," said Maria.

Bethany smiled proudly, pushing the cake closer to Tracey. Tracey's enthusiasm was so great that Marcus had to ease her into his lap, while Alexa covered the pain by placing the number one candle into the top of the cake. Everyone immediately started singing happy birthday. Tracey was entranced. The singing, the flickering candle and colours of the cake. It was almost inevitable that she would reach out with her chubby, little hand and dig it into the cake. With a look of excited curiosity, her hand went straight to her mouth before reaching out for the cake again.

"No, no, no," said Marcus quickly, grabbing Tracey's arm and pulling it back towards them while the rest of the table laughed.

Even with the cake cut and dished out on plates, Tracey did not care for anything but sinking her hands into the cake remaining on the platter. When she was forced to give up on that, her focus was on the cake on everyone's plate but her own. No one cared and no one worried when Tracey reached out for their cake as they held her. She was too adored to be disciplined on her birthday.

"You need to lie down for a bit?" asked Marcus, looking over at Alexa. "You'll need your strength to study."

Alexa rolled her eyes, hating that she could not argue with that logic. "Can we just go sit near a window in the sun?" she asked. "At least til everyone goes. Then you can put me to bed."

Marcus chuckled, but complied. He sat with his legs out on the daybed and pulled her down with him, letting her curl up against his chest. "Here," he said, unbuttoning his shirt, knowing how comforting she found the feel of his skin. As soon as he started stroking her hair, her eyes became heavy.

"I'm sorry your parents didn't come," Alexa said softly.

"I didn't expect them to," replied Marcus flatly. He had refused to talk about what happened the fortnight before when he had taken Tracey to see his parents. Rhianna had already told them about the pregnancy – and how dangerous it was – but they continued to see the union as immoral. "Our children have everything and everyone they could ever need. They made their choice. It's the wrong one, but I don't want anyone in this family who doesn't love and accept you."

"I'll try to be worth it," said Alexa sincerely.

"Worth what?"

"All this trouble."

"You annoy me sometimes," said Marcus in a heavy voice. "You're worth it, okay. Now close your eyes and try not to forget who owns the wonderful arms that are holding you while you sleep."

It was something they had been working on, not always with a lot of success, but it was better than succumbing to fear all the time. However, on important nights – like the ones before Alexa's exams – Marcus kept to the other side of the bed.

There were no celebrations when Alexa finished her exams. The pain in her pelvis had become unbearable at times that most of her study days had been spent getting tests done. Marcus met her outside her exam room and took her straight back to the specialist. The news was not good. Her uterus was not handling the strain of the pregnancy and the longer it went on the greater the risk it would simply tear.

"Every day you stay pregnant, the better it is for the baby," explained the specialist. "But we are going to watch you very closely from this point onwards. My preference would be to admit you now and you spend the rest of the pregnancy in hospital."

"I can't do that," said Alexa quickly.

"Your husband has already explained that to me, but if you want to do the best thing by yourself and your baby, that time will come. Until then, I'm confining you to a wheelchair. We'll reassess every week. More if necessary."

***

The ache in Marcus's chest built as he pulled up in front of the Whites' house. It had been difficult to accept Alexa's wish to move in with them following the last specialist appointment, but Marcus knew better than to refuse. Alexa was not herself. At times she seemed barely more than a shell, and Marcus was beginning to wish the baby born sooner rather than later.

"How's she coping?" asked Marcus softly, joining Karl in the kitchen while Tracey played with everyone else in the lounge room.

"She's not," answered Karl. "I think she's pretending this whole situation doesn't exist. I've seen her when the baby kicks – she either closes her eyes or they glaze over – go hard. It's almost like she's denying its existence – denying the pain it's causing her. We're worried she won't bond with the baby if this continues."

Marcus was thrown. He had never considered such a notion. When Alexa loved, she loved wholly, but Marcus realised it had been a long time since Alexa had touched her stomach in a loving way. For the most part she had been tolerating the situation. She had recently stopped speaking about having another child – stopped speaking about their future. The remarks had been reasonable enough that Marcus had been able to dismiss them, but all Alexa had said lately was they would have to see how things were after the baby was born.

"I don't want to imagine the worst," said Marcus. "I feel like Bethany – trying to deny reality – only see the best outcome. I don't want to think that worse can continue to happen to her."

"You're not alone," nodded Karl.

"I don't know what happens to this family if – she's the heart of us."

"This family doesn't die with Alexa," said Karl firmly. "Alexa's our daughter. You'll always be our son. We know what you've lost, but you need to recognise what you've gained as well."

When they returned to the lounge room, everyone was talking around Alexa. Bethany was on one side of Alexa, holding tight on to her hand. Hayley was on the other side, gently rubbing Alexa's stomach. Alexa had found in the earlier months that the baby would shift towards movements and sounds, so she often kept a hand near the top of her bump and tapped her fingers in a rhythmic manner. Marcus realised it had been weeks since Alexa had done that, though she had been grateful when others had.

"Hey, we have Ben lined up to stay with you tomorrow and Sam the day after," smiled Marcus, handing Alexa a juice.

"You mean babysit me," replied Alexa in a frustrated tone.

"Actually, wait on you hand and foot were my instructions," retorted Marcus.

This time Alexa smiled slightly.

Ben's shift work had proven to be a godsend over the last few weeks. With everyone else still at work, they had been rotating leave to ensure someone was always with Alexa. Marcus just needed to make it until the end of the term, then he could spend every day with Alexa. For now he had to be content with a few hours in the evening, but it was difficult to say goodbye at the end of the night and take Tracey home without Alexa. Tracey was not enjoying the separation either. It was only possible because Bethany was always there to comfort Tracey and talk to her about Alexa. They spoke so much about Alexa that Marcus had the feeling Bethany was preparing for Alexa's death as well.

Sometimes Alexa really enjoyed the way Sam could ignore things. The way he could waltz into the room with a huge smile on his face and claim to be joyous of the opportunity to chill at home was what Alexa needed right then. It was not as though she had not liked spending the day with Ben. Perhaps it was just the fact that their conversation had turned towards their past and the mood it left her in afterwards that soured the memory. She could not blame Ben. She had wanted to talk about those things. At times it made her feel very connected to the people who were her parents. Other times, she just despised herself.

Sam did not come caring for conversation. He came with the desire for food – pancakes, more specifically. When he wheeled Alexa to the dining table, she was overwhelmed by the sheer volume of food he had constructed.

"You're going to turn into a man mountain if you eat like this," said Alexa, grabbing a couple of pancakes. "Bethy'll have to start reinforcing the furniture."

"She's already done the bed," replied Sam with a straight face.

"Sam!" cried Alexa, causing him to burst out laughing. "Urgh, I hope you never spoke about us so crudely."

"Ha, Beth's right, you're so sweetly naïve. Well, I don't even have to be crude and ask you how your marriage is going. The evidence is in you." Alexa rolled her eyes, but did not look down or touch her stomach. When she just spoke of her pregnancy, but did not mentally acknowledge its existence, she found she could be quite happy with the situation. "I know it's horrible the way you lost your first baby, but I'm glad you did," said Sam in a serious voice. "If you can only have one child, then this is the one you should have."

"You never think it should've been ours?" asked Alexa.

"Yeah, sometimes," smiled Sam. "But the truth is I was only ready for that because you were. I don't regret anything we had, but I think me and Beth are the better fit. And so are you and Marc. I'm sorry I was so stupid that I didn't want to even try and see that."

"Maybe I was just there to bring you to Bethy," smiled Alexa.

"You're amazing, you know that," laughed Sam. "I've been a terrible best friend these last couple of years and yet you still think I'm good enough for Beth."

"You ever think about this with Bethy?"

"Yes and no. We've decided to focus on the near future. We're not ready for a family. We've been talking about starting a furniture-making business."

"Oh," said Alexa, trying to hide her hurt.

"Don't get like that," laughed Sam, squeezing her hand. "You're going getting out of it that easy. We decided it'd have to wait until after Beth finishes her apprenticeship, and you and me finish our degrees. This isn't something to just waste our money on. We want to make it work."

"Do you have a business plan yet?" asked Alexa.

"Ah, no, because that's not our thing. That's your thing. So you can start thinking about that in between raising two kids under two. You should have plenty of spare time, right."

"Hmm, I should look at switching my degree then," said Alexa, contemplating what their business might need. "I've done a couple of introductory accounting subjects, but if I do more I can get accredited – work the whole finance side."

"Anything to get back to those books," replied Sam, shaking his head. "I can't wait to graduate."

"Sam, where's Mel?" asked Alexa, her mind swirling back to the origins of their conversation.

"Still with Clinton," nodded Sam sombrely. "They got married pretty much as soon as he was released from gaol. I haven't heard from her since. None of us have."

"If you see her, can you tell her that I asked how she was? Let her know she can contact me any time."

"What are you talking about?"

"He's going to hurt her," said Alexa softly. "He doesn't love her. I don't know what hold he has on her, but the novelty will wear off. Whatever game he's playing – I understand – I'm the only one who will. In time, she'll know that too."

"If I see her, I'll let her know," Sam said solemnly.

"When the time comes, we'll get her out – get her away from him."

"When do you find time to even think about that?" asked Sam, wiping the edge of his eye.

"I don't ever get to not think about it," shrugged Alexa. "Every day of this pregnancy I think of him – think about what would've happened if he hadn't made me miscarry."

"I think you would've died," said Sam seriously. "You would've hidden it as long as you could've, then you would've run from anyone you didn't trust – which was basically everyone. Would've tried to do it all yourself and when you went into labour you would've died."

"You don't think I'll die now?" asked Alexa, her voice wavering.

"No," replied Sam firmly. "I think the doctors are going to take care of you."

"I'm scared."

"Yeah, I know. I'm scared too. We all are."

Once they finished breakfast, Sam decided they had had enough serious talk for the day and moved them into the lounge room to watch a movie. It was nice and relaxing. Even the way he held her was reassuring. This was the best part of the current arrangement. When Alexa could forget all her fears and just enjoy the moment, things felt great. However, reality was never too far away.

"I need to pee," Alexa sighed.

"Yeah, Marc said something about this being in my duty statement. Let's go."

Alexa slid easily from the lounge to the wheelchair, but manoeuvring on to the toilet had always been difficult. Sam helped her without complaint, but it was indignant having to pee in front of someone else. However, it was much easier with Sam than it was with Ben or Karl.

Alexa slept through most of the afternoon. Bethany arrived from work soon after Alexa woke. When Brett and Hayley turned up, it was easier for Alexa to feel like she was not being supervised. However, the additional voices seemed to wake the baby, which started moving and kicking.

"You okay?" asked Bethany. "Need me to rub?"

Alexa shook her head, tears rolling down her cheek. "I don't want to do this any more," she gasped, the truth finally spilling out as the pain became unbearable.

"I think we need to take her to the hospital," said Sam. "This isn't okay, Lex. It's worse than usual. I can see in your eyes. I know you don't want to do it, but they might be able do something to make the pain stop."

Alexa nodded. She did not want to go to the hospital, but it was the only place that could take her baby. Maybe if she begged, they would take it out of her today.

Everyone moved frantically around Alexa, but it felt like forever before she was in the car. The pain did not ease as they drove. It spiked horribly with the movement. Bethany held her hand tight. Alexa had never seen so much fear in Bethany's eyes and realised how terrible she must look. She wanted to ease Bethany's fears, but could only squeeze her hands tighter.

Sam stopped the car right outside the doors to the hospital. "You guys stay with her and get her admitted," he said urgently. "I'll park the car and make the calls."

"They're all made," said Brett. "Everyone's on their way."

Alexa took a deep breath as they moved her from the car to the wheelchair, but as gentle as they tried to be, they could not prevent the spike of pain that speared her pelvis.

"Just hold on," said Brett, quickly turning her wheelchair and rushing her inside.

The pain did not subside, and when Alexa cried out, Brett pushed her faster. They did not make it to the counter before Alexa's screams of agony drew doctors to her side, but she could not answer their questions. She could do nothing at all as the pain consumed her in a cloud of vicious blackness.

Chapter Eighteen

MARCUS RAN FROM the car. The wait for the elevator was threatening to turn him into the Hulk. All he wanted was to get to Alexa. He had never felt this sick in his life. The sight of Bethany in tears was not comforting. She had become much stronger these last few months, but this was a girl grieving.

"Where is she?" asked Marcus in a strangled voice as soon as he reached them.

"Surgery," answered Brett.

"What happened? Did she fall or slip? Reach for something?"

"No, she was sitting," cried Sam. "Just sitting. She was in so much pain and I just wanted to get her here so they could do something. There had to be something they could do. But when we arrived ..."

"I've never heard her scream like that," said Brett, looking traumatised.

"Have you?" Marcus asked Bethany. Bethany nodded, but said nothing and Marcus wondered why he had even asked. They all knew Alexa did not scream. She held her pain internally. The extremity of the situation was clear if she had screamed in agony.

"Mr Knight."

Marcus turned to see Alexa's specialist walking out of the nearby theatre. "We've delivered your son. He's been taken to intensive care for monitoring. Alexa's still in surgery. There was a tear in her uterus. She's very lucky she was in the hospital when it occurred. I'm not sure she or the baby would have survived otherwise."

"She'll be okay, though, won't she?" asked Marcus.

"Yes, she should be fine," replied the doctor, though not in the most convincing tone. "But we're concerned about complications. I want your permission to perform a hysterectomy. The damage to your wife's uterus is severe. We believe this is the best course of action."

Marcus turned around. Ben, Karl and Pam were right behind him. He knew what his answer was, but did not think he had the right to make this decision alone.

"Don't let her suffer any more," said Ben. "It's the best thing."

"We agree," said Pam, Karl nodding solemnly with her.

"Beth?" asked Marcus. "I know what I want to do. What would Alexa want?"

"We can't learn to live unless we survive," replied Bethany.

"Yes," nodded Marcus to the doctor. "Do what you need to do – anything you need to do. Just make her better."

The doctor clapped Marcus on the shoulder and nodded before walking back inside. Marcus took a deep breath, his body shaking. Reaching out to Sam, he pulled him into a shuddering embrace. "Thank you," he said. "You saved her life."

A squeal pulled them apart. Maria put Tracey on the ground as they neared and she tottered quickly towards Marcus. Marcus scooped her up immediately, holding her tight as tears squeezed out his eyes. It did not matter that the doctor said Alexa would be fine. He could not believe that until he saw her. Things with Alexa never ran that smoothly.

"Do you want me to see if you can go see the baby?" asked Charlotte softly.

Marcus was shocked that the idea had never crossed his mind, but he did not see recrimination in anyone's eyes. When he nodded, Charlotte left with Hayley and Brett.

"She'll be okay," said Ben, wrapping a comforting arm around Marcus's shoulder. "She's a fighter. Her most basic instinct is to survive. She'll pull through."

It was hard for Marcus to be convinced. Yes, Alexa was a survivor, but everyone had their limits. What she had already endured was enough to kill most people. It seemed heartless that her own child might be what finally took her life. That thought made it difficult for Marcus to walk into the room to see his son. It was not an emotion he ever thought he would feel.

"I'll hold Tracey if you want," said Charlotte.

Marcus nodded, handing Tracey over as he moved next to his son's humidicrib. Two children, two premature births. Placing his hand inside, his son's little hand curled around his finger, melting his heart. This child was not the cause of their troubles. He did not tear apart Alexa's insides. Tears started spilling down Marcus's cheeks as he sobbed uncontrollably.

"You won't be alone in this. No matter what happens, you won't be alone," said Charlotte, wrapping an arm around his heaving shoulders as Tracey tried to scramble into his embrace.

They stayed with the baby for almost half an hour. It helped to focus on something other than Alexa's surgery and the fear that was swirling in all of them. If Tracey had not become so restless, Marcus thought he might have stayed there longer, but as soon as he was away from his son, his mind could not be diverted from Alexa's condition.

"She's out. She's fine," said Karl as soon as Marcus walked into the waiting room. "Doctor came by a couple of minutes ago. Everything went well. Said from the damage that she'd been lucky to hold the pregnancy as long as she did."

"Said she should never've been able to fall pregnant," added Brett. "Never would've said she could if she hadn't already been pregnant. Said it's as close to a miracle as medicine gets."

Marcus thought about that. Alexa had been too terrified to tell him she was pregnant because it was not supposed to be possible, and yet another doctor was telling them it should not have occurred. Even if she had done more tests beforehand, she would have been left in the same terrifying predicament, never in a position to choose whether she wanted to go through this or not. Marcus was not sure Alexa would have ever chosen to terminate, almost certainly not if they had not had Tracey, but it was a choice she was never given and she was now the mother of a child she had actively withdrawn from. And there was one thing Marcus had learned about Alexa; the emotion she displayed was only a fraction of what she felt. She had never once displayed any affection for this child. The emotions she spoke about were purely theoretical, and now, after major surgery, she would have to try and bond with their son. At least this time Marcus could foresee the troubles awaiting them and swore he would be as supportive and understanding as the situation required.

***

Alexa slowly opened her eyes. It was one of the few times she had woken in hospital and known exactly where she was and why. Her hand felt warm and she turned her head to see Marcus next to her. He was sitting in a chair, his hand holding hers as he slept with his head on the side of the bed. When she wiggled her fingers, his head immediately snapped up.

"Hey, beautiful," Marcus said softly, shuffling up towards Alexa and stroking her hair. "How you feeling?"

"Sore."

"Is it bad? I'll get them to give you more drugs. You shouldn't be in pain."

"Is the baby okay?" asked Alexa, her insides shuddering.

"He's okay. A little early, but the doctors don't think there'll be any problems. He's breathing well. They think both of you'll be out by the end of the week or early next week."

"Have you named him yet?"

"Don't you think that'd be a little unfair?" asked Marcus. "He's our baby. We made him together. I think we should name him together too." Alexa bit her lip, her heart twisting. "But it's something we never spoke about, so you might have something in that space that you were too scared to talk about before. And since you almost died giving birth to our son, I'm in a pretty agreeable mood. Now's the time to tell me what's on your mind."

"I already have a name," replied Alexa meekly.

"Is it something like Dip or Kit or Chip?" asked Marcus seriously. Alexa smiled and shook her head. "Then I want to hear it."

"I was thinking Caiden Benjamin Samuel," Alexa said softly, not quite meeting Marcus's eyes.

"I like the sentiment – and the names – but it's pretty long."

"I know, but Caiden Sam Ben or Caiden Ben Sam sounds terrible," sighed Alexa. "I've tried every combination."

"Well, I'm glad Caiden keeps its place," smiled Marcus, squeezing Alexa's hand.

"Seemed fitting if we had a boy. You named your daughter after my middle name. I named my son after yours."

"What about Benson as a middle name? Caiden Benson. You simplify it, but you get to keep the sentiment."

"Doesn't work," replied Alexa agitatedly. "Then you're dropping Sam's name. It has to – all three of them need – I just want the first one."

Marcus looked at her curiously, but did not ask any probing questions. He just sat thoughtfully for a while, before smiling and sitting forward. "One last suggestion," he said, looking pleased with himself. "If you don't like it then we go with your first suggestion – no questions. How about Bensam? Caiden Bensam."

"It's not a real name," replied Alexa.

"It's a real name when we give it to him. It's real to us. That's all that matters."

Alexa liked it better too, but there was something terrifying about abandoning the choice she had spent so long constructing.

"I like it …"

"We have time to decide," said Marcus earnestly. "Think it over and go with what feels right. Our little boy will be just as perfect no matter what we call him – as long as it's not Dip."

Alexa smiled again, thankful for how kind and understanding Marcus was being. It was sweet, especially when she noticed that it was the middle of the night. Her suggestion that he could go home to bed was instantly dismissed. "My wife and child are in this hospital. It's where I'm going to be."

"What about Tracey?"

"You have no idea of the battle to be Tracey's carer," laughed Marcus. "Bethany won, but Ben and Maria are staying at the house as well. I think Beth's pretty shaken up."

"You think she'll be able to come and see me tomorrow?" asked Alexa softly, hating that she did not know the answer.

"I'd have to tie her up to keep her away," replied Marcus tenderly, stroking her face and hair. "Now try and rest."

Closing her eyes, Alexa was surprised by how easy it was to slip back into sleep. She felt Marcus take her hand and lay his head back down. It was comforting knowing she would not be alone, but when she woke again, there were arms restraining her. Terrified of what had happened in those intervening hours, Alexa jolted herself fully awake.

"Lex. It's me."

The arms immediately came off Alexa's body as she processed the words. Alexa turned her head to see Bethany lying in the hospital bed with her. Bethany reassured her, hugging her once more. Placing her arm on Bethany's, Alexa closed her eyes again and fell back asleep.

"Hey, wake up, Lex. Got someone to meet you."

Alexa opened her eyes. Marcus was back and he had a baby in his arms. Alexa's heart started thumping erratically. Bethany moved the bed so they were sitting up. Alexa could feel her body shaking as Marcus moved next to them. He did not hand the baby over immediately, just held him next to her so she could look at him. Even now, in the flesh, the baby felt so abstract. In some ways Alexa felt like it had nothing to do with her. In others, he was far too much a part of her.

"You want to hold him?" asked Bethany.

Alexa nodded and Marcus slipped the baby into her arms. It was warm and soft. Alexa just stared at him. She felt like all her instincts had been lost.

"He's so beautiful," said Bethany, reaching around Alexa and stroking Caiden's head.

Marcus excused himself to use the bathroom. Alexa was thankful. She felt slightly less pressured when it was just her and Bethany.

"I don't know what to do with him," whispered Alexa.

"Just love him," answered Bethany. "Love him the way you love me. That'll get us through."

Alexa nodded. She stroked Caiden's head the way Bethany was, but it still felt so unreal. It was strange, because when she had first held Tracey she had fallen in love instantly. Caiden should have been more special. This was where it was all supposed to click and she felt nothing. However, Alexa did not give Caiden back. She continued to hold him, hoping time would correct all these issues. Then Caiden started crying.

"He's hungry. You need to try and feed him," said the nurse who was drawn to the room by Caiden's cries.

"Do you have a bottle?" asked Alexa.

"No, you need to try to feed him," said the nurse gruffly, making Alexa feel like she was being scolded.

A few minutes later another nurse stomped into the room looking harried. She immediately ordered Bethany from the bed and started talking, but Alexa could not comprehend what she was saying as hands pulled the gown off her shoulder.

"Get off me!" cried Alexa when the nurse grabbed her breast. "Fuck off! Get off!" Alexa screamed, but with Caiden still in her arms she could not push the nurse away. The nurse was arguing with her and continued to grab at Alexa's breast, almost restraining her as she pushed Caiden's head towards her body. "No! Get off! Get off! Get off!" cried Alexa, becoming more hysterical with every passing second.

Caiden was suddenly pulled from her arms as a body pushed its way between her and the nurse. Taking her chance, Alexa pulled her gown back over her body and yanked the covers over her head, cowering out of sight beneath them.

"Touch her again and I'll fucking kill you," snarled Bethany. "She was yelling at you to stop. We're all telling you to stop."

Caiden was screaming in the background. Alexa could only guess that it was Marcus who had hold of him, because when he spoke, his voice was a low snarl. "There was no need to be so forceful with her."

"She needs to be able to feed her child," retorted the nurse in a flustered voice.

"And how does that involve you fucking manhandling her like that?" spat Bethany angrily.

"Please arrange a bottle for my son," said Marcus in a controlled voice. It sounded much closer than it had before and Alexa guessed he had moved nearer the bed.

The conversation continued in low, angry voices, but Alexa covered her ears and scrunched her eyes closed, blocking out the scene. It did not take long for the world to darken and Alexa briefly wondered if they had drugged her, but she did not really care. All she wanted was to escape.

The first thing Alexa did when she woke was ask to leave the hospital. Marcus could not blame her, and it did nothing to quell his anger. There was a hollowness to Alexa's eyes now that he had never seen before. More than that, she had withdrawn completely from Caiden. She refused to hold him, let alone feed him. The only concession they managed was Pam assisting Alexa express milk. It was horrible to watch. Alexa cried the whole time.

Pam had not been able to touch Alexa. Marcus found little comfort in the fact that Alexa was shying away from everyone, not just him. No one but Bethany could get near her. It was a level of brokenness Marcus had never seen before. He had never considered Alexa would regress this way, particularly following events that – to him at least – seemed much less traumatic than what she had already been through.

"I think at this stage it's death by a thousand cuts," said Peter sombrely. He had come to see Alexa, but after hearing the state she was in decided it was better to wait. "Far too many of her wounds will never heal. It means that every new insult, no matter how small, will cut her open that little bit further. You can't stop that. But you can help patch her wounds. You have to be the armour that protects her."

"You sure you don't want to see her," asked Marcus. The way Peter understood Alexa was phenomenal, and he thought there was much good Peter could do.

"Trust me, it's better I don't. But when things settle down, remind her that she needs to update her will. We'll have lunch. She'll like that. I'm the one who comes and digs her out of trouble with the law. When she doesn't need me professionally, let her come to me when she feels like she can impress me personally. It's more important to her than you realise. But you call me anytime," added Peter, shaking Marcus's hand.

Marcus tried to convince Peter to meet Caiden, but Peter was adamant he wanted Alexa to introduce him to her son. It was something Marcus was not sure she would ever be capable of doing. The hospital was not keen on letting Alexa go home. They wanted a psychiatric evaluation. The stress of the situation was having a very negative effect on Alexa's state of mind. She looked like she was under siege. The only good thing was that the whole family agreed forcing Alexa to endure more questioning would only do more harm than good.

"You know what they want to hear, right?" asked Sam, as he, Bethany and Marcus sat with Alexa. Alexa nodded slowly, her eyes not meeting anyone's. "Then just tell them. Make them let you go."

"She can't," replied Bethany in a frustrated tone. "You don't understand."

"Do you have to say it with words?" asked Sam.

"You want us to spell it out in hand gestures?" asked Bethany sceptically. "I've got a couple I could use."

Alexa smiled and leaned her head on Bethany's shoulder. It was beautifully sweet to see them together and it made Marcus wonder if they would always all live together in that one big house.

"I was talking about Alexa writing it down. Tell them what they want to hear in your words – your way."

Alexa's eyes lit up. She turned to Marcus. It felt like cheating on an exam, and she must have known what he was thinking, because her eyes started to twinkle slightly. The sight of her smile was more heartening that anything else could be. She was not lost, just trapped, and Marcus would support anything that helped free her.

When Alexa finished the letter, it was handed straight to the doctors. Marcus knew it contained a swirl of truth, lie and desire, and thought it better he did not read it. There was too much risk he would not be able to tell the truth from fiction and did not want to hold it against Alexa when he got it wrong. Her only aim was to get back home. From there they would reassess how she was and what they needed to do.

The letter was a great success. Thankfully the psychologists were much more sympathetic than the nurses had been to Alexa's history and the trauma recent events would have caused her. They insisted the best place for her was back at home and reassured the doctors that she was fine to leave once she was physically fit. Their doctors agreed to discharge Alexa and Caiden together at the start of the following week. They were difficult days to endure. Alexa refused to talk to any of the medical staff. She refused to have anything to do with Caiden. The only communication Alexa gave the hospital was 'LET ME GO HOME' scrawled across a piece of paper. In response to every comment and question, she held that up to them.

Alexa's stubborn defiance was something the hospital was not used to dealing with. More than once the staff came to speak to Marcus, asking him to do something about his wife's behaviour, but that kind of attitude only put his back up. He tried to explain as politely as possible why they needed to back off, but that was received only mildly better than Bethany's fiery retorts.

Marcus frequently found himself trying to calm Bethany, but was never very successful. The siege mentality that had settled over her and Alexa was drawing out their rawest mannerisms. Walking towards Alexa's room with Caiden, Marcus stood near the door as Bethany argued, yet again, with a nurse. It was then that he got a glimpse of what the hospital staff saw – two very rough, rude girls refusing to listen to advice being given with the best of intentions. They did not resemble the people he had lived with for years. They looked and sounded like the girls he would have found living on the streets.

"At it again?" sighed Ben, walking up behind Marcus. "Want me to go and quiet them down so you can take him in?"

"No, wait a minute," said Marcus, turning away from the door. "I need to talk to you." Ben followed him down the hall. It was one of the first times Marcus had seen Ben look at him without any hint of disgust. "I'm worried about what this has done to them," said Marcus. "I don't know if Beth's okay either. The way they're acting – I don't know what they're going to be like when we get home. I have to look after Caiden. I don't know if Alexa will – not straight away. But I don't want this to continue and I don't know if I'll be able to help them."

"What do you want?" asked Ben.

"Maybe you could move in with us. There're lots of rooms. They need you."

"I'm hesitant to do that. I've made so many mistakes with Alexa. I don't want to make more."

"Being there for her when she needs you is not a mistake. She doesn't know how to reach out to you. You need to be there – before she knows she needs you. The problems you two have had were never because you were too close."

"You're forgetting what happened after Bethany's relapse. I remember the hurt I caused and the way I smothered her," said Ben. "I can't make that mistake again."

"Your mistake wasn't living with Alexa but trying to live for her. Please, trust me on this one," urged Marcus. "But talk to her – not Beth. Please."

"Okay, but you and Beth need to be there. I don't want Alexa feeling like I'm ambushing her. Just maybe keep Beth quiet while I talk."

Marcus nodded, walking with Ben back to Alexa's room. The nurse had left, but Bethany was clearly agitated and Alexa was curled up in a ball on the bed facing away from the door. Ben moved to Alexa's bedside as Marcus handed Caiden over to Bethany.

"Your dad needs to talk to Alexa," whispered Marcus, walking them to seats further from the bed. "Please don't interrupt. It's really important. You need to trust us." Fear flickered across Bethany's eyes and Marcus felt a stab of pain.

"How you doing?" asked Ben, gently stroking Alexa's hair.

"I want to go home," cried Alexa.

"I know. That's what I wanted to talk to you about." Ben's voice shook, obviously worrying Alexa, causing her to sit up slightly. "Twice now – when things were the hardest for you – you've gone to live with Pam and Karl. I understand why, but I hate that I'm not the one giving you those things you need. Pam and Karl, they'll always be your parents, but I've never had the chance to be the dad I always wanted to be."

"I'm sorry," whispered Alexa.

"No, don't ever be sorry. You never have to choose between anyone in this family and of course sometimes you'll spend more time with them. That's okay," reassured Ben, leaning over and kissing Alexa's forehead before sitting back down. "I was just thinking about how much I want to be around now – I've missed so much, but there's so much ahead. I feel like the only time I'll go back to my apartment is to sleep and change my clothes because my real home is where my heart is. It's with you. With you and Beth."

"You want to live with us?" asked Alexa, pushing herself upright.

"If I could, I'd want nothing more," nodded Ben solemnly.

"Because you think I'm going to be a terrible mum?"

"No. Because I want to be a better dad."

"Bethy has to say yes too," said Alexa.

"I say yes," said Bethany with forced calmness.

"Will you be there when I get home?" asked Alexa immediately, turning back to Ben. "You pick any room you want, but talk to Char first. Don't move right on top of her. And I can pay your rent til your lease ends. You don't have to pay anything with us."

"We can work out the finances later, but there's no way I'm paying nothing. You guys all have a board system. I'll contribute to that. But I promise I'll be there when you get home. And I know it's feels like forever, but it's only a few days."

Alexa lunged into Ben's arms. He held her tight as she sobbed unrestrainedly. Bethany handed Caiden back to Marcus and joined Alexa on the bed, hugging her and Ben.

Marcus sighed. This was more than he had ever bargained on, and he understood now that loving Alexa was more than just an emotion. It was an act. Something he would have to do, not just say. He could not just live his life with her. He had to help build hers. For so long he had only looked at the part of her life she had already constructed, never attending to the fact that that only comprised such a small and untenable fraction of what she needed to be safe and secure. Looking down at Caiden, Marcus just hoped that they could build the rest quickly and soundly enough that their lives did not come tumbling down on their children.

***

It felt so foreign to be walking into the house. Alexa shuffled slowly, her abdominal region still very tender. Before the pregnancy she had been told to avoid moving irrespective of how little pain she was in. Now they were telling her to move about as much as possible, even when she felt mild discomfort. Marcus carried Caiden. They both walked into Marcus's old room and sat down on the daybed.

"You want to hold him?" asked Marcus kindly. Alexa shook her head, shuffling away from them. "It's going to be okay. It doesn't have to happen straight away."

"Do you love him?" asked Alexa.

"Yes, I do. He's our son. I couldn't feel anything but love for him," replied Marcus in a generous voice that held no accusation.

"What if I can't? What if I'm never able to?"

"I don't believe that's possible. I know your heart. No one blames you for not instantly bonding with Caiden. You spent so long fearing you'd lose him, then the physical pain the pregnancy caused you, but you can't hold it against him the hurt he caused you."

"What if it's not me he hurts?" asked Alexa, her voice shaking.

"I don't understand. Who else would he hurt?"

Alexa shook her head, curling her legs up into her body. Marcus tried to question her, but Tracey tottered into the room, crying out for each of them. Used to not being lifted, Tracey tried to pull herself up on to the daybed. Alexa helped her up before pulling her into a warm embrace. She had missed Tracey so much. Marcus started introducing Tracey to Caiden, making Alexa's stomach flip. Tracey was fascinated and poked Caiden, eventually making him cry. Quickly pulling Tracey into her arms, Alexa left the room, her heart pounding.

The house was quiet, as they had insisted on no fanfare for their return home. Unsure of where to go, Alexa started creeping up the stairs. She peered into Charlotte's room, but it was empty. She did not look towards the room in which Sean attacked her, walking in the other direction down the hallway. Tracey's arms started flapping. There were muffled noises coming from the room at the end. Alexa walked straight in.

"Hey, you're home," smiled Ben, turning around with a box in his hand. "Still unpacking, but here." Tracey reached out for him. Ben immediately put the box down and took Tracey in his arms. "Most of my stuff is in the next room. Unpacking it bit by bit. Come sit down."

Alexa moved to the lounge Ben had along the wall near the window. It looked out on to the backyard. The bed was on the other side of the room and a room divider had been put up to keep it mostly from view.

"How are you feeling?" asked Ben, bouncing Tracey on his lap. "This one must be happy to see you."

"I missed her," replied Alexa softly.

"I'm sure you did. Does Caiden like his new home?"

"I don't want to talk about him."

"Okay. Let's talk about what Beth and I are going to cook everyone for dinner."

"You and Bethy?" queried Alexa, not managing to mask her scepticism.

"Yes, me and Beth. You and Marcus have children to look after. Charlotte needs to study. Beth and I are in charge of food."

"Could we have lasagne?" asked Alexa tentatively.

"Anything you like," smiled Ben.

Alexa tried to smile, but the discomfort in her chest she had been trying to ignore had built to the point of near explosion.

"Why don't you go and see if Caiden's hungry?" asked Ben casually. "Maybe you could try feeding him. Mightn't be so bad away from the crazy nurses at the hospital."

"It's bad enough that I have to do this," muttered Alexa as she walked out of the room.

Walking to the bathroom, Alexa locked the door and expressed as much milk as she could. Sitting on the floor, she tried to find a way out of the debacle her life had become, but it was impossible. She was Caiden's mother. No matter what she did, that fact would never change. Leaving or staying would make no difference. It struck her as ridiculous that she had never considered the consequences of falling pregnant through to an actual birth. So convinced she could never have children, she had never bothered to understand how terrible it would be when she did.

Pawing through the bathroom cabinet, Alexa reached into the back corner and pulled out a razor. She did not hesitate before pushing it into her skin. Her hand shook as she cut into her upper arm. Knowing she would have to hide the cuts, she stopped before they went too far down her arm. Looking over her body, she pulled her foot up and started slicing across the inside of her ankle.

For the next fifteen minutes, Alexa found as many places as possible on her body to slice with the razor, hoping to quell the fear that continued to simmer inside her. Grabbing the bottles of milk, she was in the kitchen when she realised far too many of her cuts were visible. They were small and scattered, but her heart still lurched when Marcus walked into the kitchen.

"Hey, sweetie," he said tenderly, pulling her into a hug. He held her tight and kissed the side of her head. "We're going to get through this, okay. I love you so much."

Alexa could not tell if Marcus had seen the cuts. He said nothing about them, but stayed close to her for the rest of the day while Ben looked after Caiden and Tracey. When Charlotte came home, Alexa escaped to Charlotte's room, using the excuse that she had spent so little time with her recently and needed to catch up. The only problem was that Tracey soon found them and Charlotte was desperate to see Caiden.

The only thing Alexa could do was escape, but she was running out of places to hide – and was starting to feel like there was no way of outrunning her mistake that did not involve her permanent removal from the world. But even that was not a real solution. It only punished others.

"Hey, why don't you come up to your old room with me for a while?" asked Ben, as she wandered aimlessly around the backyard. "Escape for a bit."

Alexa could not help but wonder where this Ben had been the last couple of years. Things could have been so different if he had been like this from the start.

"It can't go on, you feeling like this," said Ben, kneeling in front of Alexa as she sat in the armchair near the balcony door.

"Like what?" Alexa asked defensively, folding her arms and hunching her shoulders.

"Scared. Frightened. Terrified. Petrified. All of those things combined and multiplied many magnitudes over. Alexa, you can't live like that. It'll tear you apart. Whatever it is you fear, we have to face it. It's the only way to defeat it – and I promise we can defeat it."

"What if we can't? What if you all love it too much," asked Alexa, tears already dripping down her cheeks.

"Why are you so scared of Caiden?" asked Ben gently. "You love Tracey. You're a great mum to her. What's so different this time?"

"Me!" cried Alexa, the pain of that confession tearing through her. "Me. I'm in him. I don't want to be his mum. I don't want him to be my son, but I can't change it. I can't get rid of the biggest mistake I've ever made."

"You having a child is not a mistake."

"But I don't want him to be mine. He's got us in his blood. He's got *him* in his blood. I hate what I've done to him so much I can't touch him. I can't poison him more than I already have."

"Okay, okay, I understand," said Ben quickly, pulling Alexa against his chest as she sobbed violently. "We'll work it out. We'll make it okay." Alexa could only shake her head, but Ben continued on with his reassuring words until her tears started to finally run dry. "I understand why you feel the way you do," said Ben, continuing to hold her against his chest. "But I want you to give me a chance to show you that you might be wrong."

"What if I'm not?" shivered Alexa fearfully.

"Then we'll work something out," said Ben tenderly. "But if you are – if I'm right – then you don't have to feel this way any more. You can have your wonderful life back."

"You think that's possible?"

"Yeah, I do, so give me a chance, okay." Alexa nodded slowly. Ben took a deep breath before speaking, grasping her hands tight. "You fear what Caiden might be or become because he's your biological son and your biological parents were pretty close to the worst you could ever ask for, right?" Alexa nodded. "But by doing that, you're ignoring that those two people – those two terrible parents – produced two amazing children – two wonderful women."

"We've been bad people too," murmured Alexa, her eyes downcast.

"I don't generally try to seek out the best in the people I've witnessed the worst from, but I often see it even when I don't want to. Your parents – neither of them were all bad," said Ben, looking pained as he spoke those words. "Your father – there's no doubt you're intelligent – but your father taught you to read. Many of the things you could do as a very young child were down to what he taught you. It was not all good, but it wasn't all bad either."

"But he still has his blood and things – they come through – things can happen – skip generations. What if I've poisoned him?" cried Alexa. "We never used protection. You told me I could never have kids, but I didn't want to use anything. I wanted to test it – see if I could prove them wrong – but maybe I was supposed to never have kids for a reason. Now I know why, but it's too late."

"I don't believe that."

"Then you're naïve!" cried Alexa, jumping up from her seat. "You can't see the best in everything and hope it's real!"

"No, but you can't see the worst in everything either, particularly yourself," retorted Ben in a firm voice, rising with her. "I'm a cop.

Seeing the good is not something that comes naturally after this many years. I suspect and distrust. You know that, but when I claim to see good in you, you try to make out like I go through life with rose-coloured blinkers on. You can't have it both ways."

Alexa crossed her arms and just stared at Ben, waiting for him to produce something better.

"Your son. Your blood. Your flesh. I struggle to see how you feel at times, because I spend my life feeling the exact opposite," said Ben, his voice wavering. "I'd give anything to be yours and Bethany's true father – and I ache with the knowledge that it can never be. I know that ache you feel – that torment. You want to tear Sean's blood, your mother's blood, right from Caiden's veins. But you should never wish your blood from him. You're a good person. Your son is not corrupted. He's beautiful and innocent and his only chance to stay that way is if you love him the way you loved Beth. You save him the way you saved Beth. If you think it's possible that Caiden will be tainted by his blood, then the only way to save him is with your love. You're the only one who can protect him from that."

Alexa felt her heart pounding, imagining Sean coming after Caiden. The idea of Sean touching him – harming him – stirred the protective instincts she had always held for Bethany. The threat that Sean and her mother posed suddenly sat external to Caiden, rather than Caiden embodying them. It was the first time she had ever been able to think of Caiden as someone she could want to be near, love and protect.

"Can you come with me to see him – see if I can – I want – I do want to," stuttered Alexa.

"Of course."

Alexa nodded and walked out of the room. Ben asked her who she wanted around when she saw Caiden. It was something she had never considered, but realised she did not want a crowd. Guiding her into the empty lounge room, Ben left her there with nothing but her swirling fears and his dizzying theories. When he returned, he was alone, but he did bring tea. Ten minutes later, Marcus arrived with Caiden. Marcus sat next to her, but did not hand Caiden over.

"You don't trust me?" asked Alexa.

"Implicitly," replied Marcus with a smile. "But not everything has to be done the painful way. We'll just go slow. Look at him. See how you feel."

Alexa turned in and looked down as Caiden slept in Marcus's arms. "He looks like you," she smiled. She had never noticed before. He had a thick mat of dark hair and the shape of his face was so similar to Marcus's.

"His eyes are light hazel brown – almost like honey – with dark rims. Everyone says how beautiful they are when they see them," said Marcus gently.

Reaching out and stroking Caiden's head, Alexa felt a pang of connection. She moved her hand to his. Caiden's hand immediately closed around her finger. He grasped it tight.

"Make him let go. Please," said Alexa urgently, her body shaking.

"You're okay," said Ben, sitting down on the other side of Alexa and putting his arm around her shoulder. "Sean's not hiding inside of him. Try holding him. Feel his heart – his soul. He has his father's face and his mother's heart. Your heart. Not Sean's. Not your mother's."

Marcus held Caiden out. When Alexa nodded, Marcus gently placed Caiden in her arms and moved closer to her side. Shifting back, Alexa laid Caiden on her chest, his face pressed against her skin. She imagined again how she would have felt if Sean was alive and around to harm them. "I'll never let him get you," she whispered. "You have to remember this is your real family. Can't let them in. Can't let them touch us."

"He's not doomed," said Marcus. "His biological grandparents aren't great, but the people he'll call his grandparents – they're wonderful. You and me, we're okay – not perfect, but good. Biology has let a lot of people down in this family, but look at us. We're more than that. We choose to be good people – do good things. Your parents, they chose to do bad things. You're the opposite of that. Caiden, he'll choose to do good things too, because we'll be there to guide him."

"It still scares me sometimes," admitted Alexa, looking into Marcus's eyes.

"I know. I don't think that'll go away completely – not straight away – we just keep working at it, okay."

Caiden started whimpering softly. Alexa's first instinct was to hand him over to Marcus, but he told her to keep hold of him while he fixed Caiden's bottle. Ben insisted she was doing well, but she felt like a fraud. Yet the longer she held Caiden the less foreign he felt.

"You want me to feed him?" asked Marcus, holding out the bottle to her.

"Neither of you think I'll poison him if I be a part of his life?" asked Alexa, looking down at Caiden. "You really think he'll be okay with me around?"

"I don't fear for Caiden the way you do," replied Ben earnestly. "I don't have your fears. I've known you and Beth as children and as adults. The contents of your blood mean nothing to me. I believe Caiden has your heart. But if you're right, and there's any chance the blood of your parents could cause him harm, I still think you're only one who can show him how to live and be good in spite of that."

Alexa looked over at Marcus. "I named my first child after you. That should tell you everything you need to know," he said, tears in his eyes. "What I think of you – I worry about lots of things, but not that – not you. I don't fear your influence on our children. I welcome it. Our son is good and pure. I refuse to believe anything else."

"Can I have some time alone with him? That be okay? I won't hurt him. I promise," said Alexa tentatively.

"I trust you implicitly," replied Marcus firmly, taking Alexa's face in his hands and nodding before kissing her.

Ben just nodded. Alexa stood up and took the bottle from Marcus before walking back to her room. Caiden did not like being put down on the bed, but Alexa did not know how to do this discreetly. She was not even sure she knew how to do it. Stripping off her top and bra, she quickly grabbed a blanket and threw it over her shoulders to stop herself feeling so exposed. Caiden was crying loudly as she picked him up, making her blood shiver. She kept telling herself that Sean was a threat external to them, not something lurking within them. The problem was that Caiden had as little clue of what to do next as she did. She could not get him in the right position and his mouth just waved around blindly, before crying loudly when it did not find food.

It did not take long before Alexa and Caiden were crying together. Alexa knew she should have fed him with the bottle, but the failure she felt was so crippling she could do nothing more than place him on the bed and sob.

The knock at the door did not even register in Alexa's mind until she felt the depression in the bed. Pulling the blanket around her body, she did not shy away from Pam's hug. Pam stroked her hair with one hand while the other tried to sooth Caiden.

"Want me to try and remember how to do this?" asked Pam in a light voice.

When Alexa finally nodded, Pam smiled and started slipping off her shirt. It was confronting for Alexa to see Pam half-naked, yet Alexa knew she could not have handled Pam touching her either. Pam picked Caiden up and showed Alexa the best way to hold him and how to position her breast. Alexa nodded, feeling disconnected from her body. Pam handed Caiden over and talked her through what she had just shown her. This time Caiden did latch on, but the sensation was so shocking that Alexa almost threw him off her.

"Yeah, it's different, isn't it," said Pam in an understanding voice. "I remember feeding Brett and thinking how horrible it felt. What helped was someone telling me that this is the true purpose of our breasts. This is what they're designed for. It's what all mammals do. And at least there's only one kid. Better than a litter."

Alexa could not help but laugh. She tried to imagine herself lying on the bed with half a dozen babies hanging off her.

"I was pretty smug after I had Brett," continued Pam with a wry smile as she pulled her top back on. "The sensation may have been unusual, but Brett feed well. He was a perfect baby, actually. Fed, slept. Was the kind of baby most people only dreamed of. I assumed Hayley would be just the same – just as easy. I don't know if it was the shock of a difficult baby, if I was unwell to begin with or a combination of both, but I didn't handle it. After a couple of months I was at the end of my tether. I'd never felt that way before – desperate – alone – lost. I call them the dark days. They felt dark. Even when the sun was shining."

"You've felt like that too?" asked Alexa incredulously.

"What you've been through is more than enough reason to feel that way, but people can go through a lot less and fall that low," replied Pam grimly. "I was eventually diagnosed with post-natal depression, but not before I got so low I took a handful of sleeping pills. Karl came home. Hayley was in her cot screaming and I was passed out in our bed. They were hard times. I didn't want help to begin with. I was ashamed."

"What changed?" asked Alexa, handing Caiden over to Pam so she could put her clothes back on. "How'd you become you – you know, strong – supermum?"

"Supermum? Ha, that's a first," laughed Pam, holding Caiden against her shoulder as he patted his back softly. "Karl helped a lot –

supported me – didn't blame me. I think going through that, it was part of the reason I wanted to foster. I got a glimpse into a world I believed was inhabited by the weak. I started to realise just how good our life was. We had a couple of short placements before you. We'd never gone into it for a permanent placement – just respite.

"When they asked if we could take you for one school holidays, we thought it'd be just like the other placements. There was something about you though. You were older than the other kids. There was something so sad in your eyes. You were very polite – but distant – detached. I saw something of myself in you – those dark times. When they asked if we could take you for a second holidays, we had no hesitation. They seemed surprised."

"You were the first people in years to take me back," said Alexa softly.

"We didn't know that then. We knew so little about you. After you ran away – when they found you – they asked us if we'd take you and your sister full-time. Nearly every day since then I've regretted saying no. It was the wrong decision, but I don't think anything but knowledge of the future would've allowed us to make the right choice back then. I'm sorry, Alexa," said Pam sincerely. "I'm sorry for what you and Bethany suffered because of that decision."

Alexa rushed to Pam and hugged her fiercely. She squeezed her eyes tight, refusing to imagine what their lives could have been like. It did not matter. This life was worth all the suffering they had endured.

Pam smiled and handed Caiden to Alexa. Alexa held him, still unsure of how to mother her son.

"When I look at you now, I see me back then. I hear them asking me if I'll take you and Bethany. I see the same fear in your eyes that I felt. I was wrong. I think you're wrong too. You'll regret not loving Caiden. It'll be hard and it'll hurt, but if you make the same mistake we did, you'll regret it the way we do – and you might not get the second chance we did to make things better."

Chapter Nineteen

ALEXA WAS SURE there had never been a time in her life when she had been so perpetually challenged. There had been worse times, but to some extent she had always been able to find pockets of escape. That was not possible any more. Everyday Caiden was waiting for her. No matter what progress she made in one day, she had always regressed slightly by the next morning.

It was tiring having to convince her mind and body over and over again that her son was not a threat. Thankfully, no one condemned her for the difficulties she was having bonding with her biological child.

Everyone had their own reasoning for why they did not fear Caiden. It was interesting and insightful, but it was Bethany's explanation that had the greatest impact. "I think I would've felt the same way," she confessed. "Only difference that if you'd told me it was okay, I would've believed you."

"Why are you okay with Caiden? If you would've felt the same, how can you be okay with him?" asked Alexa wondrously.

"Because he's yours," smiled Bethany. "I see you when I see him. How could I possibly not love him? I've never feared you. To me you're only good and to me Caiden is an extension of you – of your goodness."

Alexa imagined how this would have played out if the situation had been reversed. It was true, she could never have seen Bethany's son as a threat. He would have been too precious – too big a part of who Bethany was. Alexa even imagined how she would have felt if it had been Leo who fathered Bethany's child. Whichever way Alexa thought about it, she could not see herself abandoning Bethany's child, fearing it or doing anything but loving and protecting it. That knowledge helped to strengthen Alexa's determination to beat this, but it did not instantly conquer the fear that lurked within her. All it did was add to the slow lessening of it.

If that was all Alexa had to deal with, it would have been enough. However, the challenges of raising a newborn were coupled with their raising of Tracey. Their one blessing in this domestic madness was that

Tracey adored Caiden. Tracey wanted to be everywhere Caiden was. Maria did not mind. She was happy to continue coming over three days a week and believed there was little difference attending to two children instead of one.

"Just remember, parenthood has only recently become a single person occupation," smiled Maria when Alexa commented on how she should be able to do it alone. "I think that's the best thing about this family. We choose to care and help each other out. Friends have become family and family are our friends."

It was a concept proven over and over again as Alexa strived to be a good mother to Caiden. It was aided by their move back up to the third floor two months after Caiden's birth, and marked a momentous day. Alexa's previous visions for the floor were finally a reality. They had intended to keep Caiden in their room, but Tracey made such a fuss that they had to move him into the nursery with her. It had actually taken a couple of hours of her tantrums to realise what it was she wanted, but as soon as Caiden's cot was next to hers, she stopped crying.

"I think you have a very determined child on your hands there," said Pam. "Perhaps it's possible to inherit that through something other than blood."

"Tracey does seem to be doing her best to take after her namesake," smiled Marcus, hugging Alexa from behind.

"Better Caiden takes after you," replied Alexa softly. "Won't be a harmonious household otherwise. Need more calm people."

Caiden did prove to be more like Marcus than Alexa. His dark features were a spitting image of Marcus, with the exception of his beautiful hazel eyes, which Alexa often spent time just gazing into.

Despite Marcus and Lucy's dark hair and eyes, Tracey was continuing to display underlying fair features, leaving her strangely resembling Alexa more than either of her biological parents.

"See, can't trust biology," said Marcus. "You have to put your faith in love – choosing to love."

"Why do you choose to love me?" asked Alexa. "After everything I've put you through this year, how can you still choose to love me?"

"Because I know what it's like not to love you – to try not to love you – to live without you," replied Marcus. Alexa huffed and turned away, annoyed at the answer. "Fine. Truth is I stay for the money. I knew you won that money and I wanted in."

"I was serious," snapped Alexa angrily. "I just wanted to know the truth."

"But you chose not to believe the truth or the lie. You can't have it both ways," retorted Marcus, not quite managing to hide his smirk. "You know why I'm here. For the same reason you are. I stay for the same reasons you would if the situation was reversed."

"I don't think I'm as nice as you," confessed Alexa, sure that she would have given up on Marcus if he had been as troublesome.

"You brought me here, hired and paid for a full-time nurse, had Bethany make this place wheelchair-friendly, and all in about two days. You did that after the last time I saw you I tore your heart out. Don't think I didn't see how much I wounded you that night. I know what I did. I know what you've done. No one has endless patience and understanding, but you have more than most."

"I still don't get how you deal with me," muttered Alexa.

Marcus smiled more broadly, almost like he was about to laugh. "The love, understanding and patience I have for you is something approaching what you have for Bethany. Understand that?" asked Marcus. Alexa nodded, her heart thrumming. "You're the other half of me."

"But I can't have another half," confessed Alexa guiltily.

"I know," nodded Marcus solemnly, a gentle smile on his face.

"You're my home. You feel like my safe harbour. I feel protected when I'm with you."

Marcus pulled Alexa into a crushing hug. Pulling out of the embrace, Alexa took Marcus's hand and led him to their bed. Marcus held back, questioning if she was sure. They had not been intimate since before Caiden's birth, but Alexa did not want to continue to live with never-ending fear. She would face each challenging moment as it came – and hope they all turned out to be as beautiful as this one.

They often did. Reality was rarely as bad as Alexa envisaged, and as time wore on a strong bond began to form between her and Caiden. It was assisted by a permutation in her nightmare; Caiden joining her and Bethany in the pipe as Sean menaced them. Ben managed to kill Sean almost as often as Sean killed him. Alexa hoped that once Ben won every encounter, she would begin to defeat the nightmare itself. It felt like a process she had to live through, though Alexa sometimes wondered if it had more to do with Ben than anything else.

Ben's move into the house was remarkably smooth. Bethany was thrilled, but did not spend as much time with him as Alexa expected. With Bethany attempting to see everyone each week, she became a virtual part-time resident, spending at least two nights a week at Sam's and a fair bit of time with the Whites. The relationship with Hayley was friendly, though not close, but through Brett – who was only a week older than Bethany – she was forming strong ties to Pam and Karl.

Charlotte's life was just as dispersed, particularly when carved up between school and work. While Alexa was happy about the lives they were leading, it was very different to the cosy existence they shared in their beachside apartment. What helped to mitigate the distance was the fact that a fortnight never went by without them all gathering at one of their houses for a meal. Sometimes they were planned, but just as often they were spontaneous gatherings, with smaller ones arising in between.

It was in the quiet times that Alexa spent most of her time with Ben. He somehow managed to be around at the right times and did not make her feel useless when he did things for her. But with Alexa finally feeling like life was becoming manageable, she found herself worrying about the future again, particularly their financial situation. She hated to admit how much they needed Ben's injection of money into the household. He not only contributed to the weekly kit of money for bills and groceries, but often came home with food or things for the children. When nappies or formula were on sale, he bought in bulk. It was thoughtful and kind, but left Alexa feeling indebted and anxious about finding a job. Marcus did not want her to graduate without her honours and even offered to stay home with the kids the following year, if she wanted to go back at the start of the year.

"That's not going to help with the finances if we're both not working. You don't realise how much money we've gone through," sighed Alexa.

"Do you trust me enough to know?" asked Marcus seriously. "I admit that I'm not likely to be as pessimistic about our financial position, but I do understand your point of view."

Alexa was not keen, but eventually conceded. When Marcus started smiling at the sight of the numbers he was faced with, she knew he did not get it.

"Hey, give me a chance," said Marcus sternly. "Smiling isn't a crime. I know where you're coming from. Can you just trust me – and let me smile at how well-off we are. Don't even try and deny how lucky we are."

Alexa could never do that. What she could also not explain was the constant fear that this was all a dream – a ridiculous error that she would have to repay. When they bought things like property, the money still existed in some form. When they bought food and consumables, they were left with nothing.

"Okay, I admit, with the way it's set up, it's tight," said Marcus. "There're a couple of options though. First one is we redistribute the money so we get slightly more until the end of next year. That could hit Beth a bit hard, but Charlotte much less so."

"No," replied Alexa forcefully.

"How did I know you would say that," sighed Marcus. "Would it help to know that both Beth and Charlotte have offered such a thing to me – and by offered I mean begged. They want to help. They're both only saving the money anyway. Beth's on top of her finances now. They both have their own incomes and we can pay them back once we start earning money again."

"Absolute last resort," growled Alexa. "And by that I mean I'll have to be starving first. I won't take anything from them. They have nothing."

"While we have all been the very appreciative beneficiaries of your self-sacrificing generosity, you need to accept that at some stage people will want to do things to reciprocate. Does it make you feel better to have everyone in your debt?"

"No, but I won't be in anyone's debt ever again! Never, okay."

Marcus's arms were warm and tender as they embraced Alexa's shaking body. "Okay," he said softly. "We'll leave that, okay. It's fine. But just consider that you're not the only one who feels that way. Beth and Charlotte understand the consequences of debt too. There was one thing I thought was missing from your calculations," said Marcus quickly before she could respond. "The rent from the apartment. Where does that go?"

"Separate account. I keep it separate," answered Alexa.

"For a special purpose?"

"Emergencies. The last couple have been pretty expensive."

Marcus was smiling again. It was infuriating, but somehow he knew how to temper her annoyance long enough to get her to the next step. With his calm rationality he managed to counter her concerns and lead her slowly around to other points of view. They did not always end up on the same page, but when he left her to make the final decision she noticed that she often ended up closer to his thinking than where she started. Marcus was even impressed when she came back to him with her new plan.

"You sure you want to go back to university at the start of next year?" asked Marcus slowly.

"I thought that's what you wanted. I thought you would've been happy to have me away from the kids – you won't have to stay home and stress about them – worry I'll hurt them," Alexa mumbled.

"You know I don't think that," retorted Marcus angrily.

"Why else do you want to keep staying at home?" asked Alexa accusingly.

"I took this half of the year off because the physical strain of the pregnancy almost killed you. I'd feel like a heartless bastard if I went to work and left you to cope with that alone. I want to keep staying at home with you and the kids because I love this life. I guess that's why I was pushing a bit hard with the money. I don't want to miss out on this stuff. We live a pretty simple life. It doesn't cost much."

"I don't understand. Why do you want me to go back to uni if you just want me to be a housewife?" asked Alexa, thrown by the turn in the conversation.

"I want you to go back to university because I know that's what you want. You enjoy it. I see that," replied Marcus softly, tucking her hair behind her ear and kissing her. "I don't know exactly what you want to do after that – get a job – part-time – full-time – or work with Beth and Sam in their business. I've done most of that. It won't hurt my career to take time off to raise my family. If I can stay home with the kids and support you, then I want to do that." Alexa just stared at Marcus for a long time. He looked serious. He sounded sincere. It just did not add up. After a while she had no choice but to confess her confusion. "Men love their children – good men do," said Marcus. "Of course part of me wants us to stay home together, but I'll never hold you back from your future."

"Do you think I'm a bad person for wanting a job?" asked Alexa seriously.

"No," replied Marcus simply. Alexa just waited. "What? You need more? I'm not sure how to give you that. You didn't plan for either of these children. Because I know you won't selfishly ignore them in the pursuit of your own goals, I see no reason for you to give up what are very normal desires. Good enough?"

"I must really annoy you, huh," smiled Alexa, hugging Marcus warmly.

"It annoys me – scares me – that you believe so many terrible things. I hate that you don't see how much you deserve. But I also hate that I can never be sure that I'll be able to convince you about all these things. So just tell me how we're going to finance the next eighteen months and we'll start planning."

Alexa decided the rent from the apartment could go towards their living expenses. Marcus finally convinced her that they could also put up the rent. He then laughed when she showed him their new budget. A sizable portion of their income was set aside for savings.

"That's practically all the rental money. If we're that close, why don't we budget on not having it? Then it becomes our savings – emergency money – again. We can economise other ways."

"It's pretty tight," replied Alexa, though she was secretly thrilled by Marcus's suggestion.

"Yes, but with your Dad staying with us now, we've got more going into that kit than we need. Why don't we relook at the household budget. Maybe we can cut back there."

It all sounded so reasonable at the time, but when Alexa sat down at the house meeting she realised Marcus had tipped everyone off.

"Dad, no, you're not paying more," said Alexa firmly.

"Do you realise how much I'm saving living here?" asked Ben. "I can afford to pay about three times more than I am, so believe me when I say what I'm offering is not overly generous. Everything's cheaper living here. And if you want to start a discussion on who should be paying the most and have the most responsibility, I'll warn you now that you'll lose. I'm swallowing a lot of pride watching Charlotte and Beth put their money into this house. You're not the only one who wants to do the best by their kids."

"Urgh, fine," sighed Alexa, pushing away from the table. "I give up. You guys work out what you think's fair."

Taking Caiden from Marcus's arms, Alexa held out her hand to Tracey, who slipped off Ben's lap, and walked out to the lounge room.

Charlotte followed soon after. "I'm a kid. They don't think I should have a say," she grumbled.

"That's not true," huffed Alexa, making Charlotte smile.

"Actually, Marc and Ben started talking about me being a kid and how that meant I shouldn't pay anything. When I argued, they kicked me out."

Alexa tried not to groan. She had never wanted Charlotte to pay either, but had to admit that if she was in Charlotte's position, there would have been no way she would have felt comfortable paying nothing. Perhaps it was better she and her younger self were kept out of the negotiations. They would have to rely on Bethany to know them well enough to be their spokesperson.

"If you promise not to make a big deal out of it, I'll show you why I'm so grateful to you and Beth for giving me a home," said Charlotte as they played with Tracey.

Caiden was fast asleep after his feed, so when Alexa nodded, Charlotte offered to put him to bed and return with her evidence.

"Cayen. Won Cayen," said Tracey in a slightly distressed tone as soon as Charlotte left the room.

"Caiden's sleeping," replied Alexa. "Caiden tired. Needs to sleep." Tracey immediately tilted her head and put her hand underneath it. "Tracey sleepy too? You want to go sleep with Caiden?"

Tracey did not answer, but started to totter upstairs. Alexa gathered her up in her arms and took her up to Caiden, who was grumbling in his cot. As soon as he saw Tracey, he quietened down. Tracey squirmed to the side of her cot that was pressed up against Caiden's and slipped her arm through the bars. Holding on to Caiden's hand, they both closed their eyes.

"Are they close enough in age that they can start school together?" asked Charlotte as they walked down the stairs. "Think they might get cranky with you if you try to separate them."

"I know, but we're not in luck. Until then though they can spend every second together if they want. I don't want anyone trying to force them apart."

Charlotte squeezed Alexa's hand as she dragged her into her bedroom. Alexa liked the way Charlotte could comfort her without it being about her distress. When Charlotte turned to her, she handed over a small pile of papers.

"What's this?" asked Alexa, but Charlotte did not answer. Alexa looked at the documents more closely. They were assignments and exams. All marked and all spectacular. Alexa could not stop the scream that escaped her mouth. "Oh shit, Char. This is awesome."

"You promised not to make a big deal."

Alexa was about to apologise when Bethany burst into the room looking frantic. They quickly reassured her nothing was wrong, but after that scream Bethany demanded to know what had happened. Then it was her turn to scream. Bethany did not stop there. Still holding the papers, she ran out of the room and down the stairs.

"I think it's officially a big deal," said Alexa, though she was not able to sound too sorry about that.

When they walked into the dining room, Ben and Marcus were both looking at the papers. Charlotte just held her hand out for them.

"This is great work, Charlotte. You should be really proud of yourself," said Marcus, handing back the papers.

"It's nothing," murmured Charlotte, not looking up. "It's not like I did it all myself. You know you helped me study for heaps of these – and Ben."

Marcus groaned. "So you're still determined to take after Alexa," he said. "There are so many things I could say, but let me try what I hope is the most effective. There've been a lot of concerns about Caiden in this family, but I don't fear for him. He has wonderful male role models. But what about Tracey? The female role models she has are three women who continue to downplay all their good attributes, constantly sacrifice their own happiness for others, and refuse to believe they're worth a damn. Is that how you want Tracey – and Caiden – growing up thinking women should be like?"

Bethany, Charlotte and Alexa did not look at each other or answer. Marcus took their silence as vindication and left it at that. There was no quick fix to their problem, but they always kept it in mind. It was difficult not to with Tracey constantly displaying her proud confidence, and they did want her to be proud of her achievements. So when Charlotte came home at the end of the school year with the most spectacular report card any of them had ever witnessed, they had no excuse not to celebrate.

"You sure you didn't cheat?" asked Brett. Charlotte just stuck out her tongue. "Then you have to be some freaking Einstein. You know that, right. Nineties in everything. That's insane."

"Have you shown your report to your father?" asked Maria.

"Haven't heard back," murmured Charlotte. "Sent it, but guess it's still the middle of the night over there. At least he can see I didn't waste his money."

"He'll be very proud of you," said Karl. "Just give him the chance to show it."

"Um, yeah, speaking of Wes," said Charlotte nervously. "He said he might come over here over Christmas–New Year time. Can I invite him here? Might not want to come, but – maybe …"

"Char! You don't even need to ask," cried Bethany. "Of course they'll come here. We're a bit behind, but we'll have this house in the Christmas spirit in no time. You know you can't deny Caiden his first Christmas," she added with a smile to Alexa.

"You know there'll be no new child next year to use that guilt trip on me," retorted Alexa.

"No, but by then Tracey'll be getting old enough to understand what Christmas is, and you wouldn't want to tear that happiness away from her," replied Bethany gleefully, knowing there was no chance Alexa would condemn her children to the same childhood they had suffered.

Bethany did not wait to bring out the Christmas decorations. By the end of the weekend, the whole ground floor resembled Santa's workshop. There were decorations everywhere. They became more subdued as they went up the house, but Alexa did not resist the addition of a few ornaments in the kids' bedroom. And this year the merriment was not contained to the house. The front and back yards were decorated in tinsel and lights, but thankfully Bethany had exercised some moderation, stating that she had set herself a budget for each year to grow their stocks. The next day Alexa and Ben handed her more money – their contribution to the Christmas fund. Bethany's pure delight – and the addition of some outdoor ornaments – was worth every cent.

"Seriously, Lex. Can you stop looking so concerned every time you see the Christmas tree," said Bethany. "You agreed to this."

"Ha, I never agreed to this extravaganza," laughed Alexa. "But that's not my problem. I wanted to go and see Marc's parents. They refused his offer to join us for Christmas. I thought it'd be worth going and seeing them myself while he's out with Ryan."

"You taking the monsters?" asked Bethany.

"Of course. They're the only bargaining chips I have. They sure don't want to see me."

"Want me to come with you?" asked Bethany seriously.

"Can you be nice and not inflammatory?" asked Alexa sceptically.

Bethany smiled and shook her head. "Then I'm sticking with Tracey and Caiden. They're way cuter than you anyway."

"Good luck," said Charlotte and Bethany.

Alexa thought she probably needed more than luck. This was not a trip she was particularly keen on making, but Marcus had been so remarkably supportive over the past year that she owed him this much. The pain in his eyes when he found out that his parents would not come to Christmas had been so profound, Alexa was sure she had never seen him so hurt. Even so, there was no getting around the fact that this trip was taking her back to a world she never wanted to visit. It had been a long time since she had put herself at the mercy of people who thought so little of her and she was truly scared of their reaction.

Taking deep breaths as she drove, Alexa laughed at the lightheaded feeling that came over her. Tracey laughed with her, babbling excitedly the way she always did when they were in the car. Caiden joined in. He was usually a very quiet child, but when he was alone with Tracey he became quite vocal. His sounds helped Alexa push aside her fears. There was just no way she could confuse Caiden's vocalisations with Sean's menacing voice.

Gathering Caiden in her arms, Alexa held Tracey's hand as they walked towards the house. Alexa watched Tracey closely to see if there were any signs of recognition, but Tracey appeared oblivious until the front door opened.

"Rhanna!" screamed Tracey, lifting her arms excitedly.

"Oh, hey, Rhianna. I wasn't expecting – here – you," Alexa stuttered.

"Hey, Alexa. I was coming over tomorrow to see you guys," smiled Rhianna, bending down and picking Tracey up. "Hello, cutie. How you doing?" she asked Tracey, tickling her to make her giggle loudly. "I had some time off before Christmas so I decided to fly in early. You here to see Mum and Dad?"

"I thought I might be able to convince them to come to Christmas," said Alexa hesitantly. She was not sure she would have come if she had known Rhianna would be here. Rhianna's presence was as inflammatory as Bethany's. It was no wonder they got on so well.

"I've been trying to do that since I arrived, so come in and try your luck. The worst they can say is no."

Alexa held Caiden tighter, hoping that really was the worst they could say. It was the first time she had ever felt a stronger bond to

Caiden than Tracey. Caiden was her flesh and blood and would be judged for that just as she was judged for who she was. At least they had once loved Tracey.

"Mum, Dad, you remember Alexa – your daughter-in-law," said Rhianna, directing Alexa to a lounge before sitting down next to her. "And your granddaughter, Tracey. That one is Caiden – you know, the one you haven't met yet."

Alexa was caught between annoyance and amusement. She had not come to start a fight and the angry narrowing of Marcus's parents' eyes was not what she had been hoping for.

"Would you like to hold him?" asked Alexa kindly, holding Caiden out to his grandmother, who eyed her suspiciously. When it was clear she was not going to take him, Alexa pulled Caiden back to her chest and held him tight.

"You're going to disown your grandchildren as well, then?" snapped Rhianna.

No one answered. Alexa was not sure Rhianna's feistiness was helping the situation, although she agreed with the sentiment. Taking a deep breath, Alexa decided there was nothing more she could do than say what she planned and hope it made a difference.

"I didn't come here to fight with you," said Alexa in a soft voice, not quite daring to look at Marcus's parents. "You don't have to like me. It'd be nice if you could, but that's not why I came. I love Marc and he's so hurt you've turned your back on him. We're married, we have two children and nothing's going to change that. Please, spend Christmas with us – with our family. It would mean everything to him. Please. He's your son."

"Because of you, our family's been torn apart," said Marcus's mother viciously. "There was nothing wrong with Marcus until you came along. You turned him into … we know what kind of person you are. We know what you've done."

Alexa felt like she had been stabbed. It was strange to realise just how insulated her life had become. She had been able to slowly shed all the people who thought this way about her, somehow managing to forget they still existed just outside her front door. Lifting Caiden up against her chest, she cradled him to protect him from these vicious words. Tears stung the sides of her eyes, but she refused to cry.

"This was a good, respectable family," growled Marcus's father. "And you've torn it apart."

"That's not true!" cried Rhianna. "Alexa's great. Why won't you get to know her? How can you be so prejudiced?"

"She's a hooker!"

Alexa could not react. She could see the apologies in Rhianna's eyes, but that could not stop the pain surging through her chest. Tracey was silent, holding Rhianna's hand tightly, as she looked around the tense room. It made Alexa wonder if Tracey would disown her as her mother when she grew to know the truth.

"You seduce teachers and destroy lives," snarled Marcus's mother. "You've destroyed our son and turned him into something we can't love or respect – into someone society would lock away. You love him enough now to protect him, but what happens when you shaft him like you did that other teacher – lie and send him to gaol? Will you send our son to gaol too?"

"They didn't do anything wrong," cried Rhianna angrily. This time Tracey was concerned enough by the tension that she raced over to Alexa and clung tightly to her. "Nothing happened between them until Alexa was an adult."

"So they say," muttered his father.

Rhianna continued to argue Alexa's case, but it only resulted in bringing forth more insults. Shaking, Alexa rose, holding Caiden tight in one arm and grasping Tracey's hand in the other.

"The invitation still stands," said Alexa, her voice quivering more than she wanted it to. "I don't care if you come, but your son will."

"I'll see you tomorrow," said Rhianna quickly as Alexa turned to leave.

Alexa turned back, nodding. She was not sure if she managed to smile.

"Bye, Rhanna," waved Tracey.

"Bye, Tracey," replied Rhianna sombrely.

Rhianna came by the next day, but thankfully stayed quiet about Alexa's meeting with her parents. However, the rattled mood Rhianna was in did not escape Marcus's attention. When Rhianna explained that it was a little tense at home, Bethany immediately jumped in and offered her a room with them. Rhianna looked tempted, but eventually decided she would stick it out and try to make her parents see sense.

That thought made Alexa sick and soured her mood in the lead-up to Christmas. It was noticed, but everyone just assumed it was related to her usual aversion to Christmas. No one tried to talk her into a happier view of the world, which was good. Alexa did not feel the need to paint the world in shiny colours. There was enough bad in her life to dampen the good and enough good to lighten the bad. It left her in a generally stable state that was much easier to handle than the extremes. So when she woke on Christmas morning, Alexa was glad there was no urge to pull the covers back over her head and pray for the day to disappear.

"Merry Christmas," said Marcus, hopping into bed. "I woke up and things sounded a little too quiet," he smiled. "Monsters are with Charlotte and Beth. Beth has already taken a hundred photos of them. I hope you're in the mood to smile today."

"Ha, I thought you were coming to wish me a Merry Christmas, not tempt me to sneak out," laughed Alexa, shuffling into Marcus's arms. "How's Charlotte?"

"Pretty amped. Said she was fine. I don't know if she's nervous or excited or scared. I really hope they turn up. She doesn't deserve more disappointment. And she must be a little concerned if she refused to stay with her father while they were over."

"I think she'll go with them after Christmas," said Alexa, trying not to smile. "They're planning some travel. They invited her, but wouldn't tell her where when she kept insisting on paying for herself. Wes was a little frustrated with her stubbornness."

"What's that smile for?" asked Marcus, when Alexa's grin finally broke through.

"Nothing. Just that, as Charlotte's guardian, Wes may have contacted me to ask my permission to organise Charlotte's travel. And, as Charlotte's guardian, I may have promised that she can't go against my word."

"Very devious," laughed Marcus. "You're an amazing woman. It's a wonderful thing that you and Charlotte found each other. You and Beth, you've done so much for her, and Charlotte's been just as good for the two of you. I think she's a big reason why things are as great as they are."

"I think so too," replied Alexa in a thick voice. "And she deserves this so much. She's so amazing. She's going to do such great things."

"Yes she will, but just remember that most great things aren't the ones recognised by the world. In my world, you've done great things."

"You've been pretty great too," breathed Alexa, overcome by the burning desire in Marcus's eyes. "We don't have to get up right away, do we?"

"Absolutely not," replied Marcus, pulling their bodies close.

Even when they walked downstairs, Marcus held Alexa close, his arm around her waist. Bethany smirked as they walked into the kitchen.

"I thought we weren't unwrapping presents til later," Bethany said, grinning mischievously.

"You have a sick mind," retorted Alexa.

Bethany laughed, wrestling playfully with Alexa while Tracey squealed at their feet. Marcus picked Tracey up and held her close to them so she could join in.

"Looks like we're ready for lunch, at least. You guys have done awesome," smiled Alexa, hugging Bethany and Tracey.

"What? This is breakfast!" cried Bethany.

"Bethy! If we eat this we'll never eat for the rest of the day!"

Bethany was completely unperturbed by the excess of food. She pointed out that they had arranged for a late lunch to remove the need for dinner. Arguing was fruitless. The excesses had all but waned from Bethany's everyday life, instead directed into celebrations, as she started to question the need for many of the things she had grown up believing she had missed out on. With their financial focus on bigger things like their family business, it was easier for Bethany now to bypass those other things, but Alexa suspected Christmas would always be an extravaganza.

"We have a visitor," said Ben, walking into the dining room, where they had set the table for breakfast. Bethany was taking as many photos of the food as she was of people. Caiden was in Ben's arms, but started squirming when he saw Alexa. It made Alexa's heart warm to think that Caiden liked her.

"Hello!" cried Tracey, pulling Alexa's attention back to their guest. Tracey rushed up to Wes Cassidy and waved at him. When Wes waved back, she smiled and took his hand.

"Merry Christmas, everyone. Nice to see you again, Alexa," smiled Wes. Ben quickly introduced Wes to everyone. "I have to thank you for inviting my family and I to lunch today. It's very kind of you all. We were just hoping though that we might be able to spend a quiet breakfast with Charlotte beforehand."

"But I have to help make lunch," replied Charlotte with a concerned look on her face.

"No you don't," said Bethany, almost cutting Charlotte off. "You need to go with your dad."

Charlotte looked around the room. Everyone nodded back. A broad smile broke across Charlotte's face as she turned to race out of the room, but Bethany grabbed her and pulled her back. "Photo," said Bethany, pointing to the camera perched across the room and looking back at the table. Bethany ran over to it, pressed the button and ran back. "Smile!"

Everyone stood there waiting for the click, but none of them heard it. The result was several more attempts, producing amusing results. Charlotte pulled Bethany into a tight hug, before moving over to Alexa. Tracey demanded her own hug, which Charlotte gave with vigour, making Tracey cackle. Charlotte quickly rushed to change and came dashing back into the room so quickly she almost tripped.

"Careful. I told everyone I was picking you up in one piece," said Wes, steadying Charlotte on her feet. "Thank you again, everyone. We're looking forward to meeting you properly in a few hours."

The way Charlotte danced out of the room with her father was magical. She had grown in the past year and was now much taller than Alexa, and was even closing in on Bethany. Her features had also started to develop, lessening many of the physical similarities between her and Alexa. Alexa found some comfort in that. She did not want Charlotte to be a replica of her. She was their hope, their gift, their vision of what they could have been with earlier intervention in their lives. From the soft smile that sat on Bethany's face, Alexa knew she felt the same way.

Maria arrived just as they sat down to breakfast. They had not been expecting her until much later in the day due to this being the year her family gathered together on Christmas Day. They knew her presence could mean only one thing and Bethany and Alexa hugged her tight, each leaking a few tears at the idea that others could not want Maria in their lives the way they did. Bethany sat with Maria at the table, shifting her chair so it was almost touching. Alexa sat on the other side of the table with Ben, who had Caiden on his lap looking tantalised by the sight of all the food.

They had started Caiden on solids a couple of months earlier, when formula could no longer satisfy his appetite. It was as though he was trying to catch up to Tracey as quickly as he could. Ben tried him on almost all the food, and there was nothing he did not like, but he took the greatest fancy to the pancakes. As quickly as Ben cut up the pieces, Caiden grabbed them off the plate with his chubby fingers and pushed them against his mouth. It was an adorable sight and lifted everyone's mood as they tidied up and started to prepare the house for the invasion.

Bethany and Maria took control of the kitchen, claiming Ben as their assistant. Alexa tried to help, but she was sent away by Bethany, who seemed intent on making up for all the years she did not cook. It was probably not a bad thing. Alexa was much more of a solitary chef. The only people she could really tolerate in the kitchen with her were Charlotte and Maria. Even Marcus knew to stay out of her way. Alexa and Bethany clashed more than was sensible when they cooked together. Maria was a much better companion for Bethany and appeared to appreciate the distraction.

"What I need you to do is go and get Caiden dressed in Tracey's elf outfit from last year," said Bethany, as she shooed Alexa away from the kitchen. "I want lots of photos for the photo album."

There was something hard in Bethany's eyes as she spoke those words and Alexa guessed that her enthusiasm for family photography was helping erase the memories of the photos hidden by their mother within the security of Peter's vault. Knowing the positive impact the addition of happy images would have on Bethany's wellbeing, Alexa mustered the enthusiasm she had always been lacking. When Marcus did not question her about the change, she knew he understood why as well.

The Whites arrived just after midday, followed closely by Sam and his grandparents. The sight of Gran's frail frame made Alexa's stomach flip over. Gran's health had been failing over the past few months. When Bethany had found out the waiting times for specialist appointments in the public clinic, she had come home in tears, begging Alexa to help her afford any and all the treatment Gran might need. Sam had been unwilling to accept the assistance until the bills for the heart surgery had come through. Gran was now on the mend, but it was going to be a slow process.

As soon as things were under control in the kitchen, Bethany emerged to sit with Gran and Pop. Bethany had attended most of their medical appointments and had been there for them when Sam had been unable to get out of university. Bethany's strength and stoicism – after the initial shock – was amazing. The experience had matured her in a way few other things had. Perhaps it was because she had felt herself able to be of great use to another person. Watching her now, Alexa knew she had good reason to hope for Bethany's future. There would probably never be a day that Bethany would be free of the temptation of drugs, and the hard times would always leave her vulnerable, but to see the person Bethany was growing into was beautiful and made everything she had suffered for her worthwhile.

"She's like a different person now, isn't she?" said Marcus softly, watching Alexa watch Bethany.

"I wouldn't say that," replied Alexa through gritted teeth, not turning to face Marcus as he wrapped a gentle arm around her waist. "She's grown up and changed in that way, but her core has never changed. She's always been this brilliant. I wouldn't have tried so hard to save her otherwise."

"Most of us haven't had the privilege of knowing her core, so perhaps it's the shell that's changing – how she gets to display her core traits. I know you don't see it this way, but the transformation is amazing and I think it's even softened my views on her past actions. I've been okay with present ones for a while now, but the past has always been difficult," admitted Marcus grimly. Alexa turned to face him, making him smile slightly. "When I think about her now with that gun to your head, I'm thinking about the turmoil she was in. I think about how young she was and how terribly ill-equipped she was to deal with any of that. I think about what would've happened if she'd been brave enough to pull that trigger. I know she wouldn't have given the police any choice but to shoot her. Or shot herself. I think about how empty the world would've been, to miss out on the people you've both grown into."

Alexa threw her arms around Marcus's neck as tears burned her eyes. This was a transformation she had never expected. The divide between him and Bethany had always been so deep she had resigned herself to it never being completely bridged. The only reason Alexa had been able to accept the situation was because, even in his dislike, Marcus had always been kind and fair when dealing with Bethany.

"Hey, love bugs, we have guests," Brett called across the room.

Alexa turned to see Charlotte standing in the doorway with Wes and his family. She was shaking, but Wes was smiling kindly and his wife had a comforting hand on Charlotte's shoulder.

"Um, everyone," said Charlotte, her voice shaking as much as her body. "This is my Dad, Wes Cassidy, his wife Lindsay, and my broth– um – half-brothers —"

"Brothers," interrupted Wes, moving forward and hugging Charlotte gently.

"Yeah, brothers," nodded Charlotte. "Austin and Jackson."

"Hi," chorused the room cheerfully, before Ben took up the individual introductions.

Maria immediately offered Lindsay the seat next to her as Brett started talking to Austin and Jackson. Wes guided Charlotte to spare seats next to Karl and Pam. Alexa smiled at the sight. Caiden was in Karl's arms and Tracey was clambering into Charlotte's lap, while Hayley sat down near Charlotte's feet. Alexa had always thought of Charlotte and Hayley as small, vulnerable girls. It was strange to look at them now and see young women who were growing steadily towards adulthood. It was also a little odd to know that she was no longer the one holding this whole family together. The crisscrossing bonds between all of them were weaving them together, hopefully strongly enough to withstand the future loss of one of them.

"See, told you we needed a big house – room enough for everyone," smiled Bethany, as she and Alexa started laying out the food. There was so much that they set up a serving line in the kitchen so the table had enough space for them all to sit and eat.

"I did listen to you," smiled Alexa, waving her hand. "And I'm glad we're housing more people. Sorry it took me so long to get on board with Dad."

"It was easier for me," said Bethany. "He didn't haunt my dreams. I had no memory of him, but through you I always knew him. He was our saviour. I used to pretend he existed and would come for us one day. When you sent him – you saved me – those early years, he was wrong about a lot of things to do with us, but he was real and I felt like life was finally bearable. He'd take care of us and protect you. I wanted all that so badly I forced it to be true. I know you could never've done that, but I wanted you to."

"I'm glad it's working out now. Just wish Marc didn't have to lose his family for us to have what we do now."

"You still haven't heard from his parents?" asked Bethany, though she did not sound as though hearing from them would be a good thing either. Alexa just shook her head. "Strange Rhianna isn't here yet. You want to wait for her to start lunch?"

Alexa checked with Marcus. The stony shake of his head was very telling. They had both tried calling Rhianna's mobile, but there had been no answer. Alexa knew better than to say anything. No matter what Marcus was feeling, he refused to hear anything that might justify his parents' attitude.

"They're probably just having a late Christmas," said Marcus when they all sat down to lunch and others inevitably asked about Rhianna.

It was a good thing Tracey was positioned on Marcus's lap with Caiden in Alexa's as they ate lunch. Their antics, eating from all the plates in front of them and feeding each other kept them occupied and helped to lift Marcus's mood. When the doorbell clanged, Marcus immediately shifted to answer the front door, but Bethany jumped up, waving at him to keep his seat.

There was a very long delay between Bethany leaving and her returning with Rhianna. It was clear not everything was well when they walked in. Rhianna was much more subdued than normal, but she resisted Marcus's hints to go somewhere private to talk.

"Looks good, I'm starving," smiled Rhianna, taking a seat next to Alexa. "I hope you don't mind, but Bethany offered me the front room. I want to spent some time with the munchkins before I go back home."

"No, not at all," replied Alexa in a happy voice, wondering if that decision was what had delayed her arrival. "Tracey'll be very excited."

"Rhanna stay?" asked Tracey with wide eyes. Rhianna quickly answered in the affirmative, drawing an excited – and very loud – squeal from Tracey.

Everyone laughed and smiled, and as the eating slowed and the talking increased, the room quickly became very loud. When everyone started to disperse to walk off their overly full stomachs, Marcus commandeered Rhianna into the backyard.

"You know what happened, Marc," sighed Rhianna, before turning her attention to Tracey, who she was holding. "We had a fight. Happens every time I come down."

"So they're not coming?" asked Alexa.

This time Rhianna genuinely laughed. "I can't believe you ask that as though it's something you actually want to happen," she said. "Surely the way they spoke to you last week was enough reason to never want to see them again."

"The way they spoke to her?" cried Marcus. "What do you mean the way they spoke to her? When were they ever near her?"

"Oops," grimaced Rhianna, giving Alexa a sympathetic smile. "Guess you never told him."

"Told me what?" asked Marcus, his voice almost a growl.

"It's okay," said Alexa quickly, placing a calming hand on Marcus's arm. "You were really upset and everyone keeps saying how they'd change their mind if they just knew me, so I thought I'd see if that was true. But in case I wasn't enticing enough I took Caiden and Tracey as well. Thought they might make a difference."

"What did Tracey do?" asked Marcus curiously. "She recognise them?"

"Not that I could tell," answered Rhianna. "Tracey sat with me, but she got a bit upset when things got tense."

"They say anything they haven't already said to me?" Marcus asked Rhianna. Rhianna shook her head. "I wish you didn't go there," he sighed, pulling Alexa into a hug.

"Why?" cried Alexa, pushing away from him. "Why shouldn't I try and make a difference? Why can't I ever do something to support you?"

"Alexa, I think it's beautifully sweet what you did. I know why you went there and I love you for it. I just wish you hadn't, because I don't want you spoken to like that, especially not by my parents," said Marcus with an anguished expression. "I hate to think you might take anything they said to heart."

"Marc's right," said Rhianna. "They're way out of line. They've taken this stand and I don't think they even know why – and they don't want anyone around who doesn't agree with them."

"Oh, shit, not you too," said Marcus. Rhianna nodded, shrugging her shoulders. "I'm sorry. I never wanted you caught up in this mess, but you'll always have a home with us."

"Yeah, that's what Bethany said when I arrived a little distraught, though her choice of words was a little less eloquent," smiled Rhianna. "She's my kind of girl, really. Now, can we go and do presents. I had magical plans to corrupt your children with noisy toys, but that may have just backfired on me now that I'm staying here."

It seemed everyone else was in the mood for presents too, having sufficiently digested their feast. Karl donned his Santa hat and recruited Tracey as his helper elf. It worked for the first two presents, but when Tracey noticed Hayley and Beth opening their gifts, she decided the next one was for her and immediately proceeded to tear it open, only to be very disappointed with the contents.

"Who's that for?" asked Brett, scooting down to the floor next to Tracey. "Who should that be for? You give it to them." Tracey immediately proceeded to give the present meant for Pop to Lindsay.

Clearly chuffed by this new method of allocating and distributing presents, Brett continued to corrupt the system. The results were highly amusing, with Tracey as likely to claim someone else's present as she was to reject her own. When anyone tried to re-gift the present to the correct recipient, Tracey squealed angrily. The only person whose presents she did not allocate incorrectly were Caiden's. Every time she was told a present was for him, she handed it straight to him. For everyone else, Tracey was the arbiter of who the present was really meant for.

"I think she might be pretty good at this," laughed Pop, playing the little keyboard Rhianna bought for Tracey.

"I think we should all choose one of our gifts and give it to charity," said Bethany thoughtfully, looking down at the leather diary Pam and Karl had bought her – and that Tracey had correctly allocated.

"You don't like it?" asked Pam.

"No, I love it," answered Bethany sincerely. "That's the point. I've never been given anything so beautiful in my life, but if I wanted to, I could buy it. Maybe someone who could never afford it deserves it more than me. I know how much it would've meant to me if someone had thought I deserved their best gift."

"Sounds like a good idea," nodded Karl. "But if you gave that away, we'd want to buy it for you again, knowing how much you love it. So maybe don't give that one away."

There was slow but steady agreement around the room as they each thought about what gifts they could forego. It was not an easy process. Not one of them had shopped randomly or thoughtlessly. However, when they started to think about the people they could give their gifts to, it became a little easier. Bethany went to investigate when and where they could carry out their Christmas giving, dancing back into the room with new plans for their Boxing Day.

"We won't be able to join you," said Wes. "We've got an early flight tomorrow."

"How long are you travelling around for?" asked Pam.

"We'll be back for Australia Day," answered Wes. "We thought about having a short trip now and coming back during the summer break, but next year is such an important year for Charlotte, we couldn't disrupt her like that. But maybe we'll be able to convince her to come and see us at the end of the year after her exams."

"Schoolies in New York," hinted Hayley in an excited voice. "Might make up for you ditching me now."

"Huh?" said Charlotte. "What do – I'm not – what?"

"What Hayley means is that you need to go and pack," said Marcus. Charlotte just stared at him. "Don't blame me. Alexa's your guardian, not me."

"It came out of your board money, so you technically paid your way," lied Alexa. "So go pack. You're leaving tonight."

It was the enthusiasm of Austin and Jackson that finally got Charlotte moving. They dragged her up to her room, chatting animatedly as they went. From what Alexa had gathered in her brief conversations with Wes and Lindsay, Austin, at just eight, had had very few qualms about Charlotte's existence. Thirteen-year-old Jackson had found it a little harder to accept, but it was clear they were all trying to make this situation work.

"We do need to thank you for including us in your Christmas," said Lindsay feelingly, looking around the room. "It's more than we expected."

"You guys are family now," said Alexa. "You'll always be welcome here."

"I also want to thank you for everything you've done for Charlotte," said Wes. "Her fate should never've been left in the hands of another child. I still struggle with how her life played out. I'll be forever disappointed that I wasn't there when she needed me most – that she spent her whole childhood not knowing how loved and wanted she was."

Charlotte and her brothers edged slowly into the room. Wes and Lindsay both got to their feet and joined them at the door.

"Bye," waved Tracey. "Hi soon," she added in a demanding voice, making everyone laugh. It had been their way of helping with her distress at saying goodbye, by letting her know that they would be saying hi again soon. The concept had worked well since it was rare that Tracey went more than a week without seeing someone. Charlotte's month-long absence would be much more challenging.

"Hi in little while," said Charlotte, kneeling down and opening her arms for Tracey. "Promise."

"I'll get the thing," said Brett with a sly smile. "Don't dash off yet."

"What thing?" asked Alexa, looking confused. The fact that the only blank looks belonged to Wes and his family was disconcerting. Everyone else was trying to hide their smirks.

When Brett returned, Hayley and Bethany jumped to their feet, joining Charlotte by his side. They stepped towards Alexa, half-encircling her, making her heart thump.

"Okay, now don't go being yourself," said Brett. "But as your younger siblings, it's been a tough year watching you go through so much, especially on top of everything else you've been through."

"We wanted to get you something to help," said Hayley. "But worked out pretty quick that there was nothing we could buy that could ever do that."

"So we thought if there was something we could do," smiled Charlotte, looking like she might burst.

"It's taken us months," said Bethany. "We wanted something that would help renew your faith in life. Renew all our faith, because we realised this was something we needed as much as you. So it's not just about you, which means you can't get mad."

Alexa turned to Marcus, who just laughed and shrugged, making it clear that he had been involved in this ambush.

"All right, fine. Hand over the present then," said Alexa, holding out her hand.

Brett gave her an envelope, smirking as he did. Alexa understood why when she opened it.

One voucher for faith-renewing fun on Saturday 23 February. You are required to bring blind trust in your siblings and the willingness to take an epic leap of faith with them as we embark on a bright and brilliant future together.

Love Bethany, Brett, Charlotte and Hayley

Chapter Twenty

THE SKY WAS bright blue, decorated with fluffy white clouds. The trees and grass were radiant green and the ocean a deep emerald. Every colour seemed brighter than usual as they drove along the coast. It was the perfect scene to work Alexa into a false sense of security. Brett remained amused by the curious looks she threw him every so often. He was driving, Bethany next to him directing. Hayley and Charlotte were chatting happily next to Alexa in the back seat, talking in code to keep Alexa from understanding.

Looking behind, Alexa saw that the trail of cars carrying the rest of the family was still in convoy. It was disconcerting being the only one in the dark about what they were doing. The only hint she had been provided with was that she would be allowed to swim in the ocean at the end of it. It was a good enticement, and Alexa was sure she could survive anything that might occur before then – until Brett started following signs towards a skydiving facility.

"Um, no," said Alexa, sitting forward. Everyone started laughing at her anxiety. "Seriously, no. It makes no sense to jump out of a perfectly good plane."

"It's over the beach," replied Bethany as though that actually made a difference.

"Read your present again," said Hayley. "You agreed to have blind faith in us."

"Wouldn't have agreed if I knew we were doing this," Alexa muttered, only amusing everyone more.

"I can't believe what a great day we got," said Charlotte, smiling brightly.

It was one of the first truly happy smiles Alexa had seen from Charlotte since her father returned to the States. That month travelling with them had been a crucial bonding period and there had been a lot of tears at the airport when they left. It was then that Alexa and Bethany had started preparing themselves for the very real possibility that Charlotte would go to university overseas.

Seeing Charlotte so happy, along with the buoyant expressions on everyone else's faces, convinced Alexa to swallow her fear. Leap of faith. It would certainly be that. She was not sure it would be able to renew her faith in the world as Bethany boasted, but perhaps it could renew Bethany's, and that would be just as worthwhile.

Alexa was surprised to find out that they had purposely arrived early. Maria had very clear plans on how they were going to pass the time and immediately started laying out a picnic. It was a beautifully warm day and the smell of salt in the air instantly relaxed Alexa. With Tracey running around happily and Caiden trying to crawl after her, it was easy to believe the world was perfect, but the sight of Gran's frail frame shuffling slowly to the picnic table was the reminder that life could not be lived without pain or loss.

"I know that look," puffed Gran as she took her seat. "My doctor has more faith in my longevity than you. I politely request you don't put me in the grave before I'm due."

Tears instantly started tumbling down Alexa's face as she nodded. Charlotte was soon by her side with a comforting arm, while Sam wiped the single tear from Bethany's cheek. It kept the mood sombre as they all sat down, but Gran was having none of that.

"You know as well as anyone that death is an unpredictable, but totally unavoidable, part of life. I have lived – am still living," Gran added with a wry smile, "a very full life. That life might end tomorrow. It might end in ten years. Either way, I'll not go on to the next life full of regrets. Nor will I live each day waiting for my life to end, so I request you don't spend your days that way either."

Alexa rushed to the other side of the table and hugged Gran tight. It was difficult not to fear the future when it now promised the eventual deaths of those she loved. They were the kinds of thoughts that sometimes had Alexa in tears – and that was when there was no illness lurking. But when Alexa sat back down, Marcus holding her tight, she also knew there would be many wonderful moments like this in between the trauma, so tried to force herself to live only for those moments. However, when Brett looked at his watch and let them know that they had to get moving, Alexa started to seriously wonder if this really was a good moment – and if she would live through it.

"I can't believe you're letting me do this," Alexa said to Marcus. "I'm the person who'll crash the plane or get their legs stuck in the ropes and splat hard against the earth."

"I promise to feel very guilty for the rest of my life if any of that happens," smiled Marcus.

"Well why aren't you joining us if you're so confident?"

"I'm not one of the siblings," smiled Marcus. "And just because I think it's safe doesn't mean I've suddenly lost my fear of heights. Besides, I thought you didn't fear things you couldn't control."

"Yeah, well I was looking for ways to die back then. Not looking for that now," mumbled Alexa unhappily.

"Is it really only the idea that you might die holding you back?" asked Sam. Alexa nodded, her eyebrows raised, trying to hint that she thought that was reason enough. "Have you ever considered that the fact you're alive today means you were meant to survive – and not just long enough to die in a tragic skydiving accident."

"Trust us," said Brett seriously. "We're all in this together. And we're doing this to renew our faith in life. Consider it your swansong – closing off your rebellious past before you settle down and become all sensible on us."

"Yeah, what happened to the girl who'd simulate oral sex on her brother in a movie theatre to gee up some snotty kids?" asked Hayley with a straight face.

The chorus of cries was so loud everyone in the vicinity turned to them. Alexa blushed fiercely.

"I think I'm ready to jump out of a plane now," said Alexa, grabbing Hayley and wrestling with her. "Or at least throw you out of one. I thought you didn't realise what we were doing."

Hayley laughed as Brett filled Bethany and Charlotte in on the details in a voice loud enough for everyone to hear. The story amused everyone, even Pam and Karl. It was more difficult for Alexa to think back to that time. Marcus understood first. As soon as he heard the word Easter he was behind her, hugging her gently.

"Let me walk you over," he said softly in her ear. She nodded and they trailed behind the others. "You okay?"

"It's bad that I've been pregnant to two teachers, isn't it?" asked Alexa tentatively.

"What Clinton Marsh did to you was bad. What we have is beautiful – perfect most days," replied Marcus. "Don't start doubting our love now. We've been through too much. And I promised to stick around, so it'd be a bit awkward if you decide you don't want me now."

It was one of the first times Marcus had ever spoken about those things with such assurance and humour. The way he was smiling melted Alexa's heart. Smiling back, she pulled his head down and kissed him passionately.

"Cut it out. We're bringing her back," called Brett. "I'll even promise not to kiss her again."

"Go get renewed," smiled Marcus, gently brushing Alexa's cheek.

By the time they were dressed in their jumpsuits and had undergone the training for the tandem dive, Alexa had all but forgotten about her nerves. The confidence of the instructors was very reassuring. Coupled with the thrill of the plane ride, Alexa found herself almost excited as they cruised towards jump altitude.

"This is amazing," cried Bethany over the whir of the engines as she gazed out at the coastline. "Lex, can you take me on the plane next time you go? I think I like this."

"Absolutely," replied Alexa, feeling guilty that she had never taken Bethany anywhere.

"You can come with me when we visit Charlotte in the States," said Hayley. "I'm not letting her have all the fun."

"And while they study, we can go somewhere," said Brett.

"For a whole weekend?" asked Bethany excitedly.

"Hell yeah," replied Brett. "Me, you, strange town, cutting loose. Best weekend ever."

"All right, time to go," called one of the instructors.

The change in everyone's expression was not lost on Alexa. It was a strange reversal of their moods on the ground. Now that they were in the air, adrenalin was overwhelming Alexa's fears. It was a stark contrast to Charlotte, who had remained silent since they boarded the plane and now looked very ashen. "Suddenly this seems like a very stupid thing to do," she cried, her hands shaking in her lap.

"You'll be right," said Bethany, taking her hand. "Just remember why we're doing this. We're all about to fly in the clouds and right through heaven. All that without dying."

Bethany's comments made Alexa's heart stop. She could not understand why. Perhaps it was the shadow of death hanging over Gran, but that did not quite fit. Alexa knew exactly what Bethany was trying to say and agreed with the sentiment, yet it stirred something deeper, a memory she could not quite grasp.

"All right, let's start moving towards the door," said Brett's instructor.

Brett had volunteered to go first. Hayley was to follow in front of Charlotte, then Alexa, and lastly Bethany.

"See you all down there," smiled Brett, though Alexa saw a flicker of fear in his eyes as he looked down at the ground.

In a flash he was gone.

"Oh my God, oh my God. Oh. My. God," gasped Hayley as she moved towards the plane door. She was holding the handle at the side of the door tightly, but when her instructor tapped her hand, she nodded and let go. With another nod, the instructor leaned them out the door, Hayley's high-pitched scream trailing behind her.

Charlotte said nothing as she shuffled towards the door. Alexa watched her face harden and her shoulders pull back. Without a backwards glance, Charlotte nodded, crossed her arms to her chest and fell out of the plane with her instructor in complete silence.

Alexa's instructor nudged her forward. Her breathing came in anxious gasps. Looking down, she could see the parachutes of Brett and Hayley drifting close to the ground. Her stomach wriggled with fear, nerves and excitement.

"Ready?" asked her instructor.

"Yeah, let's go," replied Alexa softly, before realising that her instructor could probably not hear her. With a nod, Alexa quickly turned to Bethany. Reaching out her hand, Bethany reciprocated and their fingers touched briefly before Alexa started plummeting towards the earth. Her stomach flew up into her throat. It was exhilarating and terrifying. The ground was racing up to meet them and in the second Alexa began to fear the impact, her body jerked up, her legs flinging towards her head before everything slowed right down.

Alexa's fear vanished in an instant. Gliding under the parachute was so calming and the scenery was beautiful. Below them she could see two parachutes circling, with another very close to the ground.

"Would you like to fly through a cloud?" asked Alexa's instructor.

"Yeah!" cried Alexa excitedly. As a child she had thought of clouds as fairy floss; a magical place where angels lived.

They turned and headed towards a nearby cloud and Alexa stretched out her arms. The surprisingly light nothingness that surrounded them, engulfing them and taking them away from the rest of the world, was magical. It was almost incomprehensible how something that looked so thick and solid could be so different up close. Part of her wished she could have stayed in the cloud, convinced the solid magical world would appear if they were there long enough.

When they drifted out of the cloud, Alexa was surprised by how close the ground was. She could even see Pam and Karl hugging Brett and Hayley. Marcus was near them, crouched next to Tracey, pointing up at the sky. The sight made Alexa impatient to be on the ground.

Looking towards the far horizon, dark storm clouds were gathering. The sun slipped behind one, ringing it in an amazing silver. It was then that Alexa realised why Bethany's words had affected her so deeply. Back in high school Bianca had called their lottery win the silver lining they could look forward to. It was a notion Alexa had not been able to invest any faith in. Silver linings could not be trusted, not when the only way to reach them was to die. Suddenly that was no longer true. She had touched the silver lining, flown through it and been enveloped by it and she was not dead. She had never felt more alive.

Alexa could not be sure if this was what the others had envisaged when they had said this day would renew their faith in life, but she realised now that they had been right. This was what she had needed. As if catching a brief glimpse of their futures, Alexa suddenly felt reassured that things would work out fine. Their lives might never be perfect, but they would be more magnificent than they could have imagined before today. They had each other and they had each been wrapped in their own silver lining. There was no more waiting, no more wishing or hoping. Everything they ever wanted was now within their grasp.

Sliding and stumbling as they landed on the grass near the edge of the beach, the instructor had to hold Alexa back as she tried to rush towards Marcus. Finally free of her binds, Alexa bounced over to Tracey, who stood with her arms outstretched. Alexa scooped her up, kissing her as Marcus's arms wrapped around them.

"Mummy fly," said Tracey excitedly, her arms pointing up to the sky. Ben arrived with Caiden, and Alexa pulled him into her other arm, hugging him tight. "Mummy fly. Betty fly," Tracey added, seeing Bethany close to the ground.

"Mummy did fly," replied Alexa, unable to wipe the smile from her face. "We all flew."

When Bethany landed, Ben and Marcus took the kids from Alexa's arms as the five siblings gathered in a circle. They were hugging and laughing, unable to stop their bodies from bouncing.

"Woooo hoooo," screamed Brett, hugging Hayley tight.

"That was the greatest thing ever," said Charlotte with a broad grin, looking much happier with life than she had fifteen minutes earlier. "I never want to do it again, but God it was good."

They squealed and laughed for almost five minutes until the giddiness started to wear off. Alexa found herself next to Bethany and pulled her into a tight embrace. Bethany grabbed her hand and walked them down to the edge of the ocean.

"Glimpse heaven?" asked Bethany, looking back up at the sky they had just travelled through.

"Not up there. My heaven's right here on earth," replied Alexa, her eyes burning. "But it took doing this for me to realise that."

"We did it, you know," said Bethany, turning and facing Alexa. Her eyes were filled with tears, even though her voice was strong and resolute. "You and me, we made it."

In that moment, Alexa realised that, despite everything she had been through, this had never been just about her. It was about them. It always had been. From the moment of Bethany's birth, they had been linked in the most intricate and unbreakable way.

They had always known they would sink or swim together. Now they had learned to fly.

THE END